CRUISE SHIP DOCTOR

A novel by

Gerry Yukevich

PublishAmerica
Baltimore

First printing

ISBN: 1-59129-788-5
PUBLISHED BY PUBLISHAMERICA BOOK PUBLISHERS
www.publishamerica.com
Baltimore

Printed in the United States of America

To Martha, Anna, and Mike
And to the memory of Joe Millar

VALENTINE TV CRUISE ABOARD
THE *S/S NORDIC BLUE*

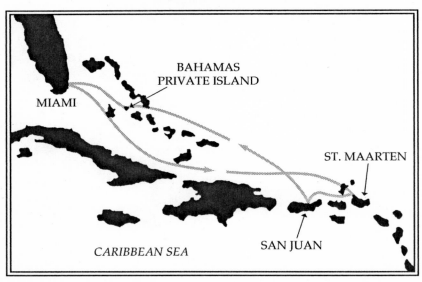

ITINERARY

DAY	PORT	ARRIVE	DEPART
SAT/FEB 9	Miami	—	6:00 p.m.
SUN/FEB 10	*Day-at-Sea*	—	—
MON/FEB 11	St. Maarten	6:00 a.m.	6:00 p.m.
TUES/FEB 12	San Juan*	6:00 a.m.	*(overnight)*
WED/FEB 13	San Juan*	—	10:00 a.m.
THURS/FEB 14	*A Glorious Valentine's Day-at-Sea!**		
FRI/FEB 15	Private Island	6:00 a.m.	6:00 p.m.
SAT/FEB 16	Miami	6:00 a.m.**	—

* Denotes live Cablevista TV broadcasts
with Farrely Farrell from the ship.
** Thank you for disembarking promptly!
Cruise on Nordic Star Lines again soon!

Brief Historical Note
about the **S/S Nordic Blue**

June 20, 1962. A sunny and jubilant day for France.

At the huge Saint-Nazaire ship yards, before more than a hundred thousand cheering French citizens, President and Madame Charles de Gaulle crack a magnum of Champagne over the lofty prow of the magnificent new **S/S Marianne***, the largest and most glamorous cruise ship of the post-war era. A legend before she hits the waves, the* **Marianne** *boasts a mammoth hull fifty meters longer than the Eiffel tower is tall! Her giant yet sleek silhouette – twin raked funnels and a long, elegantly sloped deck line – enchants the international media.*

The **Marianne** *is hailed a marvel of modern naval architecture and an icon of futuristic style. Her first crossings dominate newsreels, television, and tabloids on both sides of the Atlantic. Her passenger lists tout Hollywood film stars, European royalty, powerful politicians and business magnates, all scrambling for bookings on her breathlessly chic* **Viceroy Deck***.*

Simultaneous to the **Marianne's** *first voyages, however, the first Boeing 707's arrive on the global travel scene. The public turns fickle. The new "jet set" prefers speed and convenience to ocean liner grace and pageantry. Fares for 6-hour flights across the Atlantic soon undercut the prices for 5-day ship crossings. The fabulous* **Marianne** *can no longer fill her cabins with passengers. The ocean-going pride of France now requires subsidies from the French government to maintain her staff and itinerary.*

In 1970 Charles de Gaulle dies. His successor, Valery Giscard d'Estaing, swallows the national pride, takes the beloved **Marianne** *out of service, and sells her to Arab speculators. When the Arabs cannot find a buyer, the huge ship is moved to an obscure back pier at Le Havre, where she languishes for almost a decade. Relic of a forgotten era, the* **Marianne** *seems destined for scrap iron.*

But in the 1970's, the same Boeing 707's, which blew the ocean crossers out of the Atlantic a decade before, now open a rich market for cruise ships in the Caribbean. Runways are laid down on the islands, and passenger jets bring eager tourists to exotic Caribbean destinations from anywhere in North

America or Europe. Cruise lines begin to pull the old ships out of mothballs to be renamed and refitted for a new rage in tourism – tropical island hopping.

*Enter Norwegian shipping tycoon Stig Storjord, founder of Nordic Star Lines. Seeking a glamorous flag ship for his growing Caribbean fleet, Storjord takes a team of experts to Le Havre to examine the most fabled of all. He finds the **Marianne** fit and sound – a true iron queen despite a decade of rust and weathering. Storjord buys her and tows her back to Norway to refurbish her for a wonderful warm water career.*

June 17, 1984. A sunny and jubilant day for Norway.

*In Oslo Harbor, before a hundred thousand ecstatic Norwegians, King Olaf V smashes yet another magnum of Champagne over her prow and rechristens her the **S/S Nordic Blue**. With her majestic hull and twin funnels repainted white and royal Norwegian blue, and with her bridge manned by Norwegian officers, the grand girl slides gracefully back into the waters to regain all her international eminence and glory.*

*Since the early 1990's, cruise ships larger than the **Nordic Blue** have been built. But to her Norwegian officers, the **Nordic Blue** remains the **grande dame** of the sea. Apart from her style and dignity, the officers love her because she continues a glorious Norwegian tradition. In medieval times, the Viking ancestors of these officers routinely plundered France for treasures. This modern queen, **née Marianne**, serves prominently in a rich booty of trophies made in France to be enjoyed by the Vikings.*

*Into her fifth decade now, the **Nordic Blue** proudly continues her legendary career. Every Saturday evening at sunset, she pulls out of the Port of Miami with her adopted Norwegian flag flapping and her decks brimming with giddy passengers from all over the globe. The Norwegian officers say fondly that, despite her 98 kilotons of displacement, the old girl still sways at sunset into the warm Caribbean waters like a seasoned Parisian street professional on her way to work. Each Saturday evening as the ship pulls out and the party begins, she wishes her admiring customers a sly and seductive, "**Bonsoir et bon voyage!**"*

Ancient art has a specific inner content. At one time, art possessed the same purpose that books do in our day, namely: to preserve and transmit knowledge. In olden days, people did not write books, they incorporated their knowledge into works of art. We would find a great many ideas in the works of ancient art passed down to us, if only we knew how to read them.

G. Gurdjieff

To hunt the tiger, you must first hunt the tiger in yourself, and to do that you first make certain that the tiger is not hunting you.

Mochtar Lubis

If the fool would persist in his folly, he would become wise.

William Blake

SAT/FEB 9
The Dancing Doctor Cruises out of Miami

Oliver Loring ran his fingertips up over the three embroidered gold stripes of his snap-on epaulets. He adjusted his bow tie, slicked down his white gabardine lapels, and brushed some peanut salt from his cummerbund. The tight crotch of his new tuxedo slacks nipped at his lanky groin. Otherwise, Loring felt thrilled to be back in formal uniform – pale and prematurely balding, yes – but a thousand miles south of icy Boston and sailing out of Miami once again on a balmy Saturday night in February as Chief Medical Officer of the *S/S Nordic Blue*, the world's grandest and most legendary cruise ship.

Loring stretched back into his favorite couch near the parquet dance floor in *Club Atlantis* and wiggled his long toes in his size-13 dance pumps. Cautiously he sipped a martini.

Though a large-framed man of 39, Loring was exquisitely susceptible to the accelerant effects of even the tiniest amounts of alcohol. When his cheeks flamed hot, he set the martini down and dabbed his moist temples with a cocktail napkin.

He fingered his wrist. Pulse 110! Easy on the gin, he vowed.

But then a familiar buzz bored up through his heels – vibrations from the *Boiler Room* far below. *Whoaaaooooooooooooooooooooooooooooooh!* How he loved the constant, ubiquitous kick from those mighty steam turbines penetrating up 17 decks of the finest forged steel on the high seas! Even way up here in the plush, velveted *Club Atlantis*, Loring felt the thundering gallop of those legions of fierce, mechanical subaquatic stallions. Suddenly his spirit fused with those tireless beasts.

Yes! He really was back again! Oliver Loring, M.D., Chief of Emergency Medicine at the Boston Samaritan Hospital, was *in* the Caribbean *on* a working vacation and strictly in an *off*-call mode. He drained the martini and ordered a second – a double.

Tuesday morning in Boston, during a howling Nor'easter, Nordic Star Lines had phoned Loring's office from Miami. "We need a doctor who can dance. Desperately!"

11

"But Beth! I don't dance desperately. Ha-*ha*!"

"Oliver! Farrely Farrell insists we find a doctor who can do state-of-the-art ballroom for the cameras on the *Valentine TV Cruise*. I thought of you. Over the years you've made quite a reputation for yourself as the dancing doctor, haven't you? Couldn't you do me a special favor?"

"You know you're special to me, Beth. May I put you on hold?"

One glance out the window at the bitter Boston blizzard, a furtive peek into the mirror (Loring's wintry pallor made him gasp!), and then a quick call to Bart Novak (a colleague recently strapped by alimony payments) to cover his shifts and now – *poof!* – here he was again on the majestic *Nordic Blue* for a week of Caribbean sunshine and romantic tropical moonlight. The dancing doctor was back indeed, this time for all the glitz and dazzle of the first-ever *"Valentine TV Cruise!"*

The Samaritan E.R. nurses had drooled with envy. Loring's ballroom capers would be beamed round-the-world, courtesy Farrely Farrell, Cablevista's new Australian wag/hunk, who had recently zoomed to the top of the charts with "Love Luck," the prime time "reality television" blockbuster every American could not help but gape at and weep over.

This trophy trip proved Nordic Star Lines valued Loring's work on eleven previous cruises. And not only for his flashy ballroom footwork or for his Harvard Associate Professor status. Check the files going back five years: not a single passenger had ever cooled on any of Loring's gigs! No doctor on the fleet roster could beat that record. Who could beat perfect?

And speaking of perfect, who could beat the martinis in *Club Atlantis*? Or the ambiance?

Loring glanced up fondly at the faux-marble statue of muscle-perfect Poseidon strutting on his seashell pedestal in the aft starboard corner – with his quartz crystal beard hanging down and his acrylic trident quivering up under the eaves of the forward portico.

Yo! Poseidon!

And *Yo!* All you other statues – lusty Dionysus and wing-footed Hermes and coquettish Venus dropping her mother-of-pearl hankie in the port corner! And don't forget the ice sculpture on the long mahogany bar – a wily winged cherub poised to arch an icicle arrow at the *Atlantis* dance floor.

Yo Cupid! Dude, you rule!

Imagine! Less than 24 hours ago Loring had signed out of his Boston Samaritan E.R. with its whining medical students and its rising residue on the floor tiles of smelly (possibly infective) body fluids. Now, a free jet ride later, here he was again in his epauleted tuxedo uniform and patent leather pumps enjoying intimate eye contact with the gods in the meticulously vacuumed *Club Atlantis.*

Loring spun a swizzle stick in his palm. The wave-and-sunburst logo on the tip winked up at him in quick gold glints. He grinned. He knew that, like the invigorating engine rumbles underfoot, the happy wave-and-sunburst motif was everywhere on the *Nordic Blue.* From swizzle sticks to smokestacks, from pillow mints to *Poop Deck* cable clamps, your eyes never had to roll very far before they hit on the upbeat imprimatur of Nordic Star Lines, right down to the gilded buttons on his Chief Medical Officer sleeves.

Loring chewed his olive, spit the pit back into the glass. Tuesday night would be his round-the-world television debut. How did he look? Was he Cablevista material?

Admit it. Oliver Loring had edged perilously close to 40. (His birthday was coming up, the first of April.) Though still unmarried and losing his hair and his youth, he had not yet "gone to seaweed" as Flip Spinelli, the Cruise Director, had quipped one night last winter over several Aquavits down in the *Crew Bar.*

Loring's curly blonde hairline had retreated in recent years. That was obvious and traumatic. But he had been blessed since his Vermont birth with thick, golden, lyrically-arched brows which soon would bleach to cornsilk white as the ship cruised down the rim of the Greater and Lesser Antilles. And he had large (the Samaritan nurses said "scintillating") emerald eyes, full lips, a prominent chin, extraordinarily smooth skin with a tiny beauty mark on his right cheek, and a long nose that sloped gracefully upward at the tip. Leave it at that.

Oh yes, two more things. Oliver Loring was six-foot-four and skinny as the handle of a hoe. He was also a nail biter – a disgraceful life-long habit, which he pledged to conquer this week with help from Nadine Tulard, the gifted new French Manicurist in the *Club Roma Spa* down on *Pool Deck.*

Loring spread his fingers and sighed. On the flight down, he had gnawed all ten down to raw pink gutters. *Mademoiselle* Tulard would not be pleased.

But surely nobody at the Captain's Champagne Welcome Reception earlier down in the *Starlight Lounge* had noticed the atrocious condition of his nails – not while he served up some Cuban-style hip gyrations in a pyrotechnical merengue on center floor with Ulla von Straf, the new raven-tressed Austrian Demo-Dancer.

Ulla von Straf. Former principle ballerina and choreographer for the

Salzburg Tanzkreis! Now *there* was an eyeful for the Cablevista fans: flawless high cheeks, pouting red lips, fine spherical breasts, taut calves and muscular, smoothly-slung thighs. Loring doubted the scuttlebutt that Ulla's current on-board liaison with Cruise Director Flip Spinelli was platonic. Not Ulla. Not those voluptuous lips. Not those big, intelligent icy blues.

At the Captain's Welcome Reception, as soon as Loring had escorted the fair *Fraülein* onto the floor, he felt her lean body throb to the merengue beat. When the spotlight burned on them, her high hips hugged tight. Her supple waist melted into him. Her tongue poked out and wiggled as she took his firm lead. When he clasped her from behind in close shadow position, her bare shoulder blades rubbed seductive circles so close that strands of her long raven hair snagged his tuxedo studs. She cocked her long eyebrows, snapped back in a sly moonwalk retreat that sent the astonished *Starlight Lounge* up in a convulsive rave.

Ulla von Straf? A woman who could merengue like fire itself? In a platonic relationship with anyone?

Ballroom dictum: *"Flirting shows expertise."*

Loring's own mother had often stressed that rule at the Olivia Loring Dance Academy in Coventry, Vermont. Madame Loring, herself a Juilliard-trained *danceuse*, emphasized nuance to her classes, especially to her only child and star pupil. But earlier tonight in the *Stardust Lounge*, that pupil, Oliver Loring, had felt much more than nuance from Ulla von Straf.

And why such melancholy in the ballerina's eyes when the music stopped? (Had Loring seen tears?) And why was a *Tanzkreis* virtuoso and choreographer slumming it here as a Demo-Dancer on a Caribbean liner?

Most vexing of all: why was she doing a "platonic" with Cruise Director Francis X. ("Flip") Spinelli – the short Sicilian-American from Chicago? Spinelli talked fast, showed great tap dance chops on stage, but up close had a bulbous nose, a pencil-line mustache, bushy black eyebrows, and thick hairy wrists that always dripped tasteless gold? Plus: Spinelli was a decade balder than Loring and a foot shorter than Ulla von Straf herself!

The second martini arrived. Loring sent it back. More gin would only ignite his jealousy. He ordered an iced Perrier.

Besides, before flying out of Boston that morning, Loring had dodged a bloody nose, courtesy one high-strung beauty. Why sniff after another bruising down here in the Caribbean?

On the flight to Miami, while savaging his nails to the quick, Loring had told himself over and over he would use this cruise to distance himself geographically *and* emotionally from Dr. Anita Rothberg, his therapist-turned lover.

That morning in the swirling snow outside Logan Airport, Anita's long hot tongue had invaded his lips, shoved past his tonsils, swarmed down his throat in a burning kiss that, in fact, took his breath away. Then, without warning, she arched her neck and threw her blonde Medusa curls back. Her cheek muscles clenched sharply and her predatory brown eyes glared. "Oliver Loring! You incredible anal fixee! Why didn't you invite me for the cruise?"

"They hired me because I can dance. You can't dance, Anita. Do we have to get into this again, here?"

"You're baiting me, aren't you?"

"That's why we were never right for each other. I was raised to dance."

"Never *right* for each other? Oh, I see. You're not just baiting me. You're *dumping* me. Go ahead! Fly down to Miami and sleep with all the sluts on the ship! Leave me alone in this frigid city for what should have been our first Valentine's Day together. I hope you fall overboard, you lousy medical gigolo!"

"Thanks for the ride to the airport."

"Oliver, you are so repressed it's sickening."

"Repressed?"

"And selfish! You know I adore Farrely Farrell. I would give anything to be on that ship to meet him. I checked the web last night, and I know there are extra seats on your flight. We could fly down together. My suitcase is packed and ready in the trunk of my Saab."

"That's another reason why we were probably never meant for each other. I think Farrely Farrell is a sadistic jerk!"

"Look who's being sadistic! I hate you so much, I'm not even going to watch you on television!"

"Well, at least Olivia will be catching the show up in Vermont."

Anita's nostrils flared. She cocked her Gucci handbag over her head. "And when will you *ever* stop comparing me to your skinny old bitch of a mother!"

"I'll send you a card from San Juan."

"Why don't you cruise straight to hell? Send me a card from there, asshole!"

Loring ducked as the Gucci descended.

Whew! Thank goodness all that free-floating resentment was now freezing her lovely dimples off up in Boston.

Loring had first gone to Anita Rothberg in July for help with his nail biting. He thought he was oral. She thought he was anal. In August they did genital. Now it was February, and Loring was glad to be out of it. The Gucci in the nose, he supposed, was the most graceful exit cue he could have expected from Anita Rothberg.

Nadine Tulard in the *Club Roma Spa* would be all the help he needed for his nails, thank you very much, Doctor Anita, with your discreet little Cambridge spider web office and your adjoining condo with the mirror over the bed and the steamer trunk crammed with battery-powered sex aids.

Obviously, all along Loring had needed a Parisian manicurist for his nails – not a slinky blonde Harvard-trained wasp Ph.D. (née Anita Sloan Stewart) who had gotten a divorce two years before because she thought she was lesbian, then decided she wasn't but still used her ex's name for what she called its "professional allure."

Was it the salt air down here out of Miami or what? Loring could *breathe* again! Up in Boston with those sniveling medical students in the E.R. and with that twitchy, long-legged machine fetishist between the sheets, Loring was always asking himself, "What's wrong here?"

In *Club Atlantis* that question did not apply. There was nothing wrong here. Everything was right! And even if there were something wrong, Loring didn't have to diagnose it!

The Perrier arrived in its green, breast-shaped bottle – chilled, bubbly, lovely to hold, so very purifying as it poured into his glass. One long swig – *aaaaaaahhhhhhh!* – and he immediately felt less oral.

And up there over the mahogany *Atlantis* bar loomed the stern portrait of long-dead King Olav V of Norway.

Yo! Dead King!

And up there, over the bandstand hung the newest oil portrait of Stig Storjord, the white-bearded octogenarian owner of the whole Nordic Star fleet.

Feisty old Stig Storjord! Always with a yellow blush rose ("Imperial Fiat variety") in his lapel. Even at his age that lovable, trollish Norsky – fleet magnate and internationally-known rose fancier – had so much raw glee in his eyes, he looked like he might jump right off the canvas and down onto the dance floor.

And there, below Stig Storjord, stood Barry Cox, the little lizard-snouted sax player of Barry and the Atlantans. Barry, once pre-med at Pitt, had the sallow complexion of a dedicated urologist and could not help but snap his

16

fingers and riff out the *"Theme from M*A*S*H"* whenever he saw Loring – now for a twelfth week-long cruise – mount the *Atlantis* dance floor stairs and sink into a couch.

"Yo! Doctor Oliver! Awesome to see you on board again!"

"Equally awesome to see you, Barry."

"Hey Doc! The band's buzzing. Did you see who just stepped in?"

Loring turned, and his eyes popped. Captain Trond Ramskog – the ship's tall and dashing blonde Master with the startling blue eyes, the golden handlebar mustache, and the sensational smile – had entered *Atlantis* with the preeminent cruise couple in the ship's long history.

Truly a pair of *Nordic Blue* icons! *The* Colonel and *the* Mrs. Rockwell Snippet-White!

Medals sparkling across his long, red-sashed torso, the ancient British colonel strode slim and erect in his white shark skin uniform. Beside him glided the elegant Hildegarde Snippet-White, diminutive and perky despite her advanced age, in a lavender silk Cardin shift.

The Snippet-Whites took seats with the Captain at a table across the dance floor. Before Loring could smile politely in their direction, he was startled again.

Radiant and bare-shouldered, Ulla von Straf entered in silver lamé. Light as a breeze, she ascended to the Snippet-White table and offered her hand to the Colonel, who kissed it tenderly. The Captain, too, kissed her hand.

Loring's lips quivered. His fingers trembled. He clutched his icy Perrier as yet a third shock hit: Captain Trond Ramskog beamed at the Chief Medical Officer and beckoned him over!

* * *

The *Club Atlantis* gods stared down in envy as Oliver Loring twirled to Strauss's *"Blue Danube"* with Ulla von Straf in his arms. She gave herself to her native Viennese, murmured not a word. The perfect pressure of her hand on his shoulder, the elegant tilt of her neck, the sway of her raven locks with each revolution loosened gravity's hold. Loring felt himself float far above the parquet. His head whirled faster than his feet.

Earthy as she had seemed during their merengue in the *Starlight Lounge*, here in *Atlantis* Ulla was sylph-like, an ethereal water nymph. The mystic Danube bubbled up in her now dreamy eyes and tugged Loring, circle by delicious circle, into her undulant currents.

Peering down to the whiteness of her full breasts, he spied an amber-shaded mole – a dainty birth blemish the size and shape of a lady bug. Such an *ideal* beauty mark! Exactly over her heart, not an inch above her nipple! *Yummmmmmmmmm!* And from further below, a mysterious musk-like fragrance wafted up in pulses. How he wanted to dwell in that scent, savor the delicacies in that silver lamé.

Barry and the Atlantans were inspired, too. Maestro Cox, who had switched from sax to violin for the waltz, closed in on the last chordal cadence with a brilliant flourish of double string trills. Ulla spun through an underarm reverse twinkle, then an angel arc turn before their bow-and-curtsy combo. Her timing and balance with Loring were impeccable.

When the music stopped, the applause in *Atlantis* echoed on and on. Loring felt too out of control to return at once to the Snippet-White table. He offered his arm, and he and Ulla strolled smiling around the parquet (Madame Olivia Loring's method to milk an audience for affection) while Loring tried to compose himself.

Had they only waltzed? Yet he was sweating, panting like a schoolboy! Afraid to search her eyes, he nonetheless sneaked a glance as he dabbed his brow with his handkerchief. She was gazing at him with definite interest! Up and down his tight-crotched uniform! She was more than curious. She seemed actually turned on!

Had she seen his fingernails? Had she noticed that he had been turned on himself? Loring didn't know, could not say. All of this had happened too fast to know anything for sure.

At first, when the Captain had summoned him over to their table, the Snippet-Whites greeted Loring with surprising warmth. Hildegarde said she had marveled at his merengue with her Austrian goddaughter Ulla at the Captain's Reception. Would the good doctor care to flatter them further with an encore, perhaps a Viennese to the Colonel's favorite, the *"Blue Danube?"*

Flatter them? The disarmingly humble, scandalously rich, Snippet-Whites? Flatter them by putting his arms around the most enticing and skilled dance partner he had ever held?

Loring knew he was not hallucinating, but were not the limits of reality being stretched? His own exultant heartbeats felt real enough as he strode back to the table and saw the Snippet-Whites glow with approval.

The noted British Colonel flashed a paternal smile. He rose beside the Captain, clasped Loring's hand, bared a crooked gold incisor over his brandy snifter. "I'm not a bad hoofer myself, Doctor," he winked crisply. "But what a bloody inspired Danube! As if you've been Ulla's partner for years! I was just saying to Hildegarde, we must have you and Ulla up to *Viceroy Deck* for tea. What do you think?"

"It would be my great pleasure, sir."

"The greater pleasure would be ours, son."

Heady and gratifying as the moment seemed, Loring felt an icy tingle shoot down his spine when he looked into the old man's gray eyes and felt the insistent handshake.

It had not occurred to Loring during the waltz with Ulla, but lanky-limbed Rockwell Snippet-White did bear an uncanny resemblance to Loring's own late father. The ramrod bearing, the harpoon-shaped nose, and the crooked gold incisor were more than reminiscent of Vermont country doctor Orson Loring, who had perished almost exactly a year ago at age 88 (probably near the Colonel's age) in a skiing accident on the Killington slopes.

Bizarre! And the Colonel had even called him "son" when he shook his hand!

The past 24 hours – the escape from the Samaritan, the nasty break-up at the airport with Anita Rothberg, the jet flight south, and then Ulla's warmth on the dance floor – perhaps all of it had assaulted his senses, created an absurd visual/emotional blur between a kindly new acquaintance and his beloved dead father, who, peculiarly enough, had also enjoyed chats with his son over tea.

Loring felt Ulla squeeze his hand. She looked into his eyes. "Oliver, is something wrong?" she asked in a throaty Austrian warble.

"Ha-*ha*! Not at all! It was a wonderful waltz."

"But your face. It's red."

"I blush easily."

"Yes, you do. And I see goose bumps on the back of your hand."

"I do that easily, too. Sorry."

"Don't apologize. It's charming," she giggled. "Talented fellow, aren't you?"

Ulla cocked her head as if to say something more, but the Captain grabbed Loring's elbow firmly and pulled him away. "Might I have a word with you, please, Doctor?"

Loring excused himself from the Snippet-White table.

Once they were out of earshot, the Captain's smile faded. He cleared his throat. "Doctor, my wife Snø flew in today from Oslo. She's quite exhausted and her nerves are destroyed. Do you think you could you help her?"

"Should I make a cabin call?"

The chiseled Nordic face twitched fitfully. "Not necessary. Valium is all she needs. Ten milligrams."

Trond Ramskog – wavy blonde hair and still boyish-looking at 50 – was the most brilliant and confident Norwegian Officer in the fleet. But tonight his famous golden handlebars tilted in odd spasms, his fjord-blue eyes narrowed to a pained squint. "It's the publicity on this cruise, Doctor. Cablevista. Farrely Farrell. All this TV nonsense puts everyone on edge, including my wife. You do understand?"

"Let me run down to the *Hospital*."

"Shall we keep it a secret, strictly between us?"

* * *

Reluctant to leave Ulla and the Snippet-Whites, but duty-bound to serve the Captain, Loring tripped down four decks then proceeded forward to the *Hospital* on the port side of *Viking Deck*. He unlocked the narcotics safe (no Nurse or Paramedic in sight) and zipped back along the corridor with two 5-milligram Valium tablets sealed in a tiny wave-and-sunburst envelope and tucked neatly into his left breast pocket.

As a rule, Loring never doled out tranquilizers promiscuously, especially benzodiazapines like Valium. How often had he warned the Samaritan E.R. staff against the sneaky side effects of that over-prescribed drug, a close relative of the potent anesthetic Midazolam! But his clinical turf now was not a Harvard teaching hospital; it was the world's grandest pleasure vessel on a tension-fraught cruise.

TV star Farrely Farrell and his full New York "Love Luck" entourage and technical staff were not due to board till Tuesday down in San Juan. But already Loring had seen the advance teams in black "Love Luck" t-shirts prowling the ship to shoot on-site video promos. Tomorrow the Cablevista blimp would rendezvous over the ship to take bird's eye shots and trace their course all the way south to St. Maarten and back. Meanwhile, from Cablevista's "Valentine TV Cruise" web site, the whole world could download details of their minute-by-minute progress.

And, as if anybody needed reminders, odd little Styrofoam stickies of Farrely Farrell's wolfish grin had been posted everywhere. Over the *Purser's Desk* on *Boutique Row*, at *Licks, the Ice Cream Bistro*, in *Sails, the Glass-Floored Disco*, above the slots in *Nuggets, the Casino*, at some of the computer terminals in *"Surfs Up, the Web Cafe,"* and over the urinal in the bathroom of the *Chinese Tailor Shop*, there he was: Farrely Farrell's toothy mouth spouted his salacious battle cry in a wet Aussie drawl: *"HEY MATE! Let ME make YOU lucky in love!"*

Beginning tomorrow with the arrival of the Cablevista blimp, the eyes of the planet and the internet would focus on the *S/S Nordic Blue*. The on-board atmosphere (2400 passengers and 950 crew) already crackled with a near-hysterical charge.

From a clinical point of view, the anxieties of Snø Ramskog, newly-arrived wife of the Captain, were predictable. Cablevista satellites beamed 24-hours around the world, including to Scandinavia. Snø Ramskog certainly knew how Farrely Farrell and his tasteless "reality television" vehicle dominated the current international TV/tabloid scene. Jet-lagged after her flight from Oslo? And then to step on board and face all this?

Valium? Why, of course!

Another on board factor: for the past six years, the handsome Captain Ramskog had been in the habit of entertaining in his suite the *Nordic Blue's* leggy, red-headed Chief Nurse, Maggie McCarthy. Trond and the nubile Ms. McCarthy were the on-board item every crew member knew about – but also knew *not* to talk about.

Snø Ramskog and Maggie McCarthy would face off for the first time this cruise. Valium, anybody else?

On an ethical level, what right had Oliver Loring to lecture Trond Ramskog about drug side effects? Or about the question of potential addiction? The charismatic and highly respected Captain did not need Loring to preach to him about how Snø might develop a habit after one dose. Why quibble over ten milligrams of Valium, especially while a hundred thousand *tons* of ocean liner were thrusting through the waves under Trond's expert command? Simple arithmetic made the call an ethical no-brainer.

Also, consider shipboard politics. Traditionally, there were two Doctors and three Nurses on the *Nordic Blue*. But 15 months ago, the line had cut back funds to the Medical Department and had hired two highly competent Paramedics – Kevin Patterson and Guy Fialco, a muscular gay couple from Key West. Kevin and Guy worked out together in the *Crew Gym* every afternoon but stayed in the *Hospital* or in their cabin all the rest of the time. Kevin and Guy now did almost all the hands-on patient care and shared call with Maggie. Loring was the only Doctor in the department now, and, except in dire emergencies, his role had become largely ceremonial.

When work came his way, Loring handled the more critical and delicate cases. He sutured tendons, lanced ear drums, inserted chest tubes, and supervised the clot busting of myocardial infarctions before choppering patients off to Miami for definitive subspecialty care.

But such severe cases were quite rare. Most of the time Loring remained clinically idle. In fact, Loring relished occasional chores – like running to fetch Valiums for Snø Ramskog – if only to prove the three gold stripes and the embroidered caduceus on each of his epaulets were not purely ornamental. He certainly did not want the other Norwegian Officers to resent him as a mere uniform mannequin who was given a generous bar allowance and a luxury suite on *Viking Deck* and whose only visible duties included: (1) carry the emergency beeper, (2) check in on the *Hospital* daily to sign papers and dictate occasional insurance reports, and (3) appear sober in public areas.

Chasing down a pair of Valiums at the Captain's personal request? Nobody could do it more quickly or more discreetly!

Loring stopped for a moment and looked down the long *Viking Deck* corridor – all clear. Extending his right palm horizontally at eye level, he swung his chin over his right epaulet, gripped his left hand on his hip, and took a rigid hieroglyphic posture with both knees kinked and feet wedged in the same plane. Egyptian style in two dimensions, he then slid forward a dozen paces.

Step . . . slide . . . step!

Loring had first encountered this distinctive, if uncomfortable, ambulation style five years before in Boston. Late one night at the Samaritan, a wild-eyed, red-bearded 30-year-old Harvard grad student in Egyptology had presented in field boots and pith helmet. He was frozen in this same bizarre, rigid, two-dimensional posture. The troubled student had dipped too deeply into the preparations for his thesis defense and had returned from (an imaginary) Nile dig morphed, he claimed, into an indecipherable hieroglyph. Fortunately for this suffering patient, Loring's subspecialty was psychiatric emergencies (a discipline he had pursued during a two-year post-doctoral fellowship at the Harvard-affiliated Massachusetts Mental Institution). For this intriguing case, he knew to employ a controversial British technique called Mimic-Empathy Therapy (MEP). By mirror-imaging the tormented student's stiff gestures up and down the corridors for more than an hour, Loring (and MEP) had triumphed.

Finally, with his energy flagging and his eyelids drooping, the patient clearly showed improvement. His stony pose melted. Recovering his senses, he gratefully agreed to be locked on a ward and medicated.

Since then, Loring had often toyed with the Egyptian posture and found it, though originally inspired by schizophrenia, highly effective as a meditative calculus.

Slide . . . step . . . slide!

Coincidentally, the Egyptian mode perfectly suited the *Nordic Blue's* long hallways (1,108 meters – "longer than the Eiffel Tower is tall!") with their low, crypt-like ceilings, their visually challenging sag in the middle, and their crazy quilt, pink and blue, vomit-proof carpeting.

And why should Loring *not* meditate in motion down *Viking Deck*? Back 3,000-plus years ago, what did Ramses I and II and the rest of the Pharaohs do to amuse themselves on all those barge voyages up and down the Nile? Dynasty after dynasty? Pyramid construction site visit after pyramid construction site visit? Mummy wrapping ceremony after . . .

Slide . . . step . . .

Stepping like an ancient Egyptian – reflecting in two dimensions on water – gave Loring a timeless perspective on life's vicissitudes, even on personal debacles like his awkwardly concluded affair with Anita Rothberg.

The truth was: Dr. Anita was *all* vicissitudes but could not admit it.

Some therapist! No wonder she could not dance. Because dance means change – moment by deliciously rhythmic moment.

Olivia Loring knew this. Ulla von Straf knew this, too. Anita Rothberg did not.

Loring congratulated himself. If he had caved in earlier at Logan Airport and invited Anita down here to the Caribbean, there would have been no chance for fiery merengues or entrancing waltzes with Ulla.

No Egyptian-style stuff, either. Not with a bossy blonde ball-and-chain dragging at his heels!

And as for Dr. Rothberg's aggressiveness? Might she mellow in the Caribbean?

As a male chauvinist in recovery, Loring had taken all the rigorous gender sensitivity courses Harvard had to offer its faculty, including the White Mountains Sex-blind Winter Survival Weekend. He had been instructed, quizzed, retested on his own flaws after a Mount Washington hut-to-hut shake-down and then a blind-buddy rappel near Tuckerman's Ravine.

But who could not judge Anita Rothberg for her fierce and unpredictable temper, which was pure poison when it came to courting the likes of the Snippet-Whites?

Slide . . .

Loring snapped out of his Egyptian mode. Even Ramses II, proud Pharaoh, would not keep the Snippet-Whites and their petal-lipped Austrian goddaughter waiting in *Atlantis*.

He bounded up the stairs three at a time.

* * *

Up on *Promenade Deck* again, Loring paused outside the *Atlantis* entrance to catch his breath and savor the vision: the Colonel and Mrs. Snippet-White glided and twirled alone on the dance floor as Barry and the Atlantans played Leroy Anderson's classic *"Blue Tango."* So exquisite!

Little Hildegarde's body looked amazingly supple. She skidded up and down the Colonel's thigh in an impressive series of *duende* lift-offs. Her lavender skirt flashed while she floated, quick as a frisky dragonfly over pond water. And the Colonel *was* the erotic blue in *"Blue Tango."* He disdained her whims, glowered at his prey, offered tenderness only when she truly begged him with her eyes.

"Dance must tell a story!" Madame Olivia often stressed to her Academy pupils.

Loring knew the story behind this tango. In fact, he had heard so much about the Snippet-Whites on past cruises, he often wondered if the celebrated couple were not imaginary legends, phantoms of a latter-day sea saga. But tonight he had shaken their hands, looked them both in the eye, received their invitation to tea. He knew they were real and delicately human.

Now, looking at the Colonel on the dance floor, Loring found the old Colonel's face, except for the harpoon nose, quite fragile and vulnerable – not what might be expected of a lavishly decorated British war espionage hero who then had become a self-made billionaire and philanthropist.

The story behind this *"Blue Tango"* had begun nearly forty years ago, and right here on the *Club Atlantis* parquet, where this remarkable couple had first met. The circumstances, as Loring understood them from *Crew Bar* accounts, followed the sweet scenario of a Cary Grant-meets-Kate Hepburn Hollywood charmer.

Before the second world war, Rockwell Snippet-White, then a brilliant young math professor at Cambridge University, had invented highly sophisticated calculating devices – vacuum tube precursors of chip computers. He had served spectacularly (two Cross of Saint George awards) with British

Intelligence during the war in the top-secret *Colossus* deciphering project. After the war, he entered private industry, first in London, then New York, and parleyed his cryptananalytic skills into scores of lucrative patents in the early software industry.

In the mid-1950s he started Snippet-White, Ltd, now the computer giant Snipcon, with headquarters in London, New York, Tokyo, and Kuala Lampur. Apart from his wartime decorations, the British Crown had decorated the Colonel twice for his Snippet-White Foundation, a philanthropic megafund that founded and fostered small businesses and medical clinics in the third world.

Through all his years of professional achievements and philanthropy, the Colonel had kept his private life private. No idle schmoozing with royalty at charity galas while the paparazzi hovered. Some said the reason he had never been knighted was because he had twice snubbed invitations from Queen Elizabeth herself. (Too busy to attend. Sorry, Liz.)

The single luxury the Colonel allowed himself, however, was cruising on ocean liners where his privacy was strictly honored and protected.

The members of the *Nordic Blue* crew knew the reason behind his passion for cruising. Forty years before, on a rough February crossing from Southampton, the Colonel had first encountered Hildegarde Evans on this ship – then the *S/S Marianne* under the French Flag.

The Colonel had lost his first wife a year before to multiple sclerosis, after a 15-year, childless marriage. He was crossing alone on the *Marianne* with the sole purpose of settling some business contracts on Wall Street. He had booked the same *Viceroy Deck* suite for his return to Southampton.

The first night out in *Club Atlantis,* he spotted the perky and diminutive Hildegarde and asked her to tango.

Mrs. Hildegarde Evans was an amateur landscape artist and the daughter of a distinguished line of Boston bankers. She also had been widowed, three years before, and had no children. She had just finished a painting tour in Italy and Provence and was traveling alone and, yes, was very pleased indeed to tango.

The winter crossing proved cold and blustery, but the couple met in *Atlantis* every night. Had the gods overlooking the club's dance floor intuited that this spunky, middle-aged American lass might soothe and invigorate the still distraught English multimillionaire? The Hollywood script writers for Cary Grant and Kate Hepburn would have agreed.

Upon arrival in New York on Valentine's Day, they were married by a justice of the peace. They sailed back for England that very evening and pledged always to observe Valentine's Day by dancing their hearts out at sea, preferably on the S/S *Marianne*.

Such was the *Crew Bar* legend Loring had heard. He saw the ancient Valentine pledge still in dynamic effect as the stylish pair finished their flamboyant tango and bowed. They thrust their hands up and received the accolades of the delighted *Atlantis* patrons. Barry and the Atlantans applauded, too. Loring watched Ulla von Straf shake her head and smile, her crystalline blue eyes bright with affection.

Bursting with pleasure, the Colonel was in far too animated a mood to pause for a breather. He arched his imposing white brows, tapped his long forefinger in the air, and commanded Barry to play the old Charleston chestnut, *"Barney Google with the Goo-goo-googly Eyes,"* at a break-neck tempo.

Eager to please, Maestro Cox picked up his trumpet and snapped his fingers. The snare drum rattled. The cymbals clashed. Hildegarde laughed, raised her hands again and let her lithe hips roll. The Colonel's gold-toothed grin blazed around *Atlantis* and his feet pranced and scuffed like the paws of a manic jack rabbit.

While the Colonel cut his capers – astonishing for a man well into his ninth decade – Loring made his way back to Ulla and the Captain.

Ulla stood as he approached the table. *"Oliver!* I was waiting for you. I must run off for rehearsal. Would you like to drop by the *Starlight Theatre* at midnight and watch us?"

"A rehearsal at midnight?"

"Yes. This week all our rehearsals are scheduled at midnight – the time of our TV performance Thursday. Tosco wants everything to be timed exactly like on the night of the Valentine show."

"Tosco?"

"The magician. He has unusual power over animals. The choreography is very original," she smiled with a cryptic wink. Then she gave Loring a kiss on the cheek and disappeared.

Loring felt his heart race. He gazed on mutely as the old Colonel and Hildegarde delivered their fearsome footwork on the *Atlantis* parquet – some nifty double dagger heel swivels and British variations on the Charleston toe rattle, knee whip, and flea hop that Loring had never seen before, even at top-level competition tournaments.

It wasn't until some minutes after the remarkable Snippet-Whites had finished their amazing Charleston and both sat grinning and panting at the table, that Loring felt the Captain nudge him firmly in the ribs.

The Captain looked troubled.

"Are you feeling alright, Captain?"

Trond Ramskog gave a nervous chuckle. "I was wondering the same of you, Doctor."

"Never felt better. I know this is going to be my best cruise ever, and I'd like to thank you for being my captain, Captain."

Ramskog's glance darkened. His mustache twitched.

Loring giggled. *"Oh!* Ha-*ha!* Almost forgot, didn't I?"

He reached into his breast pocket, palmed the envelope with the Valiums deftly into Ramskog's hand.

As the Captain fingered the two pills inside the packet, his eyes brightened and his mustache steadied. "Thank you, Doctor. My wife will be grateful."

"She'll probably be feeling much better by morning, I'm sure. Once the jet lag wears off. But if there's anything more I can do, let me know, won't you?"

"Yes, there is. Please don't mention this to the Nurse."

"Of course, not, Captain. I understand. We agreed it would be confidential. If I can't take care of the Captain's wife discreetly, who can I take care of?"

"Thank you. And one thing more, Doctor. Why don't you join my honor table tomorrow night? The Snippet-Whites will be there. They like you. Their goddaughter does, too. You dance very well with her."

"Do you think? Of course, I'll be at your honor table. And again, thank you for being my captain, Captain!"

* * *

The *Crew Bar* on the *Nordic Blue* was tucked far aft and below – just over the *Poop Deck* and directly atop the boilers. The ship's huge turbines throbbed continuously under foot. Electric brass soca music thundered from the speakers overhead. Sheets of cigarette smoke, mixed with the diesel fumes in the air, pulsed bright green with neon that shouted, *"RINGNES! PROUD BEER OF NORWAY!"*

The sign taped over the bar announced, *"POWER CRUISERS STRICTLY FORBIDDEN!"* In this thick and rowdy atmosphere, Finnish Motormen, Jamaican Bell Hops, Indonesian Cocktail Waitresses, Croatian Carpenters, Scottish Casino Croupiers, Filipino Able Bodied Seamen, and the occasional Starlegs Dancer or Norwegian Officer enjoyed off-duty libations and shared scuttlebutt in raunchy sanctuary away from the passengers, a/k/a power cruisers.

Tonight the *Crew Bar* was abuzz. The jittery crowd milled at the bar and huddled in the booths. They chatted and laughed with more than the usual Saturday night zest. This was, after all, the first night of the long anticipated Cabelvista *Valentine TV Cruise,* and nobody – not even the seasoned old salts – knew what to expect.

"BULLSEYE AGAIN! Wooooooeeeeeeeeeeeeeeeeeeeee!" screamed spidery Jacques Chemin, the flamboyant Pastry Chef and Master Ice Sculptor from Port-au-Prince.

"Think I can do it again, Jacques?"

"Mais oui!" Jacques laughed in his high-pitched, nasal creole. "Tonight the Dart Doc, he has a hot hand! Tonight the Dart Doc is scary. He is utterly and uniquely *MAGNIFIQUE!"*

Darts in the *Crew Bar* had always been a boost for Loring. Tonight, a few minutes before midnight, and despite rowdy revelers squeezed tight all around him, he was in closer touch with the target than ever before.

He focused on the green and yellow concentric circles on the cork disk and zoned out all other forces. He tried to live up to the name "Dart Doc," the *nom de guerre* Jacques Chemin had given him four years back when Loring, then an unknown newcomer, had first planted his foot on the white firing line at the *Crew Dart Olympics* and walked off with the gold medal and a free case of Ringnes.

Loring could not explain it. He had been introduced to competitive darts here on the *Nordic Blue* and never played anywhere else. Yet, cruise after cruise, when he stood with his toe on the white line, his precision and consistency were, well, uncanny.

Several *Crew Bar* dart aficionados theorized that his many years of Boston Samaritan E.R. work had opened his *"dart chakra."* True: at the Samaritan, Loring routinely aimed needles into neck and groin arteries, abdomens, spinal canals, chests, and heart chambers. But, how did a fingertip feel for human anatomy relate to firing darts in a cruise ship crew bar? *Huh?*

Wasn't he more likely a variant on the *"idiot savant"* syndrome – the neurological phenomenon in which a mentally defective individual displays unusual aptitude or brilliance in some special field? Except, in Loring's peculiar case, without clinically overt mental defectiveness? (Also true – Loring had been born on April first, and his parents had often fondly called him their "fool" when he was growing up. But, to Loring's mind, being called

28

a *fool* and acting like an *idiot* were altogether different!)

Whatever the cause, Loring's skill was widely admired on the *Nordic Blue*. This shipboard renown pleased him. On the *Bridge* and in the *Officers' Mess,* the Norwegian Officers often called him "Dart Doc" with respect, sometimes even jealousy. By the pools, passenger women occasionally asked, with an intrigued glance, "Excuse me, aren't you Doctor Loring? Why do they call you 'Dart Doc'?"

"Six bullseyes of eight! *MAGNIFIQUE!* You *CANNOT* hit one more!" taunted Chemin. He wiggled his long fingers and smacked his lips in anticipation.

"Magnifique?" Loring closed his eyes before the final shot.

Yes, the scene earlier in *Club Atlantis* had been *MAGNIFIQUE*.

His heart still fluttered from Ulla's surprise smooch. And when he had excused himself from the Snippet-Whites – saying they must want to spend their first evening on board alone – they had smiled at what they called his "sensitivity to their situation." All *that* plus an invitation to the Captain's honor table tomorrow night. And a chance to watch Ulla at midnight tonight! Was the karma of this cruise not riding on Loring's own personal wave length?

He opened his eyes, winked at Chemin, leaned toward the target, whispered his aiming mantra: *"Thooooooooooooooooooooooooong."* He flicked the dart, and the feathers spun in the air three-and-a half axial rotations, as intended.

The dart junkies around him exploded.

"BULLSEYE! SEVEN out of *NINE!"* screeched Chemin. He slapped Loring's epaulets. *"Come*, Doctor Oliver. I buy you an Aquavit!"

Idiot savant or not, Loring beamed. He followed Chemin to the bar as the Haitian waved his arms and commanded, "Make way for Dart Doc, people! The man is *baaaaaaaaaaaaaaaaaaaaaack*!"

Loring enjoyed shooting Aquavit with Chemin, the talented provacateur whose dark pixie eyes and slender fingers never stopped moving – more so when Aquavit fired his metabolism.

A flashy dresser (raspberry Armani jacket tonight for the first night of the *Valentine TV Cruise*, thank you), Jacques Chemin packed panache into every gesture. Wherever he went, he did it all with signature flair – brandishing his pastry bag in the *Galley Bakery* or ice sculpting with his electric chisel in the *Main Dining Room* or wiggling his skinny pelvis under the limbo stick at the crew beach party every Friday afternoon on the Private Island in the Bahamas.

It was true that Chemin had detractors. Some dismissed him as an egotistic *artiste*. Others called him an over-sexed Haitian hustler and trickster, who had once cruised the faster alleys in Paris while training in the culinary arts and now hit on vulnerable crew women here in the Caribbean with his seductive mix of island voodoo and continental *savoir faire*. There were rumors that Chemin's Paris period had included stints as a nocturnal pick-lock and cat burglar to help meet his tuition at the *Cordon Bleu*. But as far as anybody knew, wily Chemin had never served hard time for his late night, second story Parisian acrobatics.

Loring knew for a fact that Chemin had kicked cocaine years ago. He respected him for that. And he also refused to judge him for his mere outlandishness. Yes, the tiny heart-shaped diamond, inlaid in gold on his right front tooth, was a bit over-the-top.

But so *what* if Jacques exaggerated every gesture and claimed he could read auras and tried to impress everybody with his wild antics, like blowing on his giant royal conch shell at parties to get attention? So *what* if he bragged that he could pick any lock on the ship, including the new magnetic credit card keys? Chemin was brilliant, effervescent, and entertaining. Maybe, like Loring, he had a little of the "idiot savant" in him, too. In any case, Loring liked him.

Also, his grooming habits. Forget the killer manicure. How did this dapper stud keep his round ebony scalp so slick and glistening 24/7? Bikini wax?

At the bar, they clinked glasses and chugged their Aquavits. Chemin pressed his palm to Loring's forehead and frowned dramatically.

"*Ouueeeeeeeeeeeeeeeeeeeeeeeeeh!* The *docteur* needs a second dose of the Aquavit medicine right away! Burning up with the fever? Why so very hot tonight?"

"Guess I'm just glad to be back, Jacques!"

The Haitian rolled his eyes and thumbed Loring's cheek. A sly whistle slid through his teeth. "Call the *Fire Brigade*! Dart Doc is getting a fast sunburn in front of our eyes!"

"Aquavit makes me blush every time! I think it's the caraway seeds in it."

"Caraway seeds?"

"Yes. In the Aquavit. The caraway makes me blush."

Chemin whistled louder. "*Docteur!* Don't you try to hide a romantic secret from the old voodoo king! Caraway seeds, indeed! You are burning up over a *ma-de-moi-selle*! I have seen you sizzling before on the world's grandest and most legendary cruise ship, but never this hotly!" Chemin licked his forefinger, touched the tip to Loring's nose. "*Sssssssssssssssssssst!* You better forget right away about those foolish caraway seeds."

"That bad?"

"At *least*."

Loring sighed, relieved that Jacques had not insisted on Ulla's name. Chemin was famous on board for letting things out of the bag, and Loring preferred that rumors not spread and get out of control, not this early in the cruise week.

The Haitian jerked his head back, shouted over his shoulder. "Hey, Pearly! Look who's back and burning so fiercely with passionate love!"

Pearly Livingstone, the massive Jamaican Fork Lift Master and former Heavyweight Golden Gloves champion of Jamaica, elbowed over to the bar, a green Ringnes can in his prodigious fist. His extra-extra large wave-and-sunburst t-shirt was stretched tight over his burly torso.

"In love *again*?" boomed the bearish Pearly in his deep, gravely voice. He crushed Loring's fingers in a gladiator-force shake. "You tell me that the Dart Doc, he steps on board the first night and he's already down for the count, *mon*?"

"Great to see you, Pearly!"

Pearly Livingstone, a life-long admirer of Muhammad Ali, put his Ringnes can on the bar. He raised his fists, peek-a-booed, faked a right hook to Loring's jaw. Loring countered with a gentle rope-a-dope combination to the ex-champ's squishy midriff.

Pearly rocked back against the bar. "Not bad, *mon*! For somebody in love. How do you keep your reflexes so sharp? Isn't it highly frigid up in Boston just now?"

Loring gave a fake shiver. "Snow up to your belly button!"

The Jamaican winked slowly and pointed his giant thumb down toward his crotch. "Just thinkin' about it turns both of mine to ice cubes, *mon*!" He embraced Loring in a suffocating hug and slapped him on the back. "Well, I'm glad you're back. Ready for the TV shows, Doc? Farrely Farrell's flyin' down from New York Tuesday. Gonna' make us all lucky in love, he says."

"Aren't champions always lucky in love?"

Pearly laughed and shook his head. "Not today, Doc. I was busy haulin' those big ass Cablevista computers and crates on board. We got another load of electrical gear comin' on down in San Juan. And Tuesday we're gonna' use a crane to put three new Mercedes roadsters up on *Vista Deck*, too. Prizes for the 'Love Luck' contestants."

"This cruise is big time, Pearly. They'll be watching all around the world."

"Yea, Dart Doc! Bigger than the Thrilla' in Manila!"

"And your kids? Will they be watching down in Ocho Rios?"

"You bet! Round the clock, Dart Doc! My four boys and my three girlies, they *all* gonna' see their Daddy Pearly!"

Loring winked. *"YOU NEVER KNOW UNTIL YOU KNOW!"*

Pearly roared and slapped Loring's cheek. *"YOU NEVER KNOW UNTIL YOU KNOW!"*

Loring knew what would follow – a *Crew Bar* rite.

The three men locked hands by the bar in a circle, looked into each others' grinning faces, and chanted, *"MY, MY, MY! LORDY, LORDY, LORDY! THE GOOD AND THE BAD! IT ISN'T OVER UNTIL IT BE OVER! YOU NEVER KNOW UNTIL YOU KNOW! OH YESSSSSSSSSSS! OH YESSSSSSSSSSSSSSS!"*

No sooner were they finished with the chant, than others near the bar began it again. Chemin led them all, and with wild gesticulations.

"MY, MY, MY! LORDY, LORDY, LORDY! THE GOOD AND THE BAD! IT ISN'T OVER UNTIL IT BE OVER! YOU NEVER KNOW UNTIL YOU KNOW! OH YESSSSSSSSSSS! OH YESSSSSSSSSSSSSSSSS!"

Loring's heart raced.

OH YESSSSSSSSSSSSSSSSSSSSSSSSSSSSS!

Loring adored crew chants – quirky expressions of team identity and commitment. The hard-working *Nordic Blue* crew all couldn't know each other. There were 950 people from all over the world. Many had no language in common. But that didn't mean they couldn't show tribe-like affection for each other.

The chants had oblique meanings – bits and scraps which percolated into their minds and seemed to flow together with some weird poetic thrust. This particular chant, concocted by Jacques Chemin several years back (with apologies to the New York Yankees baseball catcher/philosopher Yogi Berra) could be heard in the *Crew Gym*, the *Crew Galley*, the gang showers on *Dolphin Deck*, Loring's Cambridge apartment – anywhere the *Nordic Blue's* exuberant spirit lived.

And it absolutely thrilled Loring to bark out the chant again here in the *Crew Bar* with his Caribbean cronies.

Pearly grabbed Loring's shoulder. "Dart Doc! How about we do a long conga line to welcome you back. I have seen you lead some spirited snake dances down here. We miss havin' you with us! Don't we, Jacques?"

Loring checked his watch: 10 minutes till midnight! He wriggled from Pearly's grip. "Can't stay for the conga line tonight, *mon*."

Chemin laughed and slapped Loring's epaulet. "We cannot keep you prisoner from your destiny, *Docteur*. But before you go, one question. That new Demo Dancer. Ulla? The Austrian girl? Is it she who gives you fever?"

"There's a new Demo Dancer on board?"

The Haitian winked slyly at Pearly, pulled a Marlboro from his jacket pocket. He waved the tip at Loring. "Beautiful Ulla? With the long legs and the sad blue eyes?"

Pearly nodded. "Yes. Ulla. The whole ship is in love with her, Doc."

"Fool!" taunted Chemin. "Don't you blush at us again! You cannot keep your secrets from old Pearly and the voodoo king! When I be takin' my fresh pastries by the Captain's party tonight, did I not see you dancin' your skinny ass off in the *Starlight Lounge*?"

"It was only a merengue."

"You call *that* a merengue? *Oh la la!*" Chemin flicked his lighter, touched the flame to the tip of his Marlboro. "*Mon ami!* Be very careful! Flip Spinelli is also panting hotly for that beautiful woman. And I tell you something about fever like her. She's different from those silly caraway seeds." Chemin drew close to Loring's ear, *"YOU NEVER KNOW UNTIL YOU KNOW!"*

"Are you always so wise about affairs of the heart?"

"Affairs of the heart?" Chemin sucked saliva in from the edges of his lips, then drew on his Marlboro. Hissing loudly, he blew a hot billow of smoke against Loring's cheek. "Listen up close, Dart Doc. Ulla may go deeper than your heart. *FAR DEEPER! FAR DEEPER THAN YOUR HEART!"*

* * *

Midnight in the cavernous *Starlight Theatre*. As the house lights darken, Oliver Loring, an audience of one, settles into the back row of the third balcony. Far down in the orchestra pit, kettle drums rumble then simmer to a hum. Frenzied spotlights flash on the giant folds of the blue-on-blue, wave-and-sunburst stage curtains. Over the speakers a snappy (prerecorded) baritone.

"Thank you Farrely Farrell! Ladies and Gentlemen! It's Flip Spinelli again, your *Nordic Blue* Cruise Director, welcoming all our millions of Cablevista friends all around the world to the last stop on our tour of the fabulous *Nordic Blue*. Here it is. It's the one and only *Starlight Theatre* – the largest, most glamorous stage on the high seas! We call it our Broadway on the Blue!"

(Kettle drums roll hard then hum again.)

"Now I hope all of you have enjoyed tonight's live Valentine tour on the grandest and most legendary and sexiest cruise ship in the world. Farrely and I have shown you some amazing things aboard the *S/S Nordic Blue* tonight! Have we *not*?

"How 'bout those dancers down in the *Starlight Lounge*? And how 'bout Captain Ramskog and that exciting tour he gave us of the *Bridge*! And don't we have the finest *Hospital* and medical staff on the seven seas? And that dancing doctor? Did you catch him earlier? And the beautiful Ulla von Straf from Austria? *Oh, yeaaaaaaaaa!* Tell me about it!

"The *Club Roma Spa*? And how 'bout that fabulous visit in *Nuggets, the Casino*, with Joey Manook, our Casino Manager. *Boutique Row*? How about *Scents, the Perfume Parlor*? Or *Surf's Up, the Web Cafe?* Or the *Crow's Nest Dance Club*? Or how about *Topsiders, the Piano Bar*? Oh, *yes*!

"Guess what! Ladies and gentlemen out there on the Cablevista planet, as we say here on the high seas, *'You've hardly scratched the surface, baby!'*

"*Oh, yeaaaaaaaa!* Farrely's cameras barely had time to show you *Sails, the Glass-Floored Disco* and *Hemispheres,* our fabulous hi-tech health club – it's never too late to tone up those abs and buns, folks – and the sophisticated *Club Roma Spa* down on *Pool Deck.* Did I mention it already? Doesn't matter! The list goes *on and oooooooooooonaaaaaaah!* Ladies and gentlemen, the *S/S Nordic Blue* has a crew of nearly a thousand maritime entertainment professionals waiting to show all of you how fabulous and totally sexy a week's cruise can be.

"And speaking of sexy, how many of you out there think magic is sexy? Come on, ladies! I'm serious! Who doesn't want a little magic tonight, especially since last night Farrely showed us all how to get lucky?

"Yes, it's midnight down here in the Caribbean and we're going to cap off our tour with some very sexy and magical Valentine talent coming to you, ladies and gentlemen, right here in the sultry *Starlight Theatre!* And when I say magic, folks, I mean it! Tonight our very own Starlegs Dancers present the exciting "Love Magic" extravaganza with a new featured guest on the *Nordic Blue,* who's taking a starring role tonight for the first time in his native western hemisphere!

"You know, they say big things sometimes come in small packages, ladies and gentlemen. Well, that couldn't be more true than tonight with the star of our show. He's the little fellow with the really big super powers!

"Don't be deceived by his stature. Give *Monsieur* Tosco a few minutes with the Starlegs Dancers, and you'll see why this pint-sized guy is known as the Legend of Legerdemain, the Duke of Disappearance, the Prince of

Prestidigitation, the Sultan of Serendipity, the Pope of Poof, the Buddha of Boo, the Godfather of Golly-jee, and yes folks, a real, real nice guy, too!

"Originally from the magical island of Cuba where he grew up . . . but now coming to us directly from Paris, France, where he has his own world-famous, cutting edge circus . . . he's the one . . . he's the only . . .

"Put your hands together with the rest of us here on the *Valentine TV Cruise* of the *S/S Nordic Blue* – the world's grandest and most legendary and sexiest cruise ship . . . and welcome the guest of the Starlegs Dancers . . . the incredible and unique . . . *oh, yeaaaaaaaaaaaaaa! TOSCO! THE NEW WORLD MAGICIAN!* in 'Love Magic!'

"Here he is! The incredible and out-of-this-world magician . . . *TOSCO* and his friends . . . in . . . *'LLOOOOOOVE MMMMMMMMMAGIC!'*"

* * *

Long snare drum roll. Spotlights converge on the slit in the curtains. A sway-back dwarf creeps out from between the folds. He wears a sequined blue tuxedo with matching top hat and a red rosebud in his lapel. He tweaks his mustache, doffs his hat, bows with reverence to the empty theatre.

His face is dark, swarthy, latin. Beneath his impressive mane of silvering hair, his large eyes are luring and playful. He smiles humbly. He blows a kiss to the invisible audience, lingers on the kiss to look out at all of them. His eyes follow the kiss as though the kiss in flight has taken on a life of its own and flutters through the theatre.

Tosco puts his forefinger to his lips for silence, kisses a white dove, which he delivers from his left sleeve, kisses a purple dove, which appears from his right sleeve. The doves flap their wings joyously on his fingers, as if excited by the lip touch on their necks by their keeper, their liberator. They rise and hover in synchronized tandem just above the dwarf's shoulders.

Tosco smiles his mysterious smile and then opens his mouth, puts his palms to his belly, and begins to sing in a pleasing and robust baritone. The eerie, slithering melody rises to the upper range and then falls gracefully back into deeper tones. The unintelligible syllables are of harsh consonants and throated vowels – incomprehensible yet clearly with some deep meaning – perhaps of a primitive Indo-European or Slavic dialect or a spoken Sanskrit – *"Eeeeoooo! Eeeoooooooooooo! Wlhkravoooooooeee!"* – and the song itself writhes like an ancient, bitter lament, bringing chills, mimicking the moan of the iciest of winds over the coldest, most desolate central Asian steppes.

As Tosco sings, the hovering doves rise slowly higher. They criss-cross over Tosco's top hat, draw invisible lines in an aerial ballet, circle him in an ever-wider spiral as his voice ascends. *"Eeeeeooowhafrhatravereeeeee!"*

They drop almost onto his shoulders again before gently making their way higher and up over the invisible audience in the top balcony as Tosco's voice hushes.

Tosco spreads his short arms and the Starlight Orchestra breaks into a soaring, rapturous medley of Turkish-sounding tunes.

A flash then a huge cloud of smoke, Tosco disappears.

At once the curtains split wide and six women in black veils and leopard tights with male partners similarly clad burst onstage from behind a wall of blue smoke, give several beats of writhing to the drums and swooping flute passages for an instant before *"That Old Black Magic"* sweeps the troupe into a rock beguine that rumbles and flows *(". . . and Baby, down and down I go, round and round I go . . .")* and growls and thumps their bodies in a contorting series of leaps and somersaults, culminates with more puffs of smoke and then Tosco reappears in a black silk cape and flicks a diamond-tipped wand at the top balcony.

The beautiful white and purple doves return on command, fly down into a large round wicker basket . . . Tosco covers it with an orange silk scarf. . . and then, spinning the basket with his hands and sprinkling glitter dust on it, waves his wand . . . further drum rolls . . . more blue, now white smoke . . . lifts the orange scarf and the top of the basket . . . and Ulla von Straf jumps out in a black leotard, wrapped neck to ankle in a 15-foot reticulated python – gold and green and wriggling.

The snake clings to her ankles and wrists. It forms a wide loop as Ulla stretches out and cartwheels around the stage. They circle faster and faster, and her features blend queerly with the spiraling diamond patterns of the snake. Suddenly they seem to merge into a magnificent blur of skin and scales. The diamonds of the python glisten in rings within rings around the central black of Ulla's leotard.

They resemble a huge spinning eyeball (a human iris?) which then takes on colors – first brownish then green then almost white and finally deep blood red as they spin and spin . . . around . . . around . . . yet the inner pattern stabilizes, seems to steady and focus . . . yes it is an eye, suddenly knowing and fixed and bearing ominously right in on . . .

* * *

In . . . and . . . out . . . and . . .

Stretched high up on his toes with his eyes shut tight, Oliver Loring gripped the starboard rail out on *Vista Deck*.

Mouth wide open, he gulped in warm lungfulls of the onrushing wind. How long had he stood there in an icy sweat as the wind rolled over his damp, terrified brow? He did not know. He let blasts of salt air flow in and out and wanted to be one with the Caribbean wind.

In . . . and . . . out.

Finally it began to pass.

He opened his eyes, looked out at the horizon. The stars near the ocean wobbled at him ominously.

Wobbly stars? A vast improvement!

Minutes ago, the sky and sea had tumbled in a confluent black chaos. A thousand pell-mell heartbeats ago, he had been thrust down, spread-eagled on his hands and knees between the smoke stacks. For what had seemed a horrible eternity, he had groped around, clung to the strands of *Vista Deck's* astroturf carpet, reminded himself the *Nordic Blue's* funnels always pointed up, always pointed . . .

In . . .

He squinted at his wristwatch. A single twitch of the luminescent second hand put torque on his stomach. He closed his eyes.

No! No spinning, please! Of any kind!

In . . . and . . .

He waited then blinked out at the glittering waves. No longer were they black tongues of mocking turmoil. The sea now was a smooth, shimmering blanket that spread off in all directions. The stars twinkled as if they had been there almost forever, as though nothing had shaken them even for an instant from their places in the firmament. He slowed his breathing, took a few slow steps along the rail. Yes, it finally was passing.

In . . .

Had passed. And he hadn't tossed up a drop of Aquavit! Not all dignity was lost!

He looked east toward the Bahamas. Shaggy clouds brushed the face of the rising crescent moon. Far north and west a storm skirted the horizon where tiny lightning bolts at the edge of the front shot down at the water. They flashed dainty, cottony silhouettes high along the upper rims of the cloud banks. Yes, there was order and beauty – even a mystical sense of peace – out there in the watery world for those with a steady vision.

Loring released his grip on the *Vista Deck* rail and strode forward with renewed confidence.

See! Fore was fore. Aft was still aft. And both the *Nordic Blue's* funnels still pointed up!

Ha-*ha!* Was there ever any doubt?

And the ship was sailing south-by-southeast for St. Maarten, their Monday port-of-call. Tuesday they would overnight in San Juan, do the first evening telecast of the "Midnight Promenade," then sail out at ten Wednesday morning. Wednesday night was the "Love Luck" show. Thursday? Valentine's Day and, of course, the Captain's Cocktail Party and the "Love Magic" broadcasts. Friday was the Private Island in the Bahamas. And then Saturday, Miami again, and the flight back to Boston!

What further proof was needed? Neurologically, Loring was intact – fully oriented to person, place, itinerary, and telecast schedule. His beeper was on his belt and both his epaulets were on straight. He had not lost consciousness nor Aquavit, merely his equilibrium.

He pulled off his pumps, wiggled his toes, skimmed Egyptian-style over the astroturf. He slipped his pumps back on, twirled through Olivia Loring's standard latin dance run-down of the lower body – rumba, tango, cha-cha, samba, bosa-nova, lambada. All flawless! He snickered at the sky and loosened his neck and shoulder muscles with the ridiculous (but often requested) macarena.

He glanced again at his watch. 2:00 A.M.

Would the *Crow's Nest* still be open? Or *Sails, the Glass-floored Disco*? The Dart Doc should have no trouble finding a disco partner at this hour on the world's grandest and most legendary cruise ship!

A partner?

But Loring could think of only one partner. He closed his eyes, arched his back and felt his heart thump close to her. He turned and whistled *"The Blue Danube"* and imagined her raven hair, the touch of her hands, the fragrance inside her silver lamé, and the tempting nearness of her exquisitely situated lady bug.

At once a grotesque and rude image raced into his mind – Ulla careening around the *Starlight Theatre* stage with that scaly python tangled around her arms and legs.

Loring's head started to spin again. The revolving diamonds on the snake with the image of the eye bored again into his brain. He saw strange colors.

Fresh torrents of sweat dripped down his brow. He stopped his waltz and rushed back to the rail, gripped it tight.

Uh-oh! Relapse!

The stars started their jittery motions and the crescent moon teetered nervously again on its axis! The rows of black waves on the shaky horizon wiggled and taunted in belligerent tongues. Loring looked over his shoulder at the smoke stacks but could not read which way they pointed.

Quick! Face the wind, close eyes, stretch high up on your toes! *In* . . .

He opened his eyes. *Whew!* Gone sooner than it had come!

But Loring didn't need to remind himself: he was the Chief Medical Officer. There was no physician over him to consult. Before he dashed off to the *Crow's Nest* or *Sails, the Glass-floored Disco*, should he not take a moment out here in the salt air to reassess what had happened in the *Starlight Theatre*? He glanced up at the erect funnels and mopped his brow.

Medical fact. This could not have been a spell of sea sickness. Loring's inner ears were virtually invulnerable. Two years back, for example, during a prolonged 60-knot gale, while fruit baskets, liquor bottles and a TV went flying all over his suite, Loring had felt no need to pop a Meclizine, even while veteran Norwegian Officers were puking all over the *Bridge* and pleading for Phenergan injections.

Also, since his Vermont boyhood, Loring had been an accomplished skier – co-captained the Harvard Ski Club, sampled the trickiest black diamond slopes in the Northeast, Aspen, Zermatt, St. Moritz, never with a serious lapse in balance.

Thirdly (the clincher), Loring happened to be a roller coaster fanatic, a kinesthetic junkie. He had no-handed the lead car in death-wish machines up and down the east coast from Old Orchard Beach to Splash Mountain. Had he ever once blown his popcorn?

This was not sea sickness. Yet this nightmare – spinning, sweating, nausea, prostration – were textbook for acute labyrinthitis, *i.e.* sudden dysfunction of the inner ear. Unless – ha-*ha!* – the universe had actually spun around him.

Hold it! Forget ha-*ha*.

Ha-*ha* did not belong on the list of possible diagnoses, and cracking funny private ironies up here on *Vista Deck* did not help matters. He could not deny that down in the theatre, Tosco's magic had disturbed him to the quick.

How? Loring was confounded.

Perhaps the spell had been a freak psycho-somatic phenomenon, a meltdown primed by his emotional state. His return to the ship had thrust him from peak to karmic peak, primed his mood, dancing, dart skills. When he slipped into that top balcony seat, he only wanted to stretch back and watch the beautiful Ulla von Straf.

The quality of the show didn't matter. In fact, he had expected a Las Vegas-style orgy – feathers, rhinestones, cleavage, legs, card tricks, maybe a sword or flame swallowed and a Cupid pulled from a top hat in keeping with the Valentine theme. Listening to Spinelli's prerecorded info-mercial on the loud speakers, the show sounded like it would be the usual kitsch. But then, little Tosco appeared between the blue curtains with his silver mane, bushy brows, mustache, and those dark Cuban eyes and began to sing that strange, incongruous Russian chant to his doves.

The audience of one had been entranced by the ancient melody, the soaring of the acrobat birds. Soon Ulla von Straf twirled onto the stage with that serpent laced around her limbs, her perfect arms and legs turning like spokes on a slimy, multi-colored biological wheel. As Loring gazed, that spinning eye-like iris changed colors. Something hit him hard, stirred up a transcendent force deep inside his psyche, or even deeper beyond him – into the (ha-*ha!*) cosmos.

Up there in the balcony a strange vision jumped into his mind, accompanied by an enchanting smell – flashing lights of uncertain shape and size but of salmon pink and violet and lemon and apricot which, for the life of him, he was sure were not stage effects. Those flickers, revolving glows, spun *inside* his head, as if the python's diamonds twirled right through his eyes, ratcheted into cogs *within* his essence to churn a fabulous color palate he had never seen.

For some seconds he had been consumed in exhilaration, a tenseness he had felt only prior to tumescent sexual release. He then became aware – how he had wanted to sniff and sniff! – of succulent apples close to his nose. They were freshly-sliced golden delicious apples, rich as the abundant October harvest from the orchards around Coventry, Vermont, and of a sweetness which caused every gland in his mouth to salivate copiously.

The scent of apples? In the top balcony of the *Starlight Theatre*? Yet he had drooled for them onto his tuxedo lapels.

And then, with total authority, the spinning of the universe began.

Dazed, gyrating, he cradled his jaw in his hands, tried to hold his head in the vertical position, an act he could not sustain. From past cruises his feet knew the way out of the theatre's top balcony, and he staggered out the nearest exit and onto *Vista Deck* where he collapsed.

Now, as he inhaled the salty Caribbean air, he could neither explain the incident nor shrug it off. Magic? Is that what had convulsed his mind, viscera, the universal elements?

Clearly, the magnificent Ulla had been an accomplice to Tosco's tricks. She had invited Loring to his own undoing.

Jacques Chemin's warning about her in the *Crew Bar* rang true: *"FAR DEEPER! FAR DEEPER THAN THE HEART!"* Did the cat burglar turned voodoo king know something Loring did not?

He resumed his strides along the starboard rail, tried to erase Ulla from his mind. But he could not. There was more than a pout behind those petal lips, more than a tease behind those icy blues.

Was she dabbling with Tosco in wizardry or something like it?

He reached up and fingered the three stripes on his epaulets. How often had he walked in tuxedo uniform on this same top deck, beneath these same stars with unabashed arrogance toward the gifts which his life, the ship, the cruise, the sky offered. He tried now to stride with the same happy gait, but he felt less sure of himself.

And he took no comfort in realizing he was not the only man to be so stricken and confused by Ulla. According to Jacques Chemin, Flip Spinelli was similarly afflicted with Ulla "fever."

Oh yes, Flip – the suave crooner, tap dancer, roll-em-in-the-aisles stand-up artist. Everyone said "a genius as a Cruise Director," and "the sharpest in the Caribbean," clearly ripe for network TV exposure, if Flip had the inclination.

Loring had to admit that, center stage, microphone in hand, Spinelli's edgy charisma and his snappy verbal zingers tickled many an older audience to incontinence. But in his off-stage encounters with younger female crew members, Loring knew Spinelli was *unfunny* and as vindictive as a cut-throat Mafia don.

According to most crew members, *"Don't cross the Cruise Director!"* were words to survive by on this ship.

Spinelli even fashioned himself a mob don: pencil-line mustache, gleaming pate, flawless manicure, diamond on the pinky – the type of slick rodent who some cloudy night down on the *Poop Deck* might finish buffing his nails and shove a stick of Carefree gum between his teeth while a pair of muscular Diving Instructor hit men gagged the Chief Medical Officer and tossed him into the *Nordic Blue's* wake for shark bait.

SHARK BAIT!

Loring suddenly knew he had lost all perspective. Out here on *Vista Deck* he had free-associated recklessly, let his meditations become too vivid and personally threatening. His imaginings had hurtled him right into a hot, sweaty panic. And he knew what would come next.

No! Ha-*ha*!

It all was too cruel and familiar. He could feel his addiction rising to be fed.

At the suggestion of sharks, Loring's fingers ascended to his mouth.

He didn't fear sharks. He *identified* with them.

ORAL! He was becoming *oral* again. Acutely, uncontrollably, monstrously. Oral as any shark.

He tongued his fingertips. His lips sucked on some sprouting nubbins. He stiffened his neck, averted his eyes from the temptation, but the horrid cycle had started and would not desist. Oh no, it would not! His will was dying. He knew he could not help himself. He *never* had been able to help himself. No therapist – not Anita Rothberg, not anyone – had ever helped.

Who was he kidding? Who was Anita kidding with her therapy? Ha-*ha-ha-ha-ha*! Suddenly Oliver Loring was all mouth. His teeth gnashed. His jaw muscles twitched in spasms of craving. His incisors poised to chomp, to rip and tear in a torrid feeding frenzy.

Oh, why resist? Dr. Anita would not be around tomorrow to notice and scold and mock. Why not just let go? He had been good all day. Why not be bad now, as a reward? Give in!

SHARKS! Bring them on! Loring could teach those sharks a lesson on how to dispatch bait!

Stop! Quick!

Stand! Face wind, shut eyes, stretch up on your toes!

In . . .

* * *

Oliver Loring stretched his legs in his cabin bed on *Viking Deck*. He propped his head up on his pillow and peered out the round portholes at the moon-lit sea. Far off the port side he saw a string of tiny lights cutting a parallel course along the horizon – the *M/S Nordic Pearl*, the ship moored aft of the *Nordic Blue* that afternoon in Miami while they were onloading.

The *Nordic Peal* was only 35K tons, merely one third the displacement of the *Nordic Blue*. Every Saturday the *Pearl* picked up her passengers and supplies and then traced the same loop as the *Nordic Blue* – St. Maarten, San Juan, Private Island in the Bahamas – but in exactly the *reverse* sequence. For one hundred miles out the first night, they cruised south, played peek-a-boo across the waves.

Soon the *Pearl* would veer out of sight, head due east for the Private Island in the Bahamas, while the *Nordic Blue* steamed further south to St. Maarten in the Lesser Antilles. They would not meet again till next Saturday morning in Miami when each ship completed the weekly loop.

Till now, Loring had never noticed how the *Pearl* truly resembled her name – a tiny string of ethereal fairy glimmerings. Till now, she had always been just another ship on the horizon each Saturday night. Loring had often thought it redundant and absurd for Nordic Star Lines to send two ships in contrary directions every week. Who would cruise on the *Pearl,* a tiny joke of a ship, touch in at all the same ports, and miss a chance to sail on the grand lady, the *Nordic Blue*?

But tonight Loring actually felt fond of the *Pearl*. She was their wave-and-sunburst sister ship, a reflection – a yang to the *Nordic Blue's* yin.

At this moment on the *Bridge* of the *Pearl*, a vigilant team of Norwegian Officers guided her through the waves – just like the Deck Officers on the *Bridge* of the *Nordic Blue*. And now on the *Nordic Pearl*, night squads of Able Bodied Filipino and Indonesian Seamen were out hosing down the hull, the funnels and portholes, scrubbing the *Pearl* clean under the stars, just as the *Nordic Blue* was simultaneously being scrubbed clean.

He nestled his head into the pillow, tried to sleep.

Soon his eyelids snapped open. He sat up in bed.

Who could sleep after a personal break-through like his up on *Vista Deck* tonight? And why *not* talk about yins and yangs and invoke oriental metaphors after such a victory?

Standing alone up there under the sky, Loring had done what he had failed to do thousands of times: he had stifled a savage oral crisis!

Loring held up his hands and inspected his fingertips. In the scant silver moonlight, his nails were, admittedly, a cosmetic catastrophe. But all the injuries were twelve hours old!

No fresh bleeds! No new scourge!

Hallelujah!

The attack had started like all the others – fleeting mental images of mouth activities, what Dr. Anita called "random oral visualizations:" Spinelli chewing a piece of gum, then a shark, many sharks, had swum into the picture. Instantly, the urge was unleashed, gained momentum with its usual imperious crescendo – the urge a command, the command a raging, defiant force that refused to be denied until self-mutilation was achieved.

But, lo! Tonight on *Vista Deck* Loring had stretched up, closed his eyes, taken in those long deep breaths, became one with the Caribbean. Those were, perhaps, the most important breaths of his adult life! After many deep respiratory excursions, his fingers had fallen to his sides unmolested, the rage drained. His mouth had relaxed, felt no urge to summon those fingers up for a second try!

Astounding! The threat, the crisis, the the shark bait scenario – averted! *AVERTED!*

And with the same technique he had used against the spinning effects of Tosco's magic! In fact, while he was up on his toes, the vision of Ulla twirling with the python had again entered his brain. Instantly his oral urge had channeled into Ulla and the diamond-coated snake.

With each slow breath, up on his toes, the whirling figure blurred, faded. And with it the oral crisis.

Loring looked at his nails again and shook his head in wonder. Now that he had denied that beast inside him, perhaps he could begin to accept, even respect, things which till now had seemed almost invisible – like the little, insignificant *Nordic Pearl* – in the greater scheme of life.

He glanced again at the horizon, squinted hard, but the tiny silvery necklace had vanished from the watery rim. The *Pearl* had separated and gone on her own course straight east toward the Bahamas.

Farewell, kind sister! See you next Saturday in Miami!

He rested his head on his pillow again, reflected on the first image that crept into his head – the lady bug on Ulla's left breast.

He remembered how, when they were dancing, Ulla had seemed, among other things, the perfect height for him. As his reveries became more vivid, the lady bug spread her wings and took flight then fused into one of Tosco's doves. Another dove appeared and together they ascended in spirals, just as Tosco's birds had ascended in the *Starlight Theatre*.

Yes, blessed and comforting sleep would surely come tonight now that he had seen again Tosco's peaceful birds.

See! There was an amazingly salubrious spin-off to Tosco's powers, and Loring was feeling it now. Oh, yes! He felt the fluttering of their wings, rising on the melodic sweep . . .

SUN/FEB 10
Scherzo on the Sea

Dr. Orson Loring's credo in life had always been: *"Start each day with a cold shower and some Bach. Keeps the clinical reflexes crisp all day."*

Sleep-deprived or not, the venerable Vermont country practitioner would rise before dawn every morning and shower in icy water. Then he would shave, spray his cheeks with his favorite Nino Cerutti 1881 cologne (from the frosted glass *vaporisateur*), put on his coat and tie, and sit down at the family Steinway for baroque counterpoint – usually one of the *Partitas* or some *Preludes and Fugues* from *"The Well-Tempered Clavier."* After coffee with Olivia in the breakfast nook and a hug for sleepy Oliver at the front door, Orson would climb into his Jeep and drive off, still whistling Bach, to make rounds at Green Mountain Community.

That ritual kept Dr. Orson's clinical acumen sharp and his extensive Bach repertory solid for 51 years of solo practice, right up to his final Wednesday off-call skiing with Oliver at Killington. On that final run a year ago, the nimble doctor's ski tip snagged a spruce root. As Oliver gaped in horror, he watched his father launch out into mid-air and spin down over a 90-foot cliff. With a muffled thud, Orson's 88-year-old skull smashed on a craggy chunk of Vermont granite.

Since medical school, Oliver Loring had followed his father's prescribed regimen and tried never to skip. Even on working vacations here in the Caribbean, he took frigid wake-up showers. For his early keyboard constitutionals, he chose *Topsiders*, the piano bar up on the port side of *Veranda Deck* with its tuned-weekly Baldwin grand and its 5-feet circular portholes looking out at the sunrise.

Long ago, Loring had broken his father's Bach-only policy. Johann Sebastian deserved a lifetime of dawns. No quarrel there, Dad. But what about Scarlatti? Mozart? Schubert? Brahms? Robert *and* Clara Schumann? Poulenc? Should the sun not also rise on their exquisite keyboard epiphanies?

This Sunday morning as the *Nordic Blue* sliced east along the northern rim of Cuba, the red fingers of dawn danced off the Caribbean with hallucinatory fury.

"CHOPIN! CHOPIN! CHOPIN!" cried the wine-dark sea. *"PREFERABLY SCHERZO #1 IN B MINOR!"*

Loring – showered, shaved, cologned (also Nino Cerutti 1881 from his father's own frosted glass *vaporisateur*) and clad in white shorts and knee socks uniform – concurred.

Chopin's B minor *Scherzo* had an abundance of wavy arpeggios that rolled, vaulted, crashed mournfully, then a section of flickering chromatic chordal shimmers and a deceptively serene *berceuse* two-thirds through that rocked sweetly before the mania-driven reprise and then the final, vengeful gut thrusts of the plummeting cadenza.

Selection made, mood upbeat, Loring entered *Topsiders* and set the piano bench aside. In its place he stacked three wave-and-sunburst bar stool cushions on the carpet. He squatted on the cushions, eyes level to the keys. He straightened his spine, adjusted his crotch, threw back his head. He glanced out at the sun rising out of the waves; it glowed a rich maroon, like a giant incandescent cranberry.

His supple wrists leaped high above his head. His long fingers plunged down for the herald chord – *"FAAA-RAAAAAAAAAAAM!"* – a diminished minor ninth on the third upper octave followed by a quieter but still threatening – *"faaa-raaaam!"* – basso echo.

He lifted his fingers off the keyboard and surveyed *Veranda Deck*. His awkward position – hunkered down, bare knees tucked up in his chest and his nose brushing the keys – might seem odd to any passengers who might happen by and peer into *Topsiders*.

But not to worry. At this early hour, *Veranda* was clear. Nary a power cruiser in sight. Besides, Loring knew the giant circular portholes were embedded with a faint silvery pigment which reflected daylight like a mirror and made it impossible for anyone to look inside, except at night.

He rubbed his thumbs along his nails and felt a surge of confidence. (No, he hadn't nibbled during his sleep.) Then he tapped his epaulets three times for inspiration and let go.

"FAAAAAA-RAAAAAAAAAAAM!"

He watched his fingers pounce with an undeniable will of their own onto Chopin's liquidy arpeggios then fly back and forth.

So be it! *Scherzo #1* had begun in earnest. There was no turning back! He knew the piece intimately, and soon his hands soared through the passionate interweavings of young Fredryk's feverish lament. By the second section of chordal shimmerings, he was too immersed to care if anyone out on *Veranda*

Deck noticed him – ungainly position or not – as the first tears of pure sentiment trickled from his eyes. Tossing and swelling with each of the flowing arpeggios, he started to sob loudly.

Oh, just let go! Don't hold back! Feel the romantic volcano boiling inside you! Let your noble soul flow! Be the incandescent cranberry! Be the waves! Dance like the sun on the sea! Will yourself into the wind!

Tears had never poured down his cheeks like this – even with the B minor *Scherzo*. He knew part of it was his tightly constricted rehearsal position, borrowed from the esteemed Canadian virtuoso, the late Glenn Gould. Gould, an eccentric and a purist, had said one could maximize keyboard intimacy by stationing one's body low and close to the piano – the keys a visual/physical/emotional horizon and the fingers dancing down, as if from the sky. (The term Gould coined was the "horizontality" of the keyboard.)

A bonus for Loring here in *Topsiders* was that he *was* actually seeing his fingers pirouette on the earth's watery horizon as he looked over the piano! No wonder those tears flowed! (Plus: as any conservatory-level pianist like Loring would know, technically accurate romantic pedaling of Chopin was hell in this contorted position!)

Yet Glenn Gould's rehearsal technique could not account for all the tears and intensity. Surely Loring's fingers themselves had much to do with it! *Look* at them – whizzing with alacrity through those tricky arpeggios. But why shouldn't they whiz and cavort like ten little joyous ocean zephyrs? Those long-suffering digit tips had spent their first trauma-free night for decades. There was grand cause for the release of sentiment this morning up and down the keyboard, the horizon, and the upper extremities!

When Loring came to the tranquil *berceuse*, he slowed tempo, batted his moist eyes. He sensed the ship swinging under him like a giant iron cradle on the sea, as if the entire *Nordic Blue* shared in the delicacy of the to-and-fro lullaby. He sang the melody to himself, just as Glenn Gould might have done on his many classic recordings. *"DAH - da - dahhhh - da - Dah - da - da - DAAAAH - da!"*

More tears flowed. But with the tears, troubling thoughts.

Through the night, Loring had dreamed of Tosco's rehearsal in the *Starlight Theatre*. Only dreams could process it. Rational thought got him nowhere. And the question kept rolling back and forth in Loring's mind – *HOW DID TOSCO DO IT?*

Superficially, Tosco's magic dazzled the eye with spectacle and surprise. The unique choreography fused modern dance and melody with ancient primitivisms. Loring had sensed resonant archetypes woven into the movements which cut through his consciousness. Then, for a convulsive moment, he had been forced to escape out to *Vista Deck*, where he saw the stars spin and the sea somersault.

But what if the *Starlight Theatre* had been filled with eager spectators, as it would be on Thursday night for the *"Love Magic"* television performance? What then? Such stimulation might have subliminal – yet horrendous, perhaps violent – effects. A stampede? As Chief Medical Officer, Loring had to keep such public health considerations in mind.

Most spectators would marvel at the beauty and flow of the ensemble dancing and the tricks. But the more susceptible individuals might, like Loring, have their senses rocked to the core!

And who knew what effect such powerful shenagans might trigger on a global television audience! Did Farrely Farrell and the Cablevista executives know what they were dishing up to the viewing masses all over the world with Thursday's innocently-titled *"Love Magic?"*

He prepared for the catapulting minor fifths of Chopin's extravagant cadenza. Fingers hell-bent on a rampage, he looked out through the porthole onto the sea.

"Daaaaah-deeeee-daaaaaaaaah!"

The sun was no longer a definable red berry – it had risen fully above the horizon and now beamed a cosmic yellow-white.

"Yumph-dedeeee-yumph-deee-dump!"

The waves glowed their proper morning deep blue. Whitecaps licked playfully at each other. The cadenza would soon culminate.

"Yumph-dedeeee . . . "

Just in time. From the corner of his eye, Loring spotted a well-dressed couple strolling nearby outside – a tall woman with a very short man. Ignoring the distraction, his wrists snapped through the dramatic rolling B minor chromatic scales at the end. The final chords resounded with desperate conviction.

"FAROOOOOOOOOOOOOOOM!"

And . . . *"faaaahhh - rooooooooom!"*

He sat back, shuddered at his own bravura. Tenderly he released the sustain pedal. He turned to the waves, heard nothing but the echoes of Chopin's chords, imagined the tens of thousands of whitecaps clapping with joy and gratitude. Hot with pride, he felt certain he had satisfied them all. He took out his handkerchief, dried his eyes, cheeks and knee caps.

Chopin! You were a genius! See how the waves enjoyed your stuff?

Soon the couple he had seen came close to the porthole. They appeared to have no interest in snooping into *Topsiders*. Not at all – these two had their own agenda, their own communion with the waves. And these were not simply early bird power cruisers out for a power stroll.

The couple were Ulla von Straf and little Tosco, arm-in-arm by the rail. She had her hair braided up over her head and wore flowing black lace with a black veil. Tosco wore a white double-breasted linen suit and a white, wide-brimmed Panama. He carried a peculiar black silk pouch resembling a Victorian purse tied with a black ribbon.

They stopped, looked out toward the risen sun. Loring watched through the porthole as Tosco opened the purse, dipped his hands into it, cupped his palms above his head near to Ulla's lips.

She lifted the veil, puckered her smooth lips and began to blow a white substance out from Tosco's fingers. It was the lightest, finest white powder that flew up in puffs like smoke from Tosco's hands, joined the wind and rode in a hazy cloud sternward and away from them – less and less distinct and out into the sky and far over the blue waves. Again and again, Tosco drew the substance from the pouch and each time Ulla's petal lips pursed and puffed from under her veil – the powder soared up and away, spiraling in tiny white tornadoes – until the black silk bag lining was turned inside out to the wind. She bent and kissed his palms. They had powdered the dawn, the sea, the horizon, the mind of Oliver Loring.

When they were finished, Tosco rolled the pouch up and slid it under his lapel. As he did so, Ulla turned toward the porthole.

Loring froze, ashamed for spying. He felt assured, thanks to the silvery pigment in the glass, that Ulla could not see him watching her. But he feared any movement on his side of the glass might betray him.

She stepped near, adjusted her raven braids, which the wind had tugged during their silent ritual. Her large crystal blue eyes, tired and tearful beneath the black veil, regarded her face as she brushed her locks with her fingers and adjusted a silver barrette over her ear. But then her hands ceased, the movements of her face paused, and her fatigued yet powerful eyes bored right into their own reflection. There were tears in those magnificent eyes, yes, but there also was a deep questioning, as though she peered into herself and far beyond the veil, the mirror, the pain.

Loring had a disquieting thought. Was this the face of a woman who, at dawn, had just performed a black magic ritual? Was she a witch?

Loring tried to close his eyes, but they would not obey. A chill hit him. If not for the glass, he could easily reach out and hold her perfect cheek in his hand, touch her veiled lips. But it was not the moment to tap on the pane and say, "Whatever is in your heart, may I know it one day?"

In . . . and . . .

They turned to go. He watched every step – the graceful strides of the long-skirted ballerina and the slow, jaunty waddle of the dapper dwarf magician. They strolled out of sight down the steps at the aft end of *Veranda.* Loring put the cushions back on their bar stools and replaced the bench in front of the Baldwin.

No question about it: for the rest of the cruise, he would stick to baroque counterpoint. And no Glenn Gould contortions! Tomorrow it would be Johann Sebastian Bach again. And straight-up on the piano bench, as Orson Loring had done early in the morning for as long as Oliver Loring could recall!

Chopin was dangerous. Today Chopin had made Loring conjure up sunrise phantoms in the porthole.

But after watching Ulla peer into her own magnificent eyes, Loring wondered if – with all due respect to his father and Chopin and Bach and all the supreme composers for the keyboard – he might prefer to spend his future dawn reveries looking into the crystal blue eyes of that same woman who last night had stolen his heart and then danced with a serpent.

* * *

Loring proceeded down to *Viking Deck* and stopped into his cabin next door to the *Hospital.* He needed a moment of quiet solitude before he greeted Chief Nurse Maggie and the Paramedics Kevin and Guy, to start his day's duties as Chief Medical Officer.

Loring's Korean Valet, the invisible Mr. Kim, had already been in to tidy the cabin: bathroom tiles scrubbed, linens changed, carpet vacuumed, liquor cabinet and TV dusted, fruit basket restocked, ice bucket filled, carnations and baby's breath rearranged in their white porcelain wave-and-sunburst vase. On the clothes press hung a new formal jacket and a pair of neatly ironed tuxedo slacks with a note scrawled from Mr. Chu, the Chinese Tailor, saying *"Crotch let out to limit. Can do no more, Doc!"*

Bravo, Mr. Chu!

And *Bravo* to you, Mr. Kim! The invisible Kim knew how to freshen a cabin so that one's mind could prime itself.

Not unlike a Zen garden. Or baroque counterpoint. Ha-*ha!*

He sat down on the couch. After a few deep whiffs of the lemon-misted atmosphere, he felt more relaxed and much less perplexed.

On the coffee table, he found a note penned on the wave-and-sunburst embossed stationery from the deluxe suites up on *Viceroy Deck*. The handwriting, though shaky, was neat and feminine.

Viceroy Deck #7
Sunday – 6:00 AM (I'm an early riser. Are you?)

Dear Dr. Loring,

My husband Colonel Rockwell Snippet-White and I so much enjoyed meeting you last night in Club Atlantis. I myself find you a close challenger even to Rocky's expertise in the Viennese. (But don't worry, I haven't told him that yet!) How rare to encounter a gentleman in uniform these days who knows how to dance! I'm sure you didn't learn that at a crash course at Arthur Murray's. Or did you?

We saw your name listed as one of the guests for the "Captain's Honor Table" tonight, and we're thrilled. We want you for tea here in Suite #7 on the Viceroy Deck before we join Captain Ramskog for his gourmet feast at the oval table in the Main Dining Room. Would you be interested? If not, let me know. I understand you have medical duties. Otherwise, Rocky and I will be looking forward to your visit at 6:00 PM. (That's 18.00 hours, I believe.) We wanted to invite my goddaughter, but Ulla has a dance rehearsal at that hour. She's so busy on this cruise!

By the way, Doctor, (I meant to ask you last night in Atlantis, but it didn't really seem the setting for Boston gossip), are you related to the famous Lorings of Beacon Hill?

Most sincerely,

Hildegarde Snippet-White

p.s. – Addendum: The Colonel is feeling rather out of sorts this morning. He was, perhaps, overly exuberant with that flashy Charleston in Atlantis. I told him he outdid himself. No matter what, this is our wedding anniversary cruise and ("damn the torpedoes!") we plan to proceed with it. It's so thrilling to be back again and meeting elegant and frisky young people such as you, Doctor. Viceroy Deck hasn't changed a speck since those glorious Marianne days. We're in the same cozy suite and we're still honeymooners, but we are not shy about entertaining. So don't you be shy about visiting us.

p.p.s. – Addendum Secundum: (Nosy me! I had to ask! I understand Ulla invited you to her rehearsal last night. Well, what did you think of the little magician, Tosco? Incredible, isn't he? Rocky and I were lucky enough to catch him in Paris last September with his "Cirque Ineffable," and we think he's extraordinary! N'est-ce pas? Maybe we can talk about Tosco over tea?)

Loring put down the letter and picked up the phone. He wanted to call *V#7* to confirm tea and check on the Colonel's health. But he paused. He knew Boston Brahmins frowned on pushiness, especially by medical types, and Hildegarde seemed to imply between the lines that he should not overstep his professional bounds. Better not seem too eager to serve. He set the phone back on the table.

And, yes, he was related to the famous Beacon Hill Lorings, but distantly. Back in the 1830's and 40's, when the Boston Lorings amassed their family fortune in the clipper ship ice trade, his great-great-great grandfather Ichabod Loring had eloped to Vermont with Claudine Dupré, a comely French-Canadian scullery girl, and was promptly disinherited. Since then, all of Ichabod's descendants had stayed in Vermont – mostly lawyers, doctors, and Unitarian ministers. The Beacon Hill Lorings – now all wealthy bankers or trust fund beneficiaries/yacht club commodores – were never contacted, except for unavoidable encounters during college at Harvard or, in recent years, the occasional dinner sighting at Locke-Ober.

Was there still a feud going on after 160 years? No. But neither had there been a reconciliation. Nor was one likely. Hildegarde was from Beacon Hill and would understand.

And wasn't her letter a treat! Those quaint Latin *addenda*?

And a major relief to Loring. Because the woman's note positively *reeked* of an overly eclectic aesthetic. She and the Colonel had already seen Tosco's *Cirque Ineffable* in Paris. If anybody might be affected by invisible psychic forces laced into Tosco's act, it would be Hildegarde Snippet-White.

Had she been shocked in Paris? Had she experienced vertigo or anything else untoward? Most importantly, was she afraid to let her goddaughter perform with Tosco? Obviously not.

Tea with the Snippet-Whites? *Yum!*

Dinner later at the Captain's Table? *Double yum-yum!*

And speaking of yummies, Loring's nails had never looked more robust. They never looked more scrumptious, either.

He bit on his tongue. It simply was *not* practical to stand high up on one's tiptoes, close one's eyes and do the *"In . . . and . . . out"* routine every time one felt the urge to take a hit on one's nails.

Loring glanced at his watch. Five minutes till he was due next door at the *Hospital.* He peered around his cabin for a distraction. He spotted a copy of the *Daily Cruise News,* which Mr. Kim had left on top of the TV. He picked it up and scanned it.

The *Drink-of-the-Day* was the *Lime Limbo* – featured at each of the *Nordic Blue's* eleven bars, beginning at 8.00 hours.

Other offerings for the day: *Super Jackpot Bingo* with the Cruise Director, *Deck Sports Gladiator Combat* with the Cruise Staff, *Aerobics* with Jill, *Skeet Shooting* with Staff Captain Nils Nordström, *Super Pedigree Horse Racing* with the Cruise Director, *Kite Flying* with Shawna off the stern on *Veranda Deck, Country and Western Dancing Lessons* with Hubert (to-morrow night out of St. Maarten was *"Country and Western Night"*), *Fine Art Auction* with Franz and Marie, *Post-Superbowl Film* with former National Football League wide receiver Kahleed Stitt in the *Sports and Cigar Bar, Beginners' Internet Seminar* with Alice in *Surf"s Up, the Web Cafe, Ice Sculpting* with *Monsieur* Chemin in the *Main Dining Room, Tour of the Bridge* with Staff Captain Nils Nordström, *Auditions with Cablevista Staff* for appearances on Farrely Farrell's *"Love Luck"* telecast – everything an action-oriented and free-ranging power cruiser could want, including tonight's special after-dinner feature – the *"Roaring Twenties Revue"* with Flip Spinelli and the entire *Nordic Blue* Cruise Staff.

Loring smiled. On past cruises he had often volunteered for bit parts in the hi-jinx chorus line of *Roaring 20's.* He had donned the blue-striped blazer and boater and twirled the cane with the Cruise Staff flapper girls. He knew the canned skits backwards and forwards. They always came off as corny side-splitters, especially with lecherous Spinelli at the microphone, wisecracking with the band as the vaudeville MC:

Flip: *Pardon me, Miss, but can you tell me*
           where I can buy some talcum powder?
Flapper: *Of course, sir. Just walk this way!*
           (Vampish beat from the bass drum.)

Flip: *If I could walk that way, Miss, I wouldn't need*
to buy no damn talcum powder!
(Rim shot from the drummer. Horse laugh
from the trumpeter.)

The whole point of doing *Roaring 20's* on Sunday evening, early in the cruise week, was to get the passengers to loosen up with the Cruise Staff. Loring felt looser just seeing *Roaring 20's* highlighted in the *Daily Cruise News*. He forgot about gnawing on his nails and thought instead about a novelty number he had composed himself two years before called *"Shuffleboard Tango"* – four Cruise Staff flappers tangoing back and forth across the stage with shuffle board sticks, while Loring himself sang and danced as a mustached Argentine gaucho with a bull whip.

At rehearsal everyone had loved it except Spinelli, who scratched it from the show and shouted, "What does this Argentina gaucho crap have to do with the Roaring Twenties? Get back down to the Hospital, Doc, and lick those bedpans till they're clean!"

Undaunted in his cabin two years later now, Loring positioned himself – right elbow high in the air and left shoulder down – to relive the tango sequence.

"As I was cruising out of Buenos Aires,
A fair young señorita I did spy.
Her eyes were dark, her legs were hairy . . . "

Someone pounded hard at his cabin door. "*Oliver!* Open up! I'm gonna' beat your damn Yankee butt!"

Chief Nurse Maggie McCarthy charged in with her green eyes blazing under her red bangs. "May I cut in? Or am I interrupting something special?" she snarled. "What the frick are you doing, Dart Doc? You stupid and deceitful son of a bitch!"

"Deceitful?"

Maggie shook her head under her wave-and-sunburst nurse's cap. Pacing, she began to wave the pharmacy clipboard in a threatening manner. "Did you sneak Captain two Valiums last night while I wasn't lookin? *Did* you?"

"The wife. For the *wife*."

Maggie scowled a dark, freckled scowl. "Oh yea! For the wife! Is that what he told you? So the Captain's more treacherous than you!"

"But I thought you *liked* him!"

"I liked *you*, too. Till you shoved those Valiums at him last night, yea. Whose side of this are you on, anyway?"

"Maggie! I'm always on your side! We're friends. Don't I always send you a birthday card every September?"

"I've had enough frickin' birthday cards. I'm 34. And that damn Ramskog turns 51 in October! Neither one of us is gettin' any younger, you know!"

"Would you cool down?"

Sinewy, sharp-tongued Maggie McCarthy had been Chief Nurse on the ship for six years, long enough to know every crew member by name and crew number. In her praline-sweet Savannah drawl she styled herself the "Belle from Hell." In the *Crew Bar* everybody knew her as the "Attack Nurse." She had prominent white canines, thin muscular thighs, and when provoked, the temperament of a riled Doberman.

Nobody dared speculate re: when would Trond dump Snø for Maggie. Apparently not this *(Valentine TV Cruise)* week.

"I didn't *shove* Trond those Valiums! I signed them off to Snø. Look on the record!"

"Looks great on paper, Dart Doc! But you should see King Norsky this morning. He gulped those pills down at midnight in my cabin – thought I was asleep! *Ha!* And then he chased 'em down with a double Aquavit. Crawls in and puts his blonde head next to me on the pillow and starts snorin' like some Norwegian grizzly. Told Snø he was gonna' be on the *Bridge* all night."

"Do we have any patients this morning?"

"Trond never snored like that before. It's your V's, thank you Candy Doc! Anyone up at Harvard ever tell you about side effects? *Did* they? As long as you were dolling out benzodiazapines, why didn't you blast him unconscious with some frickin' Midazolam? Aren't you supposed to be some kind of professor or something? This morning his speech is slurred like he's plastered."

"Maggie, do we have any patients?"

"As a matter of fact, yes. I'm glad you asked. That's what I'm tellin' you. I led him down and tucked him into a bed in the *Observation Unit*. I phoned the *Bridge* and told 'em he had a fever, not the usual Norwegian flu! This is the goddamn *Valentine TV Cruise*, may I remind you? We got ourselves an incapacitated Captain and the damn Cablevista Blimp is due overhead any minute now, Doctor!"

"What did you tell Mrs. Ramskog?"

"Oliver!"

"Go easy on me this morning! I signed on yesterday!"

"Go easy on me, too. I've had a hard night. Face it, Dart Doc. This ship sucks with Snø on it! Did I ever go flyin' over to Oslo and stick my nose into her business when Trond was off on vacation and livin' with her? *Did* I?"

"Coffee?"

"Fine, Dart Doc! Kevin and Guy already took care of eleven patients. Nobody serious. Couple sun burns. Half a dozen sea sicks. That kinda' stuff. We don't have anybody waiting, except for his royal nibs. He's still sleepin' it off! I sent Kevin and Guy off to the gym."

"Maybe I better look in on the Captain."

"Go ahead! By the way, you're gettin' balder, you know! And I thought you told me last summer you were gonna' stop chewin' your frickin' nails!"

* * *

As a part-timer and an American, Oliver Loring never denied the powerful mystique of his Norwegian colleagues, whose blonde-bearded profiles graced all the glossy Nordic Star Line brochures. It was incredible how passengers succumbed to that romantic masculine vision as soon as they stepped on board and saw the tanned, silent Norsky Officers in white uniforms, gold-embroidered epaulets and gilded buttons. Loring himself was often mistaken for a Norwegian. Often he received admiring glances from women and spontaneous salutes from white-haired men 30 years his senior.

Loring often wondered why.

None of the Norwegian Officers could dance. By day, they lumbered up and down the decks with that herky-jerky (perhaps genetic?) saunter and barked into their cell phones and walkie-talkies in that ancient trollish language that echoed back like tiny invisible electronic Rumpelstiltskins. After dinners each night of reindeer meat and fish balls in the *Officers' Mess*, they all leaned back from the table and clammed up with toothpicks in their mouths and seemed to fall into some old Viking bonding/farting ritual.

Granted – all were whizzbang Refrigeration Engineers, Radar or Sonar Specialists, Boiler Room Operators, Navigators, Computer Sharpshooters, etc. But that's *all* the Chief Medical Officer knew about them. They seldom engaged in conversation beyond asking Loring how he had honed his remarkable dart skills or why he rose early every morning to practice the piano.

On his second cruise, Loring had brought along a *Teach Yourself Norwegian* book. He thought showing an interest in their language would open up his fellow officers. But every time he went up to the *Bridge* to try out a new word, the response was always, "That's the way they say it in Bergen, but not in Oslo." Or, "Why do you waste your time with our little language, Doctor?" Or, "We all belong to the sea. That's our language."

Loring became proficient enough to stumble through a few fairy tales by Jørgen Moe and Peter Christian Asbjørnson (the Norwegian Brothers Grimm) with the aid of a dictionary. But when he mentioned these, for example, to Nils Nordström, the Staff Captain snickered, "Ha! So why do you waste your time, Doctor, reading about rabbits and foxes?"

In short, the other officers discouraged Loring. It seemed they liked to keep their language to themselves. Anybody who wanted to learn it must have some other agenda in mind. Consequently, Loring learned about them mostly by watching.

Clearly they derived some odd macho pleasure from the safety drills the U.S. Coast Guard required them to perform regularly. Every other Wednesday they lowered half a dozen lifeboats to scour the waves for imaginary drowning victims, and every Saturday morning in Miami they pretended to retrieve victims of fake fires (they used theatrical smoke) in the *Boiler Room* or the *Chinese Laundry* or some other remote place.

Four times a year during the middle of the night, Staff Captain Nordström broke out the dozen high-powered semi automatic attack rifles from the locked arsenal on the *Bridge* and shouted orders while his officers ran up and down the corridors and pretended to defend the ship against a take-over by terrorists – a frightening exercise called a *"Code Commando,"* which Loring had once witnessed.

The drills were required and important, of course. But it astonished Loring how avidly the Norskies executed them – especially the mock chases up and down the stair towers, when their eyes blazed with Viking ferocity as they crouched and panted in their mylar hoods and vests, rifles at the ready, and communicated through head gear with mouth microphones that reminded Loring of the gadgets worn by hamburger caddies at fast food drive-thru windows.

Some were out-and-out testosterone junkies, notably the stocky and gray-maned Staff Captain, Nils Nordström. Nils had baggy eyes that drooped down toward his bushy gray-mustache. Unless under the influence of the caraway seed, he spoke only in deep grunts. As a younger man, Nordström had served as a mercenary in the South African/Namibian border wars, and believable rumors said that a stuffed lion's head adorned the mantel over the fireplace of his den in Bergen – a trophy to his brash, fondly-remembered soldier of fortune days.

Loring often suspected the muteness of colleagues like Nils Nordström disguised an abiding inner rage, as if only the vast, ubiquitous sea, their constant partner in meditation and reflection, could know their thoughts.

But to the passengers, the packaged formula seemed irresistible. Night after night in their white double-breasted gabardine evening uniforms, the Officers would stand like stud stallions at the chrome drinking rails in *Sails, the Glass-floored Disco*, while women scrambled shamelessly for them. Even flabby-cheeked lion hunter Nils Nordström didn't have to say a word. His mystique said and did it all for him.

Once Loring slow-danced in *Sails* with a striking blonde paralegal from Detroit. She cuddled close to him, smooched his ear, unsnapped his epaulet.

He snatched it back and left her on the dance floor.

Is that all she wanted? A piece of mystique to take back to Detroit?

But Trond Ramskog was different. Loring had cruised often with the Captain, had enjoyed jovial Aquavits with him and Maggie in his cabin, could vouch for the solidity of the man behind the mystique.

Trond Ramskog had been the youngest officer (then 28) in the fleet ever promoted to a full four stripes. Since becoming a Captain, he had distinguished himself through two decades of courageous service to Nordic Star Lines – including three hurricanes when the *Nordic Blue* had rescued victims of capsized yachts and the legendary night when the crew of the burning Venezuelan oil tanker *Enrique* had been plucked from the briny waves by *Nordic Blue* launches directed by Ramskog – a feat later celebrated at a formal dinner in Oslo at the King's Palace with Olaf V, fleet owner Stig Storjord, and the Venezuelan President.

Now in his prime at a very fit 50, Ramskog had been tapped by Stig Storjord to consult on construction and later become skipper of the *S/S Nordic Constellation* – the futuristic triple-hulled super cruiser which would dwarf the *Nordic Blue* herself.

Ladies and gentlemen! Throw the mystique overboard!

Step aside, Leif Erikson! The day of the dragon boats has long since passed. Greet the super Neo-Viking of the new Millennium!

One problem today, though, here in the *Hospital*: mystique alone would have to suffice. The bed where Chief Nurse McCarthy had left the Captain for observation was empty, the covers smoothed and the pillow fluffed. A note on the nightstand said, "Thanks, Nurse. Feel good now. Back on *Bridge*."

"Fantastic!" Maggie drawled. "First time since maritime academy he made his own bed! Oliver, he was afraid to face you and admit he did the drugs. If we pulled a toxic screen on him, they might bust his butt out of the fleet."

"His note says he's feeling good."

"He won't when I see him."

"I'll go up on the *Bridge* and talk to him."

"You kiddin me? Embarrass him in front of Nils and the other Deck Officers? No, let me take care of it. Come on, let's go get us a hot mug of Java!"

"But that's really surprising. Usually the Captain is steady and true as they make them."

"And last night isn't the worst of it! Lately that squarehead has been acting awful! Last week, we're sleepin' up in his cabin, and he wakes me up in the middle of the night, shakin' all over and sweatin' like he saw a damn ghost. I ask him, 'What's wrong, Trond,' and he gets that little boy look he sometimes gets in the dark in his cabin and says, 'Maggie, you're so long and skinny and you were holdin' me so tight, I dreamed I was sleepin' with an octopus!' Then he goes out and changes his cologne on me. Didn't say a word. Just started smellin' different! Like an Italian or somethin'. Now you always smell nice, Oliver, but you don't smell Italian. What do you wear?"

"Nino Cerutti 1881."

"Sounds Italian."

"French. Actually it's produced in England."

"Uh-*huh*? Whatever. But do you think Snø wants him to go around smellin' that way? I mean, if she gets off on Mediterranean men, why don't she just go marry herself one and make it easier for my Norsky and me? I'm sorry, Oliver, but sometimes it's hard as hell for me to keep my goddamn mouth shut about this. Hey, did you tickle the ivories this morning? You know, you look damn pale, Dart Doc. Why don't you go out and get some rays? Keep your beeper on, don't forget. Good to have you back."

* * *

High noon and cloudless on *Vista Deck*.

As the *Nordic Blue* cut her majestic course through the waves off the northern coast of Haiti, Oliver Loring strolled shirtless, his beeper clipped to his swimming suit. He gazed up fondly at the towering twin smoke stacks. Around him the azure Caribbean rippled in a fleeting pattern of rising, sinking tassels of foam. The sun blazed down and sent its limbering rays into his pale shoulders. His scalp dripped pleasurably with sweat. He slipped out of his sandals, let them dangle from his fingers against his thigh. As he strode, the astroturf tickled his toes.

Sternwards, down near the *Thor Heyerdahl Pool*, a steel band pounded out hypnotic reggae. On deck chairs everywhere, power cruisers oiled, baked, sipped *Lime Limbos*, and scanned the *Cruise News*, while their children batted volleyballs, bobbed in the jacuzzis, or tugged at wave-and-sunburst kites soaring above the *Nordic Blue's* long spangled wake.

When a huge shadow briefly darkened the ship, Loring looked up and marveled as a magnificent silver blimp hovered above. Along its broad, metallic-sheened hull scrolled the *CABLEVISTA* logo, followed by *"VALENTINE TV CRUISE!"* in large red electric letters.

The bright sun's talons still prickling his cheeks and thighs, Loring felt a surge of hot gratitude course through his veins.

This was cruising. *And* notoriety!

The Cablevista cameras sent a bird's-eye view of the resplendent *Nordic Blue* around the world. He felt luxuriant, envied.

Step . . . slide . . .

Loring recalled how improbably it all had started for him four years ago at the annual Boston Samaritan Emergency Department dinner at the Golden Dragon Pavilion in Boston's Chinatown. After the meal, all the nurses and clerks and doctors around the table insisted on reading the messages in their fortune cookies.

When Loring's turn came, he cracked his cookie and giggled. Then he recited: *"SOON HAVE NEW JOB ON HIGH SEAS!"* Clowning, he popped the piece of paper into his mouth with the rest of the cookie and belted it down with a dismissive gulp of hot saki.

A job on the high seas?

Loring had never felt the slightest urge to take a cruise, let alone *work* on a ship, and he despised the campy and sentimental reruns of the old TV show *"Love Boat."* Moreover, he had never been in the Boy Scouts or the military and, except for his regulation scrubs and lab coat at the hospital, had never worn any kind of uniform in his life.

But by some grand and ineluctable oriental force, the absurd prediction must have leached into his metabolism.

Two days after the Golden Dragon Pavilion party, his office phone rang. Beth, the secretary from Nordic Star Lines in Miami, had found his name on a list of Massachusetts emergency physicians on the internet and was cold calling to offer a paid one-week gig on the *Nordic Blue*, round trip flight included.

Loring agreed to try one cruise.

Soon he found life in the sunny Caribbean on "the world's grandest, most legendary cruise ship" replete with delights – gourmet food every night, a valet to clean his cabin thrice daily, *Crew Bar* darts, outrageous crew buddies like Jacques Chemin and Pearly Livingstone and their chants, appealing European shopgirls on *Boutique Row*, Starlegs Dancers in bathing suits, the exquisite *Club Atlantis,* and so on.

There were a dozen Baldwin and Steinway grands on the ship, each tuned *weekly*! With the Chief Medical Officer's master electric key card, Loring could avail himself of any of them (or any room or area on the ship, for that matter) at any time of the night or day.

Cruise ship doctoring became potent refreshment from his intense emergency room work in Boston. (Nurse Maggie McCarthy's first orientation tour ended with, "Well, Dr. Oliver, you've seen the *Hospital* and you've seen your cabin, and for your information I *sleep* with the Captain, so there will be no funny business between us. Got it?")

All this *plus* three golden stripes on his epaulets! For an energetic single man, could a job be any better? Quickly Loring became an addict.

Four years and a dozen cruises later, he strode along *Vista Deck* while the silver Cablevista blimp cruised through the blue noonday firmament. Chemin's chant rang in his ears: *"YOU NEVER KNOW UNTIL YOU KNOW!"*

Loring simply loved the feeling of well-being on this ship, and wondered if the rush of the warm tropical waters under the hull exerted some weird kind of buoyant spiritual dynamic. Anti-Newtonian as it sounded, could there not be a cumulative upward vector generated by the endless infinities of molecules and charged electrons sweeping under the hull?

Admittedly, for those who spent their entire professional lives on the ship – Trond Ramskog, for example – every day wasn't a reduced-gravity day. Trond, for all his savvy and charisma, had been stuck between two women for six years now. No resolution was in sight.

And all the while, Maggie agonized. She said she didn't mind that Trond never said the "L-word" about her, but she wished he would say the "D-word" sometimes about Snø.

And Loring refused to moralize about the Captain's apparent duplicity in marriage. *Or* the Valiums. What harm had been done? It wasn't the first time a Norsky had balked at revealing his feelings.

An annoying buzz near his belly button zapped Loring out of his musings. His beeper had gone off – and at a most unfortunate moment! – for across the *Vista Deck* astroturf loped Ulla von Straf in a white string bikini.

As she approached, her hand rose to shade her brow. Her eyes gleamed icy clear. She had just stepped out of the pool – all dripping – and her high bronze shoulders and long glistening thighs rolled confidently in the sun. Even the blue Caribbean could not be as vast or as deep as her eyes, Loring thought.

Hurriedly he pulled his beeper from his trunks, snapped off the pesky, insistent alarm.

Smiling, Ulla shook her head and ran both palms over her hair and down her neck. He followed the beads of water trickling past her breasts – through the wet bikini, her nipples stuck out like firm and beautiful bullets. She looked refreshed from her dip in the pool. In her eyes there was no trace of the fatigue and sorrow he had seen at dawn.

"Doctor Oliver," she winked. "I see you're not too busy today. Did you come to our rehearsal last night? I looked for you."

"I was called out in the middle of it."

"Did your beeper go off?"

"Sort of."

Ulla's eyes darkened. "So you didn't stay till the final act? That's good. We're still working on it."

"The show was wonderful, Ulla. But frankly, the snake dance made me, uh, dizzy. The spinning got to me."

She tilted her head, jumped on her heel to pound water from her ear. "Hildegarde is right. We were talking about you. You are sensitive. But as for the python, he's harmless. And very intelligent."

The three-note paging gongs sounded over the ship's loud speakers. *"MESSAGE TO ELECTRICAL CREW! DOCTOR OLIVER LORING, PLEASE PROCEED AT ONCE TO THE RADIO STATION FOR A TELEPHONE CALL!"*

"Oh, Oliver! I won't keep you. But I have a request from Hildegarde. She asked if you and I could do a Charleston in the *Roaring 20's* show tonight. For her and the Colonel."

"You and me?"

"Yes, they really like you. And they loved seeing us dance together."

"Will Spinelli permit it?"

"What do you mean? Of course Flip will agree. Why shouldn't he? I'll insist."

"Then when do we rehearse?"

"Rehearse? It's only for the cruise staff show, silly. Time is short for me today. I'm working with Tosco on some new steps. But do you know the old vaudeville song, *'Alabamy Bound?'* I xeroxed some copies for the band, and I can drop one off for you at the *Hospital*."

"Don't bother. I know *'Alabamy Bound'* well."

"*Wonderful!* Meet you backstage just before the show?"

* * *

Loring hurried forward along *Vista Deck* to the *Radio Station*.

Talk about *dizzy!* Ulla had let him look deep into her eyes – bright blue crystals spinning with kaleidoscopic whimsy – and his heart had jumped. And never had a lady bug looked more strategically placed – the wet bikini had revealed more than a *soupçon* of Ulla's taut breasts. Loring's tongue had immediately felt the wild urge to lick and confirm what his eyes saw: perfect and voluminous curvilinear symmetry.

Perhaps black magic was her game! Perhaps her boyfriend looked and acted like a mafia kingpin. Perhaps her eyes had secrets! But Ulla's glance in the full light of noon seemed to say she would hide nothing from him.

And how had she chosen that song? *Really?*

The old Eddie Cantor tune was one of his mother Olivia's favorites! She had banged out *"Alabamy Bound"* on the academy Chickering upright for her students at every Charleston competition. As a matter of fact, she and Oliver had performed it a year ago at Orson's wake – also at the Academy – where all of Coventry, Vermont, had gathered. They sent the good doctor on his way with . . .

> *I'm ALABAMY BOUND.*
> *There'll be no "Heebie Jeebies" hangin' round.*
> *Just gave the meanest ticket man on earth*
> *All I'm worth*
> *To put my tootsies in an upper berth.*

I'm just a lucky hound
To have someone to put my arms around.
That's why I'm shoutin' for the world to know
'Here I go!'
I'm ALABAMY BOUND!

* * *

"How's my favorite cruise ship doctor?"

"Anita?"

"Darling, you sound fabulously bronzed. I'm *green* with jealousy!"

"How did you find me here?"

"Oliver Loring! Do you think for one second this horny woman is going to lie naked up here all by her lonesome in Cambridge on a snowy Sunday afternoon and not try to get in touch with you down there in the sunny Caribbean, especially after I saw you on television?"

"You *saw* me?"

"Cablevista. They're taking live shots from their blimp. On the top deck near the two smoke stacks? Wasn't that you?"

"Maybe. What was I doing?"

"Looking sexy. You made me wet instantly. Oliver! I'm not going to run away from my feelings the way you did yesterday!"

"Was it only yesterday?"

"I know what you mean. It seems like forever to me, too! And you? Are you wet yet? Are you touching yourself?"

"Wet? I'm in the *Radio Station*. This is a joke call, isn't it? Or have you been doing some bubbly already today?"

"Don't make a joke out of our relationship."

"You tried to hit me with your purse. Remember? That was no joke."

"Impulse. Strictly impulse. Nothing more. You have no idea how sorry I am. And *please* don't be coy like you were yesterday at the airport. That's the last thing I need right now. I made some foolish remarks yesterday at Logan. I love Olivia, didn't mean to call her a bitch. Lovely, graceful older woman. And yes, my handbag moved faster than my heart. I confess. And I did start this cold lonely Sunday with an innocent little splash of Dom Perignon. Who wouldn't? Especially when I know where you are, and now I see where you are and where I want to be right now. Who was that slutty bimbo you were talking with near the smokestacks?"

"Anita!"

"I'm naked and on my *knees* beside my bed as we speak. And I'm asking you to forgive me. I was rude and hysterical and turbulent and hostile yesterday at the airport. Do you forgive me?"

"Anita!"

"Naked and on my knees, Oliver! And all *wet* over you! Does that *mean* anything? And I have a special surprise for you."

"You're not pregnant?"

"*Better!* I'm flying down and meeting the ship Tuesday in San Juan. I'll be there for the Midnight Promenade Tuesday night. I checked it all on the internet last night. They had one sudden cancellation, and I booked the ticket. It's all fixed. Like a miracle! We'll be cruising together for Valentine's Day! I don't think I have a window in my cabin, but you have one in yours, don't you?"

"They're called portholes."

"Yes. Do you have one in your cabin?"

"I'm busy down here."

"You didn't look busy on TV a few minutes ago. By the smoke stacks? You didn't even have your uniform on."

"Taking a break. I was . . ."

"Touching yourself yet, darling?"

"I told you, I'm in the *Radio Station.*"

"I canceled my case load from Tuesday on. The rest of the week is all for us! Can't wait, Oliver! And do you think I might be able to meet Farrely Farrell? You're an officer on that ship, aren't you? You have influence in meeting celebrities, don't you? I bet you even know the Captain. Don't you?"

"But Anita! Remember! You're a therapist!"

"Therapists have lives, too, Oliver. And not every therapist has a lover who's a doctor on the *Nordic Blue*. Especially for this cruise. This cruise is big, Oliver! Do you know how big it is? It's all over the television all the time!"

"But think of your patients! Don't people sometimes commit suicide on Valentine's day?"

"That's where I made the first mistake with you, Oliver. You should *never* have been my patient. I know I was wrong to mix therapy with all the other things we've enjoyed together over six months."

"But that's how we met. In your office."

"Fate, huh?"

"It started as nail biting."

"I can tell you're softening. I mean your feelings, big boy, not Mr. Buck-Buck. And guess what? I'm getting wetter. Can you tell? I'm so . . . grateful to you."

"Grateful?"

"I have to *thank* you for your strength in breaking away from us. It was a gesture so clear, so definitive, that I simply *had* to counter it with a strong act of my own. You can run, my lover, but . . ."

"Not a good idea, Anita. *Not* logical!"

"Are tan lines logical? I'm naked and I'm on my knees and I want to lick your tan lines. I could make them out on the television. Can you hear my tongue on the phone?"

"We broke up yesterday. You almost killed me with your purse."

"That was yesterday! I'll be down in San Juan for the Midnight Promenade on Tuesday night. Think of this till San Juan. The tip of my wet tongue on your dry, salty tan lines. And I hope you don't mind a few teeth. I'm *starving* for you already! Love you, *mmhhh!* Oh, by the way, I'm bringing my magic steamer trunk, hunk! And don't overdo it with the sun screen. I want you done to a turn."

Loring hung up. He tugged his trunks down an inch to peak at his lower belly.

What was Anita talking about? He didn't have *any* tan lines yet! There was an indistinct pink sun scald near his navel, yes, but no real line.

Still, Anita had not been joking. She was serious about flying down.

He stepped out of the *Radio Station* and into the bright sun on *Oslo Deck*. How could he ever get to know Ulla von Straf, if Anita Rothberg came on board and started crawling over him like the hives?

He had to act! There was no use phoning Anita back and begging her not to come. *Oh, no!* Once Anita Rothberg set her sites on a ship in the Caribbean? Easier to steer clear of a hurricane.

". . . We'll be cruising together on Valentine's day!"

Loring looked up in the sky at the Cablevista blimp, imagined Anita looking down on him from the camera lens. A terrible sensation of emptiness and fatalism struck him. Suddenly he was ready to give up.

Why fight Anita? Why not just give in, let her come on board and ruin his chances with Ulla?

And with life in general. Maybe he *had* tried to run away from his emotions. Maybe, in fact, he was running away from something real in himself.

After all, Loring had so very much in common with Anita.

No, Anita could *not* dance. But neither was Loring much of a computer virtuoso, didn't carry a cell phone or even have a web page and seldom checked his e-mail, didn't surf the internet furiously the way she did . (All of the appliances in her steamer trunk she had ordered discretely from the web.)

But his dancing and her computers were their only major life style incongruities. Otherwise, their similarities were profound: both were Harvard trained with faculty positions nearing tenure. Both owned condos in Cambridge, Saab convertibles, were a-political but pro-feminist. Both loved French films and positively devoured anything by Ingmar Bergman (*"The Virgin Spring"* – absolutely the best film of all time, they both agreed!) or Pee Wee Herman. (*"Pee Wee's Big Adventure"* – pure *genius*, ditto for Anita!) She and Loring also enjoyed roller coasters and skiing, loved the Club Casablanca Restaurant in Harvard Square, stealaway weekends at the Harbor View on Martha's Vineyard . . . the list was nearly endless.

Loring's right pinky slid up between his lips. He tongued the white nubbin of a tasty nail.

Perhaps Anita's words *were* logical.

Maybe they *could* start over again, do it right, begin Tuesday in San Juan, forget the nail biting altogether. Forget about the mysterious woman Ulla.

So *what* if Anita had failed him as a therapist? He hadn't been the most compliant of patients. Didn't he owe her another shot?

Anita's knees *had* sounded tempting on the phone rubbing against the smooth crimson carpet of her bedroom where they often had sported after his therapy sessions! Such *torrid* sessions! From the first moment, their verbal repartee had seemed so erotic, they had been forced (the dimpled red leather analysis couch quickly lost its novelty) to move into the mirror-ceilinged bedroom, where nail biting slid far down on the list of priorities, sometimes was even laughed at.

Despite his initial fascination, Loring eventually resented Anita's dependence on electromechanical stimulation for repeated sexual orgasms. In fact, he grew to hate the rusty creak of that steamer trunk lid when he lay there with a perfectly adequate erection, a/k/a "Mr. Buck-Buck" to Anita, while she rummaged in the trunk for her favorite *vibrateur du jour*. (He often wondered if she didn't prefer their phone sex – with the receiver in one hand and her trusty mechanical accomplice in the other – to the real, in the flesh, stuff.)

But Anita hadn't always been that way, perhaps would not always be dependent on machines. He recalled one afternoon early on, when they both were still serious about therapy and payment schedules. He had told her of his mother Olivia's early tries (when he was 6 or 7) to curtail his nail biting by painting his fingertips with oil-of-clove. He confessed that ever since then, he had always had an almost unquenchable craving for oil-of-clove. Anita had immediately led him off the analysis couch and directly into her condo's kitchenette where she took a small bottle of oil-of-clove from her spice rack, removed her blouse and bra, started spreading the aromatic substance over her meager breasts and scrawny nipples. Before long, Anita was peeling off his shirt, and his mouth was seeking out the intoxicant – symptoms of what Anita called his "delayed weaning response."

But *wait*!

Loring yanked his pinky from his mouth.

He stared out at the glistening Caribbean – almost the very blue of Ulla von Straf's eyes. He sensed a beckoning presence out there which had nothing to do with the Cablevista blimp.

He turned his head away, closed his eyes.

In . . . and . . .

Then he looked back and, yes, it still was there. Even more powerful than before. Was it in the dancing waves? In the tricky shimmerings of the sun? In the mesmerizing rhythms – syncopated choppy whites there, smooth undulating blues here, hallucinogenic glitters over there? (Had he begun to converse with the sea, the way the Norwegian Officers said they did?)

But it was more than the colors and the motions and the overall visual effect. It took on a form, indistinct but perceivable amidst the waves. Then it billowed up and became cloud-like, gigantic, dominant, seemed to have fluttering sleeves – radiant white sleeves which lofted high into the blue sky. It lacked only a voice.

But if it had a voice, Loring knew it would sound like his own voice on the ship-to-shore telephone to Boston a few minutes ago saying, "Anita, this is not a good idea!"

From out of the blue it comes! What have I been thinking? Anita Rothberg is on her way down here to ruin my cruise. And my life!

He looked at his pinky finger. No, he had not bitten off that tasty morsel. It was *not* too late.

Time to act radically!

* * *

Minutes later, the *Central Elevator* opened onto the mini-balcony of the *Club Roma Spa* down on *Pool Deck*. Loring stepped out in day uniform.

"I AM THE CHIEF MEDICAL OFFICER!" he announced loudly. *"AND I HAVE COME TO SEE NADINE TULARD! THE NAIL SPECIALIST! AT ONCE! SEE MY EPAULETS? THEY HAVE THREE STRIPES! THE CAPTAIN HIMSELF HAS ONLY FOUR!"*

Loring's voice echoed on the tiled arches of the dim, faux-Roman decor: acrylic statues, tripod torches, lounging benches, chipped fresco fragments, ferns in urns – all surrounding a rippling octagonal tiled pool. Several reclining power cruisers looked up indolently from the benches. In the fountain at his feet, water tinkled from the tiny penises of three grinning terra cotta cherubs. Loring scanned the entrances to the separate corridors which led to chambers offering massage, sauna, steam bath, mud packs, bikini hot wax, seaweed wraps, rolfing, shi-atsu, electrolysis.

No staff in site.

He cleared his throat and shouted, *"MADEMOISELLE TULARD! S'IL VOUS PLAIT!"*

Loring hated to flaunt both his rank and his French, but he had no choice. His cruise and his life were at stake.

Within seconds, Nadine Tulard, a willowy blonde *Parisienne* dressed in sandals and a Roman slave's tunic, appeared and ushered him down the corridor and into the manicure salon, sat him on the treatment chair, stretched his fingers out on the towel, brought out her stainless steel instruments with their graceful curves and edges and handles, sat there, looked him in the eye, and smiled.

That *smile* alone! It was worth the flight down from Boston!

Woaaaaaaaaaah! Had Loring ever pulled rank at the right time!

Nadine Tulard was wonderful. So French! She took him in *without* an appointment, understood everything he told her about cutting off his relationship with Anita abruptly and why it was so important that he show some sign of nail growth and maintenance before Anita arrived on Wednesday. "I have to show her I can do for myself what she couldn't do for me."

Nadine Tulard's soft hazel eyes laughed. *"Bien sûr!"*

Loring couldn't *believe* it! He sensed no issues of professional rivalry. Nadine was not patronizing him. *Au contraire!* She told him she simply didn't care if he was oral *or* anal. When it came to nail biting, she refused to adhere to any dialectic. She also appreciated the necessary cruelty involved – hitting a therapist where it would hurt – to challenge and undermine her professional competence.

"How else will you get rid of her?" Nadine wondered. "Otherwise, a bitch like that will always come crawling back to you on her knees."

"She was on her knees when she called me this morning."

"*Evidement!* See what I mean?"

"Oh, I'm so glad I came to you."

"Are you willing to do something experimental, *Docteur*?"

"What choice do I have? We must start from . . . uh . . . *scratch*. Ha-*ha*! We're not talking implants, are we?"

* * *

Four hours later, the *Central Elevator* opened onto *Viking Deck*.

Loring *already* could feel Nadine Tulard's ingenious therapy taking hold! He proceeded to the nearest porthole to view his fingers in the sunlight.

How had she done it? But *there* they were, shining in the sun! Ten tiny but distinct white crescents – still fledgling, tender – but growing at the tips of all his digits! Fresh little expressions of hope!

In four hours, Mademoiselle Tulard had achieved what Anita Rothberg had failed to do in six full months!

Loring even felt it in his toes! Why shouldn't he? What a consummate therapist she was!

After a brief introductory chat, Nadine had gone right to the task. That willowy miracle worker did not focus only on the target organs, his fingernails. She treated the *whole* patient. (So many physicians Loring knew in Boston could take a lesson from her!)

Manicure and pedicure? Just for starters. Then the seaweed wrap over the shoulders, buttocks, and thighs, the total body mud pack – face, scalp, crotch – and finally (Loring had passed on the high herbal colonic, *merci!*) a brutal steam room massage and ice chip cool-down.

Then came the *pièce de résistance*. When he had showered and dressed again, she led him into her laboratory, sat him down, closed the door.

Loring watched her with wonder.

"Do you know the scarab beetle?" she whispered, ominously.

"Like the ones on Egyptian jewelry?"

She nodded, reached into her tunic pocket for a Winston. "You are not afraid?"

70

"Of a beetle? Ha!"

"And you want your nails to grow very fast?"

"In the worst way!"

She flicked her lighter, inhaled several drags, then blew out slowly, all the while pondering him. "You want this in the worst way," she said to herself as she walked over and quietly locked the laboratory door. "Very well. This is a secret we use in Paris. It is not new. The soldiers of Napoleon brought it from Egypt. In our salon we have updated it."

"Oh, you French are always so *au courant!*"

Nadine put her Winston down in an ashtray. Out of the refrigerator she pulled an unlabeled round plastic container.

With a long pair of stainless steel tweezers she plucked out a tremendous squirming black beetle, tossed it into a smaller container and into the microwave.

Sixty seconds and three drags on her Winston later, during which tiny explosions occurred within the microwave, she took out the scarab – no longer squirming – and dropped him into an electric coffee grinder. She set the knob at *"espresso,"* flipped the switch. The blades disintegrated the hot carcass in ten seconds. Carefully she funneled a pinch of the fine black powder into a capsule, sealed it, poured Loring a cup of Perrier from the refrigerator.

"Take this one now," she said, "and another one every eight hours for a week. I'll prepare the rest of the pills and send them up to your cabin."

"It works in a week?"

"Oh, faster than that!"

"*Formidable!* You cannot be serious!"

Loring did not know how to express his gratitude, especially when Nadine said the Pharaohs themselves had taken scarabs for all kinds of cosmetological problems – nails, hair, aging spots.

"Hair loss?"

She surveyed his brow. "Don't get your hopes up."

But hope was now very "up" on his fingertips.

Regardez! Ten little sprung-out witnesses of hope! The effects were obvious, the spirit and science sound.

Mythology: rebirth, new life, rejuvenation – the scarab was all that for the ancient Egyptians.

Biochemistry: from his pre-med biology courses, Loring knew that insects, especially beetles, contain vast amounts of chitin – the polypeptide with the same molecular structure and metabolism as human chitin. Scarabs have

71

chitin in their wings, legs, claws, jaws, antennas and belly plates – the very same chitin human beings have in their nails and hair. With his nail problem and his advancing baldness, Loring suffered – clinically speaking – from an absolute total-body chitin deficiency, and scarabs were the perfect molecular remedy!

Alright, scarabs were dung beetles! A disgusting fact.

But if scarabs were good enough for the royal Pharaohs way back then and Napoleon himself not so long ago and now for all the trendy people in Paris on the cutting edge of modern cosmetology in the fashion capital of the world, why shouldn't scarabs be good enough for Loring? Hey! Let's judge that beetle by the company he keeps!

Slide . . .

* * *

At exactly 18.00 hours, the Chief Medical Officer arrived on *Viceroy Deck* in tuxedo uniform. He stopped before the full-length mirror in the corridor, straightened his epaulets, smoothed his lapels and cummerbund, buffed his nails on his sleeve. He hitched up his new trousers on his suspenders, reveled in the abundance of crotch room.

Eager to greet the Snippet-Whites for tea, he tapped the heels of his pumps and knocked at *Viceroy #7.*

He waited, knocked again, more firmly.

The door opened. A slender blue finger emerged from the sleeve of a hooded, white sable coat. Hildegarde Snippet-White blinked her mascara-laden eyes under her white furry hood and beckoned.

Loring followed her in, shivered.

Viceroy #7's expansive sitting room was richly appointed in soft pastels from the *S/S Marianne's* original mid-20th-century design. To Loring's taste, the French decorators had overdone the chrome accents in the liquor cabinet and the coffee table. They had also given an altar-like centrality to the '60s-era console TV between the huge, lozenge-shaped portholes.

But it was difficult to judge the decor fairly. Sheets of frost had formed on the lozenge-shaped portholes. The thermostat needle pointed to 32 F, (0C).

Loring's fingers shook. He stuffed them into his pockets as he noticed a nifty little Steinway ebony console tucked in the corner. He was wondering how the chill might affect the instrument, when Hildegarde slammed the door behind him.

"Welcome, Doctor," she said in a hushed voice. "Right on time! Sorry for the frosty air. I had the Refrigeration Engineers come in and lower the temperature at noon. Those Norwegian boys are so sexy in their powder blue jump suits! And marvelous technicians, don't you think? I'm sorry, but Rocky is old British stock, you know, prefers icy showers and all. And me a Bostonian? I'm used to it, aren't you? Do sit down."

Loring took a seat on the edge of the couch. Hildegarde pulled the hood further over her head and sat beside him, her trembling arms folded into her luxurious fur.

"Where's the Colonel?"

"Resting by himself in the second bedroom. Under the weather."

"S-s-still?"

She nodded. "Just between you and me, Doctor . . ."

"Call me Oliver."

"And won't you call me Hildegarde?" She leaned over to him. "Just between you and me, Oliver, I think Rocky overdid it last night in *Atlantis*. Simply hasn't been the same since. Very quiet and keeping to himself. I'd rather not disturb him till tea arrives. Tea will pick him up. Always does."

She slipped a mischievous wink from under her hood. "But perhaps you'd like some liquor, Oliver? Scotch? Bourbon? *Lime Limbo*? Warm you up? Surely *you* are not a stranger to liquor! None of the Beacon Hill Lorings are. Oh, I forgot, Oliver! We're fresh out of ice."

"I'm . . . uh . . . not closely related to the Beacon Hill Lorings, and I'd prefer to wait for tea. Uhhhhh . . . *hot* tea. Is it coming . . . s-s-soon?"

He pulled his fingers from his pockets and massaged the goose bumps on his hands.

"My, *my!*" Hildegarde grabbed Loring's wrist. "You certainly move well on the dance floor, but just *look* at those fingers, won't you! So long and graceful! I shan't say a word about your very original manicure. They told me you're a pianist as well. You certainly have the hands for serious music."

"Sometimes I putter around with Chopin and Scriabin."

"*Ha-ha!*" Hildegarde sent two spurts of white fog out from under her hood. Her fingers stroked the veins near his knuckles. "Come now, *you!* Nobody *putters* with Scriabin. His stuff is absolutely metaphysical. Sometimes Chopin is, too. Isn't he? Of course nobody's metaphysical all the time. Are they?" She pulled her head out of her hood long enough to roll her eyes. "Unless *you* are."

"Metaphysical?"

She giggled and retreated again into her fur. Loring had already appreciated her sparkly hazel eyes and her narrow, upturned nose. Up close, her natural features were fine and strangely devoid of wrinkles. But to Loring, the skin across her cheek bones had been stretched too tightly by the surgeons. In profile, the lower edges of her eye sockets had a bony whiteness that gleamed in shiny rims through her rouge. There was also a botox-induced stiffness to her lips which emphasized her Beacon Hill, hard mandible accent.

Loring had met other Brahmin *grande dames* who had been raised in the strict moral confines of the upper class and who, once youth gave out and the privileges of aristocracy ceased to comfort, cracked their emotional plaster completely. But, no, Hildegarde impressed him as a woman who had *always* been refreshingly daft.

"Cute little Steinway."

"Rocky never cruises without one. You must try it out."

"N-n-not today. He's obviously a man of many d-dimensions."

"But surely no more multifarious than you, Oliver. I can't *wait* to see you dance with Ulla tonight in *Roaring '20s*. She said you agreed. Thank you. You know, you remind me of Rocky when he was younger."

"You exaggerate."

"It's hard to exaggerate about handsome and gifted men with high hair lines. And you look stunning in uniform, if you don't mind a gratuitous comment from a wizened old stick like me. I'm 78, you know, and desperately flirtatious."

"Is your husband *really* just d-d-down the hall?"

"Indeed, he is. Do you thrive on danger?" She touched Loring's right cheek. "I *love* that beauty mark, you know."

Loring let out a volley of chuckles. The steam from his lungs pulsed across the cold air. "You're not a w-w-wizend stick, Hildegarde."

"You should see me naked. Only *kidding*, Oliver. I have always been strict on things like fidelity. I *talk* the brat, never *act* the brat. I've always been stricter than Rocky, that *roué*! Come closer. Do you like my perfume?"

"Coco Chanel?"

"It's different from the one I wore last night."

"Fernaldi, w-wasn't it?"

"She pulled back her hood and shook her tight cheek at him. "Now aren't you the olfactory animal! Don't miss a trick, do you? And so self-deprecatory about your mystical side! Just look at you. You could be Rocky's son. Same profile. Do you know that Rocky actually has some American blood? Yes. In fact his name, Rockwell, is a terribly un-English name, isn't it? Rocky's maternal grandfather was a Rockwell from Pennsylvania. He insisted on having his grandson named after him."

"I have n-n-no relatives in P-P-Pennsylv-v-v-ania."

"Well, regardless, the grandfather was quite a *roué*. Rocky, too. Are you a *roué*?"

"Pardon me?"

"I ask only because I think my goddaughter took quite a liking to you last night. Ulla is in a delicate state just now. I keep telling her she must move on, but I would hate for anyone to take advantage . . . "

There was a knock at the door. Loring went over and opened it. Jarvis Lee, the Jamaican *Viceroy Deck* Valet, wheeled in a silver-domed trolley.

"Tea at last!" Hildegarde exclaimed.

"Where would you like it put, Madame?"

Hildegarde rose. "Just outside the second bedroom, Jarvis. And thank you so much!"

Jarvis returned, pocketed a five-pound Sterling note. "Is the Colonel feeling better, Madame?"

"A bit. Thank you. Oh, Jarvis, don't bother turning down the sheets tonight. We won't need you for that."

"Shall I call the Ship's Doctor, Mum?"

"The Ship's Doctor is here and is about to enjoy your tea, Jarvis. Everything is under control. Good night. And thank you again."

"Oh, yes, Mum. Good evening, Doctor." Jarvis Lee nodded to Loring and left.

"Now where were we?" She sat down and offered her hand to Loring. "Ulla."

"Oh yes. She's from the Austrian side of *my* family. I have an Austrian lineage, too, you know – the von Strafs. That's how I came by the unlikely name of Hildegarde. From my Viennese grandmother."

"So you are related to Ulla by blood?"

"By several removals. But I'm also her godmother, which I consider more important. And not only that, Oliver! Coincidence of coincidences! Ulla's grandfather Willibald was an electronic engineer who served behind the lines in the underground in Vienna during the war. He and the Colonel used to communicate secretly in code by shortwave. If it hadn't been for some of Willibald's dispatches, the Colonel would have had a much harder time with his espionage efforts in cracking those damnable Nazi codes. Yes, Colonel worked for the Colossus project, you know. Unfortunately, the two never met, except electronically and by code. Hitler's henchmen in Austria discovered Willibald and hanged him in '43."

"So Ulla never knew Willibald?"

"How *could* she? She was born decades after the war. But that's her ancient heartbreak. Her recent heartbreak came only two years ago, and she hasn't recovered yet."

"I see a sadness in her eyes."

"Yes, you *are* another Rocky! So perceptive!"

"Actually, some of the crew members have seen it, too."

"Her sadness? Yes? Is that so? But let's not be morose. Let's lighten up. Shall we look in on Rocky before his tea gets cold?"

She rose and led Loring hand-in-hand down the hallway. "And how do you like my new white sable? Picked it out this afternoon at *Nordic Furs*. Tova, the girl in that little boutique, is so charming. I almost wanted to buy a coat for her, too. Really I did!"

The second bedroom was dark and still colder, the shades pulled down tight.

"Time for tea, Rocky," Hildegarde announced cheerfully and pushed the silver-domed trolley through the door. "Here's Doctor! Well now, will my boyfriend take some refreshment?" She drew up the blinds.

Pink beams from the sinking Caribbean sun penetrated the frosty windows and spread across the bed. The Colonel lay straight as a felled flagpole – in full uniform, bemedaled sash, and with a stiff, asymmetrical, gold-tooth grin on his face. His harpoon nose aimed up at the ceiling and cast a sundial-like shadow on his sunken cheek. He was not shivering.

Loring went over and stood by the bed. "Good evening, Colonel."

"Shake him up a little, Oliver," Hildegarde urged. "Rocky's a deep snoozer. Now, just wake up for Doctor. Be sociable, Rocky-Boy-Bebalzem."

"Rocky-Boy-Bebalzem?"

She nodded. "A term of endearment from his first wife," she whispered. "I never tried to decipher it, but it works like magic whenever I want to shock him and get his attention quickly. Isn't Boy-Bebalzem a handsome devil?"

Loring reached down and clasped the Colonel's hand.

Stiff. Gray. Cool as ice.

Loring lifted the rigid wrist – the Colonel's body rolled up and flopped back. No air was passing through the deep, hairy nostrils.

"Hildegarde? How long has he been like this?"

"He went to sleep with that silly grin last night after *Atlantis* and he's kept it up all today. Would you like some sugar in your tea, Rocky? Or will it be lemon tonight for a change?"

Loring put his ear to the frigid chest.

"How do you like yours, Oliver? Sugar? Milk? Lemon? Cinnamon stick? Rum? We can make hot-toddies. Jarvis brought us everything."

"One lump. Hildegarde, we've got to talk."

"Did I ask you about lemon?"

"Make it one lump. But we must talk."

"Just as I thought. Exactly the way Rocky likes his. I'll make two of the same. You boys are so much alike!"

Hildegarde approached, tea cups trembling on their saucers, tears streaking her Mascara. Loring took the saucers and put them down on the bedside table. He put his arm around Hildegarde to comfort her.

"Kiss me, you *fool*!" she said, falling into his arms. "You won't let them take Rocky away from me, will you? We're still on our honeymoon cruise. Hold me. Heal me, Doctor. Rocky's been with me all these years. Surely you can hold me and comfort me for a minute."

Loring kissed Hildegarde's bony cheek. Then he kissed her thin lips. Hard.

"*Oh!* You feel so warm!" she sobbed.

"When did it happen?"

"In his dreams. I felt him kicking away, like he was doing that tricky Charleston kick we did in the *Club Atlantis* earlier last night."

"The razor drop kick?"

"Exactly. Then I found him that way when I woke up this morning."

"He didn't change out of his uniform last night?"

She caught her breath. "When we came back to the cabin, all he could say was what a spectacular time he'd had, how fabulous it felt to be back on the ship . . . even said how he *adored* you and . . . wanted you up for tea, didn't say a word about chest pain or anything. And now here you are, aren't you? Drink it."

"You slept with him this way all night?"

"I didn't kill him with sex, if that's what you mean. I don't think you could prove that with an autopsy anyway, could you?"

"We probably don't need an autopsy. The ship's not equipped for a proper one."

"Yes, and Colonel would only want a proper one, don't you know."

"Why didn't you call me immediately? Don't you realize, on twelve cruises now, I've never lost a single patient! Not till now."

"I'm dreadfully sorry for you." She dabbed a napkin on her face.

Loring stirred his tea slowly, watched the steam rise in confusing spirals. Hildegarde sighed. "But face it. Even *you* could not have brought Rocky back. His heart was weak. Two myocardial infarctions and a *second* triple bypass last year? His doctors in London forbade him to take this cruise. He's on seven cardiac drugs."

"You never said a word about his heart condition last night."

"Last night was party time. And you were a dancer, not a doctor. But *go* ahead. Interrogate me. Be ruthless. I know it's your job. I have copies of all his London medical records with us, if you want to look at that."

"I'm sorry, Hildegarde. I don't intend to grill you, but I would like to look at those records, perhaps phone his cardiologist?"

"Why? He's dead."

"You mean the cardiologist?"

"No, *Rocky*! Can't you *see* that? But what's the difference? Oh, poor Rocky! What will they do with him? I met him on *this* ship!"

"We must notify the Captain. Then we must put him in the *Galley Freezer.* Temporarily, that is."

"What's wrong with keeping him right *here?* With *me?* At least for one more night? Rocky's perfectly sanitary right here in *Viceroy #7.*"

"Protocol. We're supposed to use the *Meat Freezer* for any corpses."

She sniffed and shuddered. "He's just not *any* corpse."

"I'm sorry."

"And your word *corpse.* It sounds so final."

Loring offered his handkerchief.

"Is it a nice meat freezer? Does he have to go in right away? They won't wrench him from his lover's arms on his honeymoon! Will they? *Tell* me they won't!"

"Don't you want to send him back?"

"Where?"

"To England. To London?"

"Oliver, Darling, this ship is our romantic home, always has been. Rocky wouldn't want it any other way. *He* has no children. *We* have no children. No heirs. All he has is foundations."

"And *you!*"

"Yes, and *me*! So why back to England?"

"But he's English."

"Agreed. And Rocky has had so many honors bestowed on him, just this side of knighthood. Of course, even knighthood isn't what it once was, is it? I understand it's becoming more and more difficult for the house of Windsor to muster up a campaign for any type of distinguished knighthood, what with all these rock and roll musician types coming on the scene. Seriously, Oliver, why make a knight out of a minstrel? Doesn't that seem inherently illogical to you? But does the royalty see the fallacy?"

"No matter where you decide to bury him, I have to report his death to the Captain. I should phone the Nurse, too. "

"Perfect. Why not tell Captain Ramskog at dinner? Which reminds me. We're *keeping* him and his guests! Will you wait just a twinkle till I freshen my mascara? Would Rocky want it any other way? I'm so glad he had the idea of inviting you for tea, Oliver. That Rocky always had a knack for timing. Do take a sip. It'll warm you up."

* * *

Chief Nurse Maggie McCarthy had not been included on the list of guests invited to the Captain's large oval table in the center of the *Main Dining Room*. But minutes before the opening toast, she slipped in – lean and sassy in her white dress jacket (two stripes on her epaulets) and tight black tuxedo slacks – and plunked herself in Colonel Snippet-White's empty seat beside Loring and directly across from the Captain and Mrs. Ramskog.

As the Captain's golden mustache began to twitter, Maggie flashed her white canines. "Evenin', Mrs. Snippet-White! Evenin', Captain and Mrs. Ramskog! Evenin', y'all!"

Oliver Loring – wedged tightly between Maggie and the spindly Hildegarde – sent a sociable grin around to the other eight officers and the dozen passenger guests at the table. He squirmed for leg room.

"Evenin', Dart Doc!"

"Not smart, Mag," Loring whispered. "Maybe just a tad hostile?"

Maggie sipped her Silverado Trail Chardonnay and bristled. "Well, if Snø Ramskog can sit there right beside him, why can't I poke my skinny butt down at the same freakin' table? You just phoned and said the Colonel cooled and the seat would be empty. I came down here to warm it up a little."

"I just called you to find out the protocol. You know, I never lost a patient on a cruise before!"

"Yea, Dart Doc, and you're a virgin, too, just like me."

"You couldn't resist coming down here?"

"Just *look* at her, Oliver! Who in hell does she think she is? Queen of all goddamn Norway?"

Loring followed Maggie's glance across the table and tried (as he had learned in his Harvard human resources bi-gender study groups) to avoid stereotyping and to project himself into Snø Ramskog's non-gender specific essence – never an easy feat for a chauvinist in recovery.

If Snø had betrayed rotten brown teeth from decades of chain smoking, he might have forgiven her. If she had shown burst capillaries on her cheeks from decades of private Aquavit parties alone at home in Oslo, while Trond caroused on the high seas, then Loring would have seen some vestige of suffering in the dappled skin, would have sympathized. If she had exhibited signs of an eating disorder – bullemia or anorexia nervosa or even morbid obesity or any overt signs of sacrifice/situational depression – then Loring would have given Snø the benefit of the doubt. One would have to understand and forgive her, for she had been victimized, married to the perpetually randy star of all Nordic Star Captains, paid the price of sorrow every day, knew he was cheating on her, hated him for it, hated herself, the world, you name it.

Not so.

Snø Ramskog was an elegant blonde of drop-dead classic Norwegian stock. She looked a dozen years younger than what Loring knew was her age, 46. While his eyes stared at her remarkably smooth-skinned radiance, Loring's mind went through what he had been taught in the therapy seminars – about how a woman creates her own feminine self actualizing context.

But it was clear from her bland gestures that Snø had never felt it necessary to create a context beyond her own narcissism, and tonight was no exception. She beamed up at the ship's Photogs as they leaned for their shots. She flashed smile after smile around the table, winked at Loring, seemed indifferent to her husband.

The tiara atop her blonde blunt cut and the skinny diamond necklace above her evening gown of royal blue taffeta and white lace seemed old-fashioned, but who cared? Not Snø. She could present herself as she wished – queen-like, quaint. It had to work – she was Snø.

Loring had heard that Trond first met her in Paris when she was a Dior runway model. She looked that way again tonight, but healthier, bustier. Was Loring fair in seeing she showed no regard for her husband but only for herself? Was he *accurate* when he realized, as Trond must have realized long ago, that Snø was a well-proportioned, self-admiring nightmare whose eyes lacked . . . but *wait*!

This defect was most indisposing, yet neurologically intriguing.

There it was. There it was again.

Indeed, Snø Ramskog had a sustained neurotic tic in the lower portion of her facial features which seemed to jump out unpredictably from deep inside her and, while lingering, twisted half her face into a nasty scowl. One moment Snø looked pleasant, demure, almost jolly. The next, when the tic struck, she looked cruel, sardonic, with the rear molars and the gold bridgework exposed, and her tongue whipped off to the side. She could not control the twisted contortion, especially when she looked away from the cameras and across the table at the Chief Nurse.

Maggie rocked back in her chair and sneered a freckled sneer. She said (to the back of her hand, rather than to Loring), "Now tell me you'd want to come home to that after six months at sea!"

"*Shhhhhhhhhh!* I hear she speaks fluent English."

"A minute with me, and I'd teach her some good ole Georgia trash talk real fast."

"But why are you angry at her and not him?"

"I've *had* it with both of 'em! They been jerkin' my tired ass around this ship for the past six years. It's always been *me* had to get off whenever *she* got on. Well not this time, baby! *Not* on a freakin' *Valentine TV Cruise*! If he can sleep in my bed, I can sit at his table. I want justice and I want my man. I'm tired of sharing. Especially with that!"

"Maybe deep down she's nice."

"Stop talkin' goofball, Dart Doc, and pour me some more of Captain's damn Chardonnay."

Loring introduced Maggie to the couple on her immediate right – Clyde and Blanche Cruickshank from Odessa, Texas. Clyde was the winner of an incentive cruise for being the most successful regional salesman of the year for Mercedes-Benz in Texas. He wore a white double-breasted tuxedo and a white ten-gallon hat with a large three-spoked Mercedes-Benz silver logo pin above the brim. Blanche wore a fringed white suede mini-skirt/cowgirl boot ensemble. Blanche was a busy homemaker and the gloating central face in her husband's wallet snapshot of her and the five younger Cruickshanks posed in front of the display windows of the Clyde Cruickshank Mercedes-Benz dealership in Odessa.

Clyde, the table had been told, would appear with Farrely Farrell on

Wednesday's "Love Luck" show. He would officially present the "Love Luck" grand prizes – keys to three brand-spanking new Mercedes 744K roadsters being flown now Frankfurt/San Juan and to be parked up on *Vista Deck* for the Cablevista blimp to televise round-the-world.

Immediately prior to Maggie's entrance, Clyde had hailed the attention of Kahleed Stitt, the visiting National Football League wide receiver, who sat on the other side of Snø Ramskog. Clyde informed Kahleed and Mrs. Ramskog and the other guests and officers about his own "sure-fire, kick-butt, grab-the-buyer-by-the-balls" formula for selling luxury vehicles and about his wife's nearly uncontrollable "I-got-to-beat-her-with-a-stick" gambling habit. Then he had leaned in front of Blanche's prodigious cleavage and rattled on to Loring, man-to-man, about "the lateral immobility, lack of peripheral vision, and piss-brained *ineptitude"* of the current Dallas Cowboys' defensive backfield – a topic about which Loring could not recall having requested an update.

"Nurse Maggie's from Georgia," Loring offered.

"Hey!" Clyde chortled. He tipped his hat back and smiled broadly. "*Love* them Atlanta Falcons! Mind if I touch your epaulets, M'am? You look real fine in shoulder pads. Don't she, Blanche? But why only *two* stripes, hun? I think you deserve a couple more."

"So do I," Maggie said and sipped sternly from her glass.

"Well, listen up, Nurse. Do you folks have any magic pills on board to cure compulsive gamblers? The Cruickshanks may have come on this cruise as free riders, but hell's bells, Blanche here damn near lost us our goddamn Mercedes franchise at the roulette wheel last night!"

"Hush up!" Blanche frowned.

"Well, you didn't make no secret about it last night! Just suckin' on those chips for good luck! Suckin' away like they were life savers or somethin'. It's not too good for your health, Blanche. Who knows where those chips have been? You could come down with the *Norwalk* Virus! I think it's lousy for your luck, too."

"I said hush, Clyde!"

"Can't pry her off that table, know what I mean, Nurse? By the way, what's a good-lookin' doll like you doin' still single? Total professional? That it?"

With Attack Nurse sizzling but neutralized on his right, Loring peered left.

Hildegarde had her nose in her menu but had kicked off her shoes under the table and was starting to rub her toe along the inside of Loring's calf.

She noticed his glance. "Do you like that? You feel warm. By the way, the Captain looks ghastly. You haven't told him yet, I hope."

"Waiting for the right moment."

"Let's scan the menu and see if we can find an appropriate spot. Nothing spoils good food faster than bad news. Rocky always said that."

* * *

On most evenings aboard the *S/S Nordic Blue*, Trond Ramskog's glance – thick blonde lashes over fjord-blue orbs – had the penetrating wisdom of an ancient Nordic monarch. And not only the glance! On any other evening at the Captain's Honor Table, when you saw Trond Ramskog smile and heard him wrap his tongue so charmingly around English phrases, he seemed as though he hid behind his thin heroic lips all the mystery of the Norwegian forests, the savagery of the ancient dragon boats, and perhaps a shimmering ray or two of the aurora borealis itself.

Was the Captain of the *Nordic Blue* all these things?

Nobody had ever seen his like. Trond was the country, the ship, the legend, the pageant, the mystique, the incentive cruise.

And the moment which tingled backbones throughout the *Main Dining Room* was when the good-looking Captain with the golden handlebars and the startling, fjord-blue eyes stood up at the head of the large oval table in the center of the hall, raised his wine goblet and said, *"Skål!"* in a booming baritone.

"Skål! Skål! Skål!" would shout Mahmoud, the one-armed Egyptian *Maître d'*, and all his Jamaican and Indonesian waiters.

"Skål! Skål! Skål!" would shout the multitude of power cruisers, transfixed in communion with their Captain.

What did *"Skål"* really mean?

Skål was Trond. And Trond was *Skål*. That's all anybody wanted to know on any other evening.

But not tonight. Tonight the Captain had the hiccups. Not drunken hiccups – nervous hiccups.

But who could tell the difference? Especially early on, just after the Gaspacho with Lobster was served, when the Captain rose and Staff Captain Nils Nordström tapped his water glass with his knife and the entire *Main Dining Room* hushed obediently.

The Captain lifted the lip of his Chardonnay glass the usual whisker above his mustache. His visionary blue eyes gleamed through the hall. Cameras flashed from all directions as Snø beamed photogenically by his side.

"Heeeek! Heeeek!" he squealed.

A flutter of anxious laughs rippled through the hall.

Nils Nordström's baggy eyelids drooped, and he cocked his head.

Clyde Cruickshank hitched back the brim of his hat and winced. "What Capn' say?"

The Captain lowered his glass and cast a boyish smile around at Kahleed Stitt and then at the rest of the crowd – as though he had been teasing them all.

Clyde cracked, "Some kinda' stand-up comic, is he?"

"Hush your pie hole, Clyde!" ordered Blanche. Her Chardonnay hovered reverently above her cleavage for the magic moment of the cruise's consecration.

The Captain offered his glass again, but his shoulders twitched. He emitted a more violent, *"Heeeeeeeeek! Heeeeeeeeeeeeeeek!"* His chin bumped his goblet. A profuse wave of Silverado Trail Chardonnay wandered down his neck. He reached down for his napkin and swabbed up the wine before Ezra, the Israeli Sommelier, could run to assist.

"What the hell's wrong?" demanded Clyde. "Can't hold his liquor?"

Loring felt an elbow in his ribs. "Shit, Oliver!" Maggie whispered. "Folks all gonna' think they're on another freakin' *Exxon Valdez!*"

Trond Ramskog's eyes clouded over. He looked down at his wife, whose neurotic tic had jumped into overdrive. This unleashed another salvo of violent hiccups from beneath the golden mustache.

The passengers began to stir with anxiety.

Swiftly Loring glanced at Nils Nordström and the other officers. They seemed slow, detached, fuzzy with wine, unaware that the Captain's charisma teetered in jeopardy.

Loring rose with his full goblet upraised. He held it as high as his fingertips could reach, smiled over at Snø and Trond Ramskog, as though he had heard the Captain's toast perfectly enunciated.

Then he let out from the depths of his lungs a resounding, *"YES, INDEED, CAPTAIN! SKÅÅÅÅÅÅÅÅÅÅÅÅÅÅÅÅÅÅÅL!"*

At once Mahmoud, the one-armed Egyptian *Maître d'*, took the cue and shouted, *"SKÅÅÅÅÅÅÅÅÅÅL!"*

The regiments of Jamaican and Indonesian and Croatian waiters on either side of the *Main Dining Room* followed suit, and instantly the Captain was being greeted by the usual flurry of gracious cheers.

"*SKÅL! SKÅL! SKÅL! SKÅL!*" echoed from every corner of the hall.

Trond Ramskog bowed and sat down.

"Bravo, Oliver," Maggie murmured.

The Captain nodded across the table with gratitude.

No, Loring thought, this was *not* the moment to tell Trond Ramskog about the death of Colonel Rockwell Snippet-White. The Captain had enough on his emotional plate.

But when to tell the Captain? Definitely not during the fillet of sea-bass on artichoke bottoms with light truffle sauce. Forget it! (Loring, partial to truffles, would devote that course to his own uninterrupted delight.)

Wait! Loring rubbed his eyes in disbelief as the Mrs. Maigret pheasant with chanterelles and sloe gin Massenez was served. How *could* the *Nordic Blue Galley* do it?

But *taste* those nibbly chanterelles!

Clearly they *had* done it, and most succulently!

Hildegarde rolled her hazel eyes with pleasure. "Oliver!" she exclaimed. "Do you really think Rocky and I would ever cruise on any other ship for our honeymoon anniversary?"

Loring thought further. Perhaps he could fit the Colonel in during cheeses.

"But I love a finely-aged Coulommier!" objected Hildegarde. "Why don't you just tell the Captain at breakfast," she urged as her rhubarb in puff pastry was served. "Rocky will keep till then."

* * *

Sunday evenings after dinner, the *Cruise Staff Conference Room* outside the *Starlight Lounge* converted to a dressing room for the *Roaring '20s Revue*. The flapper skirts, blazers, white ducks, straw boaters and other outfits for the hi-jinx gags hung in a sliding door closet shared by the adjoining room, the *Cruise Director's Office.*

Each *Roaring 20s*, while Barry Cox and the Starlight Band warmed up the audience out in the *Starlight Lounge* with Rudy Vallee and Al Jolson melodies, the cruise staff stormed into the tiny room, threw back the closet's sliding doors, jostled for parasols, canes, ostrich boas, teddy bears, rubber chickens.

Loring knew to avoid the cast stampede by costuming up early. As soon as Hildegarde and the Captain and his guests settled into the front row of the *Starlight Lounge*, Loring excused himself from the party and slipped into the empty conference/dressing room. He drew back the doors and picked the xx-long blazer and the 32-inch waist/37-inseam white ducks from the end of the men's rack.

When he had pulled off his tuxedo uniform, he noticed a slit in the closet doors that opened into the *Cruise Director's Office*. Through the crack he heard the Cruise Director's voice in a ruthless rant.

The Cruise Staff said vitriolic tongue lashings were routine with Spinelli, and at first Loring tried to tune it out. But through the crack he spotted the flushed neck of a tall woman in a blue-sequined flapper chemise. When she arched her shoulder, an amber lady bug peaked up above the smoothness of her left breast. Loring squinted over the costume rack and listened.

"Let me get this straight. I stand at the mike while the band plays and I sing *'Alabamy Bound.'* Meanwhile, you dance with that geeky doctor from Harvard?"

"Have you seen him dance?"

"Doc holds his own, no question."

"He's professional."

"Professionals rehearse. It's showtime. You have not rehearsed today."

"I was busy with Tosco."

"I'm scratching the number."

"Mrs. Snippet-White requested it."

"That old squat bag? So what if she's tight with Stig Storjord! Does she think she can call the shots on my ship?"

"She's my godmother. I want to dance for her. The doctor is the best dancer on board. Farrely Farrell had him recruited for this cruise."

Through the crack in the closet doors, Loring saw a hairy wrist slide up Ulla's neck.

"Don't do that, Flip."

"Is that all the Doc is to you? A dancer?"

Ulla's neck clenched, and Loring leaned closer.

Spinelli let out a rodent-like snicker. "You were in grief. It was hands off, and I agreed. But I saw the way you touched him when you danced with him. *He's* not hands off, is he?"

"Stop it."

"When will *we* touch?"

"Stop it, Flip!"

"Ever since you came on board with that runt magician . . ."

"I said *stop*!"

Loring could witness no more. He grabbed a cane from the closet and poked the tip through the crack. He swept back the sliding door and dragged a dozen striped blazers on their hangers screeching along the rack.

Ulla jumped back in fright, but Spinelli's hands gripped her wrists tight. His tiny black eyes snapped up at Loring.

"Oh, sorry!" Loring said through the closet, grinning foolishly and pretending that he had only now happened to see them. "Just looking for my bow tie!"

"Is that how you're going on stage, Dick Doc? Bow tie and underpants?"

"Ha! That would make an impression! I'm really so sorry I disturbed you!"

"And I'm so sorry, I'd like to shove that cane right up your ass!"

* * *

> *"I'm ALABAMY BOUND.*
> *There'll be no "Heebie Jeebies" hangin' round.*
> *Just gave the meanest ticket man on earth*
> *All I'm worth*
> *To put my tootsies in an upper berth.*
>
> *"I'm just a lucky hound*
> *To have someone to put my arms around.*
> *That's why I'm shoutin' for the world to know*
> *'Here I go!'*
> *I'm ALABAMY BOUND!"*

Dehydrated from their first full day of Caribbean sun, the power cruisers in the *Starlight Lounge* were easy prey for *Lime Limbos*. Tipsy or not, and whether or not they cheered mostly for Ulla, Loring loved what he heard – tumultuous applause.

He stood reveling in the delightful thunder. For all his painstaking work in medicine over more than a decade-long career treating patients, had anyone ever applauded him like this?

He loved it so much, in fact, that when Ulla's fingertips brushed his neck on their final bow, he leaned across and pressed his perspiring cheek against hers. She turned her head. In the glare of the spotlights he felt the tip of her tongue wiggle its sensuous way into his mouth. She was in intimate oral contact with him for no longer than a second, time enough for Loring to feel himself in a dizzying wet paradise.

This was no stage kiss!

In . . . and . . .

Loring stumbled from the dance floor. Ulla tugged him back for another bow and curtsy and another, much slower kiss! The audience roared again.

Loring glanced at Hildegarde in the front row. She was up on her toes, beaming and clapping madly. Had Loring done the Colonel proud?

Ulla's azure eyes burned with joy. If every dance must tell a story, this Charleston had delivered a mini-epic – every rapid phrase as precise as though the work had taken months to prepare, as if they were naturals for each other. Though not as eclectic as the English-style Charleston the Colonel had performed to mortal effect the night before, this with Ulla was ambitious, including several flashy razor drop kicks.

There had been one tricky instant, after their second razor, when Ulla's eyes had wandered briefly behind her – on Spinelli who crooned the second verse. She had paused, and Loring had felt a cringe through her body. Fear? Disgust? Loring could not say. His task was to steady her and pass smoothly in a cross step between Ulla and the audience while she had time to recover. In half a beat she was back.

Loring didn't know if Spinelli had seen the flub. The audience had not, and now they were stomping their feet and shouting, *"ENCORE! ENCORE!"*

Loring looked over his shoulder at Spinelli. The Cruise Director sent back so rough and nasty a stare, that Loring quickly escorted Ulla off the stage.

As they ran back into the *Cruise Staff Office*, Loring heard Spinelli bark into the microphone, "Let's hear it for Alabamy, folks! *Yeeeaaa! Yeeeeaaaaaaaaaaahh!* Quite the exciting couple, aren't they? *Yeeeaaa! Yeeeaaaaaaaaaaaaaaaaah!* Now our next number is a little wild west cinema re-creation, folks! Just imagine yourselves living before the days of DVD's and VCR's. Imagine, yes, yourselves sitting in a neighborhood movie hall with the flickering silent screen your porthole on the world. That's the way it was in the twenties, and it's all "Roaring Twenties" and it's all for you right here on the *S/S Nordic Blue*, the world's largest and sexiest cruise ship! By the way, if there is anyone in the audience with an epileptic seizure disorder and who might be susceptible to the dangerous stimulation of strobe lights, then our Chief Nurse Maggie McCarthy recommends that you avoid watching the rest of the show here in the *Starlight Lounge*. I *repeat*: we *do* have *strobe lights* in the show. Or else, all you epileptics, close your eyes! That's not to say that *Nuggets, the Casino*, isn't open from now till four A.M. Ladies and gents, and don't forget the *Crow's Nest* which is open all night. Now I'm proud to present a little special called 'Little Eva on the Rails!' Let's hear it for . . ."

* * *

Back in the dressing room, Loring loosened his tie and watched Ulla in front of the mirror suit up for her next spot – down with the sequined flapper dress and up with the heavy banana hat and the tasseled sleeves for the "South of the Border" number.

"Could you zip me up, Oliver? Quickly?"

Loring approached and once again sensed the marvelous musky fragrance exuding from her body. His eyes ran down the skin over her spine, now hi-lighted with a thin layer of salty moisture from their performance.

His fingertips found the edge of the zipper. Gently he tugged it up, and the dress closed at a point between her shoulder blades. For a moment he looked down along her neck and back and wished he could repeat that gesture of zipping Ulla's dress – this dress, any dress – up and down again and again and . . .

"I'm sorry," she said, startling him. She smiled over her shoulder in the mirror. "Before the show, you saw an unfortunate scene with Flip in his office. I'm sorry if you were embarrassed. I was."

"I apologize for butting in. I didn't like what he did to you."

Ulla's smile vanished as her lips pursed. She slid paper maché tropical bracelets up each wrist. "Don't apologize. You stopped it. Thank you. Things are becoming complicated. Flip has been kind, but he's used to owning people." The muscles in her neck tightened beneath her jaw. "I refuse to be owned."

"And do you refuse to be loved?" Loring stepped back. His words surprised him.

In the mirror he watched as she leaned forward and applied her lipstick slowly, precisely. "No, and I think you know that."

Loring remained silent, afraid he had seemed too intrusive. For an instant she looked into the mirror, and again he saw the pain and weariness he had seen in her eyes earlier at dawn when she looked into the window of *Topsiders*.

Then she turned to him, straightened the brim of her banana hat, rouged her cheeks thickly. The redness of her lips and cheeks made the pale blue of her eyes more icy and distant than before. "Saturday in Miami, I'll be leaving the ship. All my business here in the Caribbean will be done."

"I'm leaving Saturday, too."

She winked fondly. "So we must dance while we have the chance. Thanks again."

* * *

Loring stood alone in the shadows of the *Poop Deck* and felt the *Nordic Blue's* giant propellers churn directly beneath his feet. He gazed down at the giant white wake that stretched on and on in a turbulent ribbon trailing off to the north. Horizon to horizon, the Caribbean looked serene, the wake splendid to behold amidst the reflections of the gleaming stars and the waxing white moon.

But no matter how vast and soothing the vision, the recent minutes had cut Loring's feelings deeply. In his mind he still stood opposite the mirror in the dressing room and peered down another endless perspective – the zipper line of Ulla von Straf's "South of the Border" costume.

He wanted to touch her delicate skin again, all parts. He wanted to kiss her shoulder blades, taste the salty wetness over the muscles of her taut back, her ribs, then further down along her firm flanks. He trained his eyes on the briny splashes of the churning foam, matched his tongue's wet cravings to the propeller blades. He wondered – *ha!* – what the earth would be like, if all her grand seas were filled with a liquid as pure and nourishing as that fine sheet coating the muscles of Ulla's lean, muscular back.

Oh! To be a hardy and nimble vessel, spend a lifetime navigating each peninsula, archipelago, natural harbor, and sand bar bathed by her nutritious fluids.

He recalled Ulla's fulsome kisses on stage – deep, tantalizing. His tongue had a keen memory. As an oral person, he felt each of Ulla's lingual overtures – he still could taste them.

While their mouths had touched, their tongues had pressed together voluptuously. This was (he had sensed it for *sure*) a covert admission of trust. Loring was certain that he had felt something inside Ulla let go, open up to him. She had even laid several lightning-quick, spasmodic licks deep and then hard up onto his soft palate. He wondered if (was it possible?), despite her world-class achievements on her toes as a ballerina, if she might not be *orally-inclined* herself?

What better way to make such a confession to another oral individual than to come right out and commit the deed – wet membrane upon membrane. More to the point than whispering in the other person's ear, wasn't it? And if she was willing to make such a confession of oral lust to him, didn't that mean she liked him at least a little? Or did Loring indulge in overly optimistic speculations?

What of her reserve later in the dressing room? Deflating to say the least – as if their sensuous kisses had counted for nothing and Loring had been little more than a fellow shipboard entertainer. Then she had fled off to take her position for "South of the Border." Loring hadn't even had time to broach the subject of her godfather's death.

Her words – *"We must dance while we have the chance!"* – echoed now as perfunctory, a dismissal. Didn't she know that her searing kisses had autographed Loring's very soul?

Before he could blink back his disbelief at how ideal her body had appeared as she jumped out of one costume and into another (had two breasts ever been more perfectly formed – so round and full and ornamented so tantalizingly?) the dressing room had jammed up with cast members pushing past him to change costumes. Dazed, Loring had donned his tuxedo uniform again, wandered out into the *Lounge* and found the beaming Hildegarde.

"You're falling for her, Oliver," he heard Hildegarde murmur as he sat down beside her in the front row. "I saw that kiss! And that second kiss! Just wait till you taste her *Äpfelküchen*. You'll be a goner. You'll want more than one bite, I guarantee you that! And that Charleston truly would have made the Colonel ecstatic."

"Äpfelküchen?"

"The Colonel's all time favorite pastry! That girl bakes with the best of them. Grew up in Salzburg, remember. Makes the most scrumptious apple tart you ever put your mouth around."

Slide . . .

On the *Poop Deck*, as he strode in the shadows, he chanted out to the long and silver wake: *"ÄPFELKÜCHEN! ÄPFELKÜCHEN! ÄPFELKÜCHEN!"*

The wake did not respond. But why should it? Loring's chances to earn a tasty morsel of Ulla's *Äpfelküchen* before Miami seemed nil.

But in moments of discouragement, it comforted him to recall: *"MY, MY,*

MY! LORDY! LORDY! LORDY! IT ISN'T OVER UNTIL IT BE OVER. THE GOOD AND THE BAD! YOU NEVER KNOW UNTIL YOU KNOW! OH YESSS! OH YESSSSSSSSSSSSSSS!"

* * *

"When was the first time Rocky unzipped me? I must say, you're terribly direct, Oliver. But why not be direct tonight? Have another warm-up cocoa! And fill my mug again, too, while you're at it. Is there much caffeine in cocoa? Rocky and I never knew for sure."

Bundled in two heavy wave-and-sunburst blankets, Loring reached for the thermos. Several hours ago Hildegarde had lit a dozen candles around the bed, closed her eyes and said a silent prayer for the Colonel with each new flame. Now she sat wrapped in her sable – still holding hands with Boy Bebalzam, her honeymoon partner.

"But how about the first time I unzipped *him*? Yes . . . come to think of it . . . that was nearly the loveliest moment of my life till then, a moment Rocky and I have always hesitated to discuss together. I sort of out-did myself that night, and it really got our relationship rolling! Sexually speaking that is. As a matter of fact, we were having warm-up cocoa, too, in a lodge in Switzerland . . .

"Isn't sex a wonderful gift for God to have given all of us? We'd been skiing together at St. Moritz and many people say that skiing blends lovers by all the white majesty and the pure nature and the feeling of falling down the slope, which is rather key, I believe. Falling, I mean – it's the trick to control in skiing. When you fall, you don't give a damn and it all happens at once and there is a feeling in the Alps of surprise and wonder and peace. I was in my mid-forties – still we were busy as bees making honey. And such hot honey, Oliver, *dear*!

"Up until that night, Rocky had always been the aggressor in our love-making. But . . . how can I say it? . . . the Alpine air made me hungry for him in a way I'd never felt before. What was it? The scent of those high balsam twigs? The crunch of the snow crust echoing all over the village? I can't forget it.

"Yes. And how peculiar! We always used to joke about it. We met on the *S/S Marianne* – on the high seas, but we didn't really get to know each other well, till we married and were high up in a remote chalet in St. Moritz and as far from water as anybody could be.

"But Rocky reminded me that snow is only frozen water divided up into beautiful crystals. And all that flowing down over snow we had done on our skis that day in the sunshine over St. Moritz . . . or was it the warm-up cocoa? . . . must have given me the raw gumption to say, 'Damn it, I *crave* this man! Rocky, how does this feel?' I said.

"He was a wonderful man, Oliver. So affectionate. He really was. Always game for anything. It's such a pity we never had children. He would have loved to have children. I guess I was already too old by the time we were married. God knows, we tried hard enough. And we didn't have all these marvelous fertility drugs you young folks have today.

"You know, my goddaughter Ulla is about as close to a child as the both of us ever had. What do you think of Ulla, Oliver? But you know, I worry about that girl. She's gone through such a tragedy. It's too delicate a matter for me to discuss with you. Perhaps, if you get to know her better, she'll confide in you. Now, could you pass me another cup of cocoa? My my, how Rocky loved his cocoa! Didn't you, Rocky?

"But tell me more about *you*, Rocky. I'm dying to know. Did you say Vermont? You probably grew up on skis, didn't you? Oh, did I just call you Rocky? Excuse me. Oliver, I meant to say. You're quite sure you have no relatives in Pennsylvania? And your parents, Oliver, are they still living? Your mother and your father are . . . "

MON/FEB 11
St. Maarten Sarabande

Through the frosted, lozenge-shaped portholes high up on *Viceroy Deck*, a bleary-eyed Oliver Loring watched the bright orange rays of dawn slant onto the palm-dotted shores of half-Dutch/half-French St. Maarten.

Too immense to dock in port at Philipsburg, the quaint Dutch town on the southern coast of the island, the *Nordic Blue* lay at anchor a mile out of the harbor. Across the smooth blue water, tiny white Dutch colonial houses with red tile roofs squatted in clusters near the pale yellow beaches, while the ship's two tender boats shuttled passengers over to the restaurants, t-shirt shops and early bird casinos near the dock.

As the tenders loaded, they rocked against the ship's hull. The reverberating clangs at the water line shot straight up a dozen decks of precision-forged iron. Loring tapped back on the cold glass with his knuckles. Despite her age, this grand old behemoth was still one tightly-riveted ocean-going pleasure package! *Was she not?*

He shivered, anticipated a more doleful knock on the cabin door. Attack Nurse Maggie McCarthy was due any minute with a gurney and two Jamaican Bellhops to collect the Colonel and haul him down to the *Galley Meat Freezer*.

During the night, Loring had caught little sleep. Hildegarde had chatted on till the cocoa in the thermos had cooled to frosted mud and the candles had sputtered out. Her voice gradually withering to a raspy whisper, she led Loring through the decades of her marvelous romance with the illustrious and lusty Colonel. Finally, her eyelids batted fitfully and the muscles of her face sagged as she drifted off to sleep in her wing chair. Loring was shocked at how crone-like she looked in slumber, one hand clutching Loring and the other Rocky Boy Bebalzam.

When her snores whistled regularly in the chill air, Loring gently extracted his fingers from her bony clutch. He covered her with her white sable coat, kissed her forehead, and tip-toed out to the sitting room. There he stretched out on the couch under two wave-and-sunburst woolen blankets and fell into a fitful, dreamless sleep.

Now in the dawn orange, he rubbed his eyes, thumbed the stubble on his cheeks. He rolled his neck to stretch out a cramp. Massaging his palms, he pondered his choices for a potent wake-up tonic at the *Topsiders* Baldwin. He planned to have lunch today over on the French side of the island at *L'Etoile*, his favorite restaurant in Marigot.

Ravel? Too flamboyant. Poulenc? Too whimsical. Better stick to Bach. One of the *French Suites* would be appropriate – perhaps the first, which was baroque and contrapuntal, yet dance-like and in keeping with French colonial traditions here on the island.

He wiggled his fingers and admired the new growth on his nails.

Mais oui! Here were ten more reasons to celebrate the French!

Through the night, *Mademoiselle* Nadine Tulard's hardy squadrons of tiny scarab soldiers had marched up and down his arteries and veins, supplying his fingertips on the front lines with much-needed chitin substrate. Even the cuticles seemed replenished, almost robust.

Quel phénomène!

He went over to the mini-fridge under the liquor cabinet, found a Perrier, popped the cap. He reached into his pocket and swigged down another capsule of vital scarab essence. He had committed himself to the Tulard protocol, was deeply gratified by its efficacy.

"To protocol! And to Nadine Tulard! Skål!" he whispered. He raised the green Perrier bottle to the orange dawn and took a long fizzy guzzle. *"Aaaahhhhhhhhhhhh!"*

Re: protocol. The *Hospital Manual* said passenger remains were to be transported surreptitiously through all corridors and public areas disguised as stacks of sheets and towels on linen carts. Loring dreaded the thought of lifting the Colonel's long body off that bed and spreading him out on the cart and then covering him with stacks of wave-and-sunburst linen. But protocol was protocol, Attack Nurse was certain to assert, when she showed.

Loring hoped Hildegarde would allow the ruse. Maggie would remind her, she had no choice.

He was relieved to hear the shower water running back in *V #7's* bathroom. Hildegarde was up and stirring, which meant Maggie and he would not have to jostle the old woman out of her sleep, pry her hand loose from the grip of the dead. Would the widow follow the linen trolley down the corridors to the *Aft Freight Elevator* where Rocky would be lowered to his temporary resting place? Loring braced himself for the wailing, the clinging, the Sophoclean lament all the way to the *Galley Meat Freezer.*

But then he heard quick footsteps. Hildegarde emerged – in a straw hat, white-rimmed sun glasses, a red beach caftan with matching flip-flops. She held her paint box and collapsible easel with three blank canvases in a woven hemp bag.

"Where *is* your Nurse? You said she'd be here first thing. It's almost seven. We're not used to service like this on *Viceroy Deck*. It's rude to make Rocky wait."

"I'm waiting, too."

"Well, I cannot, Doctor. I'm off to the beach, and if I dally much longer, this beautiful sunrise will be wasted. Have you ever seen such a brilliant and meaningful orange in your life? *Glorious!* Not unlike Van Gogh's Provence? *N'est-ce pas?* We are on a cruise, are we not? We're in the Caribbean, are we *not*? Rocky always insisted a proper beach day must begin before eight at the *very* latest, don't you know!"

"Hildegarde, are you sure you're dealing properly with your grief?"

"I thought that's what our chat was for last night, silly? Didn't I get everything off my chest? Rocky would not expect me to follow him down to your *glorious* ice box, would he? And waste this magnificent orange? Vincent Van Gogh certainly would not! I'm already mixing my oils in my mind! Don't worry. Last night, before you came up and comforted me, I made all the necessary phone calls about the ceremony."

"What ceremony?"

"Don't you worry one more minute, Oliver. It's *all* arranged. And thanks for last night! You were such a chum! Give me a kiss. *Whoopsies!* Did I forget my sun screen? No, here it is. *Mwhaah! Toodles!* "

* * *

Now three days into the cruise, the *Galley Meat Freezer* was partially depleted, and Rocky Boy Bebalzam could easily have been tucked out of sight. An inconspicuous lying-in-state, however, was not what the widow had ordered. When the linen/Colonel rolled through the double doors, a team of technicians stood in jackets, caps and gloves, ready to go at him.

"Thanks, Doc! Thanks, Nurse! I'll take over from here!" shouted Mahmoud, the one-armed Egyptian *Maître d'*. "We received all our instructions directly from Storjord."

Loring shook his head with surprise. "From old Stig in Oslo?"

"A personal friend of the Colonel. *And* of Mrs. Snippet-White."

"You're *shittin'* me," Maggie McCarthy gasped as Mahmoud snapped his fingers. The two Jamaican Bellhops removed the stack of linen from the trolley and, with the help of two Venezuelan waiters, whisked the Colonel past several racks of lamb and reindeer sides to a long rectangular area marked out by a red braided cord with gold tassels and separated from the salmon section by a black velvet curtain and several large sheets of thick, protective polyethylene.

Nadine Tulard sat on her swivel chair in a thick woolen coat with manicure tools at the ready. Alfredo Pisido, the Italian Barber, stroked his leather strop. Fritz Müller, the German Florist, scurried around behind pots of roses with little Union Jacks.

"We're trying to forget nothing," said the efficient Mahmoud, who had once managed a funeral parlor in Cairo before he entered the at-sea restaurant business.

Three Filipino Carpenters rolled in a long cherry wood coffin tailored to the Colonel's measurements. "Storjord's orders," Mahmoud said. "We want everything to the widow's specifications. The Colonel's to stay in here till the burial-at-sea Friday evening after all the Cablevista shows."

"Hold everything, Mahmoud!" Loring interrupted. "I haven't signed the death certificate yet."

Mahmoud's dark, deep-set Egyptian eyes rolled. "Except for darts and conga lines in the *Crew Bar*, many of us wonder what it is you *do* on this ship, Doctor. Now hurry up and sign your name and let us get on with our work! These Carpenters have been up all night."

Mahmoud, who seemed oddly thrilled to be back in his former mortician's metier, raised his single hand to halt the carpenters. He lifted the coffin lid, reached inside, tested the red velvet. "See?" he flipped the brass-hinged head panel. "Just the way the widow wants it. Simply tip the Colonel over the side and . . ."

"*Voilà!* I get it."

Mahmoud gave Loring a derisive, dark-eyed frown.

"Oliver! You look rough!" Maggie said, as Loring handed the Egyptian the clipboard with the signed death certificate. "Hope you can catch a nap today. By the way, I told Ramskog about the Colonel this morning on the *Bridge*."

"How's Captain this morning?"

"Hiccups are gone but the wife isn't. How *you* doin'?"

"Sleepy. All I need is a little baroque counterpoint. Picks me up every time."

"Yea? Well, whatever floats your boat, Dart Doc! Hey, I missed your dance last night, but I hear you were . . . "

The *Freezer* doors flew open again. A block of ice fully five feet tall rolled in on a trolley.

"*Slide it over there! Beside the coffin!*" shouted Mahmoud. "How long will it take you, Jacques?"

Jacques Chemin stepped from behind the ice block, his electric ice chisel at the ready. "Give me three hours, Mahmoud. Hey, do I not see *mon ami* Oliver? *Bonjour, Docteur!*"

"*Bonjour, Jacques!* What's are *you* doing here?"

"Death bust, Doc. Stig Storjord commissioned it specially. Jacques is going to make it *magnifique!* Just wait and see! Hey, we missed you last night. When are you coming back down to the *Crew Bar?*"

* * *

L'Etoile, a little piece of Paris perched on a flowery veranda overlooking Potence Beach, served the only credible *foie gras* on the island. After his chilly, night-long vigil and his signing of the death certificate, Loring needed lunch in the warm sun among the white hibiscus and pink bougainvillea blossoms.

He had worked up an acute craving for *foie gras* during Bach's first *French Suite* in *Topsiders*. The D minor *Sarabande's* viscerally somber chords in a slow *andante* always haunted his abdominal organs.

"*DAAH-dah-dah-dah-dah-DAAH-da-da!*"

Had the portly and prolific Johann Sebastian experienced a digestive event the day he wrote it? A gall bladder attack? Intestinal colic? A brief diverticular flare-up? Why else would the sullen progression of minor chords compel Loring, as if controlled by Pavlovian command, to seek out *foie gras*?

Sweet? Oily? Ruinous for blood cholesterol metabolism?

No matter, the crisis was over. Loring had now devoured his second satisfying plateful at his favorite corner table and sat licking the crusts of his toast. He burped silently, pleasantly, and gazed to the west across the turquoise waters of Nettle Bay. He watched the yachts in their slips bob on the waves. He raised his Sauterne up toward the sun and squinted through the gold liquid. In the glass the boats became inverted pixie vessels dancing with their needle masts pointed down at a miniature green-gold sky.

"*DAAH-dah-dah-dah-dah-DAAH-da-da!*"

He swished tidbits of *foie gras* from his teeth, savored each, decided to indulge himself and linger there longer. Lunch had made him feel much warmer, refreshed. What a relief to be on land and dressed in mufti again! The ship and the *Galley Freezer* seemed far away.

But while shore side, one must not forget all of one's duties! He jotted off three postcards: one to his mother in Vermont, another to his colleague Bart Novak, thanking him for covering his shifts this week at the Samaritan, and a third to the Samaritan emergency nursing staff, with the greeting, *"Miss you all! Wish me (love) luck! Ha-ha!"*

Then, recalling another duty, he reached into his shorts pocket for the vial of scarab pills. Carefully he dropped one on his palm, sent it down the hatch with a quick gulp of the excellent *Château Gironde Sauterne*. He spread his white polo shirt collar and hitched up the cuffs of his shorts. He looked over at Pierre Le Comte, the jovial owner of *L'Etoile*, seated behind the bar.

"Monsieur Le Comte!" he called. *"Le foie gras! Pas mal!"*

"Merci, Docteur!" replied the rotund Le Comte in his husky, emphysematous basso.

Yo Pierre!

On previous cruises, while enjoying *foie gras* and *Château Gironde Sauterne* on the *L'Etoile* terrace, Loring had spoken at length with Pierre Le Comte. But today Pierre did not seem inclined to small talk in French. That suited Loring's mood, too.

Coughing over the cash register, Pierre Le Comte rattled his week-old edition of *Le Monde*, snuffed out a *Gauloise bleu* with his plump thumb, and grabbed the *Château Gironde* to pour himself a glass. Briefly he glanced up at the Cablevista blimp circling over the harbor, sneered, and shook his head disdainfully as he muttered, *"Les Américains!"*

A solid St. Maarten fixture, all 200-plus pounds of bald little Pierre Le Comte were encased in a mahogany hide which 25 years and three rough divorces here in the Caribbean had deposited in lieu of skin. In Pierre's paler, thinner, more hirsute days, he had played a grunting, sap-wielding thug in several *film noir* classics by Godard and Rameau. Over *L'Etoile's* bar hung a collection of framed set stills, visible proof of the *propriétaire's* former *gloire* on the silver screen. Loring's favorite was the dim shot near a Marseilles dock, where Pierre struck a match on a brick wall with one hand and fired his black Luger into the belly of a cowering *gendarme* with the other.

But the pictures showed a stocky and determined young actor, with dark fuzzy brows who bore faint resemblance – save the full lips and the dangling cigarette and the sleepy, iguana-like eyes – to the current Le Comte, the amiable, jaded, floppy-jowled Caribbean *restaurateur*.

Such were the pitfalls of being type-cast in French show bizz, thought Loring. As the Sauterne started to coat his senses, he gazed at the sea far beyond the yachts and wondered how many more retired Paris film actors were out there tending bar in the colonies and ruffling through the pages of *Le Monde* a week late.

More than a few, he guessed, but none quite as sociable nor nearly as *sympathique* as Pierre.

Adjacent to the *film noir* bar photos, hung a small shrine to the late Jean-Luc Farandouz, Le Comte's close friend and a hero of the people of little St. Maarten. Up until two years ago, Jean-Luc Farandouz had been the island's charismatic super star, the flashy island boy who had cracked the racial barriers of international Formula One auto racing. Farandouz had been killed tragically at age 34 in a mysterious accident at the dangerous Spitzring track in the German Alps.

Pierre Le Comte had supported the young driver in the initial struggles to enter world-class competition, had connected him with wealthy backers in France for his first successes on the European circuit. The shrine over the bar at *L'Etoile* was simple but poignant – the helmet and gloves from the incredible Le Mans victory and an autographed picture of the winner accepting his trophy.

Loring had discussed the photo with Pierre before at *L'Etoile* and had watched native customers fawn over it. But this time, something made him shield his eyes from the sun and take a longer look.

Was it the *Château Gironde*? Perhaps. But the woman in the photograph who stood beside the champion at Le Mans actually resembled Ulla von Straf. Black wrap-around sun glasses obscured her face, but she was tall, high-cheeked, and had the same pouting lips and the hint of a small beauty mark . . .

Nonsense!

Loring turned toward the sea and closed his eyes in the heat and fell into a deep tropical reverie. Obviously the Sauterne was playing tricks. He was imagining Ulla everywhere. Ha-*ha*!

As he meditated on her, the all-night vigil with Hildegarde and the trip to the *Galley Freezer* faded. Only Ulla's kisses on stage the night before seemed real to him now.

He felt the sun beam down on his closed eyelids. He rolled his tongue inside his mouth and tried to relive the thrill. The sun felt like the spotlight in the *Starlight Lounge* – defining a sublime moment for all the world to see, the two of them together on the stage of "*Roaring 20's.*"

I don't care if Spinelli sees us. I don't care who sees us, Ulla. All I can feel right now is your tongue in my mouth, your wet, warm, spirit-quenching tongue all over again and, yes, please do it again, please . . .

* * *

Loring's nostrils twitched pleasurably. A sweet, fascinating aroma crept into his senses, tickled him awake from his dreams. Eyes half open, he sniffed deeply.

Cigar?

But such a spirited cigar! Spicy, earthy, yet with a delicate edge, floating in from somewhere quite near him among the hibiscus and bougainvillea blossoms.

Cigarettes or cigars, though a habit for most oral types, had never been part of Loring's addictive oral symptoms. Inhalable drugs, especially tobacco, never tempted him. He preferred and practiced nail biting – benign to the lungs, cleaner, inexpensive, instantly available, and involving the incisors, tongue, all the jaw muscles, as well as the lips.

But this cigar smoke smelled pure, exotic. It beckoned, aroused.

He opened his eyes and looked around *L'Etoile*. Pierre Le Comte stood at a table nearby and held a lighter to the tip of an eight-inch cigar of a customer in a white tropical suit and a large Panama hat. Pierre lit an identical cigar for himself. They chatted in French and seemed to be gesturing toward the Farandouz shrine.

The customer, his back to Loring, wore Spanish-style boots – black embossed leather with high heels and silver buckles. He had a curious red leather and burlap sack slung under one of the empty chairs at his table. Loring cocked his head to get a better angle at the stranger under the brim of the white Panama.

When Loring's chair squeaked, the white-clad man turned and lowered his cigar. Two liquid brown eyes stared out beneath the brim of the Panama. "Pardon me, *Docteur*. Do you mind if I smoke?" he asked in a thick Hispanic accent.

The man obviously knew Loring, but Loring was at a loss to reciprocate. The swarthy, craggy face, perhaps early-60's, bore a heavy black mustache and penetrating dark eyes.

Loring struggled to recognize the stranger. "Smells delightful. Pungent but rich."

"It's my private blend. Would you care to sample one?"

He reached into his lapel pocket. The fluttering of those stumpy but graceful fingers triggered Loring's memory – he had seen the hands and smile in the *Starlight Theatre*. Another cigar appeared. The man waved it, wand-like, at Loring.

"You're . . . the midg . . . the *magician*! You're Ulla's friend. You're Tosco!"

The man's latin eyes twinkled. "And you're the Dart Doc. I know you by your reputation. You throw bullseyes in the *Crew Bar*, or so I hear."

Loring enjoyed the deep voice and the accent. Blushing at the flattery, Loring stood up. "Private blend?"

As Tosco rose to greet him, Loring stifled a chuckle. When the little man stood up from the chair, he actually looked shorter than he did sitting down. And the deep voice resonating out of such a small body – why should that seem strange or absurd? As a physician, Loring was fully familiar with achondroplasia – the gene defect that inhibits childhood growth of all the long bones in the body. Tosco certainly had all the typical body features: prominent forehead, sway-back posture, squatty extremities.

Loring's private mirth at Tosco's munchkin-like body habitus stopped abruptly when Tosco pulled off his Panama.

Loring saw long, gruesome, zig-zag scars all over his scalp, from frontal bone to occiput. In the spotlights of the *Starlight Theatre*, Tosco had sported a dense mane of long, silvering hair – obviously that had been a stage wig. Here in the full light of the St. Maarten sun, though, Tosco's pate had a steel-gray, short-cropped crew cut crossed by long, fish bone white lines, the nastiest collection of scalp scars Loring had seen since his rotations on head trauma wards.

"Cats," Tosco said, aware of Loring's stare.

He tilted his head forward and tapped his forefinger on his bumpy, cicatrixed wounds.

"Cats?" Loring felt a bizarre urge to run his fingers over the grizzly rivulets, but he backed away.

"You're a doctor. Go ahead, touch them!" Tosco insisted. His stunted fingers grabbed Loring's wrist and raised his hand to the mutilated scalp.

Loring gingerly touched the smooth surface of the center-most irregular scar. "Don't tell me a little cat did that."

"Big cat. Jaguar. Turned my back on him. Eighty-five stitches. Paris. Long ago. Jaguars are tough to train."

"Looks like he nabbed your neck, too."

"The neck's a panther. Pregnant female. Berlin. Two years later. Turned my back again."

"So you do more than magic?"

"No magic in getting clawed up, is there? Only carelessness. But I've never been mauled below the neck. I've still got all my fingers."

"Need all ten to cast your spells?"

Tosco looked up and sighed, amused. His fuzzy-browed eyes shrank to comma-shaped slits. "Give the doctor a light, Pierre." He replaced his Panama and puffed. "You see, I've done circus animals, mostly big cats, on and off for over thirty years."

"Did you ever stick your head in a big cat's mouth?"

"Why do you ask? Only an utter fool would do something like that."

"Well, when I was a little boy, I used to have dreams about it. Ha! But to tell the truth, cigars are as ferocious as I do," Loring said. He dragged tentatively on the panatella, as *Monsieur* Le Comte touched a flame to the tip.

The dwarf's rugged chin had a deep dimple, as though his leathery latin skin were tacked to his jawbone. Yet there was a softness and an aristocratic flair perhaps not expected of an individual with thirty years in the big cat cage. "Sit down, please. Do you like the tobacco?"

Loring sat down with the dwarf. "I like it a lot!"

"I grow it on my hacienda outside San Juan. Our tobacco plants are originally from Cuba. Like me."

"But you live in Paris, I thought."

"I own a hotel in Paris, and my circus is there, too."

"Cirque Ineffable?"

Tosco smiled. *"Oui.* You've heard of it?"

"Yes. I met a woman on the ship who saw your work in Paris. She says it's great."

"Good. So, our reputation is spreading."

"But you have a hacienda in Puerto Rico and a hotel and a circus in Paris? All that sounds fairly *ineffable* to me."

"Not really. Family business. Actually three hotels, *Docteur*. One outside San Juan, one in Madrid, and another in Paris."

"But why do you work as a magician on a cruise ship?"

"You have a life somewhere else, don't you? Why do you work as a physician on a cruise ship?"

The beguiling little man with the glowing cigar between his stubby fingers leaned back in his chair, crossed his silver-buckled boots, and puffed deeply. He opened his collar.

"I'm curious about the red bag. Red leather and burlap. Looks durable. Never saw anything like it." Loring said. "What do you carry in it?"

"Belongs to a friend."

"Is he dropping by?"

"I'm to pick him up on the way back to the ship. He's sunning just now. Isn't it wonderful here?" Tosco's voice in the wind was playful and cheery. "You do enjoy that cigar, my friend. I can tell."

Loring sucked on the panatella, felt the sweet sting of the tobacco at the top of his throat. The succulence surrounded his taste buds, pierced deep up into his sinuses. "Never tasted anything like it. That must be some hacienda of yours in Puerto Rico."

"It's called *Claridad.*"

"Claridad? Good name. "

"And good soil. Not as rich as the soil on our old hacienda in Cuba. But that was back before Castro."

"I see many Cuban patients in Boston."

"They all wish they were in Cuba, don't they?"

Loring exhaled. *"Yes."*

Oliver Loring was in St. Maarten, but suddenly he wanted to be in Cuba. He was tasting the magnificent tobacco from the soil of Puerto Rico, but from plants with Cuban origins. Tomorrow the ship would pull into San Juan Harbor. But Loring wished to be in Havana tomorrow.

No, now! We should be in Cuba now! I want to be in Cuba now!

Tosco made him want it, and Loring wanted to be close to Tosco. At first, Loring had wanted to ask him about Ulla. But the more he puffed, the more interested he became in Tosco himself. "You said you have three hotels in the family business. How big is your family?"

"Pleased you asked, *Docteur.*"

Tosco reached into his hip pocket and pulled out a wallet full of snapshots.

* * *

If Oliver Loring were to dabble in mystical thoughts, it might be on a safe occasion such as this – a balmy tropical afternoon, yachts bobbing in the blue distance, puffy clouds floating above, a silver blimp lazily drifting along in the sky, a fine cigar supporting his attention, and a fascinating new friend with a Panama hat covering scars on his head and a hacienda called *Claridad* outside San Juan.

The wallet snapshots of the family at *Claridad*? Tigers.

All sizes and ages of tigers. Cubs, weanlings, toddlers, adolescents, adults, gravestones. Families, full genealogies.

Siberian Amurs. Four hundred, fifty-plus pounders at maturity. Not the smaller, irresolute Bengal variety, Tosco stipulated. Siberians were critical – the same supremely intelligent tigers who were lodged in a special compound at *Claridad* and would make their Paris debut in April at the spectacular spring opening of Tosco's amazing *Cirque Ineffable*.

What an unusually devoted and (yes) wealthy man. Perhaps there were traces of metaphysical potential in these tigers, as Tosco contended. But how was that potential to be realized fully at *Le Cirque*?

Over another round of *Château Gironde*, Tosco took Loring to the very beginning.

* * *

Ramon Fernandez Garcia Jesus Tosco-Gutierez came into this world a mutant – a peculiar runt with foreshortened limbs, dark eyes, a broad, flat forehead, a nose that dipped at the bridge, and nil chance (according to the pediatric experts in Havana, Madrid, and New York) of ever growing to be more than four and a half feet tall.

But if one had to be born an achondroplastic dwarf in Cuba in 1942, then one might wish to enter a proud, well-educated family who owned sugar and tobacco plantations throughout the Caribbean, a four-star hotel in Madrid, and large fortunes in Swiss bank trust funds ripening for their two sons (Ramon and his older brother Vincente) and twin daughters (Maria and Sophia) for when the Tosco-Gutierez children came of age.

Nor would it hurt if that same family boasted the grandest riding stables on Cuba, including the finest breeding stallions in Latin America and a tradition of equestrian zeal of all kinds.

Two uncles (Pepe and Rodrigo) were famous polo players in Argentina. A great uncle (Ramon) had won top honors in the world dressage competitions in Rome. A maternal grandfather (José Nabuyel Gutierez-Lopez) had been an accomplished stunt rider in circuses of Spain, France and the United States.

And it helped the infant Ramon that the family did not feel ashamed or burdened by their fourth child's birth deformities – especially when they discovered him to be so quick and bright. Ramon was a tiny, pudgy, elfin soul whose eyes danced charmingly at his nurses and who, when left alone in his crib, chattered and sang to himself. The boy had a robust agenda for life, no matter how stingy nature had been in blueprinting his body.

It was not until Ramon turned eight and wanted to advance from riding the plantation ponies to dressage on his father's pure-bred Arabians, that his parents first insisted he wait longer than the other boys to proceed to true, full-sized horses.

How long? Ramon Fernandez wanted to know.

It was then he first heard the word *"enano"* – dwarf – spoken by his parents.

Till then, he had been tutored privately by European teachers, had been spared any jeers and taunts in the schoolyard because he was short. Ramon had heard fairy tales about *enanos*, but he knew he had nothing in common with those make-believe creatures with beards and pointed caps and who never seemed to ride horses.

No. Ramon felt secure that he was the same flesh-and-blood as his parents and his brother and twin sisters, only shorter. The servants, horse trainers, and laborers on the plantation were enchanted by the *enano's* wit and spirit, and for the first decade of his life – protected but never pampered – Ramon grew up in privilege and with very little resentment or self pity for his handicap.

At twelve the boy sailed to France with his family and began his formal education at the deluxe boarding school in Chantilly. His father opened a second family hotel – the *Hôtel de la Grâce* – in Paris. The plantation staff worried that they might never see the little fellow wandering the fields or hear him singing songs to them again.

They were right. Ramon's father Vincente had foreseen Castro's revolutionary forces would overrun the incompetent Batista government. In 1957, Ramon's father returned to Cuba long enough to sell the plantation before the communist takeover. He arranged jobs for his staff on the plantations in Puerto Rico and the Dominican Republic. Then he relocated his family and his famous stables to an estate near Chantilly.

For Ramon Fernandez, Cuba became a golden memory. But France was his new life. He was adaptable. Any *enano* (or *"nain"* as he was called in France) had to be adaptable.

From the start, his marks at school in Chantilly were superior. He challenged his teachers with provocative questions. Competitive sports like soccer or tennis were out for him, of course, but he was popular with his schoolmates, and everyone saw he had inherited the family's skills on horseback. By his mid-teens he stunned his friends with bareback antics, no longer on ponies but on the Tosco-Gutierez purebreds.

One weekend, his parents entertained a certain *Monsieur* Franconi, the renowned director of Paris's *Cirque Olympique* and an old friend of Ramon's circus equestrian grandfather, José Nabuyel Gutierez-Lopez.

Little Ramon so impressed *Monsieur* Franconi with his acrobatic stunts – remarkable to see performed so effortlessly by a sway-back dwarf high up on horseback – that the lad was invited to the next performance of *Cirque Olympique*, where he met some of the artists and joined them later for occasional workouts. The reputation of his celebrated grandfather José preceding him, Ramon was welcomed by the equestrians at *Le Cirque*. They encouraged him to hone his talents with them. He also befriended other performers on his visits – aerialists, clowns, contortionists, big cat tamers.

Young Ramon loved the Parisian circus – the blitzing array of human and animal acts and the feeling of extended family which unites circus professionals. He followed the progress of the performers, came to know them well. Tempted though he was by the challenges of such a career, he never thought a life in the ring was for him. He knew that over time the rigorous training of a career equestrian would take its toll on his vulnerable achondroplastic spine and joints. His equestrian skills were great, the thrill of performance intoxicating, but he reckoned that his appeal – a dwarf on horseback – would be mostly comical. As a proud Cuban aristocrat in exile, he did not wish to be a career clown.

Then his older brother Vincente was killed in a suspicious car accident in Geneva in 1962 – some suspected a Castro vendetta. Shortly after Vincente's death, the twins Maria and Sophia entered a French Carmelite convent. By the age of 20, Ramon realized he would be responsible for his family's fortunes. At the urging of his parents he matriculated into the select *Ecole pour les Sciences Economiques* to develop skills necessary to steward his father's businesses and hotel interests.

For several years his studies dominated his time, though he remained a circus aficionado and often invited circus friends for evenings at the *Hôtel de la Grâce*. During this time, while Ramon remained a devoted dilettante, a powerful movement began in the Paris circus. Ramon was introduced to passionate new members of the troupe who spoke with a new vision of the meaning of the circus itself. These new members said circus, though a grand effort at amusing a crowd, was also a potential forum for posing crucial questions about existence.

Ramon was intrigued. Circus – a calculus to study and explain the meaning of life? These questions were posed, not by stiff intellectuals, but rather by athletes who risked their lives for ever more dazzling effects.

* * *

Loring tapped a two-inch ash from his cigar. "But I thought the whole point of circus is spectacle, not that spectacle isn't wonderful."

Tosco puffed. The wind took his smoke toward the sea.

"I too was wary of the early *Cirque Olympique* revolution. I was a devoted equestrian until I met Tulov and his cats. You see, even for a circus person used to the spectacles, Tulov was truly incredible."

Tosco's dark eyes rolled up into the soothing blue of the Caribbean sky. Suddenly his gentle baritone began to croon a melody, the same Russian-like lyrics Loring had heard on Saturday night when the doves performed their ballet. The man's voice drifted wistfully in the breeze. His eyes took on an intense, visionary glow.

Loring felt himself transported with Tosco's singing, back to Paris, back to *Cirque Olympique*, and beyond.

* * *

Loring's medical work in Boston put him in frequent touch with life-and-death moments, so that in his leisure hours, he generally shunned meditating on the imponderables. But this had not always been true. As a Harvard undergrad, he had taken several exciting religion and philosophy courses. He also had dipped into the writings of Gurdjieff, the Greco-Armenian cult mystic who had conducted metaphysical seances in Paris in the late 1940's.

Loring had read and re-read with enthusiasm P.D. Ouspensky's provocative *In Search of the Miraculous*, which tried to explain Gurdjieff's basic teachings – that human life as ordinarily lived was similar to sleep, and that with work, an individual could rise above the usual state of consciousness and develop new levels of awareness and vitality.

Loring had argued to his college roommates that Gurdjieff's mystical wisdom suffered in translation, not from Russian into English, but rather from essence into word. Even Ouspensky's paraphrasing of Gurdjieff's words failed to convey such knowledge.

Gurdjieff: *"Those who talk do not know, and those who know do not talk."*

Music, dance, and art might serve better to invoke mystical truths which disrupt the logic inherent in spoken or written grammar. That's why, Loring speculated as an undergraduate, Gurdjieff had written music and choreographed stage pageants to impart non-verbal knowledge in a medium less rigid, more liquid, and more capable of spiritual nuance than the written or spoken, grammatically logical, word.

Why *not* use circus to transmit occult understanding? Why *not* use circus as a calculus to true metaphysical research?

As Tosco told about the developments in the Paris circus, Loring became more fascinated. It was no surprise that the radicals of *Cirque Olympique* had studied in Paris with some of Gurdjieff's closest disciples. They had ruptured off, formed their own rogue mystical cult, and after testing Ramon's trust, they had invited him to join.

The venerable *Monsieur* Franconi, the radicals insisted, was a showman. Nothing wrong with that; showmen kept them all employed in the traditions of the art. But their new and ideal circus was different – a commitment to years of dedicated study and precision and to achieving goals above ticket sales and the exchange of money for utter spectacle.

The leader of the cult was a black-bearded Russian named Vladimir Vladimirovich Tulov, a wild cat trainer from the Soviet Union, who had defected to the West when he was touring with the Moscow State Circus at the bitter height of the cold war. After acquiring and schooling a new collection of tigers, leopards, jaguars, lions and panthers, Tulov had quickly become the star of the *Cirque Olympique*.

Tulov had taken a special liking to the intense and adaptable Cuban dwarf, invited him into the cage to work the cats. The two shared discussions about the mystical intelligence of the Amur tigers.

Ramon then was in his late 20's. His father had died, his mother was ailing, and he now had inherited full control of the Tosco-Gutierez holdings. The hotels, by father Vincente's wise design, practically ran themselves. Ramon had time and financial freedom to pursue another career, the visions of his new mentor, Tulov. The cult met at the *Hôtel de la Grâce* each Sunday evening, and their ardent debates often lasted far into the night.

Critical to Tulov's cult, was the concept of manifestation. The cult insisted that the extra-natural existed within the physical and could be urged to "manifest" itself through performance brought to an extraordinary level. Tulov, for example, when working with his fabulous Amurs, had noted rare moments of ecstatic truth during which he shared telepathic identity with his cats, who also showed incredible progress in their performances. Trapeze and high wire artists concurred, though they sensed their manifestations were more like levitation, a sense of cosmic weightlessness.

Again, the very concept of manifestation was difficult to articulate in words, but the group was convinced that these unutterable realities were true and realizable to them all.

Early on, Ramon had no way to judge if the cult members had simply hallucinated at their peak moments into extra-natural visions. But how could an athlete hallucinate in mid-air from one converging trapeze to another and still maintain the necessary split-second timing critical to avoid a fatal fall? While hallucinating?

Tulov's disciples were the super-achievers in *Le Cirque Olympique*. To a soul, once they committed to the cult's strict dogma, their techniques improved. Astonishingly. Huge crowds viewed the cult members' feats with hushed rapture and tears, as if a powerful aura had seized the witnesses themselves.

Ramon watched the cult develop. He traveled with the troupe and funded their efforts. He researched other great circuses – the Beijing, the Moscow State, Ringling Brothers.

After three years of tours, reading, study, and intense meditation, he identified an area not explored by this or any other circus and which he, despite his physical limitations, could pursue: magic.

When Tosco first introduced the topic of magic to the group at the *Hôtel de la Grâce*, Tulov himself was the least skeptical. Vladimir Vladimirovich had grown up in a village near Sverdlosk in the Urals where, he recalled, certain old wise peasants practiced ancient tricks – a magic which had nothing to do with card spoofs or pulling rabbits out of hats. As a child, Tulov had seen these men and women charm wild forest bears in their tracks by singing ancient melodies – melodies which had been passed down through hundreds of generations, from magicians who, the old legends said, had practiced their craft in earliest Mesopotamia.

* * *

"Robespierre! *Descends! Toute de suite!* Come down from that tree, or I'll cut off your head!"

Loring followed Tosco's gaze up into the coconut palm. They had left *L'Etoile* and, strolling south along the tarmac road outside Marigot toward the Dutch side of St. Maarten, had stopped at a palm grove. Tosco waved the red burlap bag at the tallest tree in the grove.

"Robespierre, you have sunned yourself enough! *Descends!*"

The high fronds rustled in a fussy fit.

"I'm sorry. He's stretching. Robespierre is always cross when he wakes up from a nap in the sun. I have to intimidate him. Would you mind clapping your hands in a threatening manner while I shake the bag?"

"But you wouldn't cut off his head?"

"He knows it's a phony threat. It would ruin the act. Clap your hands loudly with me and watch him now."

Loring looked up and down the tarmac road. There were no cars in sight. He clapped his hands hard, three times.

"Louder! More fiercely!"

The high fronds ceased their fidgets. Robespierre, the python, slid down, head first, in a long lazy corkscrew that made a soft scratching sound all along the peeling bark of the palm. At the trunk, he coiled up in a fat spiral lump in the sand, his diamond-patterned hide curled tight into himself. His ribs heaved heavily, he exhaled loudly through his flat snout. The yellow eyes with their hooded elliptical pupils peered up at Loring and Tosco and then closed.

"Would you like to touch him?"

Loring's hands still stung from his vigorous claps. "You said he's cross when he wakes up."

"He won't bite. He squeezes hard but never bites. Look, he's almost asleep again. Touch his skin. He won't mind. He knows we have to put him in his bag."

"You're sure?" Loring stooped and stroked the pulsing scales, felt the slow rise and fall of the snake's lungs through his diamond skin. "Hot."

Tosco held the burlap bag open at ground level. "This boy's all reptile – just loves the sun. It's like a drug for him. We have lights for him down in the hold of the ship where we keep him, but they're not like the real sun."

In a sleepy trance, Robespierre unfurled himself and then obediently slid fluidly into the bag and coiled up again.

Tosco cinched the bag. The snake must have weighed eighty pounds. Yet the little magician knelt down on one knee, slung Robespierre over his shoulders, stood up smiling. He trudged up the road on his boot heels with his gnarly, lumpy load on his back.

"Need a hand?"

"Nobody can carry Robespierre any distance but me. Tulov and I found him in Sumatra, and we've been inseparable ever since. He's rather fastidious about who should carry him."

"Of course. But why don't you have a little trolley for him or something? That would make it easier."

"Good idea, *Docteur*. We tried it. Trolleys are bumpy. They bounce him around and make him nauseated."

Loring watched the dwarf, hunched over by the weight of the snake, lean forward and labor up the road in the sinking sun. He cast a bizarre shadow on the sand beside the road.

Foremost in Loring's mind as they walked was the question of Tosco's sanity.

Was he delusional? Messianic? Suicidal? Schizoid? Sociopathic?

But he seemed too polished to be any of those. He also seemed incredibly nice.

"I saw your rehearsal the other night, but I could not watch for long. When Robespierre twirled on Ulla's legs and arms, I got dizzy. Very dizzy."

"Yes, Ulla told me you were affected."

"Deeply."

"You thought the entire universe was spinning?"

"I didn't know what to think. I only knew I had to get out of the theatre. But, yes, that's exactly the way I felt."

"Too bad you didn't stay. The more powerful pieces come later in the show, although we still need more equipment. We'll bring it on when we dock in San Juan tomorrow."

"But do you know what happened to me when I watched your magic? Some neurological phenomenon?"

"Few individuals sense the power of what we in the cult know as ancient performance metaphysics. You, *Docteur*, obviously have a hyperacute aesthetic, and as a physician you may wish to explain it by a medical model. Go ahead, but I think you'll find that approach futile. My medical friends in

Paris have given up trying to explain it. We call it simply the visual power of the spinning serpent. How do you think Eve convinced Adam to eat the apple?"

Loring stopped on the tarmac and stood there speechless.

Tosco smiled and lowered Robespierre to the sand by the side of the road. Loring could see he was winded from his efforts.

"Are you sure you wouldn't like me to carry him?"

The dwarf pulled off his Panama and mopped his sweaty, scarred scalp. "Let's hail the next taxi. It'll be easier to continue our conversation."

* * *

"I try to keep Robespierre hidden when we're in public," Tosco explained in the cab.

Loring felt the heavy snake beside him radiate heat in slow, breathing waves through the red burlap. "I'm not surprised. As beautiful as he is, not everybody might react positively."

"If they only knew!"

"Knew what?"

"About his intelligence. His sense of humor. You believe, *Docteur*, don't you? And do you understand? After all the explaining and demonstrations, no matter where I go, sometimes I'm misunderstood."

"But it's fairly strong stuff," Loring said.

The dwarf rolled his burly-browed eyes and leaned back to watch the island landscape speed by. He smiled a tired smile. "I hope to change that one day, perhaps a day quite soon. After all, what is stronger than the truth?"

The cab climbed up over a treeless ridge and suddenly they could see the ship at anchor.

A mile out across the water – the *S/S Nordic Blue* – just where Loring had left her. She always was a visual thrill for Loring with her fluked funnels gleaming in the sun and her elegant sloped hull dipping and blending with the rippled blue sea. The view of her and the giant silver blimp reassured him briefly. Why consider ancient performance metaphysics when a perfectly enchanting sight – the foremost artistic masterpiece of 20th century naval architecture with her gleaming aerial attendant – loomed in a picturesque Caribbean setting?

Yet Tosco had said things that troubled Loring, distracted him from the beauties of the moment.

* * *

Tosco's *Cirque Ineffable* had experimented in Paris on the fringes of metaphysical performance art for six years now. With his family fortune to bankroll him and with Vladimir Vladimirovich Tulov as his mentor, Tosco had made essential advances and was on the verge, he said, of a major breakthrough.

His studies of the anthropological precedents of magic had been extreme. He had traveled with Tulov to tiny villages in the most remote regions in central Asia, had spoken with dervishes and ancient seers, none of whom seemed surprised at all when he said his cult had discovered "manifestation."

The old sages would nod their heads and agree that what Tosco and Tulov called manifestation was but a single step in the full range of superior states which resulted from keen psycho-physical concentration. If he steadfastly followed the path to the extra-physical, there was no question that Tosco could find it.

The dervishes and sages had seemed amused when he asked about magic techniques. Some had difficulty with the concept of magic. Casting spells on animals was hardly occult in some villages. There were fewer wild animals now, and so it was more difficult to keep those skills sharp. Most children were more interested in computers and the internet than with telepathic traditions. But even today, men and women in some remote villages regularly communicated with forest animals through chants and trance casting.

These elders said a state of grace had once existed among all animals and humans. Was it a state like that of the mythical Garden of Eden?

When Tosco mentioned the Garden of Eden, the old Central Asian eyes would glaze and shed tears. Some had difficulty speaking or would refuse to acknowledge his question. All knew it. Some vowed it had existed – not as a poetic metaphor of Biblical poetry, but as an actual place.

* * *

The cab paused for a stop sign at a street corner in the center of Philipsburg, near the pier. Loring handed the cabby the fare plus tip. "Uh, maybe I'll get out now."

Tosco's eyes winced. "Did I say something inappropriate?"

"No. I just have to drop my post cards in a mail box. I also have a tremendous headache. At the restaurant, the sun fried my scalp."

114

Tosco looked up at Loring's brow and squinted with concern. "You're right. Your skin is red and raw, looks like it might blister. I'm sorry, I didn't notice till now."

"It feels deeper than the skin. Hot. It's weeping. I need medication. And a hat. I should never have sat there that long!"

"Not without protection, *Docteur*!"

"And I never get headaches. How foolish of me!"

"We all lose ourselves sometimes, especially down here in the tropics."

Loring jerked open the cab door. He shook Tosco's hand, gave a cautious pat to the sleeping Robespierre.

"But thank you for a lovely afternoon," Tosco said. "Otherwise, I would have been alone. By the way, tomorrow we sail into San Juan. You'll be my guest for lunch at *Claridad*? You can meet my family, if you like."

"Do you mean that?"

"*Docteur*, perhaps you don't realize how pleased I am to make your acquaintance. Meet me at the *Crew Gangway* at ten. It's a two-hour drive up along the north coast to *Claridad*. We'll dine and then I'll show you around the grounds and give you a demonstration. We need more time together, don't you think?"

* * *

Loring watched the cab turn out of sight toward the pier. He dabbed his scalp with his handkerchief and was relieved to see only skin fluids oozing out. He had worried that blood and maybe, after his intense session with Tosco, his brains might be boiling up into the atmosphere.

Much relieved to be out of the cab and away from Tosco and Robespierre, he took several deep breaths and stretched his legs down Philipsburg's Main Street. He dropped his post cards in a mailbox and then scouted the storefronts for a pharmacy where he might get some medicinal relief from the headache. He had not exaggerated to Tosco. His headache was a whopper – pounding, resonating, deeper than a sunburn effect. Perhaps he suffered from acute and ineffable metaphysical overdose. He chuckled at the diagnosis, till sharp, acidy sparks began to descend into his neck muscles.

Metaphysical overdose, rather than sunburn, might not be such an outrageous diagnosis – not after what his mind had just been through. Tosco and his circus friends wanted to go back to the Garden of Eden's roots. Loring had trouble ridding his aching head of that little hubristic teaser.

Reestablishing a state of grace through heroic magic seemed preposterous – more crackpot than anything Loring had heard in emergency room psych interviews. Yet Tosco, honest in the face of life's complexities, called his cult *"Le Groupe pour la Réstoration d'Eden"* or "The Eden Restoration Movement."

An avowed flyweight when it came to philosophical sparring, Loring had run up against a haymaker-wielding heavyweight in the form of a genteel dwarf magician who saw new planes of existence within the real world. Paradise was right here – within any witness's perceptions. And the destiny of the new, the true circus was to show it, manifest it and big time!

As Loring stepped up the sidewalk in Philipsburg, an unshaven resident of Philipsburg stumbled in front of him and stuck a green chit of paper into his hand. The smiling man had rheumy, pink-veined eyes and a soft black face. He grabbed Loring's arm and pointed toward the swinging doors of *Blazes*, the nearest gambling casino.

"Two spins at roulette, *mon*!" he whispered, his breath rank with rum. "*Blazes* be the place!"

As the friendly drunk meandered away, Loring inspected the green paper, the size of a Monopoly bill. There was a sketch of a windmill in the middle. (A Dutch folklore allusion to the wheel of fortune?) On each corner of the bill was a large number 2 and the words, *"TWO FREE ROULETTE SPINS. EFFECTIVE TODAY ONLY!"*

Loring looked for a trash bin. Gambling ran counter to his Vermont Yankee/ Unitarian convictions, and though all Nordic Star Lines employees were forbidden to gamble on board ship, he had never felt deprived by the rule. Yet this afternoon, with an hour to spare before the last tender boat headed back to the ship, he sensed a soothing allure inside the swinging doors of *Blazes*. He ran his fingers along the corners of the pass and gazed at the quaint windmill graphic.

Before he knew where his feet led him, he was strolling through an air-conditioned labyrinth of colorful clinking one-armed bandits in a dark vault of a space which was so dim and smoky, that immediately he felt cool and dizzy and not at all guilty. The thick, opium den atmosphere soothed his sunburn immediately. He forgot about metaphysics. He was glad he had stepped out of that cab. And here he was with a chit entitling him to two free spins at roulette – a game he'd never tried!

The Garden of Eden was hard to contemplate, caused headaches.

Blazes was easy and gentle and free.

Love, really *love,* the air conditioning!

He expected to see a few familiar crew faces from the *Nordic Blue*, but he was surprised at the huge crowd from *Nuggets*, the ship's casino. Dealers, Croupiers, Pit Bosses – mostly young Brits and Scots he knew from the *Crew Bar*. There they all were – Spike, Maynard, Liz, Bess, Rupert, Ian, Nigel, Blizzard, Robert and others – hunkered over the tables. They carefully placed their chips and gazed at the action, as if *Blazes* here on St. Maarten were their first glimpse into an amazing new pursuit.

Why *not* take busmen's holidays? They all sucked cigarettes and hung in here till the last tender boat was to leave, even though, as soon as the *S/S Nordic Blue* weighed her giant anchor and shoved off toward San Juan at sunset, these same casino personnel would be back at their posts in *Nuggets*, looking stern, fab, manicured in tuxes, and hustling bets from power cruisers at the gaming tables identical to these in *Blazes*.

YOU NEVER KNOW UNTIL YOU KNOW!

Roulette. Once you were there at the green baize surface, it *did* appeal.

He watched the red and black, silver-spoked wheel spin under the lights, while that little ivory ball circulated capriciously around the rim in the opposite direction and then bounced down and tip-toed for a tantalizing instant before it nestled with a loud dry pop into one of the revolving radial slots.

How did that little ball know where it wanted to go when everything around it was moving so very fast in the opposite direction?

Not unlike Tosco trying to find his way back to Eden, while the whole history of the planet seemed to be spinning the other way!

No doubt about it. The sunburn feels better. Who really needs metaphysics when there is all this cool smoke all over your skin and fascinating, fast-paced action at hand?

He knew what it meant to be hot at darts. Did he have an idiot savant capacity to sizzle at roulette, too?

Slide . . .

He approached the bank window to trade his flimsy green freebie chit for two solid blue *Blazes* $5 chips.

"*Yo! Joey!*" he chortled, when he saw stone-faced Joey Manook, the Casino Manager from the *Nordic Blue*.

The husky Hawaiian stood beside the teller's window and barked into a cell phone, his stubby toes wiggling in their flip-flops. Joey raised an annoyed pinky finger at Loring.

Three cruises ago, Loring had treated Manook in *Crew Clinic* for pediculosis pubis (crabs) and gonorrhea, acquired here in St. Maarten. Never since had the Casino Manager offered the Chief Medical Officer the favor of eye contact. Of course, inscrutable as any 230-pound tiki god with an obvious attitude and a hidden agenda, unsmiling Manook never did eye contact with anybody. Loring, a physician first and a crew member second, refused to take it personally.

The teller slid out two ribbed blue plastic disks. Each bore a *Blaze's* windmill and *"$5"* imprints. Loring, feeling a bizarre affection for Manook as soon as he held the chips in his hand, strode excitedly past the Casino Manager and back to the roulette section – five tightly crowded tables.

Loring's palms sweated. The chips were already slippery. Why? Scion of a long line of thrifty Yanks – now with hot palms over a trivial spin or two at roulette? What would his mother say?

Olivia! Your son is far from Eden. But that doesn't mean he can't find his way back! Fascinating, this concept of reclaiming Paradise.

He spotted an opening on the far side of the crowd and sped for it. As he sidled into a spot and admired the long gold grid with its red and black numbers arrayed on the baize, the chips seemed heavier in his hand. He hadn't spent a cent for them, yet they seemed to expand and increase in mass in the sweat bath his palm had become.

But he had no right to linger and caress, while others who had paid for chips waited to wager. For several seconds his eyes were transfixed on the stationary wheel.

The brash croupier – a lean, impatient Dutch youth with a scant blonde mustache, a spike cut, and a tiny tattoo of Mickey Mouse on his left ear lobe – slid his rake to retrieve the chips and push the few winners back their payment.

Loring quickly calculated the odds: 38 to 1 on a number. But if you placed your chip on the line between two numbers, your chance to win doubled and the payback halved. Simple. What could he lose? All he had to do was think of a number and a color – red or black.

"Bets, please."

The chips started to burn hotter. Oh, they weren't burning. They only *felt* like they were burning! But he realized he was creating a stress crisis for himself. He had made recent progress on his oral tendencies, but now he wanted – was not sure *why* he wanted – but yes, he *wanted* to put the chips, at least one of them, into his mouth.

Go ahead. Put the chip in your mouth.

He recalled the chat at the Captain's Table last night with Blanche Cruickshank. Blanche actually put the chips *in her mouth* for good luck.

Would a quick suck raise his chances of victory?

Ha-*ha!*

Clyde Cruickshank said he almost lost his Mercedes dealership because of his wife's constant sucking. And losing.

Ha! Better not get oral here.

"Sir?" the Dutchman peered at Loring. "You with the red forehead!"

See, you missed your chance. You could have put it in your mouth, but now he's staring at you. Everybody's staring at you.

Loring couldn't decide. He smiled and looked up and down the grid, felt paralyzed. "But there are so many numbers."

The Dutch Croupier frowned. "Place your bet or move on!"

Loring *did* want to suck his hot two chips – *yes* – place both his gambling totems in his mouth and suck them for good luck, just like Blanche Cruickshank. Even if it meant losing everything in his hand.

Only two chips. But think where those chips might have been? Think of who handed out the chits to get the chips! Don't put the chips in your mouth! Up on toes! In . . . and . . .

"Place it!"

Loring wanted to massage those wafers, lower them onto his tongue, feel their hot bulk against his palate and . . .

Wait! Look over there! Spinelli. What number is he betting on?

Across the table Loring saw a perfect manicure and a hairy wrist in a gold link bracelet. The fingers stacked a column of "$50" chips dead center on Black 22.

Loring's eyes crept up the sleeve and forearm.

"Sir?" the croupier demanded.

Loring laid his two chips beside the tall stack.

Francis X. Spinelli had bet heavily on Black 22. If anybody knew a winner, it had to be the *Nordic Blue's* Cruise Director.

As soon as the two chips lay on the table, Loring's palms ceased to itch and sweat. His mouth stilled its longings.

Rationality had set in, chilled him.

He realized he had wagered zero. The chips had been merely a promotional gift from a kindly drunk. Nothing more. The reason he had entered *Blazes* in the first place was to cool off his skin. His skin felt cool and now – here they lay, objectified, two nylon blue circles far away from him.

Did Black 22 bear any relevance to his lot in life? No.

And his skin felt great!

But as he gazed over the betting grid and across the table, Loring saw the Cruise Director was less removed from the action, much more deeply committed.

In the *Starlight Lounge*, Loring had seen Spinelli's arrogant eyes flash around the audience – always in control, never flinching, even with the hecklers at the back bar. In a flash Spinelli could identify and humiliate any wisecracking power cruiser. But here in *Blazes*, with his tall column of chips riding on Black 22, Spinelli did not even see Loring right across the table.

As the cocky Dutchman spun the wheel then flicked the little ivory sphere into its reverse orbit, Loring watched Spinelli's face.

The dark brows arched. The eyes spun. The little veined bags under his lids trembled with each circuit. The tongue tip crept up over the lip nervously to preen the mustache. The bald pate furled, started to bob up and down. When the ivory ball dropped down from the outer rim and started its crazy tap dance around the circle, the fists came up to the cheeks, squeezed the muscles working inside. The knuckles gave thuds to both brows, countered the uncontrolled forward pulses of the head. The temple veins bulged, the lips puckered in and out with each click of the wheel.

Finally the ball fell into a slot. The steely eyes slowed their revolutions. The fists dropped. The forehead flushed.

The croupier stuck out his rake. "Red 21, thank you."

"Stop!" Spinelli grabbed the rake handle. "*Can't* be!"

"Sorry. It *clearly* rests on Red 21. Or do my eyes deceive?"

"I say it can't be!"

Mickey Mouse scanned the dozen players around the table. "Does anybody *else* think the ball does *not* rest in Red 21?"

Spinelli sneered. "You're new here?"

"Yes, I'm new. But I believe Red 21 has been around for several hundred years at least. Maybe even longer than Black 22. After all, 21 does come before 22, doesn't it? Now did red come before black? You tell me."

The croupier rolled his eyes, and the onlookers laughed.

"Shut up, asshole! I want to see the manager!" shouted Spinelli. "And where's Joey? Where's Joey Manook?"

"I assure you, sir, the manager will not alter the result of your bet. Maybe you'd rather speak with our security officers. Would you take your hands off my rake. Or does it *do* something for you? Place your bets, please, ladies and gentlemen."

* * *

Loring was the first to board the last tender back to the ship. He sat in the stern and watched the sunburned power cruisers make their way up the gangplank onto the benches for the trip back to the *Nordic Blue*. They toted shopping bags filled at the duty-free shops with bargain-priced watches, porcelains by Hummel and Royal Dalton, DVD's, electrical binoculars, along with sacks of native-carved souvenirs.

On the tenders, Loring always felt more akin to the passengers than when he was on the ship, perhaps because they all shared the joy of returning home to this huge, wonderful, double-funneled mother who loomed in the watery distance.

As the final warning toot issued from the tender's horn, Loring saw a taxi pull up and stop at the dock.

Ulla von Straf stepped out, dressed in a dark black suit. She caressed an elderly, hunched black St. Maarten native in a black tie and a navy blue suit. She kissed him and nuzzled his neck. Then, smiling tears away from her eyes, walked up the gangplank and took a standing position at the tender's bow rail.

Loring sat and watched Ulla as the tender started to bob and pull away from the port, veered over the waves back toward the *Nordic Blue*. Ulla remained standing, though there were seats available near her, and stared back, waving till the taxi disappeared from the dock.

Loring refrained from an impulse to approach her. He knew Ulla's mysteries extended well beyond this one moment, beyond his own preoccupations with her. He averted his eyes, stared instead at the sleek and beauteous *Nordic Blue*. He knew Ulla first and most intimately as a dancer. If they were to find each other as true partners, this was not a moment to cut in on her emotions.

One must assume that Spinelli, too, was huddled somewhere on this tender boat. But Flip, too, apparently knew not to bother her.

As their distance from St. Maarten increased, Loring sneaked a look at her. She stood there, eyes trained back on the island. Her dark tresses played in the wind, and her black-garbed body swayed with the waves. She looked content, at peace in some fixed vision. She looked back over Loring's head in the stern toward the island, and then she saw him. There was no doubt that she saw him. And Loring saw serenity and relief in her eyes. And when she bowed her head, as if praying in the direction of the island, Loring hoped he was in her meditations.

* * *

Monday evenings out of St. Maarten, the theme was *"Country and Western,"* the drink was the *Tequila Tornado (TT)*, and the dress code was *Denim and Pearls (D & P)*.

At sunset, as the ship drifted away from the island, newly-tanned power cruisers began to strut the decks in cowboy hats, loud shirts, neckerchiefs, boots and jingling spurs. And what buckaroo or buckarette in *D & P* would not stop to sample a *TT* in a take-it-home hurricane glass?

Caribbean and Latino waiters, wave-and-sunburst bandanas wrapped above the brims of their ten-gallon hats, fired up the charcoal in the steel drums near the two pools on *Leif Erickson Deck* for an *"Old Fashioned Texas-Style Bar-B-Q."* The mesquite-laced smoke floated above the pools, and the bar-b-q fix'ns were being put into place.

SO GIT DOWN YEEEAAAAAAWWWWWWL!

Afterward came the *"On-Deck Hoedown"* – including *Hog Calling, Rope Twirling, Miss Cowgirl Pageant, Miss Mini-Cowgirl Pageant*, and the *Square Dancing Competition* – to be called by Cruise Director Francis "Tex" Spinelli. For tonight's festivities, Jacques Chemin had sculpted a massive ice triptych: a tall and somber cigar store Indian chief in flowing feather head dress, a fierce bucking bronco, and a detailed Conestoga wagon in shiny, frozen crystal.

Strolling by at twilight in evening uniform, Loring admired each of Chemin's latest masterpieces as they were being rolled into place near the outdoor Tex-Mex buffet: tortillas, enchiladas, chalupas, burritos, and good old Sam Houston-sized T-bones aplenty.

Like I said, GIT DOWN YEEEAAAAAAWWWWWWL!

Loring whiffed the sweet mesquite smoke. He looked up as the late rays of sun played among the facets and prisms within the carved ice – glowing on the head dress of the heroic Native American and sprouting in glorious red/orange crystal feathers down the chief's back. Loring tried in his mind to straddle the defiant spine of the ice bronco as it turned purple against the sky's failing light. He huddled mentally into the glowing confines of the prairie schooner – so icy-warm against the Caribbean sunset. But as marvelous as these glazed artifacts of the American frontier were, his mind could not connect with them. In fact, country and western dancing and Tex-Mex cuisine had never satisfied Loring.

He wandered toward the bow, away from the noise, smoke, and power cruisers. San Juan lay not far over the horizon to the west, a slow night's drift away. The ship was moving barely six knots, and the warm evening wind blew gently at the bow, ideal to view a spectacular sunset.

Stretching off above the distant white caps was a low, clumpy roll of scrolling purple cumulus puffs that split the sun into a dozen vanishing vermilion shafts. Vaulting still higher was a vast periwinkle field of cirrostratus, which blanched to teal and then twisted into spidery magenta swirls directly overhead. As the sun dipped lower into the sea, it turned bloody, and then filled the darker purple clouds so they bulged and glimmered with brilliant tangerine and peach linings that played on the waves in undulating stripes.

Loring saw and decided. Even from a glimpse, it was true. Eden, for all its legendary wonders, could not top this Caribbean sunset – so rich and dramatic and fleeting. He could say without exaggeration that he was gazing at a piece of Paradise, right here and now, from the bow of the *Nordic Blue*! Eden had never seen anything better!

Until his talk with Tosco that afternoon, he would have thought it absurd to project himself into Eden. But look *out* there! Surely he was feasting on a firmament equal to any Adam and Eve could have gazed at and with exactly his same astonishment and feeling of blessedness. This was the same planet and that was the same sun, wasn't it?

* * *

Long after the sun had set and the stars had begun to shine through the frail clouds, Loring continued to gaze west. He could not stop pondering Tosco's words, as if the little man had infested his brain with one delicious paradox upon another.

He was focusing on the moon as it slipped up over the eastern horizon, when a cheery voice interrupted his thoughts.

"Well, my my *my*, Oliver! Finally I've *found* you. I've been looking all over this ship. Who would have thought *you* of *all* people would be out here staring at the stars when there's a very lively hoedown going on at the other end of the ship!"

Loring turned and saw Hildegarde Snippet-White's sprightly face. She was dolled up in a broad-brimmed hat and a snazzy cowgirl outfit – matching felt yellow skirt and vest with green piping and green cactus silhouettes embroidered on the lapels and sleeves. She clicked the heels of her fancy boots and spun around. "How do you like my getup? Feel like doing the Cotton-Eye Joe?"

"Hildegarde, I never learned Country and Western."

"Not even square dancing?"

"Sorry. I don't really like it."

"Well, you're missing out on a lot of fun. Young man, I thought you *liked* fun!"

"Country dancing just isn't for me. And I'm not trying to seem critical, but isn't this a little soon after the Colonel's death for you to go out and party hardy?"

"Don't be a pill, Oliver. Sometimes it's too *late*, but it's never too *soon* to party! Ask Rocky! By the way, have you seen the Colonel's bust down in the *Freezer*? That Haitian man, *Monsieur* Chemin, really caught the true Rocky! Just like a frozen piece of life! I've had the photographers in. Dead Rocky versus Ice Rocky. Wow! Come with me. I have to show you immediately! The hoedown can wait."

* * *

"HILDEGARDE!"

"You don't have to raise your voice, Oliver. There's nobody here in the freezer but the three of us. Rocky can't hear you. But tell me, how do you like it? Isn't it a pip? *Monsieur* Chemin *does* know how to fashion ice!"

"Let's talk about the Colonel."

"Doesn't he look *grand*? So perfect for tonight. Unlike you, Oliver, Rocky *adores* Country and Western, and he always insists on dressing up as the person least likely to be invited."

"War paint? Buck skin tunic and fringed pants? Moccasins? Feathered headband? The bow and quiver of arrows?"

"Yes, isn't he so . . . so . . . Rocky Boy Bebalsam?"

"As a Native American brave? Who *did* it to him?"

"*Did* it to him? Well, since you asked, we were fitted for the costumes in London four months ago, as soon as we knew for sure we'd be back on the ship for Valentine's. I'm sorry about that feather – it just won't go into the coffin straight. Does it look a little queer? You know, chiefs get a thousand feathers, but braves get only one."

"Queer?"

"We planned to be the winning "Country and Western" couple."

"How about the war paint?"

"Ruby Decosta. The make-up artist for the Starlegs Dancers. Didn't she do Rocky right, though? You know, Oliver, the power of the ship has *always* been incredible to me. Especially now, in my time of need. And everybody is so willing to help me out in my crisis. Ruby Decosta, for example. Knew *just* what I wanted. Said she'd do it in a flash, and look – there's my own brave!"

Loring leaned down and sniffed the gold lightning bolts on the forehead, the blue buffaloes on the cheeks, the black chin arrows – all in metal-scented, brush stroke grease paint.

"You're not planning to have the Colonel buried at sea this way?"

"Silly Oliver! This is only for tonight. Rocky's indulging me. We had looked forward to this evening for so long. Just *picture* us – *he* the handsome Native American on the prowl and then there's me, the settler's wife, lonely and sex-starved after her frigid husband set off for a two-month cattle drive. But I dress up in my finest to entertain the handsome red man when we meet in secret."

"Got it."

"Though it sounds contrived, there's so much pure chemistry in it, Oliver. Just *look* at him! Even now, can't you feel the savage? I feel some pride in knowing that I helped release it. I mean, or was it only our fantasy? What do you think?"

"Handsome outfit."

"It'll fit you perfectly, after Rocky's gone. You could have so much fun with it, Oliver. I'm sure you have the chemistry in you, too. But you haven't said a word about the death bust, have you, Oliver. *OLIVER!*"

* * *

Loring lay in his cabin bed. His teeth chattered like frenzied dice. Here he was, cruising on a balmy night in the sultry Caribbean, but never had he felt such icy rigors! Ears to toes, his entire body shook in every direction. He felt gnawed, nipped at, squeezed by demons. The tighter he bundled under his blankets, the more painfully the legions of evil took unmitigated mastery over him.

He threw off the blankets and jumped up, opened a porthole, sniffed the warm salt air deeply. He shouted to the waves, *"I d-don't n-n-eeed b-b-blankets! I n-neeeed an ex-ex-ex-orcist!"*

The chilling forces had entered him when he had looked the Colonel's death bust in the face down in the *Galley Freezer*. The huge ice effigy with the protuberant nose resembled the Colonel, but *even more* Loring's own deceased father! Chemin had copied the cut on dear Orson's prominent square jaw right down to the dimple! Loring had looked – the Colonel's jaw *had* no dimple!

And the angularity of the cheeks, the wideness of the eyes, the arch of the brows!

All of it – much more Orson Loring than Boy-Bebalzam!

Had Jacques Chemin confused the two? But how? How *could* that crazy Haitian mix up the Colonel's distinctive physiognomy with someone *he had never laid eyes on*? Freudian slip? Jungian synchronicity? Some kind of Joseph Campbell style follow-your-bliss psychic entablature?

Voodoo?

Or maybe Mozart? Was it a *Don Giovanni* father figure creeping onto the ship like the uninvited statue in the last act? (*Don Giovanni* had been Orson Loring's favorite opera. But how could Jacques Chemin have known?)

Dad! I love you! I played Bach this morning, Dad! I swear I did!

The ice head was too enormous for Loring to get his arms around, but down in the *Galley Freezer* he felt the oral urge to grab his father's huge skull and embrace him, plant a big filial kiss on his lips – as if he were an infant again and his father were the same outwardly icy, overwhelmingly warm presence he had known from his very earliest nursery memories!

What was going on around here? How had Jacques Chemin, ice sculptor, divined all that? Cozy, intimate scenes from a Coventry, Vermont, nursery transported to a Caribbean meat freezer on an overnight drift to San Juan, Puerto Rico?

When Loring stuck his lips onto the statue, Hildegarde had winced and insisted he return to his cabin at once. She offered to call a doctor, but Loring had pointed out . . . *THE FU-TI-TILITY AND RE-DU-DUN-DUN-DANCY!*

Loring dived back under his blankets. He had *never* felt so cold! He had taken two hot showers, put three sweatshirts over his pajamas, hiked his cabin thermostat up to the hilt. Nothing could thaw the vision of his father, which Chemin had carved in ice.

Furthermore, how could Jacques have guessed Loring's helplessness and shame that afternoon on the Killington slopes? All day they had skied together, father and son chatting about medicine, about Olivia, and finally about Oliver's prolonged bachelorhood. Playing the romantic field was probably a healthy emotional endeavor, Orson had admitted in the gondola on the way up the mountain for their last run. He himself had waited a long time till he had found Olivia. But after a while, bachelorhood seemed a bit narcissistic, if not wasteful, and wasn't it about time to find a mate and produce a grandchild or two for Olivia and Orson to enjoy. Eh, Oliver? Perhaps an Orville or an Orlando?

Oliver had not answered, but had climbed out of the gondola, snapped on his skis and gestured with his pole for his father to lead the way down the deserted slope.

Not ten seconds later, Orson's outside ski snagged the spruce root. His son stood speechless at the edge of the trail as his father shot out over the cliff and spun with his arms and legs extended in a silent, pinwheeling descent toward the slab of granite waiting below.

Why had Oliver not shouted, *"I LOVE YOU!"* as his father hurtled to his doom? In fact, his father's judgmental pronouncements in the gondola had stunned and peeved Loring.

As he stood watching from the edge of the trail, why could Oliver Loring not find it in himself to shout those words while his spinning father still breathed and thought, could still hear him?

In life, Orson had never gushed with affection, but he certainly deserved those words from his foolish, tongue-tied son during his final descent. Instead of an affectionate farewell, shouted passionately into the snowy ravine, Orson's only comfort in his descent into the void was the wind blowing in his ears.

Dance to *"Alabamy Bound"* at Orson's funeral? Yes. But *after* his father was dead. So was it an accident that a voodoo practitioner on a ship in the Caribbean had created a death bust of another individual who resembled his own father, then had added a chin dimple and . . . Loring rested his head against his pillow and closed his eyes.

* * *

Big cat jaws closed around Oliver Loring's wrists, clamped shut and began to rip and shake him apart till his tendons splayed out from his forearms like piano wires ripped twanging from their pinions. Long, pitiless fangs crunched his ribs, punctured his lungs, cut into his liver, bowels, bladder!

"OOOUUUUCHH! EEEOOOOWWWWWWW! HEEEEELP! HELP! HELP! AHHH! OOOOOOUCHHHHHH!"

Loring could not breathe, felt his own viscera being torn to very messy shreds. Blood, urine, feces, scrotal elements flowed out everywhere. *All* of Oliver Loring. *(As he was once known.)* Mix 'n match organs all over the bed sheets blended with large volumes of big cat saliva.

Right here on *Viking Deck!*

Ladies and Gentlemen!

Staining the whole place! The mattress, everything! The cabin reeked! Loring's own blood and shit!

Why did this cat – was it a tiger? a jaguar? a lion? a puma? – have to be so damned oral? *Oh, I get it! Death by oral! Just what I deserve!*

What will Mr. Kim do with this carnage? Why does this big cat want to chew up my insides? Where is Mr. Kim, by the way? Where is Mr. Kim ever? I've barely ever seen Mr. Kim, even though he's my own valet who receives a sizable tip at the end of every week's cruise!

Would anybody hear him? Was he lost forever? Could anybody put him back together? On a cruise ship? Was this really a *Hospital*? Was this where somebody might want to be seriously traumatized?

By a big cat, for example? No blood bank, you say? Oh, thanks a lot! And will somebody on the Bridge tell me exactly how far are we from a reliable helicopter medi-evac system? And will Kevin or Guy know how to keep my tendons preserved in salt ice till a qualified university hand surgeon intervenes?

"EEEEEEEEEEOOOOOOOOOWWWWWWWW!"

I may never play the piano again. Is anybody out there going to call a Code Commando? Hello?

Suddenly the big cat, many big cats were at him all over again. Huge claws engaged his scalp. Indefinable cats of all types.

He smelled their fur, their breath. Huge claws! They would leave the same marks they had left on Tosco's scalp. For sure. If Loring was *lucky*! Deep claws scratching in and taking hold, ripping his scalp right off his skull. He felt them now – now – now again!"

"UUUUUUUUUUUHGHGHGHHGH!"

And *where* was Ulla von Straf in all of this?

Was Ulla so involved with Tosco's magic that she was . . . yes . . she was *without* pity and he was willing to say it now . . . she's a *witch!*

A beautiful, conspiratorial witch who may be able to dance like nobody else but who . . .

"THE WOMAN'S A WITCH! SHE'S A WITCH! EEEEEEEEEEEOOOOOOW! WITCH! WITCH! WITCH!"

* * *

"SHUT YOUR FACE THIS VERY MOMENT! OLIVER LORING? DO I HAVE TO SLAP YOU TO BRING YOU BACK TO YOUR SENSES? HELL! IT'S ALMOST FOUR O'CLOCK IN THE MORNING, AND YOU'RE GONNA' YELL AND HOLLER AND GO WAKIN' UP HALF OF ALL VIKING DECK! WHAT'S THIS STUFF 'BOUT SOME DAMNED OLD WITCH? WHAT HAPPENED? DID SHE DO Y'ALL WRONG, DART DOC?"

Loring's eyes batted open. He sat bolt upright in bed.

Chief Nurse Maggie McCarthy stood beside him with his head in her hands. Her fingernails grasped him like sharp ice tongues.

"Here, honey, have a cup of some warm milk and tell me all about it. You know, I think you're taking this cruise too seriously, Dart Doc."

TUES/FEB 12
Fandango in San Juan

MEMO FROM THE BRIDGE

Date: TUES/FEB 12, 06.00 hours
From: Captain Trond Ramskog
To: All Officers and Crew
Re: "Valentine TV Cruise" Schedule

Beginning this evening in San Juan, the S/S Nordic Blue will host Mr. Farrely Farrell and his entire Cablevista Staff. We will be the center of attention for tens of millions of TV viewers world-wide. This means Officers and Crew must serve not only the on-board passengers, but also a huge audience of potential future passengers. This is not an easy task. I fully understand the pressure you all feel.

Below I have listed the upcoming events as Cablevista and the Cruise Director, have reported to me. I remind each of you please to respect the visiting Cablevista staff and cooperate in every way. I realize you are under stress, but I know you will present yourselves in a manner fitting the traditions of the S/S Nordic Blue and Nordic Star Lines.

I am also pleased to announce that Mr. Stig Storjord, the founder of Nordic Star Lines, will be coming on board tonight to enjoy the Valentine TV Cruise. As your Captain, I am proud to show him how enthusiastically we do our jobs. I have full confidence in each of you.

Trond Ramskog
Master, S/S Nordic Blue

cc: Mr. Spinelli, Mr. Farrell

* * *

CABLEVISTA VIDEOTAPING
AND BROADCAST SCHEDULE

TUES/FEB 12 (San Juan)
06.00: Arrival. Begin on-load of equipment and personnel.
Videotaping of various ship activities.
23.00: "Midnight Promenade" in the Stardust Ballroom.
Live round-the-world telecast by Cablevista.

WED/FEB 13 (San Juan)
10.00: Depart San Juan. Tour and interviews with
Farrely Farrell.
18.00: Live, round-the-world telecast of "Captain's Cocktail Party"
with Farrely Farrell.
21.00: "Love Luck" telecast in the Starlight Lounge with
Farrely Farrell and Cruise Director Flip Spinelli.

THURS/FEB 14 (Valentine's Day-at-Sea)
18.00: Live telecast of "V.I.P. Cocktail Party," Club Atlantis.
22.00: Live telecast of "Valentine Dance Gala" with
Farrely Farrell, Cruise Director Flip Spinelli, and the
Starlegs Dancers in Starlight Lounge.
00.00: Midnight show "Love Magic" with the Starlegs Dancers
and Tosco, the New World Magician, in Starlight Theatre.

FRI/FEB 15 (Private Island in the Bahamas)
6.00: Arrival.
12.00: An afternoon of rest and relaxation for Officers and
Crew on the beach. Drinks and barbecue on the Private Island
are the Captain's treat for a job well done!
18.00: Depart Private Island.

SAT/FEB 16 (Miami)
6.00: Arrival. Off-load equipment and passengers. Thanks to all!

* * *

Viceroy Deck #7
Tuesday − 7.00 hours

Darling Oliver,

I just dropped by your cabin, but your valet Mr. Kim said you were already out and about! Tickling the ivories or some such? How resilient of you! Last night you looked utterly ghastly. Especially after you kissed the Colonel's bust! I was worried your lips would stick! (They didn't. Whew!)

How I envy you your youth! Wherever you are, I'm glad you're not wasting this beautiful morning lying in bed.

What got into you last night? You are so sensitive, Oliver. Sometimes I worry about you, I really do. I said so to Ulla at the hoedown. (She asked where you were.) We had the best time square dancing, but we could have used a man − not just any ole cowpoke, you understand. We almost stopped up to your cabin. I told her you might need some warm-up cocoa.

Ulla thinks you're shy. I don't want to play Cupid, Oliver, but I would like you to take a serious look at her, and not in a medical sense. She's 32 and she has a weakness for Bohemians and fantastics. I am her godmother, you know, and I told her you're sensitive but solid − like dear old Rocky. She's intrigued, I know. By the way, she took the news about Rocky rather hard. I waited till the end of the evening to tell her − was that bad of me? Again, I wish you'd been there. I invited her for lunch and shopping today in San Juan to cheer her up. She's so Germanic, you know. She gets blue. You cheer her up. I wish you could join us, but Ulla already told me Tosco is planning to show you around his hacienda. Congratulations!

I have another little favor to ask. As you know, the "Midnight Promenade" in the Stardust Ballroom is tonight at 23.00h. Rocky and I always attended on our past cruises ever since our original honeymoon. Oliver dear, feel free as a bee in Capri to turn me down on this, but would you escort me? Please? Colonel would be pleased. And to honor him, would you mind wearing one of his uniforms? Rocky recently had a London tailor craft the finest shark skin British officer's uniform ever (in fact, it was the uniform the Colonel died in.) I'm having it cleaned and pressed. Your valet Mr. Kim (he's also a great admirer of you) said he'd look after it and have it altered by the Chinese Tailor, Mr. Chu, if necessary, and have it in your cabin when you return from your activities with Tosco in Puerto Rico today.

Really, Oliver, it would mean so much to the Colonel to know I was well escorted tonight and by a man of Rocky's proportions, especially since there may be snoopy television cameras lurking around. (Don't worry. Mr. Kim already told me about your sartorial anomaly – the Colonel always had to have his slacks let out, too! I predict they'll fit grandly. You two are so similar!) See you at eleven tonight?

XOXO/
Hildegarde

* * *

Oliver Loring stood at the *Viking Deck* rail and squinted at the white sun in the eastern sky. Hot rays slanted across the harbor onto the ancient, sprawling Spanish fortifications of San Juan. The gigantic *Nordic Blue*, queen of the current Caribbean, seemed dwarfed by the mighty stone cliffs of the immense San Cristóbal fortress, stacked up 350 years ago of slave-hewn, slave-hauled rock.

As the old walls fried in the early sun, they seemed to puff up like steroid-infused muscles. The fierce black cannons atop the balustrades poked out above the foamy waves with a phallic statement that still rang loud and fearsome through four centuries: *"OUR KING, THE MIGHTY MONARCH OF SPAIN, IS THE RICHEST AND MOST POWERFUL KING IN THE WORLD! SAY HE AIN'T, HOMBRE!"*

No argument there, *amigos*!

San Juan, their only overnight port of call, always inspired Loring. As a personal tribute to the brave but cruel conquistadors and the glorious Spanish Empire, this morning he had already logged in a frenzied hour at the Baldwin in *Topsiders* with Stravinsky's tricky, Spanish-flavored *Fandango* in B-flat minor.

Ba-rrrrrrrrrrum! ta-ta trummmmmmmm! ta-trummmmmmm! Ba-rummm!

OLÈ! Nothing like a fandango to spice up an entry into San Juan! And what a fandango mode he was in!

Bach baroque counterpoint? Pure *heresy* here in Counter-Reformational, Grand Inquisitorial San Juan!

The dawn light had miraculously purged him of his rigors and chills. The demons and big cats had fled from his cabin, leaving him fully intact and with a delightful catharsis-fired mania. He was sorry he had tugged Nurse

133

Maggie into his nightmare torments. But Maggie was a friend. She understood. Obviously Loring had *needed* those nightmares.

And perhaps Maggie had *needed* to intervene with warm milk and tender solace in a professional fashion, since her tenterhook dealings with the Captain were on slippery skids just now. Trond's hiccups had abated and he was functioning superbly on the *Bridge*, but Snø's facial tic was acting up worse than ever. The wife had confined herself to the *Captain's Cabin*, requested Aquavit to support her round-the-clock, Maggie said.

And such a nurse! Maggie had spoken calmly, supposed that Loring's brain had tried hard to process the bizarre emotional challenges which the first three days on the cruise had put before him. Why fight those dreams? Why even try to *plumb their depths*, said the expert bedside milk therapist, in so many words.

That would be like trying to plumb a *Fandango*. Wouldn't it?

Ba-rrrrrrrrrrrum! ta-ta trummmmmmm! ta-trummmmmmm! Ba-rummm!

And who, for example, after dancing a fandango for King Phillip II of Spain in his court at the height of the Spanish Empire, would then look up and quip, "Well, did his Highness plumb the depths of my fandango?"

"HANG THIS IDIOT FROM THE RAMPARTS AT ONCE!" Phillip II would shout with a wave of the royal hand, as they hauled yet another pretentious buffoon out of the Spanish Court to a dangling doom.

But enough about demons. All gone. At least most of them. Even the fierce scalding the sun had given his scalp yesterday in St. Maarten seemed resolved. No blisters. No stinging. Amazing! (Benefit of scarab therapy?)

Under the rubric of demons, Anita Rothberg *was* due into San Juan tonight. Loring spread his fingers and contemplated his nails – all ten intact. Against the backdrop of the glorious Spanish fortifications, he planned his defense. "Take a look, Anita! See what I did *without* you? See what three days *away* from you has brought about? Have a nice cruise! I'll send chocolates to your cabin on Valentine's Day. Lick your fingers, woman, but keep your tongue off my tan lines!"

Ulla was right. He *was* shy. But when Anita Rothberg showed up on the ship, he would be quite the opposite! He had almost functional *talons* now, and thanks to Nadine Tulard, they gleamed gloriously in the sun. Loring could not remember ever having so much white at the tips to flaunt.

Ba-rrrrrrrrrrrum! ta-ta trummmmmmm!

And along with the exuberant nail growth, Loring had also noticed during this morning's Stravinsky *Fandango*, an increased dexterity at the keyboard

– more than yesterday – as if his nails and his fingertips were in some newly flourishing ecosystem! And not only *on* the keyboard, but *under* the Baldwin, too! His toes had responded with authority to Stravinsky's challenging pedal notations which had always seemed elusive before. Both his soft and sustain pedal techniques had improve dramatically.

Overnight!

By no stretch of logic: if the chitin-rich insect pills could make that much of a difference in his piano pedaling, imagine what might happen to his dance technique! And where better to test it out tonight but at his favorite locale in San Juan, *El Tiburon Baillador (the Dancing Shark)*, and try out a few steps before returning to the ship to escort Hildegarde to the *Midnight Promenade*.

Tonight in San Juan he would be a dancing dynamo! He stretched his arms up to the sky, brought his fists down on his hips, and threw his head back in a bold, imperious King Phillip II pose. "Mambo, anybody?" He kicked his heels on the *Vista Deck* astroturf.

Brrrruuuum! Ta-ta truuuuuuummmmmmmmm!

Maggie had said it right last night: "I think you're taking this cruise too seriously."

Let it be understood. Never again would Oliver Loring take this or any cruise too seriously. There were only three full cruise days left. Soon they would be back in Miami. He vowed to be less shy near Ulla.

* * *

At 10.00 hours, Loring strode down the *Crew Gangway* and found the dock jammed with all the Cablevista vans and trucks. On the pavement, huge spools of cables, consoles of equipment and packaged camera units awaited transfer up into the ship.

Staff Captain Nils Nordström stood near the gangway with several Deck Officers and San Juan policemen. Casually Nils inspected the on-loading items as they passed before him. Nils, responsible for the cruise's security, looked painfully hung over and, as Loring went by him on the ramp and flashed his crew i.d. card, exuded a strong odor of last night's caraway juice. (Or was it essence of *Texas Tornado*?)

Although security measures on the *Nordic Blue* had been tightened recently, Loring could see no undue concern for the task on the Staff Captain's swollen face as he waved crate after crate of equipment past the screening x-ray machine and up the gangway. The loud rumbling and squeaks of the heavy wheels on the dollies seemed to make him wince and blink.

Monitoring this abundance of technical gear – all of it packaged in tamper-resistant containers – would have daunted the spirits of the most sharp-eyed and t-totaling bomb detection expert. The stocky Staff Captain seemed almost bothered by it all, rather than genuinely interested in detecting any suspicious-looking on-load of cargo. Hordes of Cablevista roadies – silent, muscular men and women in black – scurried up and down the gangway as they ladened the *Nordic Blue* with the necessary electronic paraphernalia. Close by, a crane hoisted a six-meter satellite dish to its station atop the ship, between the funnels up on *Vista Deck*.

As the blimp circled over the dock and looked down on the frenzy, a sweating Pearly Livingstone whirled around the pavement with a carton of computer terminals on his forklift.

Loring waved to him. "Pearly! These guys are invading us! Who the heck are they?"

Seeing Loring, the hefty Jamaican slammed his rig to a stop. He grinned and shook sweat beads off his broad brow. "Dart Doc! You old sinner!" Pearly wiped his palm on his wave-and-sunburst t-shirt. "Come here and shake Pearly's hand! Let me take a breather."

Loring obliged, then winced. "You're working hard, *mon*!"

"Hope we've got space on board for all of it. Hey, we've missed you in the *Crew Bar*! We've been lookin' for your every night. Why is that? Still in love with the ballerina?"

"Too busy to chase her, Pearly."

"*Mon*, who isn't busy with all this shit comin' up with the TV stuff? You know, Farrely Farrell's comin' on board tonight. And we still gotta' on-load those three Mercedes roadsters. Usin' that big crane, *mon*. They sure are beautiful, Doc. Wouldn't mind cruising around my island of Jamaica in one of those."

"I sort of miss you, too, Pearly!"

"Whose fault is that?"

"But this is not the same kind of cruise. It's not like before."

"I know. And, did you hear? Old Jacques has got the fever, too!"

"He's had the fever before."

"Worse this time, *mon!* Oh, yea! A new sign-on. An African this time. From the Ivory Coast. Works up in the *Jewelry Boutique*. Fatima. Nice eyes and all the rest. Speaks French. Yes, old Jacques the tom cat is prowling by her shop every day."

"Fatima? So do you think that rogue has met his match?"

"It's awful. If the fever gets any higher, we're gonna' send him up to the *Crew Clinic* to see the Dart Doc. Can you cool him off?"

"Jacques is an *artiste*. He can handle himself."

Pearly gave Loring's cheek a wet slap. "I hope so, Doc!" he chuckled. "You look a little tired, Doc. You gettin' enough sleep?"

"Tons, Pearly. Hey, have you seen the little magician, Tosco?"

The burly Jamaican clenched the throttle stick with one hand and waved the other toward the stern. "Oh yea, Doc. Sure. He's back that way. He got a lot of cargo himself to on-load, too. All goin' down to *Car Deck*. But his own people be doin' it. He won't let Pearly or my boys touch none of it."

"Thanks, *mon*!"

"He be back there, Doc. See you in the *Crew Bar*!"

The forklift pumped its load up off the dock pavement and zipped up the *Cargo Ramp*.

Loring spotted Tosco near the stern. The little Cuban looked jaunty in a felt khaki bush hat with a zebra band and the brim pinned up, Hemingway style. He wore the same silver buckle boots, but today, with safari shirt and shorts. He scampered briskly around the dock and barked commands to a team of Spanish-speaking workers in white jumpsuits as they unloaded oversized trunks from three white panel trucks emblazoned with the name *CLARIDAD* in gold script.

Loring watched Tosco direct the team. Contrary to his soft and confidential manner the day before in St. Maarten, here on the dock in San Juan, Tosco strutted around with a hurried, almost annoyed, briskness.

"Good morning, *Docteur*!" he shouted, his eyes glinting recognition. "I'll join you in a few minutes. Wait for me over there. That's my jeep." He pointed to an open white jeep beside the trucks, then he followed two rolling trunks into the *Crew Cargo Hatch*.

Loring stepped up into the jeep with *"Claridad"* gold scripted on the hood. The gas, clutch, brake pedals had all been hiked up to accommodate the owner's short legs. The column of the steering wheel was extended and lowered at an angle, customized to Tosco's reach. Loring looked into the rear storage compartment and saw a large, lumpy form resting there inside a red bag.

"Bonjour, Robespierre!"

He touched the rough burlap and felt the firm spirals of the snake heaving contentedly. "Welcome to San Juan! I hope you get plenty of sunshine today."

After the contents of the last of the trucks had been loaded onto the ship and the *Claridad* caravan had pulled down the dock road and zoomed away from the port, Tosco reappeared. He climbed up three steel rungs to the driver's seat. "Sorry to keep you," he said with a smile.

"Robespierre seems well disposed today."

"Once we're on the road, we'll let him unwind."

Tosco swung his legs under the steering wheel. He mopped his brow with his handkerchief. "Equipment! The bane of a magician's existence! Sometimes I envy you doctors. All you carry is a little black bag. And for the show Thursday night, we have to haul in more. Did you see it all?"

"Those guys in the white jump suits?"

Tosco donned chrome-lensed sun glasses and twisted the key in the ignition slot. "They are from the hotel."

The roar of the engine brought back memories of the motor in Orson Loring's old green jeep when Oliver was a boy, on his way to house calls with his father. But this jeep was very different. And this wasn't going to be a house call in rural Vermont.

"Buckle up, *Docteur*. The road up on the outskirts is tough. *Claridad* is two hours to the west. Bumpy. We'll have lunch. Then I'll show you around. You're not allergic to cats, are you? It never hurts to ask."

"Allergic?" Loring suddenly felt an urge to jump out of the jeep and run back inside the ship. "Oh, no. Ha-*ha*! I'm not allergic to anything."

What had happened?

Yesterday in St. Maarten, Tosco had seemed so soft. His voice had sounded so reassuring and convincing. Here in the jeep in San Juan, behind the chrome sheen over his eyes and with that bush hat over his brow, and with that prominent cleft chin and half smile under his mustache, Tosco's face was brusque, impenetrable, a Cuban shield – all of it!

Loring thought about his big cat dreams.

"Sure you want to come along today? You seem hesitant."

"Oh, a thousand percent sure. At least!"

"You look nervous. Is it Robespierre? We can keep him in the bag."

Loring remained pensive, sweating. "Oh, that's okay."

"You're very sure? You don't have a drug problem, do you?"

"Me? Why do you ask?"

"That wild look in your eye just now. I've heard that physicians get hooked. You know – high pressure work. Easy availability of drugs. You're not taking anything, are you? Let's get it straight, right now. I need to know. I don't want you near any of my cats if you're unstable from chemicals."

"Actually, yes."

"Yes?"

"But just vitamins for my nails."

"But you have a strange look. Deep in your eyes. Do those vitamins make you nervous? Do they give you nightmares?"

"Doubt it."

"How long have you been taking them?"

"This is my . . . second day."

Loring pulled out his handkerchief and mopped his brow, which still felt remarkably less inflamed than yesterday. But right now, in the jeep, he was sweating in torrents. The more he thought about the potential side effects of the scarab beetle pills, the more he perspired. He felt like he was on the hot seat – and not only because Tosco's jeep was parked in the sun.

Tosco had a valid point. His casual observation about Loring's nervousness was correct. And how stupid! The Chief Medical Officer had forgotten a primary rule of therapy (which Nurse Maggie had recently scolded him about) – to ask Nadine Tulard about *side effects*.

What if *anxiety* was a side effect, gave Loring an uncontrollable urge to bite his nails again! What good would it do to have his nails grow faster, if the medicine he took made him so anxious that he wanted to bite them off even faster than they grew in? That was not therapy! That was an addiction loop.

Now, more than before, Loring wanted to jump out of the jeep, run back and call Tulard for emergency assistance. But was she even *on* the ship? She probably ran off to the beach or something selfish like that. Did she carry a beeper? But Loring didn't even carry a beeper when he was off the ship! Why should he expect a cosmetologist to carry one?

"*Docteur*, are you sure you're alright today? You seemed so relaxed yesterday."

"You did, too."

As the jeep's engine churned away, Loring looked down at his nails. His mouth watered with temptation. Ten full white crescents ripe for ravishing! He was experiencing a rebound phenomenon! His mind had focused exclusively on the growth element of the equation. But now he felt an upsurge in the other factor, the fatal flaw: consummate oral fulfillment!

Even more troublesome were those chrome sunglasses on Tosco. He could not see the magician's eyes. If Loring were certain – even for a second – that

Tosco's glance was cast away from him, then a quick nibble on the right index would have allowed a little perspective on the problem. Perhaps by chewing just a tiny corner on the right index (his favorite hit), Loring could get a better sense of whether this nervousness was a side effect of the scarab medicine *or* true anxiety. Maybe Loring wasn't even *nervous* at all. Maybe this was all just scarab beetles marching up and down his veins and his extremities, and the sudden wave of anxiety was sort of a collateral damage effect. Yes. All side effects! Ha-*ha!* All a complication of therapy! *Ha!* After all, were not Egyptian scarab beetles oral creatures themselves? Didn't they eat-eat-eat all day? Since before human nails became free game for the self-abusive species?

Go ahead! Take a little bite. Who's in charge here? You or the beetles?

Tosco pulled off his sunglasses and looked deeply into Loring's eyes. "I don't want you to come along to *Claridad* if you're only doing it to humor me. You don't feel sorry for me, do you? Are you only doing this because I'm a dwarf? I sense that you're doing some kind of interior monologue that has much to do with me and your trust of me."

Loring swam for a long moment in the dark pools staring at him under the brim of the Hemingway bush hat. He sighed and felt his anxiety leave him – evaporated like the very sweat from his pores. That was it. It was there in Tosco's eyes: Tosco wanted Loring to come along, and his will – projected firmly, yet without intrusion – eased Loring's fears.

Still looking into Tosco's eyes, he breathed deeply, felt an almost joyous relief. He felt cool. Spent. Done.

Loring sneaked a glance down at Tosco's fine, round-edged nails – polished to a brilliance – each of the ten a distinct trophy of oral self discipline. Loring felt sure that someday, and perhaps a day quite soon, his own nails would be that immaculately groomed.

"I'm not nervous anymore."

"I can see. You're cool as ice."

"Ha-*ha*! Well, not *that* cool! Ha-*ha!*"

"By the way, you wouldn't by any chance be a nail biter, would you? Yours are quite short."

"I lose control. Once in a blue moon."

"Ever try scarab pills?"

"As a matter of fact, those are the very vitamins I'm taking."

"You're lucky. They helped me kick the habit long ago."

"Do scarab pills make you nervous? I mean, as a side effect?"

"What's to be nervous about?"
Tosco popped the clutch, and the jeep took off down the dock.

* * *

If Oliver Loring had harbored suspicions that Tosco was a hustler, a lunatic, or some kind of slick Cuban/Parisian *fabricateur*, the doubts dissolved two hours west of San Juan when the jeep climbed a steep ridge on a palm-lined gravel road and pulled to a halt on an overlook at the edge of a high volcanic rock escarpment.

During the trip, Robespierre has slithered out of his bag into the front seat, and now he was curled contentedly in Loring's lap – his scales were hot, but not unpleasantly so, on Loring's thighs.

Loring looked out, amazed. Far below the coffee trees on the hills, flanked to the east and west by acres of flourishing sugar cane and tobacco fields, sprawled *Claridad*. The elegant white Spanish Colonial manor house with its reflection pool stood back on a knoll above the sea. The mansion was surrounded by palms, tall willows and immense, winding, vine-covered stone walls. A wrought iron gate at the front entrance bore the letter *"C."*

Claridad was breath-taking – a vast compound of barns, cane processing plants, tobacco curing sheds, coffee sunning bins, stables, an old Spanish-style chapel, an unusual octagon-shaped granite building, a sumptuous strolling garden with a pool and fountain. Through a forest of bushy tropical sycamores and palms, Loring saw a bridle path and, further on, a separate park with rolling grass fields and even higher walls at the western extent.

Barely visible, six miles back up the white beach to the east, was the hotel compound, *Hotel Claridad:* sleek, slant-roof contemporary architecture, three swimming pools, a dozen tennis courts, huge riding stables, verdant 36-hole golf course.

"All of this is yours?"

Tosco smiled. He explained that *Claridad* was the third oldest working hacienda in Puerto Rico and one of the few sugar, tobacco and coffee plantations on the island still in family hands. His Cuban great-grandfather, Emiliano, had acquired the estate in 1898 from a displeased colonial family who moved back to Madrid after the Spanish American War.

As a teenager living over in Chantilly, France, Tosco had occasionally visited *Claridad*. The fabulous hacienda had always seemed like his early memories of the Tosco-Gutierez estate in Cuba. A decade ago he had developed the hotel complex, not only as a profit maker, but also as a reason to spend more time at the hacienda.

This dwarf was no fake. *Claridad* was no magician's mirage. *Claridad* was dignified, very real and sweet to smell as the sun-soaked cane fields let off their raw, sugary fragrance.

The jeep began to descend down the narrow road toward the manor house. Loring, the sleeping snake in his lap, closed his eyes and inhaled the delicious aromas – sugar cane, coffee berries, curing tobacco, all with a gentle whiff of salty sea air.

He felt lucky that he had stayed in the jeep two hours ago in San Juan, though his impulses had told him to flee. How cowardly that would have been! (How important was nail care, anyway?) Loring also felt a paradoxical emptiness, even regret, that his life had taken 39 years to bring him to a place as beautiful and graceful as *Claridad* – a setting so firm, sensuous, and enduring, that the glimpse of it fulfilled in him an assurance of his own identity.

In . . . and . . . out!

He opened his eyes and breathed the *Claridad* air deeply and watched Tosco pilot the jeep. Loring saw him in a new and more serious light now, and he felt relieved, refreshed at the chance. *Claridad*, here we come!

* * *

The iron gate swung open, and Tosco's jeep slipped slowly up the long, shady driveway. Loring looked around at the flamingos warbling in the reflection pool, at the beds of orange and scarlet orchids lining the cobblestone pavement, and then up ahead at the stately white columns and iron lattice work of the manor house entrance, where half a dozen house servants stood waiting for them.

Brrrruummmm! Ta-ta trummmmmmmmmm!

Loring could not keep from tapping out those cadences of Stravinsky's *Fandango* on the jeep's dash. Back in San Juan he had wanted to leap from the jeep. Now, before crossing the threshold of the manor house, he had already decided he wanted to stay for a month, lodge in for a goodly visit.

I want to get to know all the flamingos by name.

Only one request. And after they left Robespierre with the servants and entered the receiving foyer with the ancient wall tapestries and the brilliantly polished, cool red tiles, Loring saw it had been answered. There it was:

opposite the walk-in fireplace in the parlor – a 12-foot concert grand Bösendorfer whose keyboard seemed to shout, "Come over here, *Señor* Loring, and let your fingers fandango all over me!"

* * *

The *Claridad* bouillabaisse was subtle – red snapper stock with young squid, chunks of conch, octopus, scallops, Bermuda onions, unpeeled garlic, orange rinds, saffron threads – all simmered and stirred with the perfect blend of parsley, thyme, fennel seeds, and hot Caribbean pepper! Who knew what other magic was in there besides the very virginal olive oil?

Brrrrrummmmmmmmmmmmmm!

His fingers fandango-ing under the table, Loring asked for and received a second scrumptious bowlful.

Tosco ate nothing, remained silent at the end of the long oak table in the cool and elegant dining room, while Loring relished his lunch.

"Super!" Loring patted his lips with his napkin. "Tosco, you're missing a masterpiece by your chef."

"Maurice knows I never take food before a demonstration. On the tour, I will show you our latest efforts. But if one were to take food, bouillabaisse would be ideal. Siberian tigers hate seasoned fish."

"May I ask how you know?"

"Look behind you. If Daria had wanted some, she would have asked you. You can be sure she smells it. She's all Siberian Amur, that girl."

Loring glanced back behind his shoulder through the dining room archway. In the foyer lay a huge sleeping mound of furry amber and black stripes – sprawled across the threshold they had entered not more than thirty minutes before.

"Daria?" Loring whispered, trying not to disturb her deep breaths.

"You needn't lower your voice. Don't worry. She's harmless. She's my favorite. Daria has the run of the manor house."

"But she's . . . "

"Two hundred and ten kilograms. That's . . ."

"I know. About four hundred and sixty pounds. And you say she's . . . harmless?"

"Isn't she beautiful?"

Loring blinked hard.

Tosco cleared his voice. "You look very uncomfortable, the way you did in the jeep back in San Juan."

"Ha-*ha!* I do?" Loring whispered.

"I thought we already went through all that about fear back there."

"We did."

"So why are you looking like that?"

"There is a huge Siberian tiger in the next room."

"I think you should look deeply into my eyes and listen to what I have to say. Do not fear Daria. If you wish, I can dismiss her with a clap of my hands."

"Would you mind doing that before I look into your eyes?"

Tosco raised his hands and clapped. *"Allez, Daria! Dehors!"*

Loring turned his head with a jerk in time to see Daria's long striped tail sway as she exited the front door. Through the dining room window, he watched her muscular, beautifully striped form bound fluidly over the grassy mounds and the garden beds of *Claridad's* front lawn.

Slowing her pace, she ambled in the sun beyond the yard and leaped ten feet up beyond a row of coconut palms to a perch on a stone building set off with its own gardened courtyard. For a moment she stopped on the perch to yawn in the bright heat and to lick the magnificent fur over her ribs. Silhouetted against the blue sky, her huge form looked golden.

Tosco gazed through the window at his darling. "And doesn't she move superbly?"

"She weighs four hundred and sixty pounds and she's fully house trained like a little tabby cat?"

"Comes and goes whenever she pleases. My colleague, Vladimir Vladimirovich Tulov, spirited all four of her grandparents out of Siberia. Right under the nose of the Soviets! Daria will be the star of our Paris show in the spring. And what a diva for my *Cirque Ineffable*! I can say without boasting, she is the most developed tiger ever to communicate intimately with humans."

"She communicates?"

"Well, yes. When we first arrived, she wanted to come over and snuggle with you. But I gave her a signal to stay at a distance. I thought if she showed too much affection, it might take you by surprise."

"Thanks for being careful with me."

"I'm sure you'll warm up to her, *Docteur*."

His fears not diminishing, Loring stared at Tosco.

The dwarf was transfixed on the magnificent form of the tiger against the sky. "It has been an honor to research a mind like hers. And you will see the results of our work."

"At the demonstration?"

"Yes, but first look into my eyes. I want to be certain you do follow everything I have to say."

Loring looked down at the reassuring glaze of the floor tiles under his feet. "May I say something first? Even a horrible confession?"

"Feel free to tell me anything."

"Well, this *is* a confession. And now that Daria is out of the house, I want to admit it here and now."

Tosco smiled. It was a broad, wonderful smile. "I can tell you're more relaxed now. That's good. And yes, say what you want and look into my eyes."

"Do big cats know things? Things that might have happened to their relatives?"

"All the cats I have known are very familial, if that's what you mean."

"I was afraid you'd say that. You see, long ago in medical school, I was forced to perform experiments on stray cats. I stuck needle electrodes into their brains right through their skulls and gave them electrical shocks."

"The cats were . . . "

"Old Boston alley cats that we turned into 'involuntary volunteers.' We did experiments on them and then sacrificed them in the name of medical science."

"You tortured them?"

"I'm reluctant to use that word."

"But *Docteur*, you were forced to do those experiments to earn your degree."

"That's how I see it. But how do you think Daria would look at it?"

"Surely you don't believe that the family *Felidae* – which includes all the true cats: lions, tigers, jaguars, pumas, panthers, cheetahs, wildcats, and common domestic cats – might hold vendettas against humans who may have been forced to do experiments on their very distant relatives?"

"But *watch*!" Loring stood up from the table, dangled his arms akimbo on either side, let his tongue hang out, and jiggled like a demented cat.

"What are you doing?"

"That's how that cat looked! Don't you understand? Some of those experiments got ugly, sadistic. One of the cats rocketed right off the laboratory counter. I still can see him hissing and limping and salivating all over the place with his electrode wires hanging down his back. We put him out of his misery with an axe from the fire closet."

"Do you have nightmares about it?"

"Well, sometimes. And with all your comments yesterday about a common link back to the Garden of Eden, I thought perhaps it might be possible that cats, too, have links."

"Sit down. Links?"

"Thank you. Yes, links."

"*Docteur*, as we say in the movement, none of us is ever going to find the Garden of Eden if we worry about past sins. Now look into my eyes."

* * *

Maggie McCarthy had advised Loring not to take things too seriously. Did that include a 460-pound Amur Siberian tiger? In the next room? House trained or not?

And how could *anybody* not take Tosco's eyes seriously? Especially when his brows arched and his dark pupils widened and he reminded Loring that he had 17 other free-ranging Amurs on the grounds of *Claridad*. And then he said, his warm voice quivering with conviction, "Tulov and I are convinced we have brought about the end of wild."

"The end of *wild*?" echoed Loring. "Are you serious? Wild versus tame?" Suddenly the dwarf's eyes squinted shut with mirth. His nose wrinkled as he laughed heartily. "Wild versus tame. Very funny."

"Did I say something foolish?"

"You did," Tosco continued to chuckle. "And I wouldn't be at all embarrassed if you laughed at yourself."

"Ha-ha-*ha*! You know, for a moment there, I was worried you would try to hypnotize me."

Tosco's laughter subsided. "You're a physician. You know that hypnotism is a demeaning, uncontrollable art. Besides, it's superficial. Tulov and I dig far deeper into the mind."

"Of man and beast, eh?"

"Come with me," Tosco urged.

The dwarf slid down from his chair and ushered Loring into a large and intricately organized library beside the dining room. The walls were covered with ancient maps of central Asia and glass-fronted shelves filled with decrepit books, scrolls, and manuscripts, some apparently from the middle ages or

146

before, some specifically on alchemy and chanting and circus, all in sealed, locked, temperature-controlled display cabinets.

For a moment Loring was lost in contemplating the effort which must have gone into amassing such an arcane assemblage of occult material. His eyes perused the vast collection of volumes in over a dozen languages – Latin, Greek, Russian, Arabic, Sanskrit and Chinese, several of Gurdjieff's works in the original Russian.

But Tosco didn't want to talk about his books.

"TULOV!" he announced with a shout and pointed above the library fireplace to the full-length oil portrait of a tall, gray-bearded man captured in partial profile with his left hand on his hip – slender, angular of frame, dressed in a black Cossack tunic with silver buttons down the left shoulder and a black silk sash at the waist.

The eyes were large, brown. They squinted gently. The lips were thin and firmly set. The hands were large, the fingers long and graceful. The jodhpurs were maize, the high boots black with silver buckles.

"Certainly looks Russian enough. Those high Slavic cheeks? Those sharp, slanted eyebrows? Very confident in his spirituality, isn't he? That's so Russian. Or did the portraitist lie?"

"Bravo, *Docteur*! But tell me what's missing! From the greatest big cat trainer in the history of world circus?"

"He seems complete."

"That's all you have to say?" Tosco's eyes were now dark, meditative, suddenly almost tearful. "Please look deeper. Does this man look like a radical to you? Does he look insane? Tell me frankly."

"By no means."

"And yet many consider Tulov a fire brand fanatic, a true lunatic!"

"Him?"

"Yes. A wicked troublemaker in the order of the world. Of course, he has developed a strange blend of technological advances in his contraptions, which were never accepted in the circus community. But that was his context and his tradition of coming from the old Soviet Union, don't you see? And our circus has had the financial blessings of my family estate's fortunes. So we have been able to support Tulov and all his creations. You see, he started out as a metallurgist and a sculptor, then he . . ."

"I'm sorry," Loring said. "But before you say another word, I'd just like to thank you for all of this. The bouillabaisse was great, too."

"Thank you. Maurice will be very pleased that you liked it."

"Will you let me treat you to lunch in the *Officers' Mess* sometime? I feel obliged to repay the favor. Every Thursday at lunch, our chef works miracles with flying fish."

"Sounds interesting. And I'm happy that you're pleased."

"I am very pleased. Honestly, I am."

"Good. But don't you understand, Tulov was a genius in metallurgical engineering long before he even thought of going into big cats! And forty years ago, the Soviet circus felt that steel – large amounts of steel sculpture, the more the better – was visible proof of the molding of hard science and art. And I refuse to disallow those innovations, merely because of political shifts in the world! Tulov may have defected from the Soviet circus, but he has never deviated for an instant from his pure original vision."

Loring looked up and searched the face in the portrait. "Perhaps Tulov's courage is not understood."

"Courage?" Tosco snapped. "Tulov is committed, that's all. His courage is only a sign of his commitment."

"But you said something's missing. From the portrait."

Tosco's voice became loud and almost gruff. "Do you see a revolver in his hand? Do you see a whip or a chair held up against a ferocious animal? Do you see a cage? Do you see human domination over another species?"

"There's no tiger in that picture."

"Look at me. Look at my personal life. You see *Claridad*! For over 30 years, I have lived every single moment with the dedication of a religious monk, traveled to Asia to speak with Sufi seers, Indian gurus, Nepalese monks, Japanese priests. I picked and trained my animals with Tulov, developed the environment here at *Claridad*. We have three big cat veterinarians in residence, a sheep and goat farm down the road, because tigers must eat meat. Do you hear me?"

Loring tried to grin. "I hear nothing but what you say!"

"That's good," Tosco said, brushing his hand across his small belly, as if to press away an internal pang. "Yet I am forced to act here in secret, as if I commit a crime. I have never married, though I am not a stranger to romance. No, apart from the considerations which a person with my genetic condition must face before raising a family, I have devoted my heart and soul, and not a small portion of my family's wealth, to the achievement of our cult's goal."

"Your goal?"

"Not apparent?" Tosco sighed. "And you, *Docteur*, are so sensitive."

"Well, thank you."

148

Tosco's dark eyes flashed at the portrait of Tulov. The dwarf let out a loud scream of frustration there in the library.

"*EOOOOOOOOOUUUUGH!* So you *see*, Vladimir Vladimirovich! Even the most perceptive of our potential disciples is doubtful. He's bright. He's a dancer and a physician. He throws darts with precision. Yet he wishes to be *told* our goals. But *we* are certain, aren't we? We are absolutely clear on our path. And never will I doubt the vision of your transcendent gyroscope. Trust me, Vladimir! And I am certain, too, that Daria and the other tigers are *one* with us!"

Loring stood there, his eyes jumping back and forth between Tosco and the Russian, who peered back down from the canvas but did not speak. Tosco pinched the bridge of his nose with the tips of his thumb and forefinger and closed his hands in a hunched-up posture. Then he straightened and turned to Loring. "You have heard enough words."

"What's a transcendent gyroscope?"

"Come, *Docteur*. I know I ignored you briefly. You will soon see what Tulov's gyroscope is."

"And Tulov? Is he here? At *Claridad*?"

"No. Tulov is in Paris, and he's not well. He had a stroke last year and has difficulty walking. He had hoped he could make it for our performance this week on the ship, but that seems unlikely. I spoke to him this morning, and he may fly in at the last minute."

"I hope he does. I'd like to meet him in person."

"So come to Paris in the spring for the premier of *Cirque Ineffable*. But today you will meet his art."

* * *

From the outside, it appeared tall and drab: a windowless, octagonal, granite block structure, defiantly austere with a slanted slate roof and cathedral-sized iron doors fixed on a central facade.

But the interiors were draped in soft purple velvet with gold leaf etched into each of the three concentric wooden balconies. An elaborate crystal chandelier glowed over the central performing area. The theatre was, Tosco promised, an exact functioning prototype, here in the Caribbean, of the new *Cirque Ineffable* in Paris.

He had imported everything in replica to fit the Parisian theatre. The large circular, sawdust-covered performance space was recessed twenty feet below the first row of seats, and a deep drop-off trench at the perimeter gave a reassuring impression that the cats were performing at a safe distance from the audience – no cage bars to impede the eye's vision of every detail.

Loring sat alone in the middle of the front row.

Of the seven tigers in the show, Daria clearly had the best moves. The knowing head bob when Tosco dipped his forefinger at her – as a testament to their intimacy. And such a regal head to be bobbed in obedience! And that brandy tinge to her huge, brown-red eyes, every time she looked at Tosco? And they seemed so drowsy, lazy-pupiled and distracted by her inner feelings. Above the thick furry nose – so lumpy, almost bony, and with that pink triangular bulge around the nostrils! Perhaps Loring was cheating, to sit there in the front row and observe her so closely.

Was it not unfair? To Daria? Or to Loring? So *this* was the end of wild?

But why should those eyes not seem delicate behind a snout with the color and texture of a Vermont summer caterpillar and the long white whiskers threading so straight and yet beading back upon themselves, crisscross sometimes, almost despite themselves! And there was a pepper pattern in the white fur above the mouth, enhanced when her pink tongue jumped up and down, out of her mouth. The stripes on her face were nothing like the body stripes – white and orange and black and concentrically designed totally to camouflage the eyes and the ears. And the furry white beard cast its way down in a feminine whimsy onto her massive shoulders. Loring wanted to ask Tosco: was she really a tiger?

* * *

"So you touched my finest. And you care for her, don't you?"

"Daria is exquisite."

Several hours later, Loring sat in the passenger seat of Tosco's jeep and still wished to touch Daria, stroke her fur, massage her neck, feel her body heat close to his chest. The reticulated python in his lap simply could not compare to Daria.

"I think she cares for you, too. She's never had a dance partner so accomplished. Before his stroke, Vladimir Tulov could waltz, but not like you."

"Tulov must be an incredible human being," Loring said as the jeep flew along a high cliff road overlooking the sea. "And you are, too, Tosco. I am so grateful for this afternoon. It seems unbelievable to me, almost like a dream.

Now I can see why you have devoted your life to this project."

"I was hoping you would say that, *Docteur*. Would you enjoy another panatella on the ride back?"

As they cruised along the bumpy coastal highway toward San Juan, Loring puffed his cigar silently and watched Tosco's profile at the wheel against the background of the sea.

Brrrruuuuuuum! Ta-ta trummmmmmmmmm!

How he admired Ramon Fernandez Garcia Jesus Tosco-Gutierez!

Perhaps Tosco was a dwarf by birth, but he was a titan by achievement.

No, Loring had not done a fandango nor a mambo with Daria this afternoon. The waltz had sufficed – the waltz with a 460-pound Siberian Amur to Tchaikovsky's *Vagabonde* in A minor.

The speeding jeep jostled the bones up and down Loring's spine as pyrotechnical flashbacks of his hours with Tosco at *Claridad* detonated in his brain. True, there had been a few trying moments. Loring had been, perhaps, a bit too insistent on some of those underarm twinkle turns with Daria. The gorgeous feline was not familiar with the step, and her claws had dug into him when she was out of breath and he spun her a bit too fast.

But who was Oliver Loring to complain about an aspiring novice's deficiencies in technique? Or about her nails!

Even though they were dancing on four inches of sawdust, they must have cut quite an impressive figure together in that waltz. At six feet four, Loring was almost exactly Daria's length, and her front paws fit perfectly in his hand and on his shoulder. Despite the shortness of her powerful rear haunches and the faint sweet stench of raw goat meat on her lips, she was an ideal and exotic partner! Such incredible feline coordination!

Olivia and her entire dancing academy in Vermont would have been spellbound! 3/4 time held sway perfectly for Daria, even through all of Tchaikovsky's tricky Slavonic syncopations! The wagging of her tail looked, felt elegant from where Loring viewed it.

The six tigers who had performed with Tosco were not merely obedient – or "tame" as Loring might have said before he entered the theatre at *Claridad*. They not only did "tricks." They *personalized* their gestures in a way which stretched Loring's capacity to believe his own eyes. They communicated deeply – but not at all by merely mimicking human actions.

At times it seemed, rather, that Tosco was being directed by them, ordered to betray in his hands and face a sense of their their unity, their glory together! They moved in bewitching patterns to Tosco's musical voice, their stripes cascading, coat upon splendid, rippling coat, as if entire emotional landscapes were spread out and pulsing before Loring's eyes. Often at their own will! Not at Tosco's will! The spectacle was a visual river flowing of its own force in time and space, toward an ocean of delicate yet powerful emotions to touch, yes, the cosmic.

Loring sat there in the first row wondering: Is this circus? Vaudeville? Madness? Hallucination? A religion?

And when his mind stopped questioning, answers poured in. Deeper than his mind! He could not interpret whether the tigers had performed comedic sketches, dance scenarios, or slap-stick gags, although all of those cabaret conventions were included in their work.

All during the performance, a huge and onerous-appearing sculpted steel structure loomed in the darkness behind the cavorting tigers. It was an immense, chrome-plated winding tube which, supported by scaffolds, cork screwed down and around in five concentric gyres.

The bizarre tornado-shaped apparatus, beautiful yet threatening, looked like something conjured from an ancient alchemist's laboratory. At least 50 feet high and 30 feet wide at its circled top, the long chrome tube had a groove all along its surface and traversed the narrowing spirals, until it ended in a blunt-tipped drop off point at dead center, 20 feet above the stage.

On a platform high up and off to the right, where the top gyre began, perched a giant metal gyroscope with hoops about eight feet in diameter and a shimmering, see-through metallic outer shell. An inner spoked disk – it resembled a platter with fluted openings – defined the center horizontal plane. At its top pole the gyroscope hung from a sturdy ceiling chain. At the bottom it balanced on a round knuckle that nudged into the groove at the spiraling tube's summit.

Immersed in the tigers' performance, Loring had not scrutinized the steel tornado and its spherical cage in the background until both rolled forward into the spotlights on hidden wheels under the sawdust. At that moment, it corrupted the peace he had seen on stage and took on a gallows-like appearance. Abstract? Utilitarian? Early Russian Constructivist art movement?

What was so "transcendental" about Tulov's gyroscope with its crazy spinning tornado track? Loring had never seen anything like it in any museum, sculpture park, or absurd science fiction film.

A huge kettle drum was brought to the side of the stage, and Tosco picked up the mallets. He began pounding, slowly at first. The spotlight pinpointed him then shifted to Daria – her orange and black body lustrous and muscular in the light, as she ascended on a hydraulic-powered platform to the gyroscope.

Tosco's drum silenced as the spotlight caught the phosphorescent gold deep in Daria's agate eyes. She spread her front and back paws, while an attendant clamped her into place with thick velcro straps on the round central platter of the gyroscope. With a sweeping shoulder motion, the attendant began her spinning slowly on the equatorial plane. Daria lay face down as she spun three times in the huge gyroscope. Then the man stopped her, stooped over to pat her affectionately, released the ceiling chain and thrust the rim again into a spin with vigorous torque.

Suddenly a deep humming noise was heard as Daria spun faster and faster and her stripes began to roll on a central axis. An unearthly whistle could be heard – the sound of the churning device as it sliced through the air and sang through its fluted metal openings.

Tosco's drumbeat started up again and reverberated more rapidly, and he began to sing a bizarre melody at high volume. The tiger increased her velocity and descended round-and-round, through the concentric spirals, along the tortuous circular steel track. Daria became a spinning amber blur in the spotlight, attended by ominous moaning.

The tiger seemed to be in total free-fall, spinning on the rail, and Loring felt that he was falling right with her. With the house lights black, suddenly in the middle of the stage, a brilliant, seven-foot flame erupted with a roar. From the midst of the huge flame, a blazing, red-hot spike arose.

Tosco's drum swept into a crescendo, the moaning sharpened its pitch, and before Loring could shriek out loud, the gyroscope descended the final loop to the very end and, with horrifying accuracy, dropped onto the red-hot spike. When an agonizing tigerish groan rose from the fire, Loring felt the urge to hurl himself right down onto the stage to assist.

But the lights brightened. The circular rack where Daria had been skewered and fried was righted. A wet cooling cloak fell over it. With steam rising from the bonfire, Daria pranced out from behind the cloak, amidst the smoke and vapor.

Astonishing! Her striped coat was not singed in the slightest. From where Loring sat, every one of Daria's long white whiskers looked perfectly intact.

As Loring clapped in disbelief, Tosco stepped forward on the stage. "Would you like to understand a bit about our work, *Docteur*? Come down here."

"You want me to . . . ?"

"Yes, look just to your left. There's a rope ladder which you can toss out into the arena and climb down."

Loring found the ladder, threw it out into the ring, and then stepped slowly down and invited Daria to waltz the *Vagabonde*.

* * *

"You're thinking about Daria's descent, aren't you?" Tosco said as the jeep entered the outskirts of San Juan.

"Tosco, you're so very confident in your magic."

"Were you dizzy?"

"Maybe for an instant, when I identified with her."

"Do you agree the effect is marvelous? Tulov is incredible, no?"

"I never heard a tiger roar in agony before, but is that really part of your quest to reclaim Eden? When the bonfire erupts in the middle of the stage? When the blazing spike rises in the center? When the steel point cuts through the middle of the spine? I felt that crunching noise in my own backbone."

"You don't think there is passion in Eden?"

"But the spike is violent!"

"It is the fire and agony of passion."

"Daria roared in pain."

"And then she jumped off the spike in full health and beauty. *That* is the passion of Eden."

* * *

Oliver Loring stood by the aft *Olympic Deck* rail overlooking *Leif Erikson Deck*.

In a white bathing cap, Ulla von Straf's head twisted back and forth as her arms stretched lazily and her legs kicked in the *Thor Heyerdahl Pool*. There were no passengers nearby. She had it all to herself in the late afternoon sun – her lean body floated horizontal on the quivering blue surface. Loring focused on the white creases behind her tanned knees, imagined his lips there, followed the firm muscles of her thighs as they moved in their narrowing and delicious rhythm.

Loring wanted to dance tonight in San Juan at *El Tiburon Baillador*.

Talk to her, idiot! The worst she can say is no.

He had vowed to be less shy. If he could dance with a tiger, why couldn't he dance with Ulla von Straf?

In the sunlight as she dipped and splashed playfully in the pool, Ulla seemed all the metaphysics, and all the Eden, Oliver Loring would need. Ever.

"*Oliver!* Turn around! What *happened* to the skin on your back?" she called up to him. "*Look!* Those marks over your shoulder blades!"

"Waltzing this afternoon."

"Waltzing?"

"With a tiger."

"No wonder! You've been scratched! Do you need a doctor?" she laughed and dived down, squirmed against the bottom of the pool.

Loring reached back and touched the skin below his shoulders. He felt welts just beneath his shoulder. He grabbed a beach towel and covered the tell-tale wounds. Daria had left her mark on him, alright. There could be no denying those long welts, nor what had caused them! Yes, he needed to dance with a human tonight – *that* human.

Desperately!

He lost himself in the watery distortions of Ulla's image as she wiggled under the water, her legs and arms split apart in oblique, capricious reflections. It seemed at times as if her entire image could disintegrate and disappear. His mind flipped back to when he watched the tigers unfurl their cascading stripes into his mind. He was relieved when he saw her rise and splash through the surface. She smiled. A delightfully human smile.

Desperately! I want to dance desperately with her!

"And what else did you do today?"

"Isn't that enough?"

"You didn't waltz with *me*."

Ulla pulled herself up over the edge of the pool and leaned to pick up a towel from her deck chair. Her ladybug and the pale round leaf it rested on could not have looked more luscious. And with her hair hidden under the bathing cap, the stark, sculpted beauty of her face seemed even more powerful. "How was it with Tosco today? He had me there for lunch last week."

"*Claridad? Bouillabaisse?*"

She patted her forehead and pulled the towel around her shoulders. "Three bowls."

She *did* know, Loring thought as Ulla's huge blue eyes rolled up his chest and onto his face. He wondered how much else she knew.

"So let's dance this evening. Away from the ship."

"You're serious?"

"Are *you*? I have the evening off till eleven. Or will you only be satisfied with tigers now?" She winked.

"How about a mambo. I know just the place in Old San Juan."

"Shall we meet there at eight?"

"*El Tiburon Baillador*. It's a special little club hidden away at the end of the *Calle de Garcia Rey*."

"I'll find it. And Oliver, don't worry. I don't scratch."

* * *

Fax Received: Radio Station, S/S Nordic Blue
TUES/FEB 12 – 11.00 h. Dispatched 17.00h, Doctor's Cabin, Viking Deck

To: Dr. Oliver Loring, Chief Medical Officer
From: Nordic Star Lines, Oslo, Office of the Chief Executive

Dear Dr. Loring:

This morning I received a call from Mrs. Hildegarde Snippet-White, one of my most beloved friends. She told me of Colonel Rockwell Snippet-White's tragic death. She also told me that you, the Chief Medical Officer, comforted her throughout the night of her grieving in a manner which was dignified, compassionate, and in keeping with the most noble traditions of your profession. Hildegarde says you are perhaps the best doctor ever on our fleet.

I look forward to meeting you when I come aboard the Nordic Blue for the Cablevista Valentine TV Cruise and for the late Colonel's burial-at-sea. (My nephew Trygve Storjord, an emergency physician in Oslo, will be flying to San Juan with me today, and he is also anxious to meet you.)

As a token of my appreciation for what you did two nights ago for Hildegarde, I have e-mailed our office in Miami to dispatch you coupons for two (2) tickets for you and the guest of your choice for a one-week cruise at the time of your choice in the very most luxuriously-appointed suite on any of our fleet's ships. You may pick up the coupons this Saturday in Miami and use them whenever you wish.

Again, thank you. I present also a bouquet of 24 blush ("Imperial Fiat" is my favorite variety) roses, which shall be delivered to your cabin.

Gratefully,

Stig Storjord, Founder and Chief Executive Officer
Nordic Star Lines

cc: Captain Ramskog, Mrs. Snippet-White, Fritz the Florist

* * *

Bruuuuummmmmmmmmmmmmmmmmm!

Loring's patent leather pumps clicked briskly across the *Plaza de la Fontana*, echoed down ancient stone corridors, claimed the streets of Old San Juan as *his* streets.

Say they ain't, hombre!

He was wearing Colonel Rockwell Snippet-White's shark skin dress uniform, with gold buttons and medaled silk sash. In his hand he held a long-stem Imperial Fiat, a yellow bud with red blushes at the point of each petal. At the corner of *Calle de Colon* he banged a left and hastened his pace.

Destination: *El Tiburon Baillador.*

He sniffed the bud, stuck the stem in his mouth, threw his head back.

Ta-trummmmmmmmmmmmmmmmmmmm!

Why should Loring's heels not ring wildly on the old stones? Look how marvelously he was attired! And the Austrian ballerina had promised to meet him at eight at *El Tiburon Baillador,* the most romantic rendezvous spot in all of venerable Old San Juan.

Loring had discovered *El Tiburon* Baillador by chance on his first cruise and had visited regularly ever since. By now he was on first names with old Josè Lopez, the bespectacled, pot-bellied accountant and owner, and with all of *Señor* Lopez's upbeat wait staff.

The quaint grotto had candle-lit tables, an intimate dance floor, and the best latin combos in town. *El Tiburon* catered only to San Juan aficionados who took their Tuesday evening salsa seriously.

This Tuesday evening, that would include *Señor* Loring!

Would Ulla recognize him in the smoky, step-down grotto? Had Hildegarde informed her he would wear shark skin tonight? How could he know what

Hildegarde had told Ulla? But he could not refuse Hildegarde's request to wear the Colonel's uniform, especially not after Stig Storjord had sent two dozen Imperial Fiats and offered Loring a cruise.

Old Storjord had a reputation for being generous with crew. But Loring never could have expected flowers *plus* a promise of a deluxe suite for a week on any ship in the fleet! Loring might someday want to use those coupons, but with no uniform or rank, he wondered what he would *do* on an ocean liner. As a mere power cruiser?

He pulled the rose from his teeth, sped on his way. He'd better hurry. Those local *caballeros* in *El Tiburon Baillador* would surely swoop down on Ulla faster than famished barracudas after a tender tuna.

He felt his heart somersaulting ahead of him down the street. He was on his way to be alone *off the ship* with Ulla, if only for several hours. He would not only salsa with her. They might step to a quiet corner table and sit by candlelight and talk – Tosco, tigers, or the sadness in her eyes. He would not be shy about anything!

* * *

As on every previous cruise, Loring turned the corner onto *Calle de Garcia-Rey* and looked two blocks down the familiar old cobble stoned cul-de-sac. At the end of the street he expected to see the dim light bulb and the quaint sign he cherished (carved and painted by José Lopez himself) that read *"El Tiburon Baillador"* – with a corny sketch of a wild-eyed and toothy shark shaking a pair of red maracas with his fins.

But no.

Tonight Loring's eyes burned from the brightness and the change. At the end of *Calle de Garcia-Rey*, a giant orange pair of green-dotted neon dice seemed to float down from the sky onto the roof with a winning 7! A huge blinking sign in orange and green letters blazed: *"TIBURON JUGADOR! TIBURON JUGADOR!"*

Taxis lined up along the two-block length of *Calle de Garcia-Rey*. Fake palms garnished the doorway. Concussive rap music pounded out into the street. Tourists, some of them *Nordic Blue* power cruisers, spilled out and charged into the new, brightly-lit casino, now named *TIBURON JUGADOR*.

Loring stepped forward slowly. When he heard the electric buzz and tinkle of video slots beyond the street palms, his heart jumped into his throat.

Señor Lopez had retired and sold out to developers. Obvious scenario.

Since Loring's last cruise, the *Dancing Shark* had converted to the *Gambling Shark*. No smoky grotto. No intimate dance floor.

No way, José!

Way, hombre!

The *Tiburon* had switched from vintage dance club to gaudy, state-of-the-vice gambling palace. Simple and cruel as that.

But seriously! How could jovial old *Señor* Lopez abandon his loyal patrons and wait staff? Turn them all out on the street for an offer of . . .

"Oliver!"

Loring froze. In the rude glare of the new *Jugador*, his sashed uniform, his rose, and his patent leather pumps – not to mention the hope in his heart – seemed ridiculous. But *there* she was, standing alone and waiting for him and calling his name!

"Ha-*ha!*" He rushed to Ulla. "How did you recognize me?"

Her shoulders fidgeted in a low-cut, clinging black shift. For an ecstatic instant, he embraced her.

She did not kiss him hello. Her eyes, amused, roved over the badges, medals, and the sash. Then the crystal blues clouded over. "What's all this?"

"Hildegarde asked me to wear it."

"Oh, yes. And you look most distinguished."

"And you? *You? You* look *absolutely* wonderful. You see, I'm trying not to be shy, am I?"

Ulla paused, then her eyes darkened. "Yes, but I'm sorry. We cannot dance tonight."

"Not here, of course. Another place. It's a magical night. *Tiburon* used to be fabulous. I'm surprised you found it. I had planned to introduce you to Josè Lopez. He used to be the owner."

She broke from his embrace, shook his hand tightly. "I cannot. Not tonight."

Loring tried to prevent the confusion in Ulla's eyes from infecting him. "Well, not here."

"Nowhere."

"Can't we have a little chit-chat? Somewhere else? Can't we just go in and sip coffee at the bar? I'll make sure you get back to the ship in time for your rehearsal. Look, this rose is for you."

Ulla bit her lower lip. She took the bud, closed her eyes, touched her nose to the petals.

Loring felt his jaw clench. "Flip's in the casino?"

She looked up. "He met Farrely Farrell at the airport and brought him onto the ship. Then he told me he was going out to gamble. I thought he would never see us here, Oliver. You said this was a dance club."

"I didn't know it had changed. You said you wanted to dance with me, and now you're with him."

"When I was looking for you, he saw me. Flip's in trouble, Oliver."

"Losing again? Like in St. Maarten? I saw him there."

"Worse than losing. And at a very bad time."

"You don't have a moment for me? But you were all smiles earlier at the pool. You flirted with me. I vowed to be less shy. You promised we would meet and dance."

Her brows winced. "I'll see you on the ship."

"When? We only have a few days left!"

"You're sweet, Oliver. But I have an obligation to Flip. He's been kind. He needs me. Someday you'll understand."

"Someday? What does someday mean? When is someday?"

Loring looked down as Ulla rolled the stem of the Imperial Fiat bud in her fingers. The red tips of the tender yellow petals revolved, stopped to change directions, spun again.

It may have been coincidence, the exact speed and rhythm of her anxious twirling of the rose. As Loring stared into the Imperial Fiat in the flashing neon, the bud's yellow color dulled to amber, the red streaks at the petal tips to black. He had seen that undulating flow earlier at *Claridad* in the form of tigers spiraling in a multi-linear rosette at center stage.

How could she coax out of that flower the essence of tigers?

But she was *doing* it! They were there! *Inside! They danced.*

Their luxurious coats scintillated. Their tails twirled round and round. Their amber and black coats, a rotating arabesque, evoked the truest impulse toward another human Loring had ever felt.

"I like the way you twirl that rose." He looked in Ulla's eyes for a reply, but she was too immersed in the petals to respond.

"I can't help myself. I love you," she said.

Then she kissed his cheek, handed him back the rose. He watched her lower her chin and step into the casino.

* * *

On his way back to the ship, Loring ripped the Imperial Fiat apart, petal by petal. He let the fluttering remains trail behind him on the cobblestones.

160

He did not recite "she loves me/not."

He knew the answer, despite Ulla's paradoxical words of rejection as she walked back into the casino to gamble with Spinelli.

I can't believe it. She just handed me back the rose and disappeared! What does Spinelli mean to her? The man is addicted. Does she need someone with a vice? I could invent a vice for myself. Something non-oral.

But not tonight. Tonight I miss her too much.

By the time he reached the pier, the rose was fully vivisected. He threw the long stem onto the stones and ground the core of the bud into wet pulp with his heel.

Several halting paces later, his heart shrank with remorse. He gazed back at the slimy remains of the Imperial Fiat on the stones. He shut his eyes, put his right hand to his front hip, draped his left into hers, murmured a two-bar intro. (But he *had* to dance with Ulla tonight. How about a rumba?)

"Soooh-saah! Deedee ramadoo saa. Deedeee ramadoo saaa!"

Two wriggling hands gripped Loring's shoulders, held on, and a teasing nasal voice hissed in his ear. *"DOCTEUR! YOU NEVER KNOW UNTIL YOU KNOW!"*

Loring's eyes snapped open to a diamond-clad smile.

"Jacques!"

"Oui! C'est moi!"

"Bonsoir, mon ami!"

The Haitian dandy was on a break, in his galley whites – chef's toque and apron, steel thermometer in his breast pocket – and strolling on the dock.

"Lordy! I thought I saw a young Colonel Snippet-White alive again and doing a samba down the pier!"

"It's a rumba. "

"Garçon! Why would you be doin' a rumba by yourself? On a night like this out here in romantic San Juan? Did you not stay away from the ballerina who gives you the fever? Didn't I warn you about her? Eh?"

Loring shrugged. "Call me a fool!"

"Eh! Didn't I see some of these medals yesterday in a coffin? And with the red silk sash?"

"You did, Jacques. And your death bust of the Colonel absolutely overwhelmed me. You are an amazing artist."

Chemin released his grip, stepped back. "And you are not an artist? Such passionate footwork! Even when you are losing tears from your eyes, a power inspires you."

"Yes, but it's a fool's fever."

"But I have fever to match yours!"

"Pearly told me. From the jewelry shop?"

The Haitian lit a Marlboro and exhaled a wide stream of smoke. "Yes, the wonderful Fatima! In Paris I knew *all* the beautiful and snobbish West African ladies. Oh, yes. But this Fatima ignores me so rudely. I have never seen one so brutal! And she is chubby, too. I must admit, I prefer women who have full size to them."

"And you are in love with all of her? Including the brutality?"

"*Coup de foudre, Docteur.*" Chemin's thumb zig-zagged in the air and dug into his smooth black temple. "I spend every night thinking. All while my pastry oven is baking, all while I cut my ice statues, I think of her. But does she give me the time of day? When I pass by her shop, does she do more than lift her nose and spread her pretty nostrils at me? Do you think she thinks of me while she sells her jewelry? You see, to her, I am a common Jacques."

"Jacques, you are far from common."

Chemin shook his head. "And what is she doing here in the Caribbean? She should be in Paris where she belongs!"

"With you?"

The Haitian smiled and rolled his eyes, "Yes, and where do I belong? With Fatima. And with my own restaurant. I would love to fatten her up more than she is with my pastries. It is my dream. I would say to her, '*Mon Chéri*, the more I bake my cakes for you, and the more of you enjoy them, the more of you I will have to make love to.' *N'est-ce pas, Docteur?*"

"*Mais oui!*"

Chemin puffed busily on his cigarette. They strode together toward the crowded *Crew Gangway* and passed through the Cablevista personnel, security crew, and equipment. Loring had never felt the suave hustler so tender – strangely mute and with his shoulders slumped.

Near the ship's prow, two pairs of rotating klieg lights – publicity beacons for Farrely Farrell's arrival on the ship – revolved on the dock. The huge lenses shot shafts of light all about the sky. Their beams whipped over the ship's hull and onto the San Juan skyline and then up again into the black sky, where the Cablevista blimp scrolled its red letters: *"WELCOME CABLEVISTA FANS! LET FARRELY MAKE YOU LUCKY IN LOVE!"*

Loring realized that Jacques Chemin, the slick romantic savant, was oblivious to all of it – the equipment, the ship, the city, the red message in the heavens. He clutched Loring's forearm. "Look at me! I did not sleep not a wink last night!"

"But why? I thought you are an expert in such matters. Remember your advice to me about the fever?"

"Do not use Jacques' own words to mock him. Fatima excites me with a smile then frowns and pitches me down. Oh, yes! And though she is young with fresh baby fat . . . but she is still so French and so very African. I would like to do something extravagant for her. Maybe for Valentine's day, you know."

"Don't get desperate, *mon ami!*"

Chemin flicked away his cigarette casually, though his eyes were in pain. "So now you give me advice about matters of the heart? If I do get desperate, you and everyone will know about it. But will my Fatima know or care?"

"She will."

"You think so? But you don't even know her." Chemin smoothed down his apron and straightened his spine. "I hope you are right." He nodded and resumed his trademark swagger up the gangway.

Loring paused on the dock and stared. A hot beam from the swooping klieg beacons struck him in both eyes and stunned his retinas with pain. He staggered, brought his fingers to his eyes and shuddered, shook his head.

Soon the deep ache faded, and he felt oddly relieved to be shedding tears from pain, rather than from self pity about Ulla. He waited for objects to take shape – the high, cliff-like hull of the ship, the circling blimp, the trucks on the dock, the power cruisers in black tie on their way up the ramp, heading for the *Midnight Promenade.*

He regretted his willingness to pin his hopes on the smiles and odd moods of a ballerina who feigned intimacy on the dance floor.

And where is she now? With Spinelli at the roulette table!

As a dozen decks of the *Nordic Blue* loomed above him, Loring knew he was hardly unique. He peered up at the rows of portholes and wondered how many others aboard suffered from the fragility of their hearts. Was the whole cruise this week – the so-called *"Valentine TV Cruise "* – not a silly testament to the generalized folly of the whole ship and the whole world?

But Farrely Farrell, originator of "Love Luck," was certainly one creature who had the good sense to appraise the pitiful weakness of the human race and capitalize on it. In the name of "reality" television. Though Loring resented Farrely Farrell for taking advantage of tens of millions of gullible souls, he had to admit that the "Love Luck" formula was effective.

Suffering from a broken heart? Tell Farrely all about it, and he'll give you the keys to a Mercedes-Benz and 250,000 dollars cash. Then the whole world will watch and envy you as you drive off in emotional and automotive luxury. ("Love Luck" paid for five years of insurance, maintenance and gasoline. *"After that, Mate, you're on your own!"*)

The reality TV catch: during the 30-minute interview, the contestant was required to stare straight forward, point-blank at the camera, eyes never shifting, while Farrely Farrell (unseen during the entire interview) probed and cajoled and ripped layers off the individual's deeper psychic barriers. Part father confessor, part Freudian analyst and velvet-throat media deity, Farrell teased his contestants – whether street-wise New York cabbies or demure Illinois housewives or trailer park owners or stuffy Ivy League professors or carnival roustabouts – into a frenzy of shame and lurid revelations.

If the exhausted contestant turned away from the camera or begged Farrely to stop his prods, the interview ceased and the all-expenses-paid Mercedes (and the $250K) was lost. But that almost never happened.

And the drama was cruel but strangely exhilarating. Routinely, some members of the studio audience sobbed along with the contestant, which heightened the effect on the screen. Once Farrely Farrell had mangled the poor interviewee into submission, carved him/her into a state of emotional evisceration, teased every tender nerve in their near-agonal emotional carcass to submission like a pinioned lab rat, then he said delicately, "Okay, Mate! You've told your story. Now let me make you *LUCKY IN LOVE!*"

The audience would break into a laughter of joyous relief and applaud. Across America and everywhere else on the Cablevista planet, viewers rejoiced at Farrely's expert creation then release of shared tension. The catharsis was national, world-wide.

The car keys appeared close-up on Farrely Farrell's finger, jingled on their gold chain like the bells at a mass at the moment of transubstantiation. With a touch of the "winner's" forefinger, the keys slid down from Farrely (Sistine Chapel vision rip-off, anyone?) and fused into the new owner's magically morphed identity.

Loring often wondered why "Love Luck" contestants were so willing to spill the details about their torment. But what amazed him more was that, after the confession, they seemed genuinely better! *The whole country felt better!* And on a marvelous and peculiar level, Loring wondered if the entire concept might not be clinically *sound*!

Could a new Mercedes Benz (with five years of insurance, maintenance, and gasoline) and a sizable chunk of change actually cure depression? Better than, say Prozac, or Zoloft or Celexa or old-fashioned electroconvulsive (ECT) therapy? Had Farrely Farrell (who apparently had no formal degree in the psychological sciences) stumbled onto something valid in the greater clinical arena of the popular imagination and psyche?

Should results-oriented therapists look outside their usual clinical boxes for new modes of non-psychotropic, non-electrical intervention?

Stop it!

Loring knew for a fact that, even in the Boston medical community, many Mercedes owners (hard working surgeons, gastroenterologists, psychiatrists, radiologists) were depressed, and often found themselves not so very lucky in love. What salutary effect could still another Mercedes-Benz or another $250K offer such individuals?

Charlatan or not, Farrely Farrell was making "reality" television history every week. Nobody could deny his stupendous ratings. The critics said his interviews were cutting edge science/entertainment classics, though Loring saw precedent for them in the well-attended public executions of the French Revolution and its aftermath.

Spin-off discussion programs – with talking heads bickering over the exact psychodynamics of what the world had just witnessed – followed the show, often punctuated by poignant snippet replays of the interviews. "Love Luck" had become a national preoccupation, and some of the interviewees had become, in fact, celebrities in their own right – with invitations to TV talk shows, product endorsements, even high advance tell-all book publishing offers.

It seemed everyone wanted to get on the publicity and cash bandwagon of 'Love Luck," including, alas, Nordic Star Lines.

Of course, nobody ever faintly suggested that "Love Luck" had anything to do with love. Though most of his contestants used the word "love" at the start, invariably Farrely Farrell hammered hard on the same negative themes: duplicity, betrayal, divorce, abandonment, abuse, treachery, victimization, addiction and fetishism – all the crowd grabbers.

These will earn you the keys to your new roadster, Mate. Tell me about about them!

His eyes recovered now from the klieg light flash, Loring headed up the gangway. He was not in a fabulous mood for the *Midnight Promenade*, but he was an officer and knew to do his duty.

165

* * *

In the mirror-lined, triple-arched *Starlight Ballroom,* deep down on *Dolphin Deck*, the champagne corks popped like salvos of Chinese firecrackers. The three immense crystal seahorse chandeliers dangled gloriously, and the huge glassy hall, whose majestic decor tonight reclaimed all the sparkling formality of the *S/S Marianne's* glamorous crossing era, teemed with myriad reflections of jeweled power cruisers, bronze-bosomed Cruise Staff Hostesses, and gallant-appearing Norwegian Officers in their nattiest, spit-and-polish, tuxedo parade dress.

Everyone sliding across the green-swirled Florentine marble floors felt power-infused by Maestro Cox and his "Starlight Swing Orchestra." Barry and the band cavorted splendidly on the the aft stage with an enticing medley of big-band era favorites from Glenn Miller, the Dorseys, Artie Shaw and Stan Kenton.

Meanwhile, another busy horde along the starboard balcony heaped their plates eagerly at the spectacular behemoth Midnight Buffet. The *Passenger Galley* chefs had pulled out all their culinary stops: Beef Wellington, Venezuelan chicken melon, braised salmon over couscous, ragout of duck, *paella, choulibiac* with mushroom *duxelles* and *sauce vin blanc*, ham *pithiviers*, watercress salad with endive and cucumbers, strawberries *en chemise*, fresh pear sherbet, Jamaican ice cream goblet . . .

. . . *where does one begin and, more importantly, where does one stop?*

Cablevista crews lurked everywhere on the balconies and down on the dance floor. In the port forward corner, a huge gleaming quilt of 16 monitors loomed high on the wall – a single colorful vision of the real time telecast on a massive field of glowing screens. (The *Cruise News* had reported 120 monitors had been installed all over the ship so that passengers, no matter where they were on the ship, could witness the events beamed simultaneously round-the-word.)

The pulsing luster from the mirrors and monitors lent a bizarre sheen to the ballroom's vast interior and a robust, self-conscious giddiness to the revelers. The faces in the reception line could not have been more on-edge or motor-flexor stimulated to smile before the cameras, only to snap their necks up for a quick narcissistic hit on the screens.

"Is this the dancing doctor we were told about?"

"Farrely says the doctor's to be treated with kid gloves."

"Smile, uh, Sir! How do you like the love boat?"

Loring did not mind the attention, especially across the green marble dance floor where Hildegarde and he discovered each other as full-grown adult consenting dance partners.

"Say nothing, love," she murmured as they fox-trotted into a fast-paced magic step in *"Jeepers Creepers."*

"Nothing, love," he whispered into her ear, felt her bony spine on his hand as they swept across the marble in perfect tandem.

"Oliver, do you realize this is our very first dance together? By the way, what size shoe do you wear? Let me guess. 13."

"D."

"*Knew* it! You'll *never* have to buy shoes again! I've got a whole warehouse full of the Colonel's waiting for you in London! How that man could buy shoes!"

"Wow! Thank you. And I noticed yours are so dainty."

"Who cares about dainty anymore?"

"Dainty's not dead."

"Oh, *you*! Dainty has been out for decades, don't you know. Hardly anybody dares notice a woman's foot these days, even on the dance floor. Of course, you're the exception. And may I add that the Colonel himself never looked quite as stunning as you do tonight. Your green eyes seem so very deep, like giant emeralds. I think the dance floor brings them out nicely. I'm sure you look wonderful on television. And that beauty mark on your cheek, Oliver! I keep wanting to kiss it. Just teasing, silly! Do I hear a cha-cha?"

As they gave in to the infectious rhythm of Barry Cox's homage to Prez Prado's *"Patricia,"* Loring looked up at the mirrored overhead arches of the *Ballroom.* He saw Hildegarde's sapphire skirt waft down at him against the deep, smooth green of the dance floor. He was tantalized, yet the soul within the mirror image felt even lighter in his arms. She looked up into the mirrors, then over at the monitors, and giggled at his admiring glance and pose.

"Your husband must have loved you very much," Loring said, as she followed his eyes. They both craned their necks up at their reflections. "You're quite lovely in sapphire."

"All I have left of my looks is surgery. Hopefully they can't see any of it from this distance."

"And the fragrance? Gerlain, isn't it?"

"Never miss, do you? By the way, was Ulla cruel to you tonight? You seem very sad. Come on, Oliver! Smile at the cameras."

She was in her late 70s and diminutive. (Size 4B shoe, she granted.) Yet, in the middle of a double corona cha-cha swing, Loring saw her hazel eyes enlarge up over his shoulder and then flutter like a seductive teenager's. The sharp, rouged bones in her cheeks blushed, and goose bumps erupted on her skinny forearms.

Then came the firm stabs at the right shoulder blade and a barking Norwegian accent: "Doctor, allow me, please! May I cut in?"

Loring swiveled back, looked down at a small, bearded man in a white linen dinner jacket. His eyes were wrinkled but sprightly. An Imperial Fiat graced his lapel.

Hildegarde embraced him immediately. "Oh Stig!" *(Kiss.)* "Oh, Stig!" *(Kiss.)* "Oh, Stig. You found me!" *(Long lingual kiss.)*

Loring waited for an introduction, but Hildegarde, her eyes shut tight and her mouth busy with the Founder of the Fleet, gave none.

Who could blame her? A peppy woman approaching her 80's and in sudden pain, confusion, caught on the delicate cusps of marvelous old memories *versus* a bleak future of widowhood thrust upon her suddenly and . . . well . . . there they *were*, dancing as if they had always wanted to dance together. Stig Storjord could cha-cha quite well – an anomaly among Norwegians. The agile Founder took a sudden grip-rest approach to an over glide bow step. Impressive.

Norwegian!

Hildegarde responded perfectly. He challenged her with a feather brush interlock weave, and she complied magnificently, made him produce a third, then a fourth nifty turn on the weave. The cameras followed them as Loring departed.

* * *

In the forward port corner of the *Ballroom,* Loring gazed up, amazed at the hi-tech electronics as Hildegarde and Stig romped in magnified bliss. They seemed enlarged to heroic proportions – all of it revealed via satellite to the world.

He agreed with Hildegarde. On TV nobody could detect the work of the surgeons. She did not look over 65. And Loring grinned at the enormous close-up of old Stig, the rakish puckering of his wrinkled lips.

Before the cha-cha ended, the image on the screen abruptly changed to the aerial view from the Cablevista blimp.

Magnificent!

Suddenly we are air-borne. A view from the blimp. The dark harbor and the shimmering city of San Juan. The stone Spanish fort gleams golden in its floodlights at the periphery of the port. We twirl a thousand feet above the *Nordic Blue*, and we peer down through the berzerkly darting klieg beams to the top of *Vista Deck*.

Zoom down closer. Thank you.

Three silver Mercedes roadster convertibles are shown aft on *Vista Deck*, parked on a large, astroturfed circular turntable. They face away from each other at 120-degree angles, and they rotate slowly, the edge of the powerful platform ringed with glistening white lights. Viewed from the blimp, the roadsters serve as the silver spokes for a revolving Benz logo.

Clever effect! Yo you advertising mavens!

Vista Deck is also occupied by a cluster of large computer and broadcasting consoles, the satellite dish, and a full-sized remote truck wedged between the funnels.

But still, it is all breathlessly beautiful! Such a sleek and feminine ship!

Giddy from the vertiginous view, Loring dotes on the *Nordic Blue* – her grace, her power, her nautical and spiritual identity resting so self-assuredly in the warm black water beside the dock.

Gaze in envy, world! Is she not the grandest and most legendary? Switch back to the *Starlight Ballroom*. Thank you, you space age TV electricians you!

* * *

Farrely Farrell. Up close. In the flesh at the reception line.

Age 53. (A stat from the *Cruise News*). Height, under six feet, the prodigious mottled nose dead level with Loring's bow tie. Weight – two hundred plus, including saggy neck wattles and puffy love handles bulging over his cummerbund. Cheeks – bumpy badlands with scores of pocks on each side, especially under the eyes, the craters caked to the brim with pegs of pink-toned pancake base. Celebrated helmet-like hair – millions of long gray strands falling in scraggly professorial folds around his ears and over his tux collar and vaguely parted above his pocky brow at one of the hidden points where the massive apparatus glues onto his scalp.

Handshake. Uncomfortably firm.

"So here you *are*! The dancing doctor I ordered! I heard you're from

Harvard! They said you could dance, Mate, but from what I could see up there on the monitors a while ago with Mrs. Snippet-White, you do much more than that. You cast a goddamn spell on the dance floor! And you know, your eyes absolutely scintillate on the television."

"Why, thanks."

"No, thank *you!* Fan-*tas*-tic, Mate! You'll be a huge hit Thursday! Your moves are astonishing."

Loring viewed Farrell's eyes. Large and black. Quick moving. Conniving. But with an engaging glimmer of joviality.

"I think Mrs. Snippet-White had something to do with it. She was my partner."

"Simply fan-*tas*-tic! How lucky we are to have you both! So sorry for Mrs. Snippet-White, of course, about the Colonel. I heard the bad news. Did you . . ."

"*Know* him? Ha-*ha*! I'm wearing his uniform."

"Did *not* notice, Doc. *Marvelous* for you! What a tribute! Great *fit*, too! Of course, none of our Cablevista technicians will intrude on her. She knows that. Doesn't she? Will you tell her from me?"

"I'll give her your word."

"It's a big story, Doc. But we'll leave her alone. Your cha-cha was story enough. Believe me."

Loring's feelings were guarded, but he smiled at Farrely Farrell's flattery. "I didn't see what I was doing when I did it."

Farrell's left hand gave him a heavy smack on the epaulet. "Not aware of your own ability to cast a spell of fantasy?"

"I never was on TV. Not till tonight."

"Comes naturally to some of us. Never know you have it till it happens. That's what I found out. And, by the way, I hear they call you the Dart Doc. Love a dude with a sexy handle! You can be sure we'll use that one on the air. Do you know you're a real factor on this ship? Or so say a few of the lady passengers."

"A factor?" Loring felt his cheeks flame. He tried to move on, but the Aussie hadn't finished with the handshake. "Doc, could you spare time for a quick man-to-man?"

Before Loring could request clarification, Farrell's head bowed close. Loring leaned his ear close to Farrely's wine-breath lips. Farrell whispered. "Condoms." Loring's head jerked back. *"Ha!"*

But Farrely Farrell continued his whisper. "Damn it! Forgot to bring a box for the cruise. Your frickin' *Nordic Notions Drug Store* upstairs already ran out. Surely the *Hospital* . . . Doc! . . . for the crew's protection or something. Or maybe you have a few to spare from your own stash. Eh, Mate?"

Loring giggled politely. "Did you ask your Room Steward?"

"Listen. Didn't *my* Cablevista people recruit you for this gig, Dart Doc?"

"I suppose so, but . . ."

"So don't you think you could . . ."

"The *Hospital* is closed just now."

"Don't tell me you don't have a key. *Doc*, try to understand! I picked up a real fox on the flight down from New York. She's super hot tonight. Really comin' on to me. Do I make myself clear? Also a Bostonian, by the way. Claims she's lusted for me since the first time she saw 'Love Luck.' In this day and age, *who* knows better about personal hygiene than a cruise ship doctor?"

"Or a talk show host? Ha!"

"*Love* the way you think, Mate. And might you have any Viagra tablets lyin' around, too? Once in a while, my pecker needs a little boost. Never hurts to have some sustenance on board. Know what I mean? Especially for a sizzler like this one."

* * *

Loring bolted from the *Starlight Ballroom* and headed forward up the *Dolphin Deck* corridor toward the *Hospital*, two decks above. He was about to cut through the *Interior Crew Stairwell* when he spotted a lean, tall woman charging toward him far down the corridor. Her curly locks bounced on her narrow shoulders, pale and bare. She wore a crimson satin cocktail gown. A tall champagne flute brimmed in her hand, and her fine blonde brow was set firmly above her flashing eyes.

Loring slowed his pace, watched her very familiar and uniquely angular form enlarge as her scissoring legs flashed toward him through the slit in the skirt. Then he froze, did not know if he should run in the opposite direction or duck into the nearest linen closet or simply bare his nails and call her name before she came close.

That was always the problem with Dr. Anita Rothberg – sultry, evocative essence that she was. He never knew what to do when he saw her, especially when she had that leatherish, carnivorous look in her eyes.

Her glance not wavering, she raised the champagne flute to her lips and sucked in a fizzy ounce, with not a drop lost. She licked her maroon-painted lips and proceeded. Those slender hands and those thick, sultry labial muscles could do anything with such singularity of purpose!

How *well* Loring knew it! *To think!* She had flown all the way down to Miami to be with him, had dolled herself up to the teeth to impress him, to win him back, and now here *she* was, striding right back into *his* life. Was that not an expression of determined love?

Let's give credit where credit is due!

"Anita!"

Was it Anita? She didn't pause or even look up. He whiffed her bitter oriental Opium scent from ten yards away. He tried to detect an additional hint of oil-of-clove somewhere.

"ANITA!"

As she steamed past him, deaf to his voice, he stepped to the side to avoid a collision. He looked back, watched her take another strong swig and preen her hair with her other hand, before she parked her champagne flute on top of an ice machine and darted into the *Starlight Ballroom*.

* * *

Minutes later up on *Vista Deck*, Loring sank into the cushioned cockpit of a silver Mercedes-Benz 744K roadster. Lacquered walnut dash, rippled leather steering wheel cover, sensationally abundant leg room. According to the card taped to the windshield, this "limited edition" machine was "erogenously ergonometric."

How appropriate for the "Love Luck" grand prizes!

He trained his eyes on the Cablevista broadcast on the TV monitor near the revolving turntable.

A hundred yards above, its silver belly strafed by the wandering klieg beams, the Cablevista blimp hovered low and luminous. Ten decks below, festively dressed couples swirled to an old-fashioned *"Tennessee Waltz"* on the ballroom's green marble floor – all dancers in a lavish, elegantly televised fairy tale pageant.

The Cablevista wizardry transfixed Loring as he revolved in the car. He stretched back, adjusted his eyes to the glowing, shifting colors. The computer optics enlarged and mystified everything! The mirrors and the arched ceilings of the ballroom glistened and shimmered gloriously. As the cameras panned around, the giant crystal seahorse chandeliers glinted at bizarre angles. The *Starlight Ballroom,* spacious and magnificent as it actually was, seemed utterly colossal and illuminated with an eerie, combustive brilliance.

Why? On TV the ballroom appeared as airy and capacious as a mirror-lined hippodrome or airplane hanger, large enough to contain the Cablevista blimp, at least.

Yet Loring, from his seat in the roadster, glanced up and realized this was all electronic illusion. Big and generous as she was, the *Nordic Blue* could *never* house a blimp and all those power cruisers in her *Starlight Ballroom,* not all at once!

Loring had just climbed up the ten decks from that hall, and he could not believe the difference, not only in light and dimension. The revelers in the midst of the gaiety appeared idealized, glamorized, though Loring knew them to be typically inebriated power cruisers and socially awkward Norwegian Officers. Even the music wizard/lizard Barry Cox looked charismatic and sexy, well-tanned for a change, as he waved his baton and grinned in front of the orchestra.

At the center of the crowd and clamped arm-in-arm with Farrely Farrell was Anita Rothberg. She looked so at ease, resplendent. She nuzzled, ogled, cheek-to-cheeked the Aussie superstar.

The camera focused above the pearl necklace, avoided any shot of their egregious footwork during a rather pedestrian rendering by Barry and the boys of Glenn Miller's *"Chattanooga Choo-choo."* From the craning of the necks around her, everyone on the dance floor seemed to wonder who she was.

New York actress? Malibu starlet? Australian runway model? Who *was* this brown-eyed mystery blonde in pearls and scant crimson who, quite obviously, had stolen Farrely's world-coveted fancy? Would Farrely himself get lucky in love tonight?

Loring took scant delight in being the only person on the ship who knew her. Minutes before, down on *Dolphin Deck*, Anita Rothberg had blown past him like a steam engine in heat. Had she rendered the common civility of eye contact? Even when he smelled her perfume and called her name? Had Dr. Rothberg noticed the condition of his nails? Doubtful.

Oh, yes. Loring knew Anita Rothberg – the Ph.D., the *M.O.*, the web site – very well, and it all seemed obvious and typical now. And a tribute to her computer expertise – that Anita had webbed out the whole strategy, consulted airline bookings on the net, then on her way down to Miami switched planes in New York, intercepted Farrely Farrell with a first class ticket on his flight from JFK.

The rest was all now fast becoming reality TV history.

And she did look uncharacteristically happy, didn't she? The close-ups enhanced her features, especially the profiles. Loring had never appreciated the charming, out-and-out dip in her jaw when she gave a full, open-mouthed smile. Or the slant of the tip of her aquiline nose when her lips pursed and she tried to stifle a laugh at one of Farrely's inaudible witticisms. And there was a sensuality of muscle tone in Anita's upper forearms that had always aroused Loring whenever she grabbed for anything, like just now, for Farrely Farrell's crooked bow tie.

Confession: Loring felt no guilt that he had not delivered condoms (or tablets of Viagra) to Farrely Farrell. From personal experience, he knew Anita practiced the safest sex this side of a Florentine nunnery: double-bag condoms, dental dams, whatever was on the market, she made it part of the build-up. She stocked her steamer trunk with a full supply of all the latest hygienics/lubricants, along with her trusty battery-powered phallic commandos.

Relax. Not to worry, mate. She orders all the latest items from the web's adult-only interstices. *Enjoy! Both* of you!

And about the Viagra, Farrely. The *Hospital* formulary is fresh out; Viagra's a much-requested medicine on board. But Anita may already have told you that impotence is one of her professional specialties. She has a deal with the drug salesmen, and she uses the free samples herself as a "research nutritive."

Loring yawned and pulled his eyes away from the TV screen. He stretched his fingertips up on the steering wheel of the roadster and scrutinized his crop – those ten miscreant digits that had put him in contact with Anita in the first place – all displayed around the steering wheel magnificently. As if they were new organs. Organs he had never envisioned, had always tried to gnaw off, lest they seek destructive tendencies of their own, their individual acts of self-renewal.

Loring sang to himself with paternal content while his offspring danced before him:
One little, two little, three little Indians.
Four little, five little . . .

* * *

174

Loring might have dreamed. He suspected he had dozed for several hours at the wheel, because all the lights around the ship were off and the circular platform had stopped rotating. A moist layer of sea dew coated his hands. A long strand of clear drool strung out from the corner of his lip and down to several medals near the Colonel's sash.

The string quivered and broke when Ulla von Straf slammed shut the passenger door beside him. She was in a black leotard and with a white silk shawl over her shoulders. She was fragrant and slightly sweaty from her rehearsal. She wiggled her toes in her ballet pumps.

"So I found you!" she said. "I looked all over the ship. First of all, I am sorry. But first I must kiss you. Yes. Thank you. Here, let me clean up your face with my handkerchief. There, that's better."

He might have dreamed.

Or he might have heard Ulla's words as truth when she lit up her Winston filter tip, licked her petal lips and said, "Do you mind if I smoke?"

Of course she smokes. She's oral. Like me. And isn't it beautiful how she holds that Winston between her lips?

"Go ahead. And talk to me. Tell me everything, Ulla."

"Flip is out of control. He's in big trouble. And I guess I'm in trouble with you. Do you remember what I said tonight? Outside the casino?"

"You said you loved me."

She inhaled deeply, let all the smoke out up into the black, starry sky. "Do you want proof?"

"Talk to me."

"You know so much about me, even though we are almost strangers. I could tell how much you knew from our first dance together."

"Your touch feels wonderful."

"Oh, you feel so much in me, don't you? I could feel how you knew. May I kiss you again first? I love the way your mouth feels."

"And will you tell me about Tosco and his tigers?"

"But first, a kiss."

* * *

"I was the last person to touch Jean-Luc Farandouz alive. At the Spitzring track. At the start of the race he crawled behind the controls and before he put on his helmet, I leaned down and kissed him and told him I would love him always, always, always. Two hours later they could not even find all of his body. The wreck was scattered all over the track and far beyond. He was more than burned. He was disintegrated.

"Oliver, do you believe there is a continuous link between the physical and the spiritual worlds? Later the engineers said that he had actually defied certain laws of physics, just before he died. I saw his car levitate, fly up in a red cloud. But it was not a cloud of flames, not at all. And the pathologists who examined his body said, when they looked at his tissues under their microscopes, they could not account for some of the changes. The changes were new to science.

"His body was not only burned. Some of his tissues under the microscope showed no evidence whatsoever of burn destruction. The individual cells themselves had unlinked and come apart. You are a doctor. You perhaps would understand better than me. They said parts of him had simply vanished, the internal organs were not burned at all, but showed some random disintegration. Right down to the chromosomes.

"I always warned Jean-Luc that he was too serious. And Tosco himself felt that his metaphysical studies should never be applied to a sport such as automobile racing. It was Vladimir Tulov who first attracted him into the group. Vladimir Tulov urged Jean-Luc to meditate deeply in the cockpit, and then he started winning race after race. Including Le Mans. The Spitzring race, high in the German Alps, was the one he wanted most, the most grueling and exacting course on the circuit. See that! He wanted it most, and I believe he simply meditated too hard.

"I met Jean-Luc two years before in Paris, when our troupe from Salzburg was performing at a summer festival. There was a reception after our first performance. He was different. Handsome, of course. Extremely delicate and boyish and with dark, dark skin and sparkling blue eyes and this very charming Caribbean accent when we spoke French. I didn't know who he was, but one of my friends said he was a well-known racing driver.

"He invited me to the circus, and of course I was fascinated, especially after I saw their astonishing performances. He told me he was involved in some spiritual studies with these men Tosco and Tulov. He said their cult met every Sunday night at the *Hôtel de la Grace* and that they were followers of the teachings of Gurdjieff. I could not become involved, because my troupe was returning to Austria. But he followed me there, and soon we were lovers. I could not help myself. Jean-Luc was not shy like you. And he had fire deep in his eyes, too much fire, really.

"No, it was Tulov who excited him with the idea of applying the spiritual

176

techniques at the racing track. To this day, I condemn Vladimir for coaxing him into it. Jean-Luc had enough talent and courage without mixing in metaphysical effort. He had come from nowhere – a poor black island boy from St. Maarten, who won over everyone, including his French backers, with his abilities and his marvelous grace. But he wanted too much too fast, and Tulov showed him how to try for it.

"When Jean-Luc first told me about his ideas, that the Spitzring would be a place for a metaphysical experiment in his Porsche, I dreaded his thoughts at once. He and Tulov had felt certain that at such high altitudes, and with such a devastatingly difficult track, he would have opportunities to focus his powers that would be unavailable on any other track anywhere. I didn't want to go and watch him try. I told him that, as a dancer, I believed in meditation. But you see, Vladimir Tulov had studied these Muslim dervishes closely in central Asia. That was an important part of his theories. He believed that the dervishes attain a state of ecstatic purity, achieved through swirling motions and intense meditations, and for two hours that afternoon at the Spitzring, Jean-Luc was so far ahead of the other drivers, he could have coasted in and still finished in the lead.

"Then I remember him trying to accelerate just beyond the last sharp hair-pin turn, and the approach to the final straightaway. His engine roared just out of the turn, then, as I said, his car started to give off a red cloud. But it was not smoke or flame – no, it simply hovered around him, this strange bright color, then his entire car rose from the track. There was no sound whatsoever as he scattered into pieces. They recovered what they could of his car and his body, but as I said, much of it was missing. Even some of the DNA from his cells.

"When the doctors were finished with him, I had his body cremated completely, to the finest dust possible. A few days ago Tosco and I finished spreading particles of Jean-Luc into his beloved Caribbean Sea. Yesterday on St. Maarten I said farewell to his parents, and we left a few pinches of him in the palm grove beside their house."

"You mean Jean-Luc Farandouz simply etherealized?"

"He was winning the race. He didn't have to die."

"Red smoke?"

"It wasn't even smoke. Smoke doesn't glow like that."

"And you came here to the Caribbean with Tosco . . ."

"Yes, as a pilgrim. Tosco and I blew the last of his ashes into the sea, and the next day I met his father."

"So you've been on a farewell mission? That picture over the bar at the restaurant, *L'Etoile*? It was you at Le Mans with Jean-Luc, wasn't it? So that's why you came to the Caribbean."

"Do you know why you came here?"

"Something to do with a *Fandango*. Are you familiar with Stravinsky's nifty little piano piece with . . ."

* * *

In delicious silence they promenaded hand-in-hand on *Vista Deck*. All of San Juan – palm-lined streets, sculpted fountains, lapping harbor waters, floodlit citadel, the memory of a forsaken dance grotto – passed gently around them.

Hours ago the blimp had disappeared, tethered somewhere out of sight to be refueled, one supposed, and the klieg lights had been snuffed. So now the sky was pure for them – no logo or message beamed down, except billowy clouds, white stars, and a reticent half moon falling to the west.

Ulla smoked, sighed into the warm, windless air. They took another turn around *Vista Deck*. Loring closed his eyes.

In . . . and . . .

Did Ulla actually walk beside him? Had she not poured out a confession about the death of her lover? Did Loring dare believe the metaphysics? The metapathology? Whatever it was called?

The Farandouz Porsche, far in the lead, rises high off the Spitzring. Red smoke shoots from the disintegrating man and machine. Forensic analysis verifies the driver's cryptic attenuation – right down to the microscopic absence of cells in his organs, loss of gene substances from his chromosomes. Was it a plasma physics event? Was there a meeting place between the spirit and . . .

In . . .

Loring opened his eyes.

Ulla stared up at him, her jaw firm, her eyes the lucid blue of a bright mid-day sky. "You don't have to believe everything I just told you. All of it is fairly unbelievable, I know. But I love you. Believe that, please."

He drew her to him. "Yes, I want to."

He watched her black eyelashes flutter, moisten. Her lower lip swelled. Her eyes closed and she rose up on her toes to kiss him. "Oh, Oliver," she blurted out. She shook her head and tears spilled over her cheeks. Their faces came together slowly. He took the sweet tears on her lips onto his tongue. "I feel dizzy," she said after a long kiss.

"I can't think of anything more real than this."

"Oh, there's more, Oliver. Kiss me again."

MEMO FROM THE BRIDGE

Date: WED/FEB 13, 06.00 hours
From: Staff Captain Nils Nordström
To: All Officers
Re: Cablevista Interviews

Today the Nordic Blue will host two live television shows, the Captain's
Cocktail Party at 18.00 hours followed by the "Love Luck" telecast at 21.00h.
There will also be several informal interviews earlier in the day with Farrely
Farrell and various department chiefs.
It has come to the attention of the Bridge that certain Officers have tried
to "steal the show" by nosing in front of the cameras and trying to dominate
the interviews with their unwelcomed comments or by waving to the cameras
and making other types of behind the scenes "monkey shines" not befitting
an Officer.
Such misconducts will be punished by cancellation of vacation leave.
Those of you out there know who you are, and you will be punished if this
continues.
This memo does not apply to the Ship's Doctor, whose dancing has been
highly praised by Farrely Farrell on the air.

Nils Nordström,
Staff Captain, S/S Nordic Blue

* * *

Sleep? *Ha!* Not this red, soul-ripping morning!
The rising sun glowed a fierce crimson. Long streaks of flaming cirrus
vapor arched high from horizon to vermilion horizon. The vibrant San Juan
silhouette baked in an unearthly dawn radiance. The ancient fortress of San

Cristóbal looked fire-forged in a massive blazing kiln, while a seething red brine boiled at the base of her bulwarks.

Thank you, sky and ocean, for your surreal and inspirational hues.

Thank you, *Nordic Blue* decks, for being almost deserted. A single hooded jogger, his fists punching weirdly at the red morning sky as he charged forward (where *do* these power cruising lunatics come from?) spoiled the otherwise pristine vastness of the *Promenade Deck* planks.

And thank *you*, young Wolfgang Amadeus Mozart, for your glimmering *Sonata #12* in F major.

It simply *had* to be Mozart this dawn. Who *else* could pen lyrical melody to match the joy vaulting wildly in the chambers of Oliver Loring's restless heart?

Though Loring's head had not touched his pillow, a nippy shower and a brisk post-shave spritz of Nino Cerutti 1881 from the frosted glass *vaporisateur* on each cheek had catapulted him up out of his cabin to the Baldwin near the *Topsiders* portholes.

By this penetrating redness through the circular portholes, he had sat fully upright on the piano bench and immersed himself in young Wolfgang's whimsically syncopated *Allegro*. Then came the succulent *Adagio*. And *now* he cavorted with the scintillations of the final *Allegro Assai* with those mesmerizing right hand runs and reverses that wove and broke, seemed to free fall, until an innocent minor motive floated by, almost out of nowhere, to buoy up the whole dreamy monument and pin it elegantly in the timeless imaginative firmament.

Ba-da-daah-daah-dah, dah da daah dahdah . . .

What good was a Mozart melody, if not forever?

What good were Loring's feelings this dawn, if not forever?

Alas, why is this intoxicating red dawn herself not . . .

Ba-da-daah-daah . . .

With his passion for Ulla as the wind and the music of Mozart his wings, Loring flew to Salzburg. Glorious, quaint, Mozartian Salzburg! Loring had always felt identity there. Now he knew exactly why! And it wasn't the Von Trapp family escapades, although he had always been partial to that marvelous Rogers and Hammerstein movie, too.

Long ago, during his college summer vacations, he had backpacked in the nearby Austrian Alps and lodged at the youth hostels. With the music festival crowds, he had paid his fervent respects at the Mozart residence at *#9 Getreidegasse.*

Indeed, fully two decades before Loring had ever danced with *Fraülein* von Straf, he had rambled giddily through her native haunts in the lovable Baroque streets. He had lingered at outdoor cafes, sampled pastries, sipped *Kafe mit Schlagsahne,* greedily absorbed the melodies wafting from the windows while the festival performers rehearsed.

Why had his heart always beat so deliriously in Salzburg? Had he sensed Ulla's presence there? And had their paths crossed by chance back then? Had he seen her strolling through the streets – a pre-pubescent, pig-tailed girl in a laced bodice and pleated dirndl skirt?

But he knew for certain that he had not made eye contact with her then – even a casual glance from those gleaming blues would have been indelible, would have shot an unforgettable, permanently-haunting bolt of electric rapture through his soul.

Had Ulla's eyes betrayed sadness back then? Would Loring have understood?

Through the huge portholes of *Topsiders*, the red ramparts of San Juan's own San Cristóbal morphed magically to faraway Salzburg's prominent Benedictine abbey and fortress atop the Mönchsberg.

Then, with a flutter of Mozart's chromatic runs, Loring found himself transported there with Ulla. He took her hand and clambered up the stone steps to the old abbey, zig-zagged giggling with her in and out of the sacrosanct corridors. They stood by the parapeted walls, surveyed her town, Mozart's birthplace.

How he thrilled, as Ulla's laughter floated freely into the fragrant, balsam-laced Austrian ether! Loring wanted to gallivant everywhere in the world with her, but yes, especially to Salzburg. He wanted to see where she danced, strolled, enjoyed pastries and sipped her *Kafe mit Schlag,* smoked her Winstons.

Sonata #12 broke into a lightly-bounding canter/carousel melody.

Tee-ropa-tee-ropa-tee-ropa!

Oh, how busy their tongues had been all night as they walked the vast outer decks of the *Nordic Blue*! Busy talking, yes. But busy, too, exploring each other's inner needs.

Tee-ropa . . .

Ulla had proved herself more deliciously oral than Loring had ever imagined. Her mouth was dynamic, comprehensive – an *Allegro, Adagio* and *Allegro Assai* of Mozartian delicacy.

Lip to lip, they had matched the tongues of the Caribbean waves, had tirelessly tasted, massaged, quested for ever-more gratifying mucosal caresses. Her magnificent lingual muscle was long and thin and of a warm, silky intelligence, such as Loring had never known. And she was not afraid to suck hard, till he hurt. He *liked* that.

By the time the night's stars faded behind the high pink cloud bank, the folds under Loring's tongue felt frayed and sore. But such pleasant pains were wounds of love – lingering evidence of how lonely they had been for each other until . . .

Tee-ropa-tee . . .

Oh, how he had wanted to lick her lady bug! Often, as they cuddled, Ulla's round breasts with their bullet-hard nipples pressed tight against his chest. Once, as they nuzzled in the shadows near the stern, his nose followed the fragrance of her body, down past her chin and over her smooth neck and lower still. But he stopped, dared not meet the ladybug, feared to explore any further.

Through the night, between the kisses, there had been tears for Jean-Luc. Ulla said she had grieved enough now, was overwhelmed that Loring had excited such playful and erotic feelings in her, sensations she had been numb to since Jean-Luc's death. Time and again she shook her head away from Loring, laughed up at the stars and then turned back to him, sighed, kissed him more fulminantly.

The loss of Colonel Snippet-White had also brought fresh trauma, though she seemed to accept it as anticipated. Hildegarde had spoken with her about the code she shared with Rocky Boy Bebalzam – that at their advanced ages, life must be embraced to the fullest and with whatever strength one has, death being only a reminder of life's blessings.

Ulla's eyes had beamed a beatific blue as she smiled and said, "You know, Oliver, he died dancing – as he would have wanted."

As much as Loring desired her, wished to lick the ladybug, he knew this had to be a night for condolence, not concupiscence.

Finally, with a thick layer of sea dew coating both of them, he had escorted her down to the *Viking Deck* cabin she shared with Spinelli. Silently they kissed again at the door, and Loring noticed fresh tears on her cheeks.

But behold the red dawn!

"NO TEARS THIS MORNING! NOT IN SAN JUAN OR SALZBURG, EITHER!" declared the joyously manic voice of Wolfgang Amadeus Mozart!

Ba-da-daah-ddah, dah da . . .

At least Ulla had true feelings for him. That was a start.

"SHE CERTAINLY DOES HAVE FEELINGS FOR YOU!"

As fragile as she had remained for the past two years following Jean-Luc's death and the bizarre discoveries of the forensic investigators, there were signs of recovery. She said she had not been with a man since Farandouz's disintegration. Well, she certainly had *been* with Loring during their night stroll, was still deeply with him, had promised to meet with him at noon today in the *Starlight Lounge* for a rehearsal of their dance routine for tomorrow night's televised spotlight.

Ulla said a mambo would turn the audience on.

Oh, dear mambo gods! Wherever you are, up above this brilliant red Caribbean sky, please bless us and our mambo!

The mambo was a start. But would Saturday morning in Miami be the last time he would ever see Ulla? Would Miami be the end of it? Would she disappear from his life like a Caribbean mirage? Would they never see Salzburg together?

"NO TEARS THIS MORNING!"

Thank you, Wolfgang! For your confidence and your inexhaustible hope! But should I remind you? When you were alive, the mambo hadn't been invented. And now you're dead.

"DO I SOUND DEAD AS YOU PLAY MY SONATA?"

Point well taken! And I'll trust your word, as a native Salzburger, that the Fraülein at least likes me.

"BUT YOU MUST NOT BE CONTENT WITH DREAMING ABOUT HER! TOMORROW IS VALENTINE'S DAY!"

"So what should I give her?"

"SOMETHING BEAUTIFUL AND PERSONAL! TRUST ME!"

"If I can't trust you, Wolfgang, who can I trust?"

"AND I DON'T MEAN A HEART-SHAPED BOX OF CHOCOLATES!"

"Not even the little ones wrapped in foil with your name and face on them? And marzipan in the middle? Ha-ha!"

Tee-ropa . . .

Loring fingered the final, lilting 6/8 cadences and their frolicking reprise of the carousel motif. He bowed his head and closed his eyes at the keyboard. Out of respect for Wolfgang, he agreed not to shed tears of self absorption this morning.

For reassurance, he slid the tip of his tongue down under and licked his sub-lingual bruises.

I must follow Mozart's advice. Seize this glorious red dawn and prove

your love to Ulla. Find something beautiful! Something personal!
In and . . .

* * *

Ba-da-daah-daah . . .

Loring jumped down two levels of the *Central Stairtower,* turned starboard on *International Deck.* He stepped out onto the polished flag stone pavement of *Boutique Row* and looked up and down the broad, glittering promenade mall, where the display windows of two dozen deluxe shipboard stores enticed power cruisers to add to their cruising pleasure by making power purchases at duty-free rates.

Tee-ropa-tee . . .

Something beautiful!

Loring's gut response to Mozart's suggestion was, of course, perfume.

Scents, the Fragrance Salon, featured the latest Paris and Milan had to offer: Guerlein, Versace, Lanvan, Paco Raban, plus several obscure Italian houses. On past cruises, Loring had pestered the clerks in *Scents* to let him sniff all their exotic wares.

Often he had strolled out of the shop, his pockets full of circular filter paper blotters imbued with fascinating samples. In the privacy of his cabin, he had taken leisure to decide which fragrance to bring back duty-free to please his current Boston *amante.*

Loring had learned, however, that perfume was risky. A new essence, which might smell subtle and intriguing on the blotter and look spectacular in its tiny crystal decanter, later might mix hideously with any woman's particular skin oils.

Result: confusion over the gift, perhaps insult, with unpredictable emotional repercussions and, often, permanent damage or termination of the relationship.

Perfume, though beautiful and personal, as specified by Mozart, could jeopardize much. Also, Loring had no right to impose an aroma with invisible layers of meaning and presumptuous power messages on Ulla. And why should he think of doing so? Till now, he had not detected *Fraülein* von Straf's own preference for a scent. (Did she even wear one?)

In fact, he enjoyed her own natural, rain-water sweet, unadulterated essence. For example, last night after her strenuous rehearsal, her moist, salty glow had mixed intoxicatingly with the stingy tobacco of her Winston kisses.

No, Ulla smells fine as she is. Something else personal and beautiful, please.

Tee-ropa...

Officially, because the ship was still docked in port, the duty-free stores on *Boutique Row* were not supposed to do business. But Loring knew most of the shop clerks and managers would be inside this morning to take pre-departure inventory. The stores were closed to passengers. But, as an officer with three stripes on his epaulets, he could probably knock on any door and buy what he wanted.

But what did he want? A garment or accessory from *Trends*? A painting or an etching from *Belgravia*? Certainly not a watch or a porcelain figurine from *Margueritte's Boutique*!

Ba-da-daah-daah ...

As he strode by the shop fronts, he passed clusters of power cruisers on their way to and from breakfast. They all seemed to regard him with unusual interest. Twice he turned his head and noticed glances, smiles, and murmurs of his name, as if they all knew exactly who he was.

"Was that the Dart Doc?"

"I'm sure it was."

"Yes, that was Doctor Oliver. From Harvard."

Why was that? Ha-*ha!* Was the old axiom true about everybody loving a lover? Did they see it?

Did his face gleam with an obvious romantic luster? Did the manic speed with which he clicked jauntily along the *Boutique Row* flagstones, his eyes casting hasty probes into the shop windows, betray the fact that he had spent the entire night cuddling and chatting with the voluptuous Ulla and couldn't wait to buy her something personal and beautiful? Could everybody tell from his body language alone, that his joyous heart had just flown to Salzburg on Mozart's melodic wings and he wasn't, actually, quite back on the ship yet? Oh, so what! Loring hoped to be in love with Ulla for a long time, and he might just as well get used to people smiling and nodding familiarly when they saw his obvious elation.

Please, please, mambo gods!

Tee-ropa...

He stopped in front of *Flair, the Jewelry Salon.*

What did he want? What exactly did he want?

"Oh, Doctor! Do you mind? May we have your autograph, please?"

Loring turned.

Behind him stood three pale, chubby blonde women in matching pink jogging suits. The middle woman pulled a crumpled copy of the *Daily Cruise News* from her wave-and-sunburst fanny pack. She smoothed the paper out and handed it to Loring along with a wave-and-sunburst ballpoint. "I'm Doris. This is Kitty and Babs. We're the Spaulding triplets from Cincinnati."

"Well, good morning, Cincinnati! My autograph? Shall I sign three times?"

The Spauldings giggled in triplicate. "Just once. Right here on the first page by your picture, if you please?" said Babs.

"Oh, is my picture in the *Cruise News* today?"

"Show him, Doris," grinned Kitty. "You're right there with Farrely, Doc. That's *you*!"

Loring perused the paper and winced at the profile shot of him shaking hands with pendulous-lipped Farrely Farrell. (It was the moment when Farrell was requesting the condoms.)

"And you're all over Cablevista, too," added Doris. "The camera just loves you."

"And we do, too!" Kitty beamed. "Our friends back in Ohio are going to be so jealous!"

"Will we get a chance to dance with you at the cocktail party tonight?" asked Doris. "Cablevista calls you the Dancing Doctor. And some people call you the Dart Doc. Why is that?"

Loring hastily penned "Happy Valentine's Day to Doris, Kitty and Babs!" along with his name under the photograph. "It's a secret, ladies."

"Oh, just be satisfied we got his autograph for now," said Babs.

Loring handed back the *Cruise News*. "I'm flattered, ladies."

"If you give us a kiss now, we won't bother you for a dance later," said Doris. "Just think of it, girls! Last week we swam with the dolphins, and now this!"

"A kiss is better than a dance," added Babs.

"Quicker, too," winked Kitty. "Bet you never kissed triplets before, did you, Doc?"

"As long as your husbands don't mind."

Doris laughed loudly as she fumbled in her fanny pack. "Husbands, hell! We all three married skunks. Divorced 'em soon as the kids hit high school. Here, let me find my goddamn Nikon. My friggin' neighbors are not gonna' *believe* this! We gotta' make copies right away, girls! Wish we had one of them damn digitals!"

* * *

After kissing and squeezing the Spaulding triplets for repeated snapshots and then mugging at the camera with a pair of newlywed lawyers from Lewisburg, West Virginia, and a butcher and his wife from Boise, Idaho, Loring knocked on the door of *Flair, the Jewelry Salon.*

The broad-shouldered, mocha-skinned clerk with a tiny gold ring in her right nostril smiled and opened the door. *"Oh la la*! But aren't you popular!" She had a fetching French accent. "Oh, I know *you*. It's Oliver."

"Seems everybody knows me this morning."

"Did you come in to shop or to hide from your fans, Dart Doc?" she winked.

Loring glanced at the full-figured creature's i.d. badge. "Fatima. And I've heard about you!"

Her lips were large, finely-curved and sensual, and she had a soft, amused glance in her big brown eyes that quickly put him at ease. Her majestically high brow was rimmed by meticulous corn-rows, gold beaded at the tips. She abundantly filled out her royal blue pleated skirt and beige wave-and-sunburst print blouse, yet there was a dimpled daintiness, elegance, to her generous bearing.

"And has not everyone heard about you? You've become an overnight television personality. Cablevista keeps flashing your picture on the screen, saying you are the ship's dancing doctor."

"I never watch television."

"Even if you're *on* it?"

"Never thought about that."

"But, don't you want to know what people are saying about you?"

"I didn't really come in here to talk about myself."

"I know. You probably want to buy a Valentine's gift. And you probably have to be down at the clinic soon."

"Well, yes and yes."

Fatima walked around the counter with large, authoritative steps. "Might the gift be for your dancing partner, Ulla? Now look! You're blushing."

"I'm sorry. I can't help it. But yes."

"Have anything special in mind?"

"Something personal and beautiful."

"Could you narrow that down a bit?"

Fatima's teasing edge did not bother Loring. *Flair* was officially closed, and she was, in fact, doing him a major favor by letting him shop. And he could sense why Jacques Chemin was so absorbed in her. As she moved gracefully around the store and pointed out various jeweled rings and bracelets, necklaces, earrings and broaches, she seemed marvelously content with herself and her robust-sized femininity. "Let me think now. What would I love to wear if I were Ulla?"

"Something personal and beautiful."

"You said that."

"I'm sorry. I'm nervous about it."

Fatima searched his glance. "You love her, that's obvious," she winked. Then she put her fingertips to her temples. She closed her eyes, raised her chin, and took in several deep, meditative breaths.

Loring stood with his hands on the counter and admired the very smooth chocolate contours of her pudgy cheeks and the enormity of her breasts.

"You don't want to shock her," she mused, her eyes still closed.

"How did you *know*?"

Fatima's shoulders shook, but her eyes remained squinted tight. "*Docteur*, my job is to help you."

"You're great, Fatima!"

"Ulla can glance at a ring or a bracelet and think of you, of course," Fatima smiled. "But a necklace is a much more elegant statement of affection, no? Each breath she takes while she wears it will be embraced and enhanced by your gift."

"Oh, I *love* that. Do you, by any chance know Nadine Tulard? Please open your eyes."

Fatima blinked and gave Loring a skeptical glance. "Of course I know Nadine. We two are cabin mates."

"You seem to have the same style, you know?"

"*Bien sûr!*"

"Yes, and Nadine says '*bien sûr*' a lot, too."

"She's French."

"*Bien sûr!* Ha-*ha!* Just kidding! No, I mean you two are room mates and style mates, sort of."

"Don't you have a clinic to attend, *Docteur*? And would you care to look at something quite special? We just received it in San Juan."

Loring tried to suppress his delight. He felt totally confident in Fatima. "Please. Yes. Ha-*ha!*"

"I think it would look exquisite on her."

The necklace was of a rare and milk-pale lapis lazuli – mined in the limestone-streaked mountains near Ovalle, Chile, Fatima reported – strung alternately with gray-white natural pearls on a thread-like silver link chain.

Loring had never seen lapis so powdery blue and delicate, with goldlike flecks sprinkled throughout, resembling the faint scattered stars of a cloudless pre-dawn sky – much like the Caribbean sky they had watched, arm-in-arm, only hours ago. The smooth lapis spheres and pearls reflected gently into each other with a unique radiance. Loring couldn't wait to see them adorn Ulla's elegantly sloped neck. How would that unique blue play with the crystal blue ice of her eyes?

Speechless, he slid the necklace through his fingers and caressed each of the lapis orbs and pearls. Finally he sighed, *"Magnifique."*

"Is it personal and beautiful enough for her?"

"Yes. Oh, I'm so grateful."

"Special Valentine gift wrap?"

"Bien sûr, Mademoiselle! Merci!"

* * *

Tee-ropa-tee-ropa-tee-ropa!

Loring glided giddily over the smooth flagstones of *Boutique Row.*

Ba-da-daah-daah . . .

He found it difficult to believe his impossible luck in happening into *Flair* and finding Fatima. Of all the thousands of terrific gifts all these stores on *Boutique Row* offered, he had clearly selected the most personal and beautiful of all! Thanks to Fatima's inspired consultation.

Yo fabulous, full-sized African woman!

Fatima had conjured for him a gift which was the starry essence of his feelings for Ulla – a virtual piece of the sky. (The necklace hadn't even made it into the display case yet. So, without Fatima's clever reckoning, Loring would never have even *seen* it.) The box itself felt as light as the dawn air. He held it up and tried to make out his reflection in the *Flair* silver foil wrapping paper with the gold foil bow. And, of course, as light and airy and sky-like as those milky blue stones inside shone, there was in Loring's heart a universe of starry feelings alive and turning with celestial constancy for Ulla.

Tee-ropa-tee . . .

No wonder Jacques was entranced with Fatima. The woman was amazing. And remarkably intuitive, like Chemin *lui même*!

At one point, while she had snipped the gold strands on the gift box, Loring inquired in French, perhaps impertinently, if she herself had a favorite Valentine.

"Pas du tout!" she giggled with a slight batting of the eyelids.

When Loring mentioned Chemin by name, however, her gaze steadied, and her face blanked into an indisposing, Sphynx-like stiffness.

Loring left it at that, silently handed her his Visa card. With a cheery and sincere, *"Merci mille fois!"* he slipped out of *Flair*.

Ba-da-daah . . .

As he floated aft down the polished flagstones and then turned into the *Central Stair Tower*, he glanced at his watch. Ten minutes till clinic. Plenty of time to trot up to *Topsiders* again for a reprise of the *Allegro Assai* and perhaps a quick telepathic indulgence to Salzburg. He simply could not rid his system of that bubbly Mozartian bliss. Why fight it? Why not ride that cascading melodic motif another time before meeting the power cruiser patients?

"Dart Doc!"

"Yes?"

Loring looked down. On the landing he saw a freckled, green-eyed frown bearing up at him. Maggie McCarthy was charging up the stairs, panting.

"Good morn . . . "

"Good?" She paused to catch her breath, then whispered, "What the frick's *good* about the Captain going AWOL on us?"

"Captain?"

She nodded and scowled. "This ship is due to leave San Juan in two hours, and his Norsky nibs Ramskog is nowhere to be found. No word to me or to Staff Captain or anyone. Guess he couldn't take the news about Snø."

"Is Snø alright?"

"More than alright, Doc. Didn't you hear? Queen Snø? Oh, yea! Snø's gonna' be on the frickin' *Love Luck* show tonight. Yep. Gonna' trash mouth me at the *Cablevista* cameras and pick up one of them new Mercedes roadsters and a cool $250K."

"Couldn't the Captain keep that from happening? He *is* the Captain."

"You can't command a ship you're not on, can you? Even *he* can't do that!"

"Not even on the ship?"

191

Maggie rolled her eyes. "Plus, do you know you got world famous overnight? You heard me. You probably haven't seen the reruns from last night? I know, you always say you never watch the frickin' boob tube. Well, no matter, Cablevista has your face plastered all over the frickin' screen this morning. I guess your dance with old Mrs. Snippet-White caught everybody's eye. Cablevista headquarters in New York is hyping you up somethin' hideous. Harvard Med and an eligible bachelor and kind to old ladies and all that stuff. Even started callin' you Dart Doc. We got us a long line of old broads, just waiting to have their pictures taken with you at clinic this morning. Do they want to meet Kevin and Guy? Hell, no! And what's this stuff about a TV tour of the *Hospital*? Farrely Farrell's camera crew is down there nosin' 'round at everybody."

"Did I promise Farrely I'd lead him on a tour this morning? I don't . . ."

"And did you think of mentioning any of this to the Chief Nurse? Turn your head. Everybody's yakin' it up about the doctor's profile. All the power cruisers want to meet you. All they want to do is see Doctor Oliver and get your autograph. They keep showin' your profile on Cablevista. Boy, you got a *nose* on you! For sure. They say you look like Leslie Howard. Now who in hell is he?"

"You're from Georgia. Didn't you ever see *"Gone with the Wind"*?"

"Oh, *that* guy! You mean Ashley? Well, shit! You do. Sort of. But you're a Yankee!"

"They think I look like Leslie Howard?"

"And wasn't that Leslie Howard English, anyway?"

* * *

Loring had given personal tours of the *Hospital* on previous voyages and always enjoyed hamming – gags with the cardiac defibrillation paddles ("Oh, that always makes me feel *so gooood*!" or *"NUURSE! IT'S WOOOORRSE!"*) or the usual urine or orifice jokes, whatever came to mind as he pointed out the Art Deco particulars of the facility, which the original French naval architects had crafted so enduringly on *Viking Deck*. But to lead the tour in front of TV cameras with a flock of fans milling out in the *Passenger Waiting Room* and down the corridor?

"Be yourself, mate! Sorry I forgot to mention this to you," added Farrely Farrell, who quickly appraised the narrow environs of the *Hospital* and saw that a question and answer interview format was not practical.

"Better for you to lead us through it solo, Dart Doctor," he said. "You certainly have the star power to sustain it by yourself! And by the way, the producers in New York simply *love* you, man! You're our latest blast image."

"Blast image?"

A technician fastened a microphone to his collar and a small transmitter to the back of his belt.

"Forget the make-up!" shouted Farrely Farrell. "You're on, Oliver."

"I'm on? Ladies and gentlemen out there in Cablevista country, welcome to the *Hospital* of the *S/S Nordic Blue*. I'm Doctor Oliver Loring, and I'll be your host for a brief vision of what we have to offer you here, should you have need for medical assistance, on your otherwise pleasure-filled dream cruise on the world's grandest and most legendary cruise ship.

"Farrely Farrell has probably already shown you many of the incredible facilities here, and – not to worry – we have some of the finest medical facilities afloat anywhere. And now, without further ado, let me lead you viewers from around the world through a facility that . . ."

Just pretend you're Flip Spinelli. Parrot all his usual expressions. Play to the audience as if they were only so many insects in the palm of your hand. You could crush them with one swift squeeze of your fingers, and they know it, but they are so grateful that you don't. You know that tone and that pace. Keep talking smoothly and without an interruption, as if you've done it a hundred times before . . . and stop repeating that word "facility."

"We'll start off off in the *Passenger Waiting Room*, move right on into *Radiology*, and then on down to the *Treatment Rooms*, the *Observation Unit*, and *Intensive Care*, a quick peek into our *Hospital Kitchen* and the *Nurse Quarters* and then a look-see into the original deluxe *Plastic Surgery Suite* which the crack team of French naval architects did in high Art-Deco style. And then, ladies and gentlemen out there in Cablevista land, I'd like to invite you all down the corridor into my own private suite for a few final words about why our ship, the *S/S Nordic Blue*, cannot be rivaled by any other afloat for . . ."

For seven minutes of the tour, Loring was total master of his domain, with the cameraman and sound technician following his every gesture and syllable. He pressed flesh in the *Passenger's Waiting Room*, glided swiftly into *Radiology*, where he deciphered images of a Brain CAT Scan – pointing out shadows of blood that indicated a brain bleed in the left temporal lobe and the necessity of air evacuating a patient on a recent *(thank our lucky Nordic Stars! – not this!)* cruise. He showed the *Hospital Kitchen* in all its sanitary brilliance. He discreetly displayed the flowered counter area of Maggie McCarthy's cabin boudoir and briefly opened the sliding glass doors of the Plastic *Surgery Suite* with its three curious claw-footed, sterilizing pressure ovens.

"Now is that some kind of French style or *what*, heh?"

No detail was too precious or obscure, and Loring would have been willing to elaborate generously. But time was a factor, and he wanted an opportunity near the end to celebrate his own philosophy of cruising in his own private suite. But this was not to be.

As he was about to lead the cameras and Farrely Farrell into the *Passenger Examining Rooms*, Loring heard a loud thump at the port *Emergency Entrance*. The door blew open. "Doctor! We need you out here. *Stat!*" Maggie shouted urgently from the aft corridor. "And no cameras, please, damn it!"

"I'm sorry, Farrely." Loring unsnapped the microphone wires from his collar and belt. "Looks like our tour has to come to an end. Nurse wants me."

"*Do* what you *must* do, Doctor Loring! I know you have incredible responsibilities on this ship. And thank you. We'll catch up with you later at the Captain's Cocktail Party. Yes, and isn't that Dancing Doctor fabulous, ladies and gentlemen? Let me see where we can take you on our next visit around . . ."

* * *

"DOCTOR! THEY WATCH THAT SHOW IN NORWAY!"

If Maggie McCarthy and Staff Captain Nils Nordström had not been out there in the corridor to identify the hooded figure running in place and cursing belligerently under his breath, his hands cuffed behind him, Loring might have passed the creature off as a crazed power cruiser.

Loring had seen this same incensed creature at dawn out on *Promenade Deck* – the jogger oddly pumping his fists up at the red sky. But at dawn, Loring had considered him only a harmless curiosity, perhaps a martial arts enthusiast out for an intense morning work-out.

A concerned passenger had phoned the *Bridge* to report the individual's bizarre, possibly dangerous, behavior. On the *Bridge*, Nils Nordström had dispatched Security Agents Nigel Cooper and Nick Fenwick to *Promenade* to investigate.

Agents Cooper and Fenwick, both retired London Bobbies, radioed back that the hooded man refused to speak to them and appeared to be harmless but "dingy as a doorbell." Nigel and Nick asked Nordström if he thought Captain Ramskog would want them to haul the weird lunatic up to the *Bridge* or down to the *Hospital*.

When Nordström called the Captain's Cabin, Trond was not with Snø. Nor was Trond with the Nurse. Nordström then realized that none of the Officers had, in fact, seen Trond Ramskog since his brief appearance the previous evening (without his wife) in the reception line at the *Midnight Promenade*.

Unaware of the identity of the frenzied jogger, Nordström ordered Nigel and Nick to secure the troubled man and bring him to the *Hospital* for a medical evaluation. Meanwhile, he ordered half a dozen Officers to fan out over the ship to find the elusive Ramskog. Not until Maggie McCarthy confronted the sweaty, bundled-up kook grunting and hiccupping in the corridor, did anyone realize the handcuffed jogger and the missing Captain were one and the same.

"HOW CAN SHE DO THIS TO ME? LOOK AT ME! I CAN'T STOP!"

Loring was no stranger to moments when waves of pernicious influence took possession of events in a clinical arena. Mental aberration in any of its devious forms – mania, hysteria, paranoia, frank depression – could quickly infect anyone near the process. The astute clinician had therefore to isolate the source immediately to prevent spread of an insidious dynamic. To deny the presence of the pernicious influence – due to amazement or disbelief – invariably led to trouble.

Loring looked back inside the *Hospital* corridor. The Cablevista personnel had cleared out with their cameras and microphones. "Take him into *Examining Room One*," he whispered, "and remove the handcuffs."

Loring had scarcely been given time to consider the Captain's reported absence, and it was a quick relief to see Trond Ramskog on board and accounted for. But the Captain's condition shocked him.

"We better medicate him at once," Maggie said, as the Brits, followed by Nils Nordström, led the Captain into *Examining Room One* and took off his shackles.

"Let him jog as long as he wants!"

"But he's been running all night, Oliver! At least let's get some of his clothes off him."

"Go ahead!"

"Probably needs fluids, too."

Loring stood back in amazement as the Captain shuffled, rather idiotically, in place. His black sunglasses obscured his eyes, and a towel covered the parts of his face not already hidden by his black hood.

With difficulty Nurse McCarthy peeled off the layers of his disguise. Finally, his moist blonde head with its wet, matted mustache, and then his sweaty, hairless torso were unveiled. Flushed and lathered in a full night's perspiration, Trond glared forward, continued to jog, the well-defined sinews in his arms rigid and drenched. His ribs heaved and bulged with every pace. His abdominal muscles tightened spastically.

The 50-year-old brow was riven, bereft of its gracious sweep above his boyish upturned-nose. Down his cheeks, stony, sweat-dripping streaks of muscles tightened into his fixed jawbone. His thin lips pressed together. His nostrils flared with each panting breath. The seething, fjord-blues blazed with blow torch force.

"SHE'LL TELL EVERYTHING! THEY WATCH THAT GODDAMN SHOW IN NORWAY, YOU KNOW! HEEEEEK-HEEEEEK. HOW CAN SHE HEEEEEEK DO THIS TO ME? HEEEEEEEK."

See that! A perfect example of the denial instinct! You noticed him out there earlier. But you were too busy cavorting with Mozart and Ulla in Salzburg to perceive who he was and how seriously depraved he was. Obvious denial, Dart Doc! You should have recognized your own Captain! You were up buying jewelry while Nick and Nigel were strapping him in irons. Your Captain in irons on his own ship!

"DOCTOR! I CAN'T STOP!"

"We'll get you through this, Captain!"

"SHE WANTS TO DESTROY ME! ALL FOR A GODDAMN AUTOMOBILE!"

Loring waved Nick and Nigel out. Then he looked at Nils Nordström. "The Nurse and I can handle things here, Staff. Why don't you head back to the *Bridge*."

Nordström chewed on his gray mustache as he watched the Captain's grotesque movements. "You'll transfer him off the ship right away?"

"Not just yet. Let me see what I can do with him here."

"Here?" Nordström's lower lip curled. "Doctor, this is a very important cruise. The Captain needs all his faculties. His mind has gone frickin' psycho! Look at him, man!"

"I'm well aware of that, Staff Captain. I'm *looking* at him."

"Get back up to the *Bridge*, Nils, or wherever you're supposed to be!" Maggie insisted. "Aren't you supposed to be supervising security? What?

Do you think this Captain's gonna' hi-jack his own ship? You gonna' call a *Code Commando* on him?"

"We sail in one hour," Nordström said.

Loring glanced at the three and a half stripes on each of the Staff Captain's epaulets. "Maybe that will be enough time, Staff," Loring said.

Maggie glared hotly at Nordström. "And shouldn't you be doin' your frickin' job? You're not the Medical Department. *We* are. And you're *not* the Captain. *He* is."

"I think I just call an ambulance. In case Captain needs one."

"Yea. You *do* that, Nils. Just in case. We'll let you know if Captain needs one. And by the way, I don't think he needed the handcuffs, either. You should be ashamed of yourself."

Maggie sneered as Nordström shook his head angrily, stepped out and closed the door.

"That fat son of a bitch would love to take over command. He'd love to make it four stripes at Trond's expense."

"But look what we've got on our hands."

"FOR ONE DAMN AUTOMOBILE! SHE WANTS TO DESTROY ME! HEEEK!"

"We'll get you through this," Loring insisted. "I'll be right back."

"Where the hell are you going?"

"Stay right here with the Captain, please."

* * *

At the Boston Samaritan, Loring sometimes found it useful to remove himself briefly from difficult patients to define a separate emotional space for himself and to find fresh therapeutic vision. Often a quick glimpse out his office window at the clouds in the sky or the people in the street was enough to offer relief and insight. To distance himself from the current turbulent clinical arena, Loring stepped down the corridor into the adjacent *Examining Room Two*.

He took a seat on the examining table and peered out the porthole. Although he heard the Captain stomping and raving on the other side of the wall, he tried to focus on his exterior environment.

The intense redness of the early dawn had dissipated, and the slowly moving cumulus shadows of a partly sunny Caribbean morning now speckled the surrounding San Juan cityscape. So much for distraction from the weather.

Everything else Loring saw outside the porthole only cranked up his anxiety. Preparations for the departure from San Juan proceeded full tilt. The *Passenger Gangway* teemed with reporters, photographers, San Juan police, ship security agents, curious onlookers and power cruisers.

Rearward, supply vehicles jammed the on-load area. Cablevista teams dragged more equipment consoles and cable spools up the ramp. In the middle of it all was hard-working Pearly Livingstone, sweating through his wave-and-sunburst t-shirt as he wheeled his forklift through the maze of vegetable crates, liquor cases, bundles of fresh cut flowers, and mail bags.

And up above, three news helicopters flitted over the city and the port. They dived and ducked crazily around the blimp, whose message glowed a loud electric: *"FAREWELL SAN JUAN! HELLO CABLEVISTA WORLD!"*

Meanwhile, the commander of this magnificent, history-making voyage was jogging in place, stripped to the waist and ranting at the nurse in the next room.

"DOES SHE WANT A NEW MERCEDES? HEEEEEK. OR DOES THE BITCH WANT TO CUT OFF MY BALLS?"

Loring could do it the safe and easy way: medicate the Captain and transfer him off the ship to a psychiatric facility in San Juan, as the prickly Staff Captain wanted. Five milligrams of Haldol intramuscularly would do the trick – dope Trond deep and then whisk him out in disguise. But a hasty fix with anti-psychotics, though expedient, could spell catastrophe for Trond's career. Mental stability, particularly for a Norwegian Officer's reputation, meant everything, even if an Officer's wife were about to go on international television and slander him to little tiny womanizer smithereens.

On the other hand, keeping the Captain on board in his present agitated state risked burdening the *Hospital's* limited capacities and putting severe emotional strain on all the ship's personnel.

Loring had always taken Ramskog's suave, trademark smile for granted, and most Officers and crew members felt the same. As surely as the powerful steam turbines in the boiler room propelled the ship, the Captain's positive beaming countenance motored the morale of the *S/S Nordic Blue*. But how could Loring restore that famous smile – and that magnificent Norwegian paragon of captainly qualities – back to his usual super Viking self? And quickly, please!

The Captain's psychiatric diagnosis? Acute reactive, agitated depression. His practical diagnosis? Rage.

Loring shuddered at the cruel paradox. Trond Ramskog, the skipper of legendary fortitude, who had displayed steel-strong nerves through hurricanes, ship fires and numerous other grim catastrophes, had now regressed to an ineffectual, blithering babbler by the threat of humiliation by his jealous wife.

"NURSE! SHE WANTS TO CUT THEM OFF!"

"We're not gonna' let her do that, Captain!"

To treat a rage reaction with anti-psychotics seemed extreme. An alternate approach, which Loring had used with excellent results at the Samaritan, was Auto Dialogue Therapy (ADT), developed by the ingenious Dr. Hartmut Forgascher at the respected Berlin Psychiatric Institute.

Highly effective with professional executives in severe emotional crises, whether from domestic problems or accounting irregularities in the corporate workplace, ADT employed no drugs but simply the creative use of any standard hand-held mini-casette tape recorder and a rigorous auto-feedback technique.

The theory behind Dr. Forgascher's innovative ADT involved the creation of a "therapeutic mirror." The point of ADT therapy was to allow the deranged patient to record and then play back his or her own insane ravings over and over again. Once placed in isolation (as short a period as one hour sometimes sufficed) with the tape recorder, many individuals in crisis – particularly executive types with professional track records of superlative performance – displayed a "cathartic horror" when they were forced to listen to and objectify the stark nonsense of his or her own documented depravity.

ADT required a compliant patient, an individual with enough intelligence and ego strength to intellectualize and take an interest in the process itself. The initial "bonding period," during which the therapist introduced the patient to the recorder and sat through the first dialogue exchanges, was delicate and critical. In Forgascher's own ground-breaking research, therapeutic success depended on the patient's trust in the "self-to-self bond."

Variations on Auto Dialogue Therapy had fluxed in and out of fashion in the emergency psychiatry literature for close to a decade. Loring had been skeptical of some case reports. But experience had shown him that when the "bonding period" was effective and a bona fide "cathartic horror" occurred, therapeutic results were dramatic, prompt, gratifying, and – very importantly here in the Captain's situation – drugless.

Trond Ramskog had the brilliance and ego strength to comprehend the psychodynamics of ADT. Now it was Loring's task to engage that noble but troubled Nordic brain in some frank self-to-self discussions.

His strategic meditations nearly concluded, Loring peered out the porthole again. He smiled when he saw Tosco down by the *Crew Gangway*. Three white *Claridad* vans were pulled up close to the entrance, and the unflappable dwarf was hopping around in his jaunty khaki safari outfit. He held a clipboard in one hand and waved the other as he supervised the on-loading of several large wooden crates and over-sized trunks through security.

Ha! Now *there* was an inspiring vision. *There* was an individual who would never need ADT. Tosco had lived his life with ever stronger conviction and courage, had never shirked from questing further into the frontiers of emotional reality.

And Tosco had never been afraid to use whatever equipment was necessary to pull off an effect. Look at all that stuff he was stowing on board!

Equipment for Loring in this case? Easy. And in perfect compliance with Dr. Forgascher's specifications. The *Hospital* had two little Sony pocket dictaphones – the hand-held machines Loring occasionally used to dictate insurance reports. One of these would be ideal for the Captain's ADT session. *("Hold it in the palm of your hand, spill your nutty guts, Trond!")*

In fact, Loring recalled that the Captain had an identical fleet-issue dictaphone in his office on the *Bridge* for his own daily memos. So there should be no confusion with the mechanical details of which button to push when the crucial "bonding period" was under way. The esteemed *Herr Doctor* Forgascher would approve.

* * *

"Believe me. It works. Especially in executive types."

"Executive types? You want that damned square-head Norsky to sit in there alone and blab his feelings into this little frickin' tape recorder?"

"It's worth a try."

"Honey, I've been sleepin' with the man regular for five years, and I never once heard him mention a truthful word about feelings. I always figured, he didn't know what he felt, so how should I know it, either. Somethin' like that."

"So, what do you want me to do? Drug him to a zombie state and haul him off the ship? You know his career would be ruined. Do you want Nordström to command the ship?"

"But why can't we haul that neurotic bitch of a wife off the ship? *She's* the problem. The poor guy has needed a wife-ectomy for years."

"Should I approach Snø and ask her not to appear on the show?"

"Fat chance of that, Dart Doc. That woman has her mind set on tellin' the world about what a two-timin' bastard he's been. And you know Farrely Farrell is gonna' pick her memory for every little kinky thing. Funny, isn't it? That man hasn't got a clue about his own feelings and his wife wants to tell hers to every body from here to Tokyo and frickin' back. I saw some shots of her on their TV promotionals already. No *way* that dame is *not* appearing on 'Love Luck.' That queen bitch is loaded for bear. By the way, you might peek in on *Examing Room Three*."

* * *

With a virgin mini-casette and three fresh AA batteries snapped into the hand-held Sony, Loring tiptoed down the corridor from the *Nurse's Office* toward *Examining Room One*. He paused when he saw a pair of dark, almond-shaped Polynesian eyes staring at him from the partially open doorway of *Examining Room Three*.

Stone-faced Joey Manook blinked out. "Flip's in shit, Doc. Can you help?"

"Spinelli? In *there*?"

"The Nurse said to bring him in here."

The door opened enough for Loring to slip in past the stout Hawaiian.

Stinky with all-night cognacs and cigarettes, Manook was still dressed in his last night's tuxedo. He clenched a styrofoam coffee cup in his fat, trembling fist.

Sniffing another source of rank vapor in the room, Loring pulled up the porthole shade.

An unshaven, unbathed Flip Spinelli sat in black speedo underpants on the examining table. He was curled monkey-like on his haunches in a tight muscular clump. The Cruise Director stared forward blankly, his tiny black eyes even smaller under his knitted brows. Mounds of curly chest hair billowed up between the thin moist straps of his sweat-stained undershirt. His arms rigid as rocks, his fists cocked tight against each thickly stubbled cheek, he heaved forward into a bellowing snort through his arched nostrils.

Stone faced Manook shrugged his shoulders at Loring.

"Joey, isn't Flip supposed to help out with some of the Cablevista broadcast? I thought he was to be Farrely Farrell's right-hand man tonight."

"Not like this. He's been this way since he came back from the casino last night. Didn't Ulla tell you?"

The Hawaiian raised his hand and shook it in front of Spinelli's eyes, but the Cruise Director did not respond.

"Like I said, Doc. He's in some deep frickin' psychic shit. But probably not as deep as he thinks." Manook clamped his large hand onto Spinelli's head and tilted him to the left. Spinelli rocked over to the side and then wobbled back onto his haunches. "Like the frickin' Hunchback of Notre Dame."

"You mean the gargoyles?"

"Yea, frickin' whatever."

Before the Casino Manager could repeat the tilting stunt, the mute Cruise Director's eyes widened and he brought his thumb to his mouth. His large Adam's apple bounced in his neck. His rodent-like teeth gleamed as he began to nibble on his forefinger nail. Loring saw blood crusted on the cuticles of several fingers.

"Stop that, Flip."

"Go easy on him, Doc. He's in some deep frickin' psychic . . ."

"Would you mind not saying that? I'm trying to think."

"Like a frickin' hunchback."

"Shut up!" Loring glared over at the Hawaiian. "I'm sorry, but I've been up all night."

"Who hasn't, Dart Doc?"

"How did this happen?"

Manook grabbed Loring's forearm. "Can you keep a secret?"

Loring looked into the almond eyes. "Nobody can hear us."

"How about that noisy asshole two doors down?"

"Don't worry. That guy's making too much noise to hear us. Come on, Joey, help me here."

Manook glanced over at the squatting Spinelli, shook his head in disbelief. "Not a peep to anyone?"

"Strictly confidential."

"Okay, then, listen up." Manook loosened his grasp on Loring's arm. "You know what a skim is?"

"A skim?"

"A casino skim? Flip and I were in a little agreement with a couple shore side operations. *Blazes* on St. Maarten and a new one here in San Juan. We've been doing it for three months. We had an understanding with the casinos. Each week we come into port, Flip sends them passengers from the ship, he gets rewarded at the roulette table. Simple as that."

"Sounds innocent enough."

"Yea. But we got busted last night."

"Police? FBI?"

"Hell no!

"Thank goodness."

"In-house. That's why I'm not worried. But Flip is."

"I see that."

"Listen, it wasn't much more than a grand or two a week at each place, but over the months, it would've added up. Nobody gets hurt. Just an innocent business understanding, see? Paid at the tables. Casinos do it all the time."

"How'd they find out?"

"Some old asshole in San Juan named José. When they converted that dance club into the *Tiburon Jugador*, the old owner insisted they keep him on as a part-time accountant. Part of the sale deal. So this asshole José sniffed us out when the books didn't add up. The bastard called St. Maarten on us, too."

"José Lopez blew the whistle?"

"You know José?" Manook searched Loring's eyes.

"Hey, Joey, there must be a hundred guys named José Lopez in the San Juan phone book. Don't you think?"

"I guess you're right. You won't tell anybody? Like Captain Ramskog?"

"Oh, I'm sure the Captain has enough to deal with today. What with the ship leaving port and all?"

"So I can leave Flip with you?"

"Sure. I'll put him back into shape."

"No word to anybody? Well, Ulla knows. She said she'd come by later."

"Ha! I always keep strict confidence with my patients."

Loring saw that Manook had to leave quickly. As soon as the *Nordic Blue* cleared harbor, Joey explained, *Nuggets* would open for business. He had to be back up on *Sunfish Deck* overlooking his staff at the gaming tables.

"No problem, Joey!"

"I need to take a shower before I go to work."

"Great idea. Your staff will be thankful. Believe me, I can keep a secret."

* * *

"Flip, I want you to to hold this tape recorder in your hand, then push the little red button, and speak into it. I know you've been through a very traumatic event. You might even consider me a rival on this ship for the favors of Ulla von Straf. But I understand that you lost at the tables. I was *there* at *Blazes* in St. Maarten. I saw you lose big time. Manook tells me you lost big time in San Juan, too."

"You saw me in St. Maarten?"

"Flip, this is a tape recorder. The microphone is inside."

"Ulla's been after your skinny body ever since you . . ."

"Remember, Flip, I'm a doctor, and I can help you. I want you to think about what you're feeling. And after you've thought about it, please speak into the machine. This isn't a deposition. This is a simple conversation with yourself. This will stick with us, actually between you and yourself. Once you've expressed yourself, just press the rewind button and listen."

"I was worried. She didn't show up till dawn this morning. Then she says she was up with you all night."

"Just speak into the machine, Flip. Remember, several minutes ago you were in a catatonic state. Joey says it's because you were exposed for your skim with the casinos. Also, remember that Farrely Farrell expects you to be performing at your top level later this afternoon. The skim is nothing. Joey says everything's covered up and you can't get into trouble. It was all in-house. The police and the FBI were not involved."

"You sure?"

"Sure, Flip. Remember: the Farrely Farrell connection means everything to your career."

"But did you get into her pants?"

"How about if I press the red button and leave the rest up to you? Get to know yourself, Flip. For your sake. For everyone's sake."

* * *

Loring would have wished for a more complete bonding period with Flip Spinelli. *And* with the Captain. To begin with, he didn't have a clear diagnosis for Spinelli. Catatonia? Pseudo-Catatonia? Conversion Reaction? Acute Regressive Reactional Depression? Also, Loring needed time to suppress his own inner skeptical voice, which screamed in disbelief that the Captain and the Cruise Director could experience simultaneous emotional crises at this critical moment.

As he felt the vibrations of the *Boiler Room* turbines begin to churn up and fire at full power to pull the grandest, most legendary cruise ship afloat out of San Juan Harbor, here were the two most important individuals on the ship incapacitated in his *Hospital*.

In emergency medicine, pondering unlikelihoods was, of course, the clinical equivalent of navel gazing. Loring knew not to dwell on the how-could-this-happen and stick to the this-must-be-done. Listening to his own inner skeptical voice was clinically counterproductive and ethically reprehensible – just another version of frank and dangerous denial.

Yes, perhaps if Loring had paid closer attention to the evolving psychodynamics with the Captain and Spinelli, such an unlikely coincidence might not seem so surprising. Could he have taken pro-active measures to prevent these simultaneous crises? Could he have foreseen the Captain's stressful state with the hiccups? Could he have predicted Spinelli's break-down when he saw him let loose at the young Dutch croupier back in the casino on St. Maarten?

In any case, Loring had no time for such diversions. Nor was he granted time to hover outside the *Examining Rooms* to eavesdrop and make sure Ramskog and Spinelli bonded with their tape recorders.

"NOW HEAR THIS! THIS IS THE CAPTAIN!" Loring overheard from *Examing Room One*.

"LADIES AND GENTLEMEN! DID I LEAVE ANYBODY OUT?" Loring oveheard from *Examing Room Three*.

But minutes after the turbines began to spin and the ship sailed out of harbor, the cityscape of San Juan shrinking to the south outside the porthole, Loring's belt beeper buzzed with three angry electric blasts: the code signal for cardiac arrest somewhere on the ship. Loring darted out into the corridor.

"Blackjack tables up in *Nuggets*!" Maggie McCarthy shouted from the far end of the corridor. "Joey Manook says a power cruiser's turning blue. Better get your butt up to *Sunfish Deck*. Kevin and Guy will cover the Captain and Flip."

Loring grabbed the cardiac code knapsack and darted out of the *Hospital* and down the *Viking Deck* hallway with Maggie toting the portable defibrillator behind him.

* * *

Oliver Loring's long legs vaulted up the *Central Stair Tower* four steps at a time with Maggie McCarthy at his heels. They dashed forward half the length of *Sunfish Deck* to *Nuggets* and traversed the maze of jingling slot machines to the blackjack area.

A thick swarm of gawking passengers huddled near one of the low stakes tables in the rear portside corner. Two Cablevista technicians held their cameras high above the crowd and aimed down at the flurry of fumbling forms and faces. Amidst the confusion of heads around the semicircular table, a white ten-gallon Stetson with a silver Mercedes Benz logo jerked and bobbed desperately.

A frantic, red-faced Clyde Cruickshank yelled, "When is that damn doctor showin' up?"

"Let me through! I'm here, Clyde!" Loring shouted, as he tugged at the shoulders barricaded in his way and wedged forward.

"Clear out everybody!" yelled Maggie.

"Yea! Don't nobody touch her!" bellowed the frenzied Clyde. "Let Doc get in here! Shit Doc, hurry!"

Loring reached the corner table, where the large form of a chubby blonde woman in a tight white leisure suit lay sprawled sideways across the green baize of the gaming surface. Among the cards scattered over the playing area, the prodigious gluteal hemispheres of Blanche Cruickshank quivered fitfully. Her disarrayed platinum page boy jerked in spasms.

"Stopped breathin', Doc!" roared Clyde, his palms upright to the Cablevista cameras. "Christ almighty!"

Loring scrambled over the table to the dealer's side and saw Blanche's pudgy cheeks change in fading pulses from purple to slate gray. Above her pink lipstick, her ashen nostrils flared. Here eyes bulged and wandered in desperate jerks. Her stubby fingers clutched her neck as she struggled to gasp in air.

Loring felt for a pulse in her wrist. "Something in the throat!" Loring screamed. "We might need to cut into her trachea, Maggie. Let's try a Heimlich first."

"I'm right here!"

"Grab her legs and help me get her upright."

While Maggie McCarthy struggled to swing the stricken woman's large knees to the outer edge of the table, Loring stretched his forearms around Blanche's ample waist and hoisted her into an upright position. He hitched his weight forward onto the table from the Dealer's position and knelt, his knees on the table and his thighs and pelvis flush against her rump and torso. With Blanche's heavy breasts drooped over his wrists, he locked his fists deep under her rib cage. He felt the jerks in her chest and neck dwindle to a slow, feeble shudder.

"Give her your best shot, Doc!" hollered Clyde.

Loring nestled his nose deeply into the overwhelming scent of Shalimar in Blanche's stiff platinum locks and braced himself. As the crowd around the table stared on in a paralysis of dread and the two Cablevista cameras whirred on, Loring inhaled as deeply as he could. He rammed his fists up through Blanche's belly and higher into her diaphragm and let out a strident grunt. *"GHOOOOOOOOOOOOOOOOOSSHHH!"*

From the woman came a tiny, high pitched whistling whimper, *"Wheeeeeeet!"*

Flicked free, a wet blue $100 poker chip suddenly lofted up five feet in the air and arched out over Maggie McCarthy's head like a tiddly wink.

"SUMBITCH!" hollered Clyde, as he watched his wife gasp. *"SUM-FUCKINBITCH!"*

After several jerking breaths, Loring felt Blanche's head move of its own accord. He stood down off the gambling table and watched her eyes blink to awareness and her complexion perk up to a rosy flush in front of the bright headlamps of the Cablevista cameras.

She looked across at her husband. "I saw a white light. Where am I ?"

Clyde Cruickshank tipped his Stetson back, came over to give Blanche a kiss on her sweaty, pinkening cheek, and faced the cameras. "Honey, you're on the Cablevista Valentine TV Cruise and you're havin' the time of your ever lovin' life!"

* * *

An hour later, as Blanche Cruickshank lay breathing comfortably in the *Observation Unit* of the *Hospital* – oxygen prongs in her nose, cardiac monitor electrodes on her chest, intravenous drip in her arm, and the fawning Clyde at her side – she had ample opportunity to re-live the gruesome details of her terrifying near-death experience for her reality television fans. The Cablevista monitors all over the ship, including the screen at the foot of her bed in the *Observation Unit,* flashed replays of her ghastly gray face and the sudden awkward jerk of her head as the blue disk spurted up out of her neon pink lips and flipped into the air.

Caught in slo-mo and greatly enlarged, the chip – which Blanche had been sucking on for good luck and inhaled just as she realized she had a perfect 21 (two queens and an ace) – arched high in a graceful parabola and froze, spinning back and forth, at its zenith. As the chip flipped back and forth on the screen, the engraved words, *"Nuggets, S/S Nordic Blue"* could be read circling the central wave-and-sunburst logo.

Then the tape fast forwarded to the exchange between the dazed, resuscitated Blanche and her husband. "I saw a white light. Where am I? . . ."

"Honey, you're on the . . ."

As a sound/visual bite, the event was pure gold. The Cablevista editors quickly seized on it as a spot advertisement. They replayed it repeatedly with Farrely Farrell commenting in amazement at every frame, including ". . . the raw courage which Doctor Oliver Loring used to dislodge the chip in Blanche's wind pipe and thus create a thrust and torque necessary to effect the life-saving extraction . . . and now here's a preview of what Cablevista has to offer you later tonight when we interview three fabulous guests on "Love Luck" and I get a chance to make each of them, just as I want to make *you*, Mate, wherever you are on the Cablevista Planet, *lllllllllllllllllucky in llllllllllllllllllllllllllllove!"*

* * *

Loring paused at the door of *Examing Room One* and listened. No rants or stomps. But no dialogue, either. Had the verbal interaction purged Captain Ramskog of his anger? Had his agitated depression abated already? Or was he sleeping? Had he escaped? Loring knocked and opened the door slowly. Trond Ramskog sat naked, except for a jock strap, on the examining table. The Captain breathed heavily, stared intently out the porthole. He clasped the dictaphone firmly in his right hand. As the sunlight flickered off the moving waves onto the Captain's pursed brow, Loring listened for a whimpered confession. A deep grimace remained across the Nordic jaw.

Loring stepped into the room. "Captain?"

The Captain glared directly into Loring's eyes.

Loring stared back. "Any questions? About the technique?"

With a sudden downthrust of his fist, the Captain sent the Sony smashing onto the floor. Then he jumped up and stomped on it. Whatever clinical data had been recorded on the tape (Loring doubted if there was much) soon became irretrievable, as Ramskog crushed the device under his bare heels. *"PURE BULLSHIT!"* Trond shouted, as Loring looked at the flattened apparatus.

"Be careful! You'll cut your foot! And, by the way, that's a fleet-issue dictaphone you're stepping on."

"*HEEEEEEK. FUCKING BULLSHIT, DOCTOR!*"

"Don't leave. I'll be back in a little while," Loring answered.

His heart beat furiously as he retreated out into the corridor and locked the door of *Examining Room One*.

It dismayed Loring that Trond Ramskog had been so cavalier about the dictaphone – very *unlike* the Captain.

When he passed *Examining Room Three*, Loring became even more dismayed. And not a little insulted.

Outside the threshold, the Sony mini-dictaphone, which Loring had presented to Spinelli as an opportunity to ventilate verbally, now leaned submerged in amber-colored liquid in one of the *Hospital's* clear plastic hand-held urinals. Remarkably, the tiny recorder spools still spun and churned up bubbles and foam.

* * *

"Where the hell do you think you're going?"

"Twelve o'clock. Mambo rehearsal. Gotta' get into my pumps and head down to the *Starlight Lounge*."

"You're gonna' run off and dance, while I sit here and play nursemaid to a couple of jibbering kooks?"

"Kevin and Guy can help watch them. Neither one of the patients is going anywhere. That's obvious."

"How about your frickin' tape recorder therapy?"

"No therapy works a hundred percent of the time. You've got to cut me some slack."

"You're asking a lot of me, Dart Doc."

"I've got my beeper."

For anyone who considered dancing mere recreation, rather than a meditative act, Loring's hasty abandonment of the Captain and the Cruise Director in their current states might seem irresponsible. But he felt no qualms as he left the *Hospital* to rehearse with Ulla. Puzzlement over cases at the Samaritan occasionally forced him to retreat to an empty room for a few quick shuffles, rolls and jives. Besides, he *had* responsibilities to the fleet to perform as a dancer at a professional level in front of the television cameras. In this case, rehearsal was critical.

More importantly, when Loring returned to the *Hospital* after his rehearsal, the Captain and Spinelli would surely benefit more from a therapist newly reinvigorated by some deep dabblings in the kinetic, terpsichorean mode. It worked at the Samaritan. Why not here? And especially since Terpsichore herself, the modern dance muse, was waiting for him in the *Starlight Lounge*!

* * *

Ulla had chosen the zippy, syncopated classic *"Mas que Nada"* for their televised showcase mambo number. When Loring arrived, she was already running through the routine with Barry Cox and the band.

The boys were hot into it. Nimble-fingered Venezuelan percussionist Fernando Uribe popped his conga in a frenzy, while *Señor* Cox's trumpet sizzled with spicy Hispanic trills and accents.

Her hair up in a tight bun, Ulla wore a simple black ankle-length leotard and latin-style stiletto heels. Loring entered slowly and watched as the woman pulsed, swayed, tingled, triple dipped, did a rumba slide variant, all in rhythmic intimacy with Fernando's driving conga ecstasy.

Mambo gods! Thank you for this sanctuary! After that sickness up in the Hospital and the Casino, do I ever need a dose of healthy movement. And oh, doesn't your high priestess have splendidly healthy movements!

He admired her fluidity, knew he could not match it. But when she saw him step toward the stage, she winked, went over to him, and grabbed his hand. Before Fernando Uribe had delivered a dozen feverish beats on his incandescent conga, Loring's patent leather pumps began to glide nose to nose with those fabulously clicking stilettos.

Skin prickles flowed over him in electric waves as he felt her touch and gave himself to the bracing thrust of the almighty mambo. Her long lean trunk and muscular buttocks shot forward and back in tantalizing swivels, as he embraced her and then ran his fingers along her flanks. How exquisitely her hips thrust and her shoulders bobbed! And always with such briskly defined precision and cunning anticipation! At peak moments of tenderness, her eyes batted shut. Then they'd open wide with a wild and joyous, almost defiant blue glare, as Fernando's staccato conga riffs soared louder, more commanding.

When they'd finished the final triple-turn reverse carry, she grabbed a towel from a chair and laughed as she panted. "Wonderful, Barry! *Gracias,* Fernando!"

She mopped the moisture from her flushed face and her shoulders. The *caballeros* in the band smiled.

"What do you think, Oliver? Of course it's only a sketch so far."

"It needs some knee slides on the final refrain. Or would that be cliché?"

"Why cliché?"

"Watch this."

"Da-dooooh, mambo dooooooo!" Loring hummed as he slid forward for her on his knees, his back arched and his neck cocked resolutely.

"Like it!" she exclaimed. She tossed the towel back over the chair and joined him. "So, I'd probably cross over like this and follow up with an open arm . . . maybe a . . . shuffle weave? Like this?"

"And then meet me right back here on . . . *mas que nada* . . . "

* * *

Did the pure kinesthesia purge Loring's mind? Or was it the stimulation of collaborating with Ulla and the band in planning their number?

Total professional rectitude – not a word about their night strolling the deck or even mention of Flip Spinelli's precarious emotional condition – only mambo, mambo, mambo.

Or was it the occasional heady rush he felt when he looked into her eyes and took a mysterious whiff of that familiar balsam-flavored Salzburg air? Of course the mambo was unknown to Mozart, but could the ubiquitous and irrepressible spirit of Amadeus have influenced the roots of its Afro-Cuban development?

Absurd thought? Perhaps. But after three run-throughs of the routine, *"Mas que Nada"* was solid musically and tight choreographically. Though he was out of breath and sweating profusely, Loring's head felt as dry and clear as that of any discerning Enlightenment philosopher strolling around the Austro-Hungarian Empire.

"Let's try to fit in another rehearsal tomorrow afternoon?" Ulla suggested as Barry and the band put away their instruments and stepped down from the stage.

Loring toweled his brow, removed his pumps. "Do you know what tomorrow is?"

"It's our television performance," she said, drying off the flushed nape of her neck.

"Besides that?"

Ulla blinked twice, looked down at the dance floor and up into his eyes again.

"Do they celebrate Valentine's Day in Salzburg?"

"Yes."

"Well, would you be mine? Just for tomorrow?"

Heated as she was from her dancing, a deeper red blossomed on her high cheeks and then flowed in a wave down her neck.

"Only for a day. But longer if you'd like. You see. I don't feel shy at all with you anymore."

* * *

Halfway down the *Central Stair Tower* to the *Hospital*, Loring was movement incarnate. The enlightening effects of the mambo were in full force, and his hoped-for cure for the Captain of the *S/S Nordic Blue* hit him full blast, point blank.

Kinesis. I must put my will into action, full physical action. I must focus my kinesis, just as my physical meditations with the high priestess of the mambo gods focused my will. Kinesis. Kinesis. Kinesis.

"Tee-ropa-tee . . ."

Loring had no new idea of how to rehabilitate the Cruise Director. Spinelli was, after all, a singular and off-putting case.

But Captain Trond Ramskog, on the other hand, had better be ready for a bullseye therapeutic maneuver fitting to the will and wiles of the somewhat sleep-deprived, but newly charged-up, Dart Doc.

It would not be elegant. Neither would it be pleasant for either of them. But as surely as the mambo gods had lived and reigned in the *Starlight Lounge* a few minutes ago, Loring was about to cure the Captain.

* * *

On the port side of *Viking Deck*, Loring ducked into his cabin adjacent to the *Hospital* and stripped naked. He jumped into his shower, fired it up to the hottest water temperature he could tolerate, lathered completely, and then jammed the faucet into full-force icy. Skin tingling from the shocking reversal in temperature (Loring also dipped into his ice chest and rubbed some cubes all over the chest, abdomen, inner thighs and calves). Then, shivering, naked, and dripping wet, he went out of the bathroom and lifted the bunch of Imperial Fiat roses from their wave-and-sunburst vase.

He grabbed the 23 roses by the clumps of their stems in his fists and began to flail himself across the shoulders and spine.

"OUWWWW! EUUUUUOOOOOHH! OUWWWWWWWW! HARDER! YOU MUST BE MERCILESS! TOTALLY MERCILESS! YOU CALL THIS KINESIS? YOU REALLY CALL THIS . . .

"OUWWWWWWWWWWW! EUUUUUUPH! HARDER! MERCILESS! DID YOU HEAR ME? I WANT YOU TO DO BETTER THAN DARIA DID WHEN YOU WALTZED WITH HER! OUWWWEEEEEEEOUUUUUHHHH!

"YOU NEVER KNOW UNTIL YOU KNOW! LORDY! LORDY! LORDY!"

Again and again he self-flagellated, until his back smarted horribly, rose petals were strewn all over the cabin, and streaks of blood had started to show up on the rose leaves. (Fritz the Florist, usually a meticulous de-thorner, had left a few token jaggers on some of the stems. Thanks, Fritz!)

The private ritual lasted five minutes by the clock. Loring could not have endured 30 seconds more.

But now I feel fully imbued with kinesis. Raw, raw, raw Kinesis!

And he needed all the preparatory purging and power packing he could get. After all, he was about to confront one of the toughest Viking creatures the seven seas had ever seen. And yes, he was borrowing from Ingmar Bergman – a Swede, not a Norwegian. And yes, in *"The Virgin Spring,"* Max von Sidow tears down a birch tree and shears its branches into stinging switches for the flagellative device.

But so what! Max von Sidow needed to be spiritually pure to wreak vengeance on the three hoodlum shepherds who raped and murdered his virgin daughter and then wandered to his house and tried to sell him her mother-made, gold-threaded garments.

So what if it was not a perfect match? Imperial Fiat roses, not Swedish birch branches. Loring *had* all these roses and he had *no* Swedish birch switches. Modern Norwegian ship captain, *not* ancient folklore Swedish land owner. Direct and definitive psychotherapy, *not* mortal vengeance!

Ersatz ritual scenario or not, down at gut level, Trond Ramskog *was* an old-time Viking, and he needed some old-time Viking medicine, albeit folk lore medicine. Loring was certain of it. The same principle of kinesis was active and relevant, and Loring knew it would work.

He padded his back welts with a towel till the blood stopped oozing. Then he redressed, donned his epaulets, picked up the frosted glass *vaporisateur* and spritzed on some refreshing Nino Cerutti 1881.

Kinesis! Go for it!

* * *

Confident and fully focused, Loring entered *Examining Room One*. He found Trond Ramskog still jogging in his jockstrap – furious and obsessed, but with a posture slumped and with fists now weakening and barely raised. Fortunately, someone had swept the floor free of dictaphone fragments.

The Captain revived at the sight of Loring. His pace quickened and his fists rose. Despite the fatigue of his body, his brow creased with fury, and his blue eyes flared, intent and indignant.

Though words were strictly ornamental to the treatment Loring was about to effect, he paused and said, "Captain, be a captain!"

Ramskog arched his head back, first in surprise then defiance. It was the ideal angle for Loring. With one quick step forward, he raised his open right hand and, feeling the power of all the ritual rose lashes now mounting to a near omnipotence within his therapy chakra, he uttered his dart-aiming mantra – *"Thooooooooooooooooooooong!"* – and cuffed the Captain broadside on the cheek.

For the briefest of instants, Loring thrilled at the physics of the slap. His large palm popped along the Captain's lower lip line, up across his cheek bone, and his fingertips reached back across the Captain's curly golden hair well behind his ear. The Captain's jawbone bore the brunt, and Loring could feel the rear molars in twin ridges register across the center of his palm. Loud and high-pitched, but with no crunch to it, the full impact torqued Ramskog's head slightly on his neck.

Loring heard the Captain's low-pitched grunt, *"Uggghhh!"* Tears of pain welled in the squinted fjords. A delicate stream of blood rippled down from the corner of Ramskog's mouth, and his left cheek welted up in a raised crimson, finger-streaked patch. Twice Ramskog's head bobbed down. His nostrils opened wide as he breathed in deep lungfuls of air. All the while, he stared steadily into Loring's eyes.

"I'm sorry," Loring said, as his palm began to smart. He watched the Captain turn his neck and try to regain his bearings. The jolt had gone deeply into Ramskog's senses, as Loring had intended.

For a long while, the Captain did not blink, but simply stared forward, statue-still. Loring stepped back from him, worried Ramskog might fire off a blow of retaliation. Then, quite oddly, Loring thought he could distinguish in the Captain's eyes an actual tiny human figure approaching him from deep in the blue firmament of his gaze. Sure enough. There appeared a minuscule running man, an incubus creature, who charged forward toward him.

Loring stepped closer and gazed deeper into Ramskog's eyes, watched as the figure grew in size, as if closing the distance between them. The tiny character was out of breath, jogging forward and almost as if running uphill.

Loring rubbed his own eyes in disbelief. (Was this like a communication with the blue of the sea? But the sea inside the Captain's eyes?) Then Loring shuddered as he recognized that the figure was the Captain himself.

"Captain! I think I see you. I think I see you in your own eyes."

But as soon as Loring spoke, Ramskog blinked. The figure disappeared, and in its place the gracious glance of Captain Trond Ramskog returned, spread its glorious Scandinavian beams across his brow, his cheeks and his face. Ramskog, fully alert and cognitive, said, "You're right, Doctor. I must be a captain. And a man."

Yo Enlightenment!

Loring saw it, felt it, rejoiced in its radiance.

The greatest Viking since Leif Erikson, the beloved but troubled Captain of the *S/S Nordic Blue*.

Enlightened again! Even the subtle vibratory drone underfoot of the *Engine Room's* stallions seemed once again steady, fully spirited and functional.

Loring watched the Captain's shoulders spread. He straightened his spine. He stepped to the mirror over the *Examining Room* sink, spat blood mixed with saliva into the drain. "Could you send Nurse in, please," he said as he looked up and surveyed his wounds. "I'll need an ice pack and some help cleaning these wounds."

Loring sighed as he watched the Captain shake his head at his own grizzly visage. "Oh, and Doctor," Ramskog added, "tonight my wife appears on the Cablevista television show. It's called 'Love Luck.' She'll be talking about me to the entire world."

"I know, sir. Nurse told me."

"She'll be saying things that might hurt. I plan to watch the show in my cabin. Would you sit with me through her interview with Farrely Farrell? I may need your support."

"It would be a privilege, sir."

"Not a privilege, Doctor. It's an order from your Captain."

"But Captain. You're the Captain. Couldn't you just order her not to appear on the show?"

"You've never been married. Have you, Doctor?"

* * *

"How'd you get that jackass to see the light?"

"Slapped him."

"Good work. Been wantin' to do that for years myself. Think he needs some fluids now, too?"

"He'll cooperate. Three liters, maybe more. He probably ran the equivalent of a double marathon, but he says he wants to be back in shape for the Captain's Cocktail Party at five."

"I'll move him out into *Observation*."

"Mrs. Cruickshank can probably go back to her cabin now."

"Yea, I suppose. I've got to hand it to you, Dart Doc. But what are we gonna' do now with frickin' Flip? He hasn't said a word all day. By the way, Mr. Kim stopped by. He says somebody broke in and trashed your cabin, tore up some roses and threw them all over the place. Didn't look like anything was missing, though. Man, this trip is weird! Who would do a thing like that?"

* * *

Security agents Nick and Nigel had already come down for an investigation of the crime scene. Photos were taken and reports filed up on the *Bridge*. Then Mr. Kim vacuumed up all the petals and stems and tidied up to the customary pristine. When Loring entered, not a trace was left of his meditative rampage. Every corner of the cabin sparkled, lemon mist graced the air, and white carnations and baby breath sprigs adorned the wave-and-sunburst vase on the coffee table. A note from Mr. Kim read: *"Lock cabin all times! TV cruise! Be sure somebody did not take your passport!"*

Loring refrained from calling the *Bridge* to clarify things. He did look into the bottom dresser drawer and checked that his passport was still stowed under his socks. (In case Mr. Kim might ask again.) Then he sat down on his bed and gazed out the porthole. The afternoon sun bobbed behind low clouds that shadowed down on the water in gray and green patches. Far to the south, the low cliffs on the northern Puerto Rican coastline had begun to slip beneath the horizon.

"Farewell, *Claridad*!" he whispered fondly, as he gazed south and imagined Daria sunning herself lazily in the grass near the reflecting pool. He wondered if, in her dreamy tiger mind as she gazed at the flamingos, she had any memories of him from their waltz yesterday. "Bye, Daria! I'll see you in Paris in the spring."

He opened his porthole and felt the warm air stream through as the ship headed north. He closed his eyes and breathed contentedly. And not without pride. Inspired by his mambo rehearsal with Ulla and then enhanced by his Bergmanesque ritual, Loring's kinetic momentum had obviously struck a resonating psychic chord, so much so that Trond Ramskog felt he needed to command Loring's presence to support him through the challenge of witnessing "Love Luck."

Had Loring perhaps stumbled upon an entirely new therapeutic modality? Call it Kinetic Momentum Therapy (KMT)? Data would need to be collected, but Loring knew that no less far-fetched concepts appeared regularly in the emergency psychiatry journals. Skeptics might criticize KMT as a technique borrowing from widely disparate, non-medical disciplines, such as pugilism. Likewise, ethicists and forensic specialists might ridicule a method which required the infliction of corporal pain on the subject. (He could hear his detractors already!) KMT risked dental fracture, gingival avulsion, tongue laceration, intra-sinus hemorrhage/fistula formation, orbital blow out fracture, and tempero-mandibular dislocation. Or worse.

But before Loring gloated too long about his success with the Captain or considered putting his own professional reputation out on a shaky limb by publishing Ramskog as a sentinel case report (he *did* enjoy the way the stacked consonants KMT jumped off the tongue), he reminded himself: he had another patient in the *Hospital*.

Should he apply KMT to the catatonic Cruise Director?

To begin with, catatonia of pseudo-catatonia was intrinsically static. Loring had doubts about applying major psycho-kinetic dynamics to a willful and headstrong subject. Secondly, for all of Spinelli's marvelous professional gifts, the Sicilian-American would probably be insensitive to Scandinavian folkloric influences, no matter how therapeutic the intention to apply them.

Lastly, Loring felt conflicted that he might actually *want* to hurt Spinelli for personal reasons.

Should he bother to treat Spinelli at all? The Cruise Director had slimed his own way into this syndicate skim. Perhaps getting busted injured Flip's pride, rather than his conscience or his psyche. Was it Loring's duty as the ship's Doctor to treat the shocked ego of an egomaniac?

Well, yes. Hippocratic tradition called upon the physician to treat according to his/her abilities and judgment. Picking and choosing patients was lousy ethics in fifth century B.C. Greece, just as it would be on a twenty-first century ocean liner, especially when the world's grandest and most legendary pleasure vessel was in the spotlight.

But if not KMT for Spinelli, then what?

For any clinician, deep regressive catatonic states were notoriously difficult to unlock. Loring had fooled himself, not Spinelli, with the great Dr. Forgascher's Auto-Dialogue Therapy. Unfortunately, the psychotropics and mood elevating drugs were either useless or frustratingly slow in taking effect, and the application of electroconvulsive paddles to Spinelli's brain was impossible and inappropriate.

Loring must search outside the conventional armamentarium for a safe, quick-acting therapeutic modality. But where?

Loring leaned forward toward the porthole, closed his eyes and breathed in the Caribbean air. He listened as the waves slapped crisply at the venerable iron hull at the waterline below.

"You should congratulate yourself!" the waves said, in their licking voices. *"The Captain requested your help to sit beside him and watch the TV show tonight."*

"I know that," Loring answered, pleased with himself.

"If the great Captain can look for help with a problem, why can't you?"

"You mean a consultation? But where should I look?"

"Try looking south."

Loring opened his eyes and glanced southward, toward Puerto Rico. "You mean *Claridad*? But he's a magician. Besides, he's not back there. He's on the ship."

"Look up his cabin phone number."

At Maggie McCarthy's desk in the *Hospital* Loring thumbed through the print-out of the *Crew Roster.*

"Tosco-Gutierez, R*amon. Magician and Entertainer. SD #05."*

Starfish Deck. Hmmmm. As low-as-you-can-go down at the prow, near the Crew Weight Room.

SD #05 seemed an oddly humble address for an aristocrat who owned a Puerto Rican plantation and an international hotel consortium. On past cruises Loring had made cabin calls down on *Starfish* – Jamaican, Indonesian, Croatian, Algerian crew members bunked three-on-a-wall, six-to-a-unit, four decks below the waterline.

Was there anything *not* unpredictable about Tosco? Most of those cabins didn't have telephones, but *SD#05* did. Loring rang up Tosco.

"*Docteur*, I would be pleased to help you in any way possible, but this afternoon I am a bit . . . "

"I know you are not a human psychiatrist, but I have need of your insight. I'm in a bit of a jam. May I come down and talk to you? The Cruise Director! He's depressed, catatonic."

"Yes, Ulla told me he was acting strangely."

"He's utterly unreachable. And we need him to be at his best."

"I do have a suggestion. Come right down. Do you think you can find my cabin?"

* * *

From *Viking Deck* Loring descended nine levels of the *Central Stair Tower* to *Starfish Deck* and followed a long, dimly-lit starboard corridor forward through three sets of spring-trigger, water-tight iron bulkhead gates, past several crew lavatories and gang showers and further up a serpentine tunnel that skirted the *Chinese Laundry* and the 50's era French plumbing ductwork that surrounded it and the *Carpenter's Shop*. Near the slanting iron plate liftoff of the *Crew Uniform Warehouse* and the *Paint Shop* near the prow, Loring proceeded still forward.

He felt the rise and sink of the bow, heard the sea smash against it, as the waves pounded several decks up and 17 inches the other side of the forged steel.

"See, I found him," he whispered through the hull to the waves. He caught his breath and tapped at *SD #5*.

"*You won't be sorry,*" the waves answered. "*Don't bother to knock. Just look down!*"

On the cabin threshold sat a styrofoam container the size of a shoe box. Loring read the message written hastily on *Claridad* note paper and taped to the top.

Docteur –

I suggest you feed the Cruise Director half a kilogram. There's a full kilogram in this box. Ulla will help you. She'll meet you in the Hospital. We feed this to our tigers whenever they are out of sorts. Sorry, but I had to run out. Let me know if I can help. Chef Maurice prepared it just this morning.

Tosco

Curious, Loring stooped and opened the container. In a plastic bag, surrounded by steaming cakes of dry ice, he found several pounds of raw meat diced into smooth cubes. The meat looked visceral – an unusual purplish-yellow color. The bag was sealed with freezer tape and labeled with magic marker: *"Foie de chevrette, mariné, 13 février."*

As he retraced his steps aft down *Starfish Deck* while toting the styrofoam container, Loring recalled how, only several days before on the sunny veranda at *L'Etoile* in St. Maarten, *foie gras* had profoundly improved his own humor. Could marinated Puerto Rican goat kid liver possibly share a mood elevating (even anti-psychotic) therapeutic effect with its Alsatian goose counterpart?

Loring had next to no knowledge of the constituents of goat kid liver, but he certainly trusted Maurice, the bouillabaisse master. Cross-species application of tiger to human metabolism and pharmacology might seem unorthodox, even radical. But face it: Spinelli was in a radical dilemma.

Loring had visited *Claridad,* and, not unlike his quest for emancipation from gender-biased prejudices as a recovering male chauvinist, he felt committed toward species blindness. Isn't that what *Claridad* and the *Cirque Ineffable* were all about? And why not use a big cat tonic to treat a little catatonic? Ha-*ha!*

Loring stopped at the base of the *Central Stair Tower* and scolded himself. He knew that a flippant or insincere approach to any patient often jinxed therapy, no matter the methodology. His success barely an hour ago with KMT *vis-a-vis* the Captain had relied heavily on solemn ritual and momentum for its potency.

He stood at the base of the stairwell, the styrofoam container under his arm, and closed his eyes. He took a slow, deep breath. Suddenly another concern – partly ethical, partly gustatory – occurred to him: shouldn't he sample the marinated kid liver himself before feeding it to Spinelli? What physician would risk the integrity of a therapeutic gesture without benefit of testing it on a control subject? There seemed to be plenty of the stuff, and there was no other control subject in sight. Besides, though Loring was far from falling into a catatonic state, he *had* skipped breakfast *and* lunch.

Before his eyes had fully opened from his meditation, his stomach knotted with hunger. He opened the box and unsealed the inner bag. It emitted a pungent, herb-heavy odor. His bare fingers slithered through the cool, oily-cornered chunks inside and scooped a liberal handful of the savory, purple/yellow viscera into his mouth. He closed his eyes again to eliminate extraneous sensory input and slowly closed his lips over Maurice's delicacy.

Carefully and ever so reverently, his incisors, bicuspids, molars touched upon each other, felt the quivering cubes squish between his teeth and his tongue, burst their tender, exotic contents all through his enraptured and wildly salivating orifice.

The effect: instant, fulminant. Maurice's *foie de chevrette, mariné* was an oral epiphany! An explosion of delight! An *out-of-mouth* experience! Talk about seeing the white light!

As fabulous as the chewing and tasting were to his lingual muscles and taste buds, suddenly another imperative – the swallowing act – declared itself. Maurice's *foie de chevrette mariné* slid down Loring's throat, soothed and massaged the lumen of the entire length of his esophagus, wiggled into his stomach and coated it with a blessed warmth and richness.

Was it meat? Fruit? Narcotic? What was it? Loring's gut had never felt so caressed. Then Loring started counting to himself.

One . . . two . . .

He had to open his eyes, find his exterior bearings.

Yes, he was kneeling at the base of the *Central Stair Tower* at the bottom-most habitable level of the ship, *Starfish Deck*, dead middle in the strong iron belly of the ship. He had the open styrofoam box firmly in his keep, steaming up onto his face. Nobody around him. No voice or footstep could be heard. Nothing could be seen above him more significant or dramatic than a grim series of bare electric light bulbs wired in their cages and a disappearing sequence of upward-reaching steel struts and stairs and the adjacent iron bulwarks.

Everything around him was as mundane as anything could appear on a cruise ship. Yet his interior bearings *quaked* with a fabulous energizing power.

Up and down his veins flowed a fulminant, triumphant force – a growing and undeniable exuberance. He had not had a full night's sleep since he arrived on the ship, yet his eyes were open now with the freshness of a thousand dawns. *Love* that goat kid liver! Love *you*, Maurice!

* * *

Nine decks up, with the styrofoam container and its chilly treasure under his arm, Loring exited the *Central Stair Tower* and lunged aft down the *Viking Deck* corridor toward the *Hospital.* He now knew why those tigers at Claridad thrilled from the taste and effects of Chef Maurice's *foie de chevrette mariné*. Loring could feel his long legs stretch and bend, stretch and bend again. He had leaped Amur-like up the *Central Stair Tower*, breathed easily, as if no rhythm – save the silent and sustained rhythm of his vibrant metabolism – could keep pace with him.

Double Ha-ha! So much for his previous theories – particularly his recently-invoked Kinetic Momentum Therapy, which had been so effective in the cure of Captain Trond Ramskog!

Loring had never suspected till now that, for all its ritual and catharsis-mimicking power, KMT relied heavily on a punitive therapeutic message. Marinated Kid Liver Therapy (MKLT), in contradistinction, stood on a much higher ethical plain. MKLT had *no punitive qualities* whatsoever and was, at its core, *sharing* therapy.

Loring had quivered to his very substance with the effects wrought nine decks below by the taste and texture and psychotropic effects of MKLT. His ethical approach to the waiting patient, Flip Spinelli, was therefore as an equal, a co-participant.

As he loped aftward down the *Viking Deck* corridor, he slowed his pace, prepared his mind for the application of the therapy, switched from tiger to Egyptian mode.

Slide . . .

* * *

"You took some, didn't you, Oliver?" Ulla asked.

"I had to be ethical. So what? Tosco's note said you would help me, not grill me with questions."

"I will. I'll feed it to him myself. He's more likely to cooperate with me."

"I'm sure Flip's never tasted anything like it."

"Who has? Maurice is a magician."

"A magician's magician in the kitchen! Ha-*ha! Ha-ha-ha!*"

"How much of it did you eat?"

"Maybe half a kilo."

"*What?*"

"I had to be sure there were no side effects."

"Thank goodness Tosco has much more of it in his cabin."

"Flip won't need more than a pound, do you suppose?"

"Let's see."

Spinelli's tongue shoved the purply-yellow viscera up between his incisors and palate. Then his mouth closed.

His eyes, which had stared forward blankly for the past four hours in *Examining Room Three,* rolled up weakly under quivering lids. His jaw muscles began to clench. His chin rose and his tongue massaged the tiny dice-sized chunks of meat.

Ulla cupped her fingers in front of his chin and offered more.

He blinked slowly, looked at her, first darkly, then with a brighter gaze. He swallowed. His oily, unshaven cheeks flushed slightly with pink. He nodded, opened his mouth wider. She popped in another handful of the cubes. Saliva began to well from the corners of his mouth. He smacked his lips as his tongue tip prowled up under his gums for particles. Slowly he rolled his neck and shoulders, stretched up on his back.

Spinelli would never have taken the goat kid liver from Loring's hand. Only Ulla could deliver the cure, as Tosco had anticipated.

And deliver it she *did.* Her intent glance never wavered as she forced more and more of the healing substance into Spinelli's mouth.

Loring stood back as the Cruise Director regained his animation and intensity. The effect was slower than the Captain's cure, and there was no jogging incubus figure in Spinelli's eyes. But within ten minutes, Spinelli had changed from the rigidity of a stone gargoyle to the kinetic pliancy of, yes, a cat.

He stretched his arms and legs, yawned with a smile. He jumped down off the examining table and moved with agility about the room, his eyes gleaming with his restored, devilish sparkle. If he'd had a tail, he would have waved it in delight.

"What *is* this shit, Doc?" He scooped up gobs of the meat and stuffed them into his mouth.

"A secret preparation."

"Haven't had anything this good since I visited my uncle's farm in Sicily back when I was a boy. They fed me goat kid liver. Tasted just like this. Is that what this is?"

* * *

The day's events had raced at a dizzying pace, and late in the afternoon Loring felt the need for tranquility and reflection.

Tea with the Colonel? Long overdue.

Donning long pants and his wave-and-sunburst tennis sweater, Loring stopped by the *Officers' Mess* to brew up a piping hot thermos of fragrant, lemon-laced Darjeeling. Then he descended to the *Galley Meat Freezer*.

The automatic doors slid back silently, and Loring stepped along the rows of reindeer sides toward the Colonel's secluded bier. The deceased lay in chilly, candle-lit repose.

His white shark skin uniform had again been dry cleaned, ironed, and fitted without a wrinkle onto his long frame. Each medal and ribbon on his chest and sash had been precisely arranged. The candles surrounding his coffin reflected a serene, reverent and geometric tidiness. The glint of the crooked, gold-capped incisor played delightfully in the flames. Chemin's huge ice death bust gazed over his cold flesh twin and glowed with a solemn, flickering vigilance.

With all the lunacy rampant elsewhere on the ship, Loring felt sure he had come to the right place to collect his wits. Here in the wavering glow, Rocky Boy Bebalzam seemed at peace in both static embodiments. As opposed to some of the primary members of the ship's personnel, the Colonel certainly needed no therapeutic interventions, except for the seasoned skills of the finicky, one-armed ex-undertaker, which were clearly on display.

Thank you, Mahmoud!

Sensing respite, even fellowship, Loring unscrewed the thermos top and poured two steaming cups of Darjeeling, one for the Colonel and one for himself. He had planned it this way – two cups – in an effort to reclaim the chat he had never enjoyed with the Colonel in life.

But as soon as the second cup was poured and the cinnamon stick inserted, Loring felt conflicted. Which Colonel should be offered the tea? The actual dead Rocky or the artistic rendering? The corpse or the ice bust? Which was the real Rocky?

As Loring set the teacup down at the head of the casket, in the middle distance between both the Rockies, he realized the dilemma was trivial at most. By perceiving a duality of the Colonel's presence here in the frigid

Meat Freezer, Loring's mind was simply being too busy. He had come here in search of simplicity. Immediately he had complicated matters. No, he would not settle the issue by running back up to the *Officers' Mess* for another teacup. Come to think of it, Loring's father had always told him his mind was too busy. And since Colonel Snippet-White reminded him of his father, and the ice bust was a *dead* ringer for Orson, wouldn't it be the obsessive and polite gesture to bring back down a fourth teacup from the *Officers' Mess*, include Dad in this little seance, eh?

Stop. Close your eyes. Breathe in the steam.

In and . . .

Now take a slow sip of tea, good, and kneel by the casket. Bow your head and meditate. Slow down your mind. You've been flying, Dart Doc.

In . . .

Loring eliminated all exteriors, forced himself to concentrate. Not even a faint Mozart riff should be allowed to drift in and violate the interior vacuum.

Superb. All you feel is the vibrating romps of those myriad stallions far down six decks below. All else is peace. Let the tea enter your metabolism. Now be the tea. Say, "Tea."

"Tea."

Doesn't that sound exactly the way you feel? Have another sip and say it again.

"Tea . . . tea . . ."

Do you like that feeling?

"Yes. Tea says it all."

Tea does not say it all.

"But I mean, tea says all that needs to be said right now."

Well, what else would you say right now?

"Coffee. How about *coffee*? Ha! Ha-*ha*!"

Stop laughing. You're spoiling everything.

"I can't help it! Ha!"

You are being disrespectful of the dead.

"Look at him. He's grinning."

He died grinning.

"How do you know? Were you there?"

If you had been there, he might not have died.

"Oh, right. Super doctor, eh? The guy had a dozen cardiac reasons for dying."

Which guy?

Loring considered excusing himself from the *Freezer* for a few minutes to collect himself, but he remembered he had come here for that very reason: to collect himself. Was he too slap happy to meditate reverently in front of the dead?

"Ha-ha! Ha-*ha!*"

Or did you eat too much goat kid liver today?

He picked up his teacup and slowly inhaled some soothing steam, tried to keep it deep in his lungs, but then he burst out again with laughter. That simply would not do. He took in a full mouthful of tea, tried to hold it within his mouth, was halfway through a deep swallow when another fit of convulsive mirth hit. The laughter exploded and issued as a fine white mist of Darjeeling fog droplets – the cloud hung out a few inches over the Colonel's array of medals.

"Oh, excuse me!" he shouted, laughing heartily as he leaned further forward and waved his hand out over the corpse to disperse the moisture before it congealed and tarnished the Colonel's decorations.

He heard a voice, not his own. "That's quite alright, Oliver. You're certainly excused."

Loring's head jerked back. Directly behind him stood Hildegarde in her white sable fur with Stig Storjord beside her. Loring was afraid to ask how much of his casket-side soliloquy they had witnessed, but Hildegarde seemed not to care.

"Oh Oliver. You two seem to be getting along quite famously together, aren't you? Imagine how much more fun you'd be having, if . . ."

"But that's not going to happen, is it?

"No. But what *were* you talking about, really?"

"Nothing in particular."

"Oliver, I don't think you've actually been introduced properly to Mr. Storjord, have you?"

Loring stood to shake hands with the Fleet Founder, who nodded suspiciously. "You're feeling alright, Doctor?"

"Oh, maybe a little frazzled. I've had several difficult cases today."

"Yes, and I understand you've done quite well with all of them. But could it be time now to look after yourself? Mmmmh?"

"Oh, Stig!" Hildegarde scolded, "I don't think Oliver needs advice. Rocky spent a lot of time talking to himself. I used to love eavesdropping on him. Oliver, don't listen to Stig."

"Doctor looks tired."

"Well, why shouldn't he? He romanced my beautiful goddaughter all over the ship last night! By the way, Ulla doesn't look quite buff herself today! And then, from what I hear, he put the Captain and the Cruise Director back into shape. In the meantime, he brought a woman back to life in the casino. No wonder he looks tired! All that, plus he's on television all the time."

"He looks more than tired to me."

"Well, he needs more tea. Don't you, Oliver? Tea always picked Rocky right up."

"I wish I had more cups to offer . . ."

"Oh, don't worry. My valet Jarvis is bringing tea down to us directly, Oliver. Drink up, boy! We love to have tea with Rocky, don't we, Stig?"

"Mr. Storjord, I'd like to thank you for that nice memo and those roses you sent me."

* * *

At the Captain's Cocktail Party Loring stood with the other Norwegian Officers in full dress and sipped on a Ringnes at the back bar in the *Starlight Lounge*.

Up on stage Barry Cox and the Starlight Dance Band amused the crowd of tippling power cruisers with the usual medley of upbeat Broadway show tunes from *"The King and I," "Oklahoma," "Brigadoon"* and *"Camelot."* Meanwhile, Filipino and Indonesian Waiters scurried around the club tables with the featured alcoholic concoction: the *Bermuda Rectangle (BR)* – a variation of planter's punch with strong rums from four different islands. Amidst all the giddy preliminaries, Cablevista technicians crept up and down the aisles, cameras cocked and running.

When Loring caught the eye of the Captain, Ramskog winked back at him with a jovial blue twinkle. That kingly visage displayed only the slightest of discolored bruises at the upper edge of his left cheek. Otherwise, Trond looked totally captainly. All-systems-go. Loring smiled and saluted.

As his hand dropped from the salute, Loring sighed and took a deep gulp of Ringnes. Trond Ramskog appeared once again handsome, his golden handlebar mustache as straight and even as the horizon itself.

And the recently catatonic Flip Spinelli was also back up on stage looking shiny and frisky in his tuxedo. The Cruise Director bantered off-mike with the band members, clearly restored to his show-time sharpest.

Loring himself, however, despite his clinical victories of the day, felt nagged by doubt.

His uncontrolled outburst of private hilarity down in the *Galley Meat Freezer* had not flustered Hildegarde in the slightest. The widow saw no reason whatsoever why a person should not chat heart-to-heart with a corpse, especially a deary like Rocky Boy Bebalzam.

Stig Storjord, in contrast, had not shared the levity and seemed clearly concerned. The wiry little Norsky had said few words over tea, but often he looked up at Loring with glances that seemed skeptical and worried.

The messy monologue over the corpse might have appeared intemperate. But hadn't Loring already proved his clinical prowess clearly on three separate and very challenging occasions today? Wasn't Loring an expert on the treatment of psychiatric emergencies? He hoped the boss did not suspect the Ship's Doctor himself was experiencing mental instability, just because he became a bit unhinged over the coffin.

Unhinged! Over the coffin! Stop it!

And what did Loring have to fear from Stig Storjord's skepticism? The Founder's instincts were famous. He had built Nordic Star Lines, the modern sea-going empire, on his own gut take on markets and ships, true. But mostly on people.

Loring reckoned that as Ship's Doctor, he wanted to be valued and respected by that same magnate. If Loring prided himself on anything, it was on his competency. It seemed unfair to judge a doctor by what he or she said or did on his/her knees in a meat freezer when he/she thought nobody could see or hear.

Back in that same meat freezer, Loring had almost asked Stig Storjord what was that doubtful look in his eye. But he refrained. He worried that Stig might consider such a direct question further proof that Loring's emotions had tipped ever so slightly over the rails, if not overboard, toward paranoia.

Norskies! Why don't they talk? Don't they know the meaning of tea? Teach him, Hildegarde.

One Norwegian on board *did* have an urge to talk. Unfortunately. And shortly after leaving the *Galley Meat Freezer,* Loring had stopped up at the Captain's Cabin and, in a last-ditch strategy, asked Mrs. Ramskog not to appear on the "Love Luck" show.

Snø rejected his pleas, said it was her "chance for a lifetime," and would Loring be polite enough to leave her alone. She wanted to collect her thoughts for several hours in private before Mr. Farrell interviewed her. Loring pointed out that, begging Snø's pardon, he noticed how she had a tendency for unusual, perhaps awkward, facial expressions when she was nervous. Would she really want to run the risk of showing those nervous tics to a mass international television audience? As a specialist in psychiatric conditions, he was worried she might have a variant of Tourette's syndrome. Had she ever asked anyone in Oslo about that? Would she want to take a tranquilizer?

Snø said she had not asked for his advice and she resented him pestering her. No, she was quite certain she did not have Tourette's syndrome or anything else wrong with her, and would Doctor please leave her alone? Then, after flipping her face inside out a couple times and spasmodically showing off her gold bridge work, Snø slammed the door.

He had tried. And it took a certain amount of mental stability to go up there and confront Snø, didn't it? In fact, it might have required some mental fortitude – and an appreciation of the big picture – for Stig Storjord himself to go up there and talk some sense into Snø Ramskog. But apparently that was not the Norsky way of running a cruise line.

* * *

Prior to Loring's first stints on the *Nordic Blue*, pseudo-military apparel had always struck him as potentially buffoonish. But at the Captain's Cocktail Party, when the band struck the opening martial beats of *"Anchors Aweigh!"* and he marched in file with the other Norwegian officers from the rear bar of the *Starlight Lounge* right up the middle aisle to the stage, Loring felt proud to strut tall and show off his three-striped epaulets and gilded buttons before the audience and all the Cablevista cameras.

This *was* the world's grandest and most legendary ocean liner, he thought exultantly, as the officers stood at attention in a semi-circle before the cheering audience, and he *was* her Chief Medical Officer! The *S/S Nordic Blue* was barreling full steam ahead through the Caribbean waves with her major operatives restored to their rightful and eminent posts on, undoubtedly, the highest profile cruise of her recent history.

And speaking of profiles, Loring glanced at the Norwegian Officers standing to either side of him – all 14. How competent they appeared! How delighted Loring felt to share in their pageantry! Even the deeply pouched eyes of Staff Captain Nils Nordström seemed to glint with a game sparkle.

Loring saw Hildegarde Snippet-White and Stig Storjord grinning behind champagne flutes in the first row. He also spotted the flaming red head of Maggie McCarthy near the bar at the rear and the coiled blonde locks of

Anita Rothberg at a table near Farrely Farrell. The shiny black head of Jacques Chemin could be seen popping up and down as he stood on his toes and craned his neck for a better view from the rear port doorway.

And wasn't the Captain himself handling things marvelously! The *old* Trond! He smiled without a single jiggle of his mustache, bantered with the audience, joked about the number of TV cameras and monitors all over the ship, laughed about the pressure the officers and crew felt, wondered how many of the Norwegian Officers standing behind him were ready to sign Hollywood contracts – an oblique stab at wit, which the audience obligingly chuckled over.

Despite his on-stage confidence, Ramskog knew that back up in his own cabin, all the animosity accumulated over twenty-four years of a dysfunctional marriage was rolling herself up now into a tight coil of spite for her reality television debut. Snø, former Paris runway model, would be back in the spotlight again. She was about to proclaim herself in explicit terms to the Cablevista viewers around the world as a fitting recipient of a *"Love Luck"* grand prize.

How did the Captain *do* it? Had Loring's therapeutic slap helped Ramskog get in touch with his inner Viking? This evening, while the gale-force winds were revving up in Trond's own cabin, his fjord-blues beamed around the *Starlight Lounge* with unshakable assurance. "And ladies and gentlemen, I'd like to introduce a very special passenger to all of you. You may have seen her earlier on the Cablevista replays of her difficult medical situation some hours earlier here on the *S/S Nordic Blue*. Her name is Mrs. Blanche Cruickshank and she has agreed to join us tonight and give a special award. I think by now all of you know who that officer is who will receive the award."

Once Blanche Cruickshank had left the *Hospital*, Loring had been too engaged all day to think much about her and her poker chip. In Loring's mind, his actions earlier that morning in *Nuggets, the Casino*, did not merit international attention. However, his execution of the principles of resuscitation science had apparently embedded itself, courtesy Cablevista, on the international charts of satellite-transmitted heroic gestures.

His cheeks heated with surprise when Trond called him forward from the semi-circle of Norwegian Officers, shook his hand firmly. Farrely Farrell and Flip Spinelli came at him from the right flank, and then Clyde and Blanche Cruickshank ascended the stage from the left. Finally, the Fleet Founder mounted the *Starlight Lounge* stage to join the circle of admirers.

"Doctor Oliver Loring, you saved my life!" Blanche Cruickshank's trembling voice said in front of the audience, the photographers, and the cameras. She gave him a wet kiss on the cheek.

"Let's hear it, folks, for the Cablevista hero of the day!" Farrely shouted into the microphone as the flash cameras went off. "And don't forget, this doctor can dance, too! He'll be featured tomorrow night on our Valentine gala show, folks!"

"And we have a special presentation to make to him, don't we Farrely?" Spinelli added.

"We certainly do, Flip. Would you like to do those honors, Mr. Storjord?"

Loring's own eyes teared up when Stig Storjord stepped to the microphone and Mahmoud, the Egyptian *Maître d'*, approached the stage. Mahmoud held high in front of him a scale model of the *S/S Nordic Blue* – a hand-fashioned wooden replica of the ship. Her keel rested on a shiny mahogany brace with an engraved plaque that read: *"To Dr. Oliver Loring for inspired service to the S/S Nordic Blue."*

Loring received the trophy from Stig Storjord and Blanche Cruickshank. He remained speechless as the glasses of champagne were passed around the stage and the Captain commanded, *"Skål!"*

The entire *Starlight Lounge* stood and toasted him with a thunderous and reverberating, *"SKÅÅÅÅÅÅÅÅÅÅÅÅÅÅÅÅL!"*

* * *

"And tell us, Snø. When did you first suspect he might be cheating on you?"

"The third night of our honeymoon he didn't come back to our hotel. The bastard stayed out all night on me."

"No apology? No excuses?"

"Mr. Farrell, he's been giving me excuses since that third night of our honeymoon. I've had enough damn excuses."

"Yet you've hung on with him through all these years. Amazing, Snø! Absolutely heroic of you! Is that what your friends say about you?"

Loring sat before the 27-inch screen in the *Captain's Cabin*. He shifted his eyes between the huge glowing close-up of Snø's spastically contorting face while her husband – not two feet from the screen – stared on silent and implacable.

"I've given three children and most of a lifetime to a man who . . ."

"Wouldn't you also call it painful? I want you to tell me about the agony, Snø. Won't you?"

"You want me to talk about how I suffer?"

"Yes. Why didn't you ever consider asking for a divorce?"

"I've been waiting for him to ask me for one."

"But he never did?"

"No."

"Do you think he ever will?"

"No."

"Yet, he keeps treating you in the same humiliating fashion."

"I know."

"Are you ready to make that breakthrough now? Here? Tonight on *'Love Luck,'* Snø? Are you ready to ask him before the whole world?"

"I doubt that he's watching this program."

"So you think it's too embarrassing for him to watch? He doesn't even have enough respect for you to . . ."

Snø's spastic facial expressions could rival a flip-book by Picasso at his most anatomically defiant period – jerky, grotesque twists that startled the viewer's eyes. Her eyes popped around in jerks, and her nose seemed at times to jump around on her face. For her sake, Loring wished she had taken him up on his offer of Valiums.

"I can't take it anymore!"

"Too painful, isn't it, Snø? I can see it in your face. It's written over and over again, all over your beautiful face. All the years. All the betrayals. All the trumped-up excuses. Perhaps we should talk more about the pain before we talk about the divorce. I don't think you've gone into enough detail. You need to get it out, all out. And tell us about sex with this monster. I'm sure people want to know what sort of bedroom life you two have shared over the years. And I know you won't mind revealing it. Try to keep your eyes on the camera, Snø. What happens when he comes home from four months at sea? For example, do you still get aroused when you meet him at the airport?"

As he watched beside the Captain, Loring fondled his replica of the *S/S Nordic Blue*. From time to time, he looked down and admired her twin fluted funnels, the feminine slope of her hull, the tiny renderings of the portholes on all his favorite spots on the ship. *Club Atlantis. The Crow's Nest. The Crew Bar. Boutique Row.* His own *Viking Deck* cabin porthole and the adjoining *Hospital.*

He was grateful for the gift. It seemed curious, though, that he had been

232

awarded a 12-inch wooden model boat for saving a human life, while Snø Ramskog would receive one of the finest deluxe sports cars Europe could produce, along with two hundred and fifty thousand dollars, for trash-mouthing her husband to the world.

"After we have sex, he tells me he pities me. Can you believe that?"

"*Pities* you? I think he's the one who should be pitied, Snø."

To Farrely Farrell's credit, the name Ramskog was not mentioned. He identified Trond only as a cruise ship captain on a ship "very much like this ship."

"Talk about the pain, Snø. Let it out. Let it go."

But would they wish any ship's captain on the high seas to be cursed with a wife like the one on the screen – dazzlingly gorgeous and intelligent, but full of hate to the point of neurotic disfiguration.

How this interview could be considered entertainment seemed bizarre to Loring. What thrill did the Cablevista audience possibly get out of such sadistic picking away at emotional scabs? The mutilatory process was formidable, especially at three-times life size and in blazing color. Pain on the face, hate on the tongue.

Loring, who over the years had shared his Cambridge apartment with several women for longer than get-acquainted relationships, refused to judge anyone who had entered into matrimony, particularly a Norwegian Officer. He knew Trond and Snø Ramskog's story was hardly unique. Perfidy to one's wife back in Oslo or Bergen was virtually *de rigeur* to maintain a modern Viking's sanity, what with all the alcoholic, string bikini escapades fostered on board.

What gnawed Snø to the core was the fact that, within this temptation-laden, sybaritic context, the Captain had stayed true to Nurse McCarthy for six years. If he had romped with a succession of power cruiser movie starlets or a series of Filipino Chambermaids, Snø said she would have considered such behavior forgivable, expected of the modern day equivalent of a feudal baron, whose word made those around him jump to please. But this "shameful and immoral arrangement" with the Nurse had insulted their three children, Runar (21), Kristian (19), and Trygve (17), and brought Snø to the "height of dishonor" among her friends in Oslo.

She now saw a psychiatrist daily, had invited the children into therapy with her, begged the Captain to enter into group couples therapy. Under protest, she had resorted to taking anti-depressive medications, suggested the children try them, too.

(Why hadn't any of those busy Oslo psychiatrists diagnosed her Tourette's?)

"Surely you've considered looking outside your marriage, Snø? If for no other reason than to find relief from your pain?"

"Looking? What do you mean by that?"

"Looking and maybe finding."

"You mean sex? You mean have sex outside my marriage?"

"Try to calm yourself, Snø. Look at the camera, please."

"What the *hell* do you mean *'looking'*?"

A wave of dark crimson surged into Snø's cheeks and forehead. Her already distorted features fragmented further. Farrely Farrell's question, in no way voiced as accusatory, had stepped on a mine field of deeply conflicted emotions.

"Please, *please* calm down, Snø. I didn't mean . . ."

The Captain jumped up. *"I KNEW IT! LOOK AT THAT!"* he shouted as he pointed at the screen. *"SHE'S HAD SOMETHING GOING IN OSLO FOR THE PAST THREE YEARS! I KNEW IT! IT'S OUR NEIGHBOR KLAUS NILSEN!"*

The face on the screen began to shake and disintegrate. Snø's lips snarled, her tongue extruded, her neck began to jerk about, so that the muscles in her chin quivered in quick pulses. Then, in violation of "Love Luck" rule number one ("You must always stare straight at the camera throughout your interview!") Snø's eyes began to twirl in their sockets like a pair of pinwheel fireworks.

As her eyes spun, she shouted, *"YOU CAN TAKE YOUR GODDAMN MERCEDES! WHAT DO I NEED WITH A NEW CAR? AND THAT GODDAMN SON OF A BITCH CAN HAVE HIS NURSE, TOO!"*

"Snø, *please!*" Farrely tried to soothe her, "Don't worry! You can have your new Mercedes. I think we'll cut this interview off now. You've been under enough strain as it is. You've told us so much."

"I CAN HAVE THE CAR?"

"Of course, dear. My whole purpose in interviewing you is to make you lucky in love. That's the name of the game, mate."

Snø's head slowed its trembling. Her eyes converged again straight at the camera and long wet tears spurted down her cheeks. *"I REALLY CAN HAVE THE CAR?"* she sobbed.

"With all the blessings of Cablevista, Snø!"

The Captain shook his head and laughed in front of the screen, *"OH*

SURE! GODDAMN IT! SO NOW SHE AND KLAUS NILSEN CAN RIDE
ALL OVER GODDAMN NORWAY WITH THE TOP DOWN! HA!"

* * *

The *Bridge*. 23.00 hours. Darkness. Chapel-like silence. Vast view through
the ship-wide windscreen of the starry heavens, the shining sea, the constantly
escaping horizon.

Tonight Juan Enriques, the bright-eyed Filipino Assistant Navigator, stood
vigilant at the central helm of the ship's nerve center. Before him the broad
consoles of gently glowing computer screens, sonar and radar monitors, gave
witness in gently twinkling shapes and digits to the ship's position and
progress.

And tonight, as this hushed sepulcher hummed and shimmered efficiently,
the Captain entered with the Ship's Doctor. The half dozen silent Deck
Officers, gratified with the restored authority of their peerless commander,
greeted Trond Ramskog with smiles and handshakes. Loring, too, received a
cordial reception. They nodded their delight at the ship's replica Loring held
proudly in his hand.

It was no secret to any of them, of course, that the night before the Captain
had briefly split his emotional seams and that Loring had helped him collect
his confidence. They also knew watching Trond's wacky wife on international
television was a torturous gauntlet none of them would care to run, though
several of them probably could have been vulnerable to a similar exposé.

Loring watched their eyes follow Ramskog affectionately. Then they
returned to their work, stepped mutely about the *Bridge*, touched the buttons
and levers, shot glances off toward the horizon as their beards and foreheads
reflected the green and orange panel lights. The Captain moved past each of
them, inspected the meters, nodded at each Officer, saluted Juan Enriques.

Loring clutched his model of the *Nordic Blue*, felt a prideful rush to be
even an oblique part of what these men did here on the ship's silent, all-
seeing central nervous organ. On a small TV monitor near the coffee maker,
he saw the blimp's eye shot of the three Mercedes roadsters on the astroturf
of *Vista Deck* rotating in a 3-spoked carousel circle, a delirious Snø Ramskog
waving from the cockpit of one of the trophy cars.

"Thanks for being my captain, Captain," Loring said.

Ramskog grinned as he shook Loring's hand. "Thanks for being my doctor,
Doctor. I owe you."

"I hope I didn't hurt you earlier."

The Captain rubbed his cheek with his thumb and winced. "Nurse should have done that to me years ago."

"Will you be seeing her later?"

"Things seem to be under control here on the *Bridge*. I thought I might drop down to the *Hospital* later, if I have my doctor's permission."

Loring smiled. "Permission granted, Captain."

* * *

Loring dropped off his cherished *Nordic Blue* trophy in his cabin and proceeded down the *Rear Crew Stairway* to the *Crew Bar*. It was near midnight, and the joint was jammed but subdued. No darts. No dancing. The heads at the bar and in the booths all cocked eagerly toward the nearest TV.

On the glowing screens Farrely Farrell and a witty, animated Flip Spinelli co-hosted a flashback review of the day's activities: shots from the blimp, highlights from Farrely's various tours, scattered interviews with passengers and crew members. When Pearly Livingstone *did* get his chance to say hello to his "boys and girlies" in Ocho Rios, the gang applauded with shouts and catcalls.

The *Crew Bar* regulars lapped up every scene and sound bite. If a crew member appeared during one of the sequences, everybody at the nearby booths giggled and toasted. Then a hush would fall instantly, till another familiar face appeared and the teasing and toasting began again.

Unnoticed, Loring strode over to the end of the bar for a Perrier. He watched the others, shared their excitement, especially the crew members whose faces, sometimes only fleeting images, were broadcast now all over the globe to family and loved ones in tiny home towns across Latin America, Europe, Western Africa, and Asia.

Give the talkmeister devil his due. The broadcast was a living post card. Farrely Farrell had set this all up, allowed these hard working souls to be seen by their families far away, though the first family of the *Nordic Blue* itself had undergone a traumatic and humiliating rupture, apparently, courtesy Mr. Love Luck.

"As an insider on the ship, Flip, what has been the highlight of this week's cruise so far?"

"Farrely, here on Cablevista's *Valentine TV Cruise* on the *Nordic Blue*, I just don't know where to begin. Know what I mean?"

"Sure do, mate! I've been here only two days, but I wish I could spend much, *much* more time getting to know this grand old ship. So many fabulous details. It seems on every deck and down every corridor, there's a new surprise."

"You're welcome anytime, Farrely, and so are all your Cablevista fans out there."

Remarkable. The make-up technicians had smoothed out and de-greased Flip's complexion, nearly eliminated the forehead lines and jowl creases. Lid shadow and lash thickener had enlarged the tiny black eyes. They seemed farther apart, less desperate. Little could be done for the bulbous nose, of course, but the techs had widened and spiked the pencil-thin mustache upward – more edge to the upper lip, less overhanging Sicilian beak. And when the camera focused closely on him, the camera crew cut off his bald pate entirely. This gave Flip an intensity of gaze. He looked strong of cheek and chin. Loring wondered if marinated goat kid liver, rather than stage rouge, might have lent the boyish blush to Spinelli's face. And didn't Flip and Farrely exude mutual chemistry?

Yo! Slime meisters!

"Thanks, Flip, for the invite! And can you give our viewers a little taste of what we'll be offering tomorrow in the way of live entertainment here on the high seas?"

"Love to, Farrely. And first I should mention tomorrow night's extravaganza. To start off, we'll be having a wonderful romantic dance show with the Starlegs Dancers. And haven't we received all kinds of e-mail about those Starlegs Dancers?"

"We sure have, Flip. This afternoon our web site had hit after hit."

"Fab, Far! And we're going to have the dancing doctor, Oliver Loring, on for a special spotlight."

"Hey, wasn't the doctor great in the casino today? He saved that woman's life, as you well know, Flip."

"Sure did, Farrely, and would you let me ask you one silly question, Farrely?"

"Shoot the moon, Flipster!"

"Well, Farrely, do *you* think magic is . . . ugh . . . sexy?"

"Ha-ha! I love the way *you* think, Flip! Tell me more."

"The reason I ask, Farrely, is because tomorrow night upstairs in the *Starlight Theatre*, the place we call Broadway on the Blue, we're going to offer our Cablevista viewers something very special and very sexy."

"You mean *'Love Magic,'* of course. Tell us about it, Flip! I hear you've got a magician who . . ."

"Not only is he a magician! You're not going to *believe* this little guy. His name is Tosco. Originally from Cuba. Runs a circus in Paris."

"Do you have any clips to show us?"

"I think we do, Farrely. Let's roll that first set . . ."

Loring nursed his Perrier at the bar and waited to see what promotional hype Tosco might be given for the Cablevista viewing audience. Not surprisingly, "The New World Magician" had not granted Farrely Farrell an interview. After a few standard publicity photographs of Tosco and Ulla and several group shots of the Starlegs Dancers, Spinelli was forced to speculate about the content of Tosco's midnight show.

"Farrely, this little guy has kept everything under wraps. Not a word to anybody. And I'm the Cruise Director. Takes his magic very seriously, eh?"

"Looks like one of the original munchkins, doesn't he? Yes, but look at his fabulous dancing friend. Isn't that Ulla von Straf?"

"She's our new Demo Dancer here on the *Nordic Blue*. From Austria."

"Can you tell us a little bit about her? Our web site has had more hits on her than any of the other dancers."

"Sort of a mystery, too, Farrely."

"Well, I'm sure our viewers will want to tune in to find out everything they can about Tosco. And about the beautiful Ulla, wouldn't you say?"

"Check out these shots of Tosco loading up his stuff onto the ship early this morning. Can you get any clue from . . . "

Loring felt a gentle elbow to his ribs. He glanced over to see Jacques Chemin decked out in an orange silk blazer, white mock turtle and worsted white slacks. On a gold chain around his neck, he wore his giant royal conch shell. The Haitian slid the chain off over his head, sat the conch on the bar, and ordered an Aquavit.

Loring shook Chemin's outstretched hand. "May I?" he asked, and then he reached for the shell. He ran his fingers over the spiny points and the smooth pink flare of the opening. Loring had heard the magnificent royal conch from a distance on the beach of the Private Island. When Jacques blew the shell, it sounded like a cross between a French horn and an ambulance siren.

"So, Jacques! Your fabulous trumpet!"

"Yes, *mon ami*. I was just tooting on her out on the *Poop Deck*. That's the only place on the ship where I can let loose with her."

Loring raised the giant shell to his lips, but Chemin's fingers blocked the gold-gilded nozzle. "Nobody but old Jacques blows this baby, *Docteur*. I'm sorry."

"No, *excuse* me!" Loring echoed, surprised at Chemin's touchiness. He placed the royal conch carefully back on the bar. "I've only heard you blast her a couple times, but boy is that an amazing sound."

"Yes, *Docteur*," Chemin smiled, admiring his instrument. "When she blows she really blows, that one. Sometimes, you know, I just love to let her speak to the waves. They like her. That's where she came from, you know. From the waves. They are like her sisters. And tonight I just felt like letting her talk to her sisters."

Loring took a sip of his Perrier and regarded the unusually pensive Haitian. "Speaking of sisters and waves, did you catch our brother Pearly on the air waves?"

"*Mais oui!* And look at him, over in the corner. Yes. He is very proud of himself. Of course, I told him he should go back immediately into intense physical training. He looks fat on the television, don't you think?"

"But it's been a few years since he was down to lean fighting weight for the Golden Gloves."

Chemin's lip curled above his incisor diamond as he stared up at the monitor. "You are a *docteur*. You should advise him. Pearly has too many of those Ringnes beers every night. Did you see the man's belly on the television?"

Loring surveyed Chemin's unsettled face. The Haitian's eyes flipped up and back between Farrely Farrell on the screen and Loring beside him.

"Are you jealous of Pearly?"

Chemin reached into his pocket, snapped his lighter to a Marlboro, drew in on it slowly. "Just because he shows his face on the damned booby tube?"

"*Oui. C'est vrai!*"

"*Pas du tout!*" Chemin inhaled, puckered his lips and sent a perfect smoke ring up toward Flip Spinelli's face.

"Or is it Fatima who is troubling you again? By the way, I met her this morning."

"You met my Valentine?"

"She's fabulous. She's a little like you. Intuitive, I mean."

"Oh, I know she is fabulous."

"So what's eating you?"

The Haitian's brow wrinkled. "Who do you think you are tonight,

Docteur? Farrell himself? Do I win a Mercedes if I look you in the eye and tell you everything?"

"Look at me, Jacques."

For an instant, the Haitian's confident sparkle glazed over with doubt. Then his head shook, as if a button clicked, and the broad, ingratiating smile reappeared with all the brilliance. He puffed and winked. *"YOU NEVER KNOW . . ."*

"*Stop* that. What does that smile mean? Are you going to surprise us?"

"And Fatima, too."

"I guess we'll never know . . .

"*. . .UNTIL YOU KNOW! OH YESSSSSSSSSSSSSSS!"*

Exasperated by the Haitian's tease, Loring watched as Chemin picked up his Aquavit and his royal conch, winked again, and swaggered off toward Pearly Livingstone's booth in the corner.

As Loring wondered what new trick the Haitian might have up his sleeve, he looked up at the monitor over the bar. The screen showed other flashback views of the day's activities all over the ship. *The Bridge. The Boiler Room. Boutique Row. Club Atlantis.* There was even an aerial shot of the top decks and that solitary hooded jogger plying the planks and punching the sky.

Loring caught a few shots of the "blast image" conducting the *Hospital* tour with an impatient Maggie McCarthy behind him. There were several dramatic views of the blimp from the ship, and vice versa.

As Loring watched and sipped, one view caused him to snort up some bubbles of Perrier. The screen showed a chance pan of the dock with an overhead close-up of Tosco scurrying up the rear cargo gangway – the outback hat and the quick stride identified him. Seeing Tosco was not what sent a frothy Perrier wave up into Loring's nostrils. What made him choke was the large wooden crate in front of the little Cuban. The crate moved up the ramp on its own power. No *Claridad* workers could be seen pushing *or* pulling the crate.

A closer view came a minute later. This time, the camera had been panning from one of the upper decks, probably *Promenade*, and the same crate could be seen rolling down the back of one of the white *Claridad* vans, again on its own power.

The crate was at least eight feet long and four feet high. It rolled along on four over-sized bicycle wheels, but the underside of the crate had pleated black curtains draped all around the bottom at wheel level. As the crate moved, the curtains waved on the ground, and Tosco could be seen muttering words near the crate. Apparently at Tosco's command, the crate stopped to allow Pearly Livingstone's fork lift to pass, and then glided forward gracefully again, untouched by human hands and motored, apparently, from within.

Shortly after the large object scooted smoothly up the gangway, Loring saw another disturbing scene: one of the *Claridad* workers rolled an older, distinguished-looking man with a white beard and in a wheel chair up the ramp.

Jacques Chemin nudged Loring. "*Docteur!* I'm back and I see your Perrier is finished. Now, can I treat you to a very fine Aquavit? Non-fattening, you know. The boys in the corner would love for you to come over and join us."

Loring glanced at his watch. Twenty after midnight. "I hate to run out on you, Jacques. But . . ."

"Again?"

"But I need to get up to the *Starlight Theatre*."

"You are a hopeless case."

* * *

As Loring sprinted up seven levels of the *Rear Service Stairwell*, tiny electric quiverings ran up and down his spine and shoulders and refused to subside. The higher he ascended, they seemed to curl around and make their way into the pit of his stomach. His legs simply would not move fast enough. Every third or fourth pace, his heart flip-flopped. The armpits of his tux jacket became swamps of sweat. Why this drenching, guilt-ridden fit?

Why hadn't he thought things out? Was there any chance that his suspicions of what he had just seen on the video monitor down in the *Crew Bar* could be unfounded? Could his eyes have deceived him? Could that auto-propelled, big cat-sized crate have contained some heavy and self-moving mechanized appliance necessary for Tosco's elaborate tricks? Could that elderly bearded man in the wheelchair have been someone other than the famous Vladimir Vladimirovich Tulov, one of the world's preeminent big cat tamers?

The electrical quiverings centered in Loring's stomach seemed to think not. Perhaps something in his belly would quench those annoying visceral sensations. Loring reached into his vest pocket for his scarab pills, quickly bolted one down without water.

You should have figured this out several days ago! And by the way, I noticed you're not walking like an Egyptian tonight.

Several paces later, he noted that the stomach quiverings had, in fact,

241

diminished slightly, (Thanks, scarab squad, for covering that front!) but the mere pressure of his fingers against his lips had suddenly engaged an old passion in him. Before he could command them otherwise, his right index and middle fingers had levitated into his mouth. His lower incisors and his tongue touched the generous cleft between the ungual shelves and the tufts of his fingertips, and he felt his lips twitch with temptation.

Now, that's more like it. Chow down! Look up the corridor. How many fingers can you dispatch before you reach the entrance to the theatre?

Oh, *why* hadn't he paid closer attention? Maybe Tosco *had* hypnotized him over lunch at *Claridad* two days ago. Or maybe it was that first day on St. Maarten, without Loring even realizing it. Or had Ulla von Straf bewitched him? The first night! With her merengue and waltz! Maybe Loring had, in fact, been in some kind of hypnotic trance this whole cruise! What else could account for his blindness? His ignorance? His stupidity? His culpability? What else could explain his inability to anticipate and prevent what he feared was being rehearsed right now on the stage in the *Starlight Theatre*?

Oh, mambo gods! Make it not so! Or undo it! Or something! How did I let this happen? Did I leave my entire brain back in Boston? Tosco said the tiger act was going to debut in Paris. In the spring. I had already planned to go over there and see it. Perhaps with Ulla.

For a moment Loring stopped, spread his fingertips in front of him.

Maybe tasting just one might bring you back in touch with your old self, before you went into this cruise trance. The last time you used your brain was on the plane down here, when you concluded, beyond a doubt, that you had to get out of the entanglement with Anita. And you were chewing your nails all the way down, remember? You were thinking lucidly back then – something you used to be able to do!

His fingertips glowed up at him, in need of a trim.

And the fact the Anita is already taken care of by Farrely Farrell, and you don't have to deal with her anymore, don't have to show off your nails to her, makes it all the more dangerous to keep on abstaining. Get back to your old self, Loring! Take just a little test nibble and get yourself out of this debilitating trance before it's too late!

Eeeeeny . . . Meeeeeny . . . Miiiiiiiiiiny . . .

* * *

THE STARLIGHT THEATRE
"BROADWAY ON THE BLUE"
REHEARSAL IN PROGRESS – DO NOT DISTURB
ENTRANCE ABSOLUTELY FORBIDDEN TO PASSENGERS OR
CREW!

Loring stood outside the entrance to the *Starlight Theatre*. The quivering tingles persisted. Plus heart palpitations. Plus throbbing temples and a burning forehead. Hot acid seared his entire stomach and leaped up his throat. Lower down in his gut, sharp mocking pincers tweaked at him from inside his belly. (That scarab squad he'd sent down the hatch had been wiped out.)

Despite his rage and embarrassment, he had fought off the urge to nibble. He looked down and inspected – all ten of them long, white, mature, now deliciously ripe for a quick oral harvest. How could he indulge in the thought of mutilating himself? Tosco had already embarrassed him to the core. What else should Loring have expected? Magicians *trick* people. Loring should be feeling astonishment and pleasure – not humiliation and fury.

He took several paces around the foyer outside the doors and checked his watch. Thirty minutes past midnight. Of course nobody was permitted inside.

OF COURSE!

In and . . .

Why had he even needed the television for evidence? The *evidence* had been circulating within his very own *metabolism* since early in the afternoon when he took his first fistful of *foie de chevrette, mariné.*

WHY DID TOSCO HAVE ABUNDANT SUPPLIES OF BIG CAT TONIC ON DRY ICE IN HIS CABIN DOWN ON STARFISH DECK? HAD LORING NEVER CONSIDERED THE MEANING OF WHAT HE ATE? OR OF WHAT WAS PROVIDED BY AN INTERNATIONALLY RECOGNIZED AND APPLAUDED CON ARTIST?

Out and . . .

"YOU NEVER KNOW UNTIL . . . "

It could be that Tosco hadn't really smuggled a tiger on board after all. Or, even if Tosco *had* sneaked a tiger on board that morning in San Juan, there would now be a huge cage all around the *Starlight Theatre* performance area, so that nobody in the audience would feel threatened by the presence of a big cat on board. If that were the case, as Chief Medical Officer, Loring would not have to worry about a generalized uproar in the *Theatre* and on board the ship. No stampede. No power cruiser panic. No real chance of an on board catastrophe. No public health issue whatsoever.

Ha-ha! What, me worry?

And maybe Loring had *imagined* that gaunt Russian-looking man in the wheel chair, who just happened . . .

You might as well bite your nails as try to pretend you didn't get suckered in and allowed all this to happen! At least you would enjoy biting your nails.

Loring put his ear to the doors. He heard the steadily growing drone of the kettle drum and Tosco's eerie voice in its plaintive moaning.

"Eeeeeooowhafrhatravereeeeeee!"

* * *

The hall was dark, and Loring's eyes had to adjust slowly. Tosco's pulsing tympany rolls and his haunting vocal strains puffed up the space to heroic, invisible dimensions.

And suddenly there she was. Daria – striding beastly and beautiful, alone, center stage. For several paces the spotlight followed her magnificent and graceful gestures as her luscious amber and black stripes twirled upon each other. Each nod of her massive head, each prowling step of her paws, each languid flip of her tail, appeared knowing, supremely intelligent. She looked gigantic and omnipotent. Her huge agate eyes were not of a tiger, but of a tiger god.

And yes, Loring believed in her, and for a moment he also believed he was back at *Claridad* in the seductive dream of that gorgeous afternoon he had spent (was it only a day ago?) with Tosco.

But as Loring looked above Daria to the threatening, tornado-shaped apparatus wheeling its way from the background forward onto the stage, his senses were jarred ominously. At once he recalled he was not at *Claridad*. He was on the *S/S Nordic Blue* in the middle of the Caribbean with nearly three thousand passengers and crew members under his keep on a *Cablevista TV Valentine Cruise*, and he did not want to allow even the slightest chance of a disaster to slip by him, not *now* when he could do something to prevent it. As opposed to *later*, when a hundred trauma surgeons wouldn't be enough to repair the mess.

Why hadn't Tosco talked this over with him before? Tosco had been nothing but charm. And big cat food.

Loring knew how refined and genteel, how delicate, was Daria. But how could she possibly be perceived that way by any power cruiser? There was *no* cage around the *Starlight Theatre* stage. That's all an inebriated horde might need as a triggering image to to turn into a rampaging, screaming, panic-stricken . . .

Why hadn't Tosco . . .

In . . . and . . .

"MAY WE HAVE THE HOUSE LIGHTS, PLEASE!" Loring shouted as he stepped down the center aisle toward the stage.

"I SAID, MAY WE HAVE THE HOUSE LIGHTS?"

The *Starlight Theatre* brightened at once.

"AND TOSCO, WOULD YOU PLEASE HAVE ONE OF YOUR PEOPLE SECURE THE TIGER? DOES THE CAPTAIN KNOW ABOUT THIS? I THINK NOT. AND LOOK AT MY EPAULETS, PLEASE! THE CAPTAIN HAS FOUR STRIPES AND I HAVE THREE. THAT GIVES ME ENOUGH POWER TO TERMINATE THIS REHEARSAL RIGHT NOW! DO I MAKE MYSELF CLEAR?

"AM I BEING OBNOXIOUS ENOUGH, PEOPLE? HELLO? DO I HAVE TO NOTIFY THE BRIDGE AND CALL SECURITY? NOW I DO NOT WANT ANY OF YOU PERFORMERS TO LEAVE THIS HALL UNTIL I HAVE SPOKEN TO YOU. MAY WE HAVE SILENCE PLEASE? THAT INCLUDES ALL MEMBERS OF THE STARLIGHT ORCHESTRA, THE STARLEGS DANCERS, AND ALL TECHNICAL STAFF. I'M SORRY, BUT I ABSOLUTELY HAVE TO CALL A HALT TO THIS REHEARSAL FOR REASONS OF THE PUBLIC HEALTH OF THIS SHIP!"

* * *

The musicians, the dancers, and the techies seemed solid when they agreed not to breathe a word of Tosco's tiger to anybody, especially the Cablevista people. Several members of the cast were genuinely relieved when Loring countermanded the final Flaming Tiger Transcendental Gyroscope. Tosco had apparently kept the act a secret from them till tonight's dress rehearsal. A python was interesting, they said, but the tiger was scary. While Loring engaged the cast, Tosco and Ulla took Daria herself down the *Rear Freight Elevator* in her disguised van to the padlocked hideaway area on *Car Deck*. They said they'd be right back, wanted to talk things out with Loring.

Talk things out? *At least!*

As the light and sound techs in the booth finished their final adjustments and clean-ups from the rehearsal, Loring strode about the empty *Starlight*

Theatre stage and struggled with his feelings. He paced the same spot where, twenty minutes before, Daria had exulted in her full splendor, goddess-like in the center stage highlight. No, there certainly could never be another tiger quite like Daria. And yet Loring had not even addressed her by name. That had been rude.

The gold embroidered cadeusis and the three stripes on his epaulets bore down heavily on his shoulders at this moment, human that he was. He would have loved to allow Daria her moments to dazzle the world with her shimmering coated magnificence. Loring knew, without a doubt, that she sensed in her tigerly way the full impact of her appearance. And Loring himself had already seen and felt the shock of the Flaming Tiger Transcendental Gyroscope at *Claridad*. The whole world *should* see the Flaming Tiger Transcendental Gyroscope.

But *not* tomorrow night! And *not* from this particular stage! *Not* with a live tiger who could threaten the safety of the entire ship and possibly the sanity of the world!

Loring turned and stared up at the giant stainless steel structure at the rear of the stage. So many bizarre twists and funneling dimensions! It *was* beautiful in all its baleful majesty. Even a casual glance at its huge concentric gyres swept the eye into an abyss of dread, foreboding, and death.

How had Tosco possibly managed to sneak all this finely-crafted hardware on board and then reconstruct it so sturdily here in the *Starlight*? *And* with its hydraulic lift to allow the tiger to ascend to the lofty gyroscope itself?

Little by little? Piece by piece? Furtive step by . . .

Step . . .

Here I am, trashing the moment of a lifetime for this Cuban dwarf. Who do I think I am, really? And where the hell is Tulov, anyway?

For a moment Loring looked out at the empty rows of red velvet seats, three upper tiers of them, and imagined himself as Daria, imitated her ambulatory style. Several paces later, he stood rear stage right on the hydraulic platform that was supposed to lift her up to the gyroscope itself.

I hope those people are coming back. Where are they? Oh yes, it does take a while to get down to Car Deck. Especially with a tiger in tow.

He noticed a large button – black ceramic and paw-sized, just at tiger eye level. Loring looked around the empty theatre – all clear. He pushed the button and rose, as Daria might have risen, up, up, beside the gyres of the stainless steel tornado, up to the perch of the gyroscope itself forty feet over the stage surface.

He stepped off the platform onto a high thin ledge beside the gyroscope. For a moment he gazed around and wondered how, on such a small steel plank, Daria could adjust herself and stretch out onto the central metallic plane of the gyroscope before the velcro straps were clamped around her paws in preparation for her descent.

He grasped the long steel tube of the structure. Incredible! Not the slightest quiver to the entire apparatus, even when Loring applied some forceful jerks to it. He tapped the tube with his knuckles, and a sweet and musical tone rolled all down the length of it – with a pipe organ's heft and authority.

Curious at the size and structural integrity of the sculpture (for it was a powerful piece of art), Loring peered around toward the back of it, where several long black curtains of thick felt draped the iron balancing scaffolds, which the viewing audience could not see. Loring bounced up and down on the thin steel plank. Not a single vibration could be felt from the structure itself, but as he steadied himself and curled his toes within his shoes, he felt the distant but certain vibrations of the ship's turbines so far below!

So thin and elegant, yet solid! Ingenious! And noble in all aspects of its design and execution!

It did seem a waste to scrap such an enormous sculptured work of genius, which had been brought aboard with such effort and stealth, albeit not a word to any of the officers (including the Chief Medical Officer). Loring put his hands on the circular tubes of the gyroscope itself and grasped them. They were forged with the same precision and integrity as the gyre tube itself, rang with a solid and noble ping when he tapped with his fist.

Yo Tulov! Wherever you are! Old Russian dude, you sure can sculpt steel!

Loring turned the gyroscope on its vertical axis and then peered around behind the central plane, the underside of which was wrapped, as the rest of the structure, in thick black theatre felt. A heavy fold of the fabric slipped open, and suddenly Loring's grip loosened, his head grew dizzy with what he saw.

A full-sized tiger – a Daria double – lay spread-eagled out on the undersurface of the gyroscope's inner plane.

Woooooooooooooooooooaaaaaaaah! What have we here?

He nearly lost his balance. He grabbed the overhanging tube to collect his senses. He saw that, though she looked exactly like Daria, the tiger was not moving.

She was a dead tiger, a full-sized stuffed corpse.

"DOCTEUR! WHAT ARE YOU DOING UP THERE?" Loring heard from

the back of the theatre. *"PLEASE COME DOWN RIGHT NOW! I MUST EXPLAIN EVERYTHING TO YOU IMMEDIATELY! AND I HAVE SOMEONE I WOULD LIKE YOU TO MEET."*

Loring looked back at the theatre entrance. Tosco strode down the middle aisle. Behind him Ulla walked slowly on the arm of a tall, angular, dignified man with a hooked nose, a long white beard, and a silver-tipped walking cane.

The fiery, determined glance, the long white eyebrows that slanted up and out like satyr horns – no doubt about it. No illusion. Vladimir Vladimirovich Tulov, the genius sculptor himself. With obvious effort in each step, but his gaze never wavering from Loring, the old Russian proceeded toward the stage.

"But how do I get down from here?" Loring shouted.

"PUSH THE BUTTON, DOCTEUR!" Tosco called, *"AND THE PLATFORM WILL DESCEND. WE HAVE QUITE A BIT TO DISCUSS."*

Loring pushed the button. As the platform descended slowly, he watched the three from the *Cirque Ineffable* proceed silently toward him from the back of the theatre.

Was he still in a trance, or did they *really* not resemble an odd trio from a Mozart opera? Loring had started this day in Salzburg with Mozart, and now, here at midnight he was being approached by a Cuban baritone, a Russian basso profundo, and an Austrian contralto. The three of them looked for all the world like they were about to pipe up into beautiful and conspiratorial, Mozartian harmony. Did they somehow intuit that Loring had greeted the dawn with young Amadeus, and that now, after midnight, he might be in the mood for more? Actually, he *was* in the mood for more Mozart.

"THIS ISN'T ONE OF MY OPERAS, OLIVER. THIS IS THE 'CIRQUE INEFFABLE,' AND YOU'RE IN THE MIDDLE OF IT. THESE FOLKS ARE USED TO STAYING UP VERY LATE AT NIGHT TO POUND OUT THE IMPONDERABLES."

But I'm not the imponderable sort. That Russian scares me. See the way his face glows with a dominating lucidity? Never takes his eyes off me.

"NOW YOU KNOW HOW HIS BIG CATS FEEL."

Thanks, Wolfie! I notice the cat up on the back of that gyroscope gizmo is dead.

"STICK WITH THEM AND BE CREATIVE!"

Oh? Was that your slogan in life?

"INNOVATION! IT WORKED DURING THE ENLIGHTENMENT."

I'll try it. But one question.
"WHAT NOW?"
Am I in some kind of a trance?
"TEE-ROPA-TEE . . ."
That's all the advice you can give me, a melody?
"MELODY IS MY METIER. AND BY THE WAY, I HONESTLY HAD
ABSOLUTELY NOTHING TO DO WITH THE INVENTION OF THE
MAMBO. SOMETIMES YOUR MIND IS SIMPLY TOO BUSY. DIDN'T
YOUR FATHER TELL YOU THAT?"

* * *

The trio took seats on folding chairs in the middle of the stage. The apparatus for the Flaming Tiger Transcendental Gyroscope loomed behind them. As wily Wolfgang had predicted, they seemed intent to hammer out the imponderables.

Tosco knit his brow, chewed his lip, looked cross-eyed – hardly, for once, the controlled aristocrat or the steel-nerved big cat trainer. But how could Tosco *not* reveal his discomposure? Loring had nixed his big caper here on the *Nordic Blue*, for reasons that seemed obvious and fundamental to Loring. Then Tosco had returned to the theatre to discover the Chief Medical Officer bouncing on Tulov's magnificent metal sculpture with the irreverence of a schoolyard brat on a jungle gym. Worst of all, and perhaps the ultimate insult to a magician, Loring had snooped without permission into the workings of the Flaming Tiger Transcendental Gyroscope.

Tosco was so agitated, he forgot to introduce Tulov. But Loring didn't want to point out that breach of etiquette. What did etiquette mean, anyway, in the *Cirque Ineffable*?

"Well, *Docteur*! Since the trick is off anyway, you might just as well know how it works."

"Yes, I would like to know."

Tulov nodded and tapped his cane in great irritation, while Tosco walked Loring through each step of the trick. They ascended again to the gyroscope on its perch. Tosco demonstrated the circled panel of the gyroscope's center, which had two surfaces – one for Daria and the flip side, invisible to the audience, for a stuffed tiger.

"But this one looks exactly like Daria."

"She's Daria's mother. Her name is Veda."

"She doesn't look old, though."

"No, Veda died just before her prime, shortly after she gave birth to Daria. In fact, Daria now is seven, older than her mother was when she died."

"But Veda looks perfectly healthy."

"She's dead."

"I know. But I mean, she doesn't look diseased or wasted or anything. Her hide is luxurious."

"Like her daughter's. Veda perished quite by surprise, cracked her neck while attempting a trapeze jumping stunt in Paris."

"A trapeze? A tiger on a . . . "

"Fell thirty meters. Cracked her head. The safety net broke."

"That's exactly how my father died last year. In Vermont."

"He fell from a trapeze?"

"No. Skiing. But he fell about thirty meters. Ninety feet. Just like Veda."

"I'm sorry for you."

"Yes, and I'm sorry for Daria, too. I bet she didn't have a chance to say good-bye, did she?"

"We're getting distracted. Don't you want to see how the trick works? Look behind you."

"A sliding board. So that's how it works?"

"Yes, you see, after Daria is strapped onto the center plate, the whole unit is revolved three times, then quickly flipped. The four velcro restraints on her limbs snap loose, and she slides down on the invisible circling ramp behind the gyre. She then appears behind the bonfire spike and jumps out, unsinged and perfectly alive."

"Meanwhile, Veda spins down through the gyres, onto the flaming spike."

"Voilà!"

"But that spike goes right up through the tiger. Back at *Claridad*, I'm sure I saw that spike go straight up through her!"

"It does. Look here." Tosco pointed at the middle of Veda's spine.

A circular, bored-out channel and lined with a metal cylinder – slightly larger in diameter than the spike – penetrated the base of the lower thoracic vertebra.

"So that's where the spike fits, right?"

"Slides perfectly up into the center of the animal."

"Through and through?"

"Exactly."

"Magnifique!"

* * *

Loring marveled at the care with which Tulov and Tosco had envisioned and constructed the Flaming Tiger Transcendental Gyroscope. The closer he examined the giant structure – surfaces polished down within milimicron variances, joints fitted vacuum-tight, thousands of rivets smoothed to undetectable borders upon the chromium surfaces of their beds – the more Loring realized that no detail had been too insignificant (forget the whisker-by-whisker exactitude of Veda's taxidermist) to elude their picayune attention. And the kinesthetics of a spinning tiger's descent along a concentric series of gyres seemed to defy Newtonian principles of torque, balance, velocity – all the gyroscopic concepts Loring had once pondered in premed physics. Yet despite all the sophisticated metallurgy (the sphere itself was forged of a titanium alloy used only in advanced Russian astrophysical projects) and aerodynamics, the structure itself was merely a means to an end: the revelation of metaphysical truths.

"Yes, it stunned me profoundly at *Claridad*," Loring said, leaning over the back of his chair when they all were assembled again in the circle.

"I recall how affected you were."

"But why all this incredible effort and, if you don't mind my saying, subterfuge to present the Flaming Tiger Transcendental Gyroscope on international television? You're dealing with an audience from the masses. Did you see what they watched earlier tonight? 'Love Luck?' It's a show about betrayals and failures. It's what they call reality television. How is the Flaming Tiger Gyroscope going to make sense to them?"

Tosco cleared his voice. "I think you're being elitist, *Docteur*."

Tulov shook his silver-tipped cane in the air. *"SENSE? HA!"* His eyes flashed. *"WE DO NOT WISH MAKE SENSE! MAKE SENSE IS FAR FROM WHAT WE WANT DO! YOU UNDERSTAND THAT?"*

"Making sense doesn't make sense?"

Tulov's dark eyes flamed. His satyr eyebrows arched in rage as his face blushed to a deep Russian crimson. "Do not trivialize our goal, *Docteur*!"

Tosco cast a worried glance at Tulov. "Sit down Vladimir Vladimirovich. Doctor Loring laughs when he's uncomfortable."

"Yes, *yes*!" Loring apologized. "I wasn't trying to demean anybody in any way. I was making a joke to express my discomfort."

"How American!"

"Well, *yes*. Ha-*ha!* And speaking of uncomfortable, I do not like the idea of having a tiger jump around here on this stage with a full theatre and three balconies packed with panic-stricken passengers. You people have figured out every detail possible to this marvelous stunt, but you forgot to visualize the bigger picture. People see a tiger in front of them and they panic and stampede all over each other to get out. Simple as that! There's absolutely nothing metaphysical to the public safety of this ship."

Tulov shook his head angrily. "Daria never not harm *nobody*."

"*I* know that and *you* know that. The four of us sitting here on this stage tonight *know* that! But imagine an audience out *there* tomorrow night who *doesn't* know that! And I'll be the one expected to pick up the pieces! You understand that, don't you, Ulla?"

Ulla nodded hesitantly. "Vladimir, he has a point."

"We reassure," Tulov said.

"We cannot risk that," Loring said.

Ulla stood and put a hand on Tulov's shoulder. "Please calm down, Vladimir."

Tosco frowned. "Yes. Settle down."

Tulov began to shake. His bony shoulders trembled. His face flushed purple. Loring could hear his knee and elbow joints crack with uncontrolled trembling.

"Okay," Loring offered. "Just for the sake of continuing our discussion, what goal did you actually hope to achieve? Pretending, only for a second, that I allowed you to go ahead with the Flaming Tiger Transcendental Gyroscope performance tomorrow night?"

"Ah! Thank you, *Docteur*!" Tulov gasped.

"I'm speaking *theoretically*!"

"Understand."

"I mean, you folks have your own circus over there in Paris. Why not just wait and pull off everything in a perfectly safe venue, as I thought you had planned to do."

Tosco stood. "Vladimir Vladimirovich, I think you should let me explain." As Tosco began to speak, Loring sneaked a glance at Tulov, breathed a sigh of relief. The old Russian had sat back in his chair and no longer bored into Loring with his penetrating stare. In fact, Tulov's eyes glued now, and with no less intensity, onto Tosco.

"*Docteur*," Tosco began, as he strolled about the stage, "I have told you about our work in Paris with the Eden Reclamation Project. But tonight I must make a confession to you. Our movement is desperate."

Tulov's eyes softened, began to glow fervently as Tosco spoke of their cult. Loring watched the old Russian with increasing tenderness. To think of the experience knitted into that venerable face! The years growing up in Sverdlosk under the Stalinist regime, then the war, his education as a metallurgist and then his hero's career in the Moscow Circus, his defection to the west, and now three decades of occult circus studies and the spiritual impetus for *Le Cirque Ineffable*! To mention only the professional side of him.

And look behind him at his own chromium-surfaced artistic monument! Hauled, piece by piece, and constructed secretly here in all its magnificence in the *Starlight Theatre*. It actually might not be appropriate to have it standing there – so ominous and mute – behind the other segments of the performance without it, at least, serving some functional purpose in the show.

"Look around this ship, *Docteur*!" Tosco continued. "You see technology running wild with civilization. We are very far from Eden."

"But most people on board are having fun."

"*IDIOT!*" Tulov shouted. He glared again at Loring.

"Vladimir, quiet down!" Tosco insisted. "The *Docteur* is no idiot. He's only new to our movement."

"Hold it!" Loring interjected. "I'm not part of the Eden Reclamation Project."

"Of course, you are," Tosco replied with a confident smile. "I sensed your loyalty to us from our very first discussions in St. Maarten."

"Sympathy yes. Loyalty no. Hold on just a minute! Look what the Eden Reclamation project did to Jean-Luc Farandouz! Maybe he was in the same kind of trance I'm in right now."

"Don't speak foolishness, *Docteur*. You are not in a trance. The story of Jean-Luc is very sad. We warned Jean-Luc about using our techniques with a racing machine," Tosco countered.

"Ulla says Farandouz was vaporized or something!"

"We take that as further proof of the validity of our studies."

"Well, what do you call that thing up there on the metal perch. Isn't that a machine?"

"Yes," Tosco said. "But you saw the act at *Claridad*. Nothing hurt Daria. This magnificent metaphysical sculpture celebrates life, it does not take away."

Loring stood for a moment, took several deep breaths. He looked around at the three faces gazing intently, expectantly at him. "You say the movement is desperate."

Tosco nodded. "Don't you think we should be? As I said, take a peek around this ship! All this television nonsense! Having people slander their own spouses publicly! Giving away automobiles as comfort for emotional loss! There's even a huge electronic blimp overhead all the time taking pictures of this catastrophe and broadcasting them all over to infect the entire planet!"

"But here you are wanting to use the same technology to . . ."

"Exactly, *Docteur*! We are so desperate to counteract the effects . . ."

"That you're willing to use the tactics of those you perceive as your enemies."

"We must."

"And you think that by broadcasting this fantastic Flaming Tiger Transcendental Gyroscope trick show around the world . . ."

Tulov shook his cane. "If only dozen souls see work and digest message, all efforts worth it. Individuals will know. Will seek movement out in Paris. We get youth and energy. Look at me, *Docteur*. Old."

"A dozen individuals out of hundreds of millions watching?"

"Remember, *Docteur*. Jesus Christ himself needed only twelve to start."

"Yes, but the world is . . ."

"And we are certain that the form of the spinning tiger stripes and the gyroscope's descent onto the flame will be proof to many, not just twelve, *Docteur*."

Loring looked back and forth between Tosco and Tulov. He felt himself melt under their glances. Ulla's icy blues, too, seemed urgently to be invoking his sympathy for their cause. "One more question, fellows. How did you get this gig, anyway?"

"This gig?"

"How were you booked to be the entertainment on this cruise, anyway?"

Tosco nodded to Ulla. "Mrs. Snippet-White. She's one of us. And she is a close friend of Stig Storjord, the owner of the Nordic Star Lines."

"Hildegarde?"

"Yes," Ulla nodded. "The Colonel was a member, too."

Loring ran his palm over his brow, his fingers over his epaulets. He looked up at the magnificent shining sculpture behind them on the stage and then faced this circle of the *Cirque Ineffable*. Whether or not he was in a trance, he decided to follow Wolfgang Amadeus's advice: *"INNOVATION!"*

Granted, they were all a long way away from the Enlightenment. But they were a much longer way away from Eden.

"Let me make myself clear," he said. "I am *not* a member of the Eden Reclamation Project. I personally doubt the heroic performance of circus acts can bring anybody closer to realizing an Eden-like state."

"How would you know?" Tosco objected.

"IDIOT!" Tulov raved.

"Please, listen to *Docteur*, Vladimir!"

"I may never know. But since Mrs. Snippet-White is sympathetic to your movement, and since I now know how the trick works, I do have an option."

"What sort of option?" Tulov demanded.

"Does it absolutely have to be a tiger that spins around on that gyroscope?"

THURS/FEB 14
Russian Resurrection

"Play! Play! Play!" cheered Hildegarde Snippet-White, as the dawn sun scattered dizzying flickers of rose, orange, yellow and turquoise through the lozenge-shaped portholes.

"Again?"

"Yes! And *molto fortissimo*! Don't worry. These *Viceroy* cabins are perfectly sound proof. Nobody can hear your Scriabin. *Or* our hair dryers."

"I've played it four times. I know other Scriabin. How about a different *Etude*?"

"But I want the *D Sharp Minor*. So much rich Russian intensity. It's Rocky's very favorite Scriabin. Look! His shoulders and hips aren't loose yet. Play till Colonel's all warm and jiggly. That's the way you want him, isn't it?"

Loring stretched back his shoulders, rubbed his temples, shook the cramps out of his hands. (He too was a bit stiff, but only – ha-*ha!* – from lack of sleep.) His wrists coiled back and his fingers pounced yet again into Alexander Scriabin's cascading chords on the obedient keys of the Snippet-White ebony Steinway upright.

Ba-baaaam, ba-ba-ba-ba ba baaaaaah ba-bam!

With the late Colonel stretched out on the beige carpet in his white sleeveless silk undershirt and maroon paisley boxer shorts, Hildegarde and Ulla kneaded his joints, tried to pry them into some semblance of flexibility.

Loring had chosen Scriabin for this morning's pianistic adventure in deference to Vladimir Tulov, with whom he had grown attached during the night. *And* for the piece's own soul-searing and unremitting melodic insistence. This was, after all, a stunt to be pulled off for a radical cause, the reclamation of the Garden of Eden itself! If what they needed was a Russian Resurrection, Loring knew Scriabin could provide it, if anyone could.

Scriabin's *Twelfth Etude*, *"Patetico"* in D sharp minor (Opus 8), written in 1896, shortly after young Alexander Nikolayevich graduated from the Moscow Military Cadet School and entered the Moscow Music Conservatory, fairly shrieked with the malevolence and regret of a battlefield cataclysm. It was Loring's favorite Scriabin Etude, too: five innocent-looking pages of music manuscript, but replete with muffled explosions, soaring rockets, an interior section bitter-sweet as a soldier's farewell love letter, and then a stuttering, staggering, wildly erotic orgasm-like recapitulation before the despairing chordal bellow at the end.

Ba-baaaam, ba-ba-ba-ba ba baaaaaah ba-baaaaaam!

"LOVE IT, OLIVER!"

When the eccentric Scriabin performed, in order to heighten the ecstatic charge, he had sequences of brilliant colors projected onto stage screens during his performances in Moscow and Paris. That was similar to this dawn performance in *V#7* in the Caribbean, where the rising sun and bounding waves bombarded the walls with a dazzling, mind-assaulting mix of tropical pastels and aquamarines.

And the battlefield theme applied perfectly, didn't it? Kneeling with their hand-held General Electrics blasting at high heat on the Colonel's armpits and hips, Hildegarde and Ulla trained their guerrilla efforts against four days of *Galley Meat Freezer* temperatures *and* another foe – that ubiquitous frequenter of battlefields – rigor mortis.

"Give that left leg another good crank, Ulla, darling!"

Da-da-da-daaaaaaaah, da-da-dahhhh da da da daaaaaaaaah-dah! (soldier's farewell love letter section.)

Loring let his gaze drift over to the kneeling Ulla. Her raven hair was pulled back in a bun, and she wore a white wave-and-sunburst t-shirt and white shorts. In the spangled reflections of the dawn sun through the portholes, her tanned calves and thighs, so muscular and firm, contrasted cruelly with the cadaver's stiff-skinned upper legs. As Loring's fingers stroked the drifting chords, he watched her sweating hands knead the hard, dry flesh around the Colonel's creaking groin. Loring smiled at the care and resolution in her brow as she worked. She was a woman who, though an artist of extreme talent, could also commit to the basics, the menial – right down to nursing the dead to a semblance of life, if necessary, for an important cause.

When her eyes looked up, she let out a glorious girlish twinkle. Preposterous as this cause might seem, Loring welcomed the chance to work for it with Ulla, wondered if other causes might arise for them to share, causes less peculiar and grotesque than waking up the dead.

And how *fabulous* it felt to be playing the Steinway for Ulla. At dawn, too! He liked her in white as the colors of the sea and the sky flickered on her moist shoulders, across her breasts, down her arms.

Yes, please, more and more dawns with Ulla!

Da-da-da-daaaaaaaah, da-da-dahhhh da da da daaaaaaaaah-dah! (More farewell love letter – *piu piano*.)

The Colonel lay at attention. There was only so much he could do, while the determined pair of women pried at his frozen joints and tugged at his long, chilly limbs. His eyelids were locked shut, and the blotchy purple and beige mottling of his bony cheeks looked appalling. (Even after several shaves by Alfredo Pisido, the Ship's Barber, he *did* have a white whisker fuzz on his chin – new growth or skin shrinkage around the dry pores? Curious.) But his gray lips were separated in a grimace that gave his face an almost jovial, if zombie-like, look, especially when Hildegarde, still in her pink silk bathrobe and working up a few beads of elder sweat, prodded at his underarm. The gold-capped incisor glinted, as though she were tickling him.

Boy Bebalzam's facial expressions, however, were unimportant. What counted was the extendibility of his arms and legs, so that he could be stretched out on the central circle of the Flaming Transcendental Gyroscope to serve as Loring's flip-side double, just as the stuffed mother tiger Veda had been intended to serve as Daria's flip-side double in the original trick.

Hours ago, Loring had communed with Mozart for *"INNOVATION!"*

But now he must commune even harder with Scriabin and inspire the others for, *"RESURRECTION!"*

Ba-baaaam, ba-ba-ba-ba ba baaaaaah ba-baaaaaam! (Recapitulation.)

Loring had derived this variation on the stunt during his night-long discussions on the stage of the *Starlight Theatre*. Tosco and Tulov both had seemed skeptical of his compromise, till Loring pointed out that he had danced with Daria, knew the dimensions of her extremities, and that he and the late Colonel – physical, if not spiritual, *Doppelgängers* – fit perfectly into the same clothes and would, therefore, strap on nicely to the gyroscope's spinning inner platter.

As long as the dear widow gave her permission, what was *their* problem? How often did a corpse that matched a living human volunteer's body type come along? Especially *within* the Eden Restoration group?

Tulov had objected for mechanical reasons: each tiger weighed more than twice as much as her human counterpart. Therefore, the centrifugal force of the lighter rotating bodies would be diminished, could foul up the trajectory of the gyroscope along its monorail course.

Well, Loring countered, why not put ballast weights around the rim of the central platter? That would equalize the revolving masses and assure that the gyroscope would stay right on course. Tosco admitted he once had envisioned the trick as a human conveyance but had never had a suitable corpse available to him.

"Of course, a *HUMAN!*" Loring replied, "and how much more compelling and immediate the effect!"

To this, Tulov had chewed his beard reflectively and then looked hard at his loyal protegé.

If Tosco and Tulov insisted on replica tiger stripes for reasons of optical nerve stimulus, then both the Colonel and Loring could be fitted with amber body stockings. They could both be painted by Ruby Decosta, the *Starlight Theatre* costume designer and make-up expert, to resemble the striped hides of Veda and Daria. What were Tosco and Tulov waiting for? Did they want to reclaim Eden?

INNOVATION, GUYS!

Da-da-da-daaaaaaaah . . .

And when Loring shot up to Hildegarde's cabin in the middle of the night and woke her up to pitch the project, she was enthralled.

"Wonderful, Oliver!" she had giggled, explosively. "That's the best idea I've heard for a long time. You know the Colonel would love to go out in a blaze of glory like this. And who cares if his spine is punctured by the steel spike? He won't need it anymore, not where he's going on Friday, eh?"

"So you'll let the Colonel participate?"

"He'd *love* to! And you know, Oliver, this *amazes* me," she said as she started to relish the idea. "Such a coincidence! Do you know that drawing by Leonardo Da Vinci – the one with the determined man stretched out, all spread-eagled, in the middle of a circle, to illustrate the ideal dimensions of a human being, some say? Well, don't you know, the Colonel absolutely *worshiped* that drawing, said he always felt haunted by it all his life. Some sort of Renaissance vision, I suppose, on Rocky's part."

"I love Leonardo. And that drawing! Always have."

"Now we know why, don't we? And to think now Rocky will have a chance to be that very man, just like Leonardo had in mind!"

"Me, too!"

"You're fabulous! I'll wake up Ulla. First we need to have Rocky hauled back up here. I shall alert the Bellhops. Then we'll all get right to work! In secret, right?"

"That's the way Tosco and Tulov operate."

"Splendid, Oliver. And thanks so much for inviting us to join in the fun.

Rocky will be so proud!"

Ka-rooooooo, da-rooooooh, (Scriabin's culminating chordal stutters of conclusion) *da faaaaaaaaam* . . .

The frantic resurrection had been going on for an hour now in *V#7*. Down in the *Starlight Theater*, Tosco and Tulov were busy with Tulov's laptop as they calculated the necessary modifications on the gyroscope and the gyre track. Their preliminary estimates all seemed to jive with Loring's instinctive vision.

After all, it was their only option in this rather unique situation, Loring judged, and an inspired improvisation at that, if he didn't mind flattering himself. Otherwise, they would either have to tear down the entire giant chrome sculptured structure *or* just leave it up there in its magnificent tornado-shaped ineffability for all the Cablevista world to puzzle over as a poorly thought-out, possibly unsophisticated, set design enigma.

No, Loring's spirited volunteerism was the perfect solution.

. . . *da roooooooh* . . . . *ba* . . . *baaaaaaaaaammm!*

Loring finished the final, resonating measures of the *Etude*, kept the sustain pedal down for several poignant beats, then broke for the refrigerator and sucked down an iced Perrier. "Anyone for some refreshment?"

"Let me call down to Jarvis and see about some coffee and scones. Look here! Rocky's arms stretch out even with his shoulder now. Come on, Ulla! Let's attack these hips now. Hey, what's that? You know, I never knew the Colonel had a mole back there."

* * *

"Don't you dare move one muscle!" insisted Ruby Decosta, the *Starlight Theatre's* chain-smoking costume artist from New York, as she carefully stroked Loring's rump with her brush tip. "I want this side of your butt to look exactly like that side. It's amazing what you can do with black acrylic on spandex fabric, you know. Dries fast as shit."

Loring lay on his belly in his amber body stocking – nose-to-nose with Veda, arms and legs stretched out on the cold floor of the *Starlight Prop and Costume Shop*. Ruby Decosta, a perfectionist, had wanted him in that position – opposite Veda's stuffed remains, so that she could see "a direct visual template" to guide her in replicating the stripes.

From the corner of his eye Loring watched the ashes from Ruby's American Spirit Menthol waft down onto the floor near his elbow. He decided this wasn't the time to lecture her about the evils of tobacco, even the native American brand.

"Hey, I saw that video of you saving that fat broad's life. Good work! Your buns ain't bad, you know. For a thin man, that is. Gay, are you?"

"What?"

"Gay? Are you, like . . ."

"No."

"Well, how the hell *old* are you and still a bachelor, right?"

"39."

"God! I'm 31. Been married twice."

"Should I say congratulations?"

"Would you like to be gay? I mean, at your age and all. Pardon me, but we . . . well, *I* run into a lot of gay guys in theatre work, dancers and the like, and they're sometimes not sure about a lot of stuff."

"Not gay. I'm not gay."

"But why are you doing this magic shit? Aren't you supposed to be a doctor? Don't they call you the Dart Doc?"

"I can throw darts pretty well. At least in the *Crew Bar.*"

"Some doctors are gay."

"I know. Could we change the subject? It makes me nervous, especially when you're . . ."

"Hey, your butt's twitchin away on me. Try and hold still."

"Well, change the subject."

"Okay, another question. What the hell am I supposed to do about your tail? And doesn't this whole outfit look a little frickin' ridiculous without a real tiger mask? Who are we fooling here, Doc? You want me to make a mask that looks like this Veda and fits with the rest of you? Or, do you want I should shut up?"

"No, don't."

"I'm mouthin' off to you."

"I'm grateful, Ruby. Ha-*ha!*"

"What's wrong?"

"Tickles."

"Sorry. Trying to be thorough."

"Just paint my stripes, okay?"

"We're almost done. You gonna' dance in this outfit?"

"No, this tiger stuff comes later."

"Cool, Doc. Now hold still."

* * *

At 9.00 hours, proceeding aft down the port corridor of *Viking Deck* on his way to morning *Passenger Clinic*, Loring pondered Ruby Decosta's question: why was he doing this?

Why *would* he pitch in on such an antic in a tiger suit and perhaps make an utter fool of himself in front of millions of television viewers? To Ruby, a hardened New Yorker, it seemed *(ha!)* ineffable. Was he only doing it to humor two mystical circus performers who hoped to proselytize their cult beliefs to the world through the subliminal effects of a psycho-kinetic stunt? But that wasn't all. Did he *really* expect to reclaim any part of Eden through participation in Tosco's ritual?

Loring's Unitarian upbringing had exposed him to a gamut of religions – Christian, Hebrew, Muslim, Shinto and Buddhist, and also Greek/Roman polytheism and primitive native South American and African creeds. He had perused the assigned passages in the *Torah*, the *Koran*, and the *I Ching* with the Unitarian purpose of helping him pick his own spiritual path. Those original texts, plus his religion courses at Harvard undergrad, had mentioned versions of the Eden myth, and the South American religions sometimes suggested a paradise-like consciousness through rituals with hallucinogens. There were also the Utopian philosophers, like Thomas More and Francis Bacon and the French Montaigne, to consider.

But Loring could not recall any faith or philosophy he knew applying circus stunts to reclaim the lost paradise.

Let's face it: the link between the physical and the spiritual realms has never been so deficient in proof. And these modern charismatic prophets invoke heroic circus performance as a testament, what they call a manifestation! They want to orchestrate a manifestation in the middle of a decadent (but technologically proficient) media phenomenon known as the Cablevista Valentine TV Cruise. "Love Luck" epitomizes the triumph of materialism over spirituality itself. Yet here they are – mystic guerrilla fighters Tosco and Tulov, and their latest disciple Loring – in the thick of the enemy camp.

Did Loring feel guilty for not allowing Daria to complete the stunt?

Doesn't that smack of species bias?

Yes and yes, but Loring's conscience as a physician simply could not allow a formula for a certain public health catastrophe to unfold before his eyes.

Love for Ulla?

Oh, stop it!

If Ulla had not ventured onto this cruise ship, I would be enraptured with the Tosco-Tulov conundrum anyway, would have gladly volunteered for the Gyroscope, would have put my bones on the line for Tosco and Tulov. My love for Ulla is separate entirely from all this metaphysical daredevilism.

So now you're a cult member? Something missing from your life?

Not rewarded by your profession? Dissatisfied by your repetitive (some might think stereotypical) activities in Boston? Beginning to understand Scriabin a bit better? Wondering about the microscopic evidence of the disintegration of Jean-Luc Farandouz's protoplasm in his most unusual demise while trying to win at the Spitzring? Do you think he died in a trance like yours?

Ba-baaaam, ba-ba . . .

* * *

"Have some hot Joe, Dart Doc. Looks like you need some. Get any sleep at all? You were smart to duck in the back door. There's another horde of power cruisers out there say they want your autograph. Man, are you popular these days."

"It's only a cruise, Maggie. We shouldn't take it too seriously. Anybody sick out there?"

"Not like yesterday, thank goodness. One lady with palpitations. She's from Boston, too. I put her in *One*. EKG's normal. She can wait till you drink your java."

Loring noticed a fresh lilt to Maggie's voice and a renewed gleam in her green eyes. "And how's Captain this morning?"

Maggie arched her back and stretched her arms with a confessional grin. "Captain's at his best, thanks. I've got to hand it to you, Dart Doc. You did right."

"Farrely Farrell did him the most right."

"You think so? I couldn't believe it, Oliver. That bitch is big time disturbed. Did you see her eyes shootin' around like a pair of whirligigs?"

"Maybe she got it all out of her system last night. Now she can fly back to Norway . . ."

"And get off Trond's and my ass."

"You really think that will happen?"

"After what she said last night on Cablevista? Ramskog's mine. He invited me to sit beside him at dinner tonight."

"Now that *is* progress."

"And this morning he even mentioned the D-word again. Snø can just suck on her damn Mercedes keys, far as I'm concerned."

"Don't let her choke on them."

"Wouldn't bother me. She's lucky in love now. Hey, shouldn't you be seein' some patients? Start with that lady in *One*. Palpitations, she says. Boy, now that broad's got some skinny legs! I thought mine were bad."

* * *

The Gucci was parked on the medicine stand.

"*You're* having palpitations?"

Loring watched Anita Rothberg suspiciously. He did not kiss her. She was his patient now, so it seemed.

She leaned on her elbow, chin in hand, clad in a powder blue wave-and-sunburst hospital gown. Her freshly-tanned legs stretched out on the examining table with all the sensuality and nervousness he had remembered from a life and a confusing crimson-carpeted bedroom he left five days ago.

"I lied to that rude bitch, your nurse. Just wanted to be first in line to get in here and see you. You once said the quickest way to see a doctor in an E.R. is to complain of chest pain or palpitations. We have a few things to talk about, Oliver. By the way, how is my cardiogram?"

"You could have phoned my cabin."

"I tried a dozen times. You're *never* in your cabin. Oliver! And I know you too well to expect you to answer me any other way than face-to-face! Can you experience this as an act of love?"

"Now *I'm* having palpitations. Call the nurse, will you?"

"By the way, you don't look bad in a uniform. Know that? And now you're a TV star, too. By the way, Farrely wants to recommend a friend of his to be your agent. You absolutely *must* acquire an agent as soon as possible. Do you hear me?"

"You and Farrely are . . ."

"A couple."

"Quick."

"Not like *us*, eh?" She pulled the gown down low on her neck. "Aren't you going to listen to my heart, at least? Isn't it odd that now *I'm* your patient and *you're* my therapist? I find that so . . ."

"Ironic? Symmetrical?"

"Yes. Symmetrical. I'm the therapist on the way in, and you're the therapist on the way out. It's a veritable . . ."

"Palindrome."

"I guess we had a palindrome of a romance. You could even call it a palindromance."

"Able was Oliver ere he saw Anita?"

"You don't want to listen to my heart?"

"Anita, I will miss the word play between us."

"In retrospect that's what I think we were, mostly."

"Did you notice my nails? That's where we started."

"Well, shiver my timbers, lad! I'm so impressed."

"Scarab pills. I've been on them for four days now."

"Scarab pills? You mean *dung* beetles?"

"A rich source of chitin."

"Really? How disgusting! But I guess they work better than word play, don't they? Well, do you mind if I turn a few words on you? I'm not playing anymore."

"Go ahead. But leave your handbag where it is."

Anita Rothberg smiled then turned and shook out her blonde curls to full medusa length, a gesture that usually signaled she had something apocalyptic on her mind. She perked up her posture, looked Loring closely in the eye. "There's talk that you'll be participating in the magic show tonight. Any truth to that?"

"Who said anything about . . ."

"Farrely, of course. By the way, he's offered me a job as his consultant. I'll be flying down to New York every week to consult for his show. Isn't that wonderful?"

"I'm sure the money is."

"So is the sex."

"Well, congratulations! New job, new positions . . ."

"You're hurt, aren't you?"

"I am not hurt, Anita."

"But I didn't come here to talk about sex. Even though you *are* my therapist, Dr. Palindrome."

"Waiting."

"Oliver, ballroom is one thing. You've always had the exhibitionist in you. And the whole world saw the way you saved that woman's life up in the casino yesterday. The chip popped right out of her, and now half the world is gazing at it like some kind of wondrous space satellite shot. But shouldn't we just leave it there, while your reputation is . . ."

"I was doing what anybody . . ."

"That's why Farrely and I think you need an agent. Before you do something disastrous to harm your show business career. "

"Career?"

"Look at me, Oliver! A *magic* show? Is the magician going to saw you in half or levitate you or something like that? They'll laugh you right off the Harvard Medical Faculty. Have you lost all your sense of physician-like conduct? Do you trust the Dean of the Medical School not to observe your nutty antics along with the rest of the world?"

"It's more than magic."

"You're always escaping, Oliver. At your piano every morning, for example. This cruise was an escape from me. I see that now. But I can forgive. And, as you know, I got a new job and a wonderful new lover out of it. And I'm sure you feel a sense of escape on the dance floor, too. But what the *hell* kind of escape can you expect from performing in a tin horn magic show? Escape from your faculty position at Harvard?"

"I love Harvard."

She shook her finger at him then reached for the Gucci.

Loring stepped back.

"I'm not going to hit you. I'm frustrated you won't listen to reason. So I want to give you something sweet."

Her hand went into the bag and pulled out a small heart-shaped box of chocolates. "Happy Valentine's Day, Oliver."

"Ditto, Anita. Do you believe there ever was such a place as the Garden of Eden?"

"For us?"

"It's part of a certain religious cult's understanding of heroic gesture."

"Do they eat dung beetles as a sacrament or something? Oliver, what has *happened* to you?"

"It hasn't happened yet. Ha-*ha!* Maybe tonight it will."

"I'm not going to say a word to Farrely about this. Trust me. But, please, as your former therapist and your ex-lover and your fellow Harvard faculty colleague, please don't do anything really, really stupid. I still love you in a way. And I worry about you. Admit it. I know you're sensitive about being born on the first of April, but sometimes you really do act like a goddamn fool."

* * *

For most of an hour, a long line of power cruising autograph seekers pressed into the *Passenger Waiting Room*. Loring remained cordial, smiled into their flash cameras. While his eyes smarted with flickering retinal shadows, he asked if all were enjoying their cruises.

It seemed all were, and some had requests. Several wanted his e-mail address. ("Don't have one.") A blue-hair from Tulsa wanted his stethoscope for her premed granddaughter. (Granted.) A brunette from Houston wanted his epaulets. (Not granted.) One couple from Johnstown, Pennsylvania, brought in a pair of $5 gambling chips from *Nuggets* and asked if he would kiss them for good luck. ("I only kiss $50 chips. Just kidding. *Mmmmwha* and *Mmmmwha!*")

"You know, Dr. Oliver, I might just make a pair of cufflinks out of these for him. Wouldn't that just set the town talking?"

By the time the last autograph was signed, most of the morning had fled. Loring sneaked back to his cabin and found another memo from the *Bridge* under his door.

MEMO FROM THE BRIDGE
Date: THURS, FEB 14, 10.00 hours
From: Captain Trond Ramskog
To: Staff Captain Nils Nordström and All Officers and Crew
Re: Suspension of Duties, Chief Medical Officer

Effective immediately, Dr. Trygve Storjord will take over as Chief Medical Officer for the remainder of the cruise.

I have relieved Dr. Oliver Loring from duties as Chief Medical Officer. He will stay on as "Honorary Chief Medical Officer" and will be allowed all the privileges of Officer's status, including his cabin.

Dr. Loring's involvement with the entertainment aspects of this Valentine TV Cruise has made it necessary to free him up from his official medical responsibilities.

Trond Ramskog,
Master, S/S Nordic Blue

cc: Chief Nurse McCarthy, Mr. Stig Storjord, Mr. Farrely Farrell

Loring pulled a Perrier from the refrigerator and swigged it. Then he belted down a scarab pill and settled onto the couch to reread the note.

He had heard stories of cruise doctors getting canned before – practitioners who simply could not adjust to the perpetual proximity of alcohol and thong bikinis without letting loose some long latent drinking or fondling tendency. But he never imagined that he, Oliver Loring, yesterday's recipient of a scale model of the *S/S Nordic Blue* and a deafening ovation in the *Starlight Lounge*, might be asked to step down before the ship pulled back into Miami.

Silently drummed from the ranks! Stripped of status. Just like that!

The Captain's laconic Nordic style in the memo left much to interpolate. What was behind this? As an Officer, honorary or otherwise, didn't he deserve a fuller explanation than just his "involvement with the entertainment aspects of the cruise"?

Should he have done things differently? Should he have presented himself in a more professional manner? Had he become too immersed in his work?

Try as he might, Loring could not immediately see the advantages of his newly acquired honorary status. He felt a prickle of perturbation, then frank outrage took hold of him.

He *did* deserve an explanation, and he would not wait around for one. He would storm up to the *Bridge* (the place where this demeaning epistle had been issued) and confront Trond Ramskog once again, this time with no therapy intended. He chugged the remainder of the Perrier and was about to head out the door when his cabin phone rang.

"Stig Storjord here."

"Sir? Mr. Storjord?"

"Yes, Doctor, I was wondering if you'd like to shoot some skeet with the Captain and me this morning?"

"Shoot skeet?"

"We're heading down to *Atlantic Deck*, stern. Care to join us? Our appointment is in ten minutes."

"I never went skeet shooting before."

"Time to learn, don't you think? See you down there in ten minutes?"

* * *

Loring had heard that in Norway a tradition among men was confidential chats during hunting expeditions, not unlike the American custom of business executive golf outings. In Norway, if you were asked to go hunting, whoever invited you probably had something important to say to you.

To Loring, who had never been invited before to shoot skeet (he didn't golf, either) firing shotguns off the stern of *Atlantic Deck* had always seemed an ugly waste of resources and time. Power cruisers were charged upwards of four dollars a round to blast clay disks out of the sky – thus polluting the fragile Caribbean biosystem with porcelain detritus and buckshot.

For an unattached woman who might yearn for a Norwegian Officer's arms around her waist as she aimed and popped one off, the activity was apparently cost effective. Loring had seen the technique of the gold-bearded Norskies on the *Atlantic Deck* stern – Viking mystique in action and a sellout attraction.

Did skeet shooting also serve as the seagoing equivalent of a manly walk in the Norwegian woods with the intention of confidential male conversation? Loring had no experience to judge. He knew, however, it would be rude to turn down the Captain and the Fleet Founder.

When he reported at the *Atlantic Deck* stern, however, he was greeted only by Staff Captain Nils Nordström, who told him Storjord and Ramskog had spoken to him on his walkie-talkie and would be detained a few minutes.

"So I'll come back later."

"No, no! Doctor. Stick around. Hey, don't they call you the Dart Doc? We all heard about what a hot shot you are down in the *Crew Bar*." Nordström presented Loring with a semi-automatic, open bore 12-gauge Smith and Wesson, a carton of shells, and a pair of ear muffs.

"Yes, they call me that," Loring admitted. He tested the unfamiliar heft of the shotgun and mimicked Nordström's manner of grasping the rifle.

Nordström's tired eyes, injected with nasty clusters of hangover veins, seemed to taunt Loring. "I say darts are for children. So let's see how you do with a man's weapon, eh?" He pulled his ear muffs down and loaded up.

"Lousy. I can assure you, Staff. I haven't fired one of these since I was a boy at summer camp. And that was only a .22."

"You say you were 22 last time you fired a shot gun?"

"No, I was . . ."

"PULL! PULL!" Nordström did not wait for the calculation. With two sharp concussions of his weapon, the powdery fragments of a pair of clay pigeons blew down over the *Nordic Blue's* glistening white wake. Despite his obvious headache, Nordström gave a jowly grin and reloaded. "Mind if I shoot till I miss?"

Loring was amazed. If the blood vessels in the Staff Captain's brain looked anything like the tangled red webs visible in the whites of his eyes, then the last thing his cerebral circulation needed was the pounding echoes of repeated gunshots.

"Sure, go . . ."

"PULL! PULL!"

Ears ringing, Loring inhaled the sweet puffs of gunpowder and watched a dozen spent shotgun cartridges flip out in sequence onto the smooth *Atlantic Deck* planks from Nordström's rifle."Twelve in a row. Gosh! You're quite the sharpshooter!" Loring yelled. Suddenly his ears began to ring fiendishly.

"Ha! Think you can do that good, Dart Doc?" Nordstrom shouted. He flipped the release and cricked the gun barrel over on his forearm, the butt wedged firmly into his paunch.

"Not a chance. You know my ears are ringing already. And I haven't even pulled the trigger."

"But I thought they called you the Dart Doc. Ha!"

The conversation had nowhere to go, except out into the wake with more fake pigeons and buckshot. Nervous from Nordström's derisive looks and not wanting to irritate a man in obvious need of some hair off the great dog Aquavit, Loring slid two cartridges into the firing chambers. He lifted the rifle to his shoulder and shouted, *"PULL!"*

As before, a clay disk flew up and aft a hundred feet into the sky. Loring aimed and pulled the trigger. Then he pulled again hard. Uninterrupted, the spinning black circle continued its downward parabola into the waves. Loring faintly distinguished Nordström's deep bellows below the high-pitched ringing in his ears. *"Nincumpoop!* You forgot the safety button. That's a waste of a good target!"

"Sorry, Staff!"

"Don't apologize, man. Release the damn button. Here, let me show you." Nordström grabbed Loring's gun by the butt and thumbed the button over the cartridge chamber to reveal a small red dot. "Now do it."

"You have big thumbs!" Loring said.

"CAN'T HEAR YOU!" Nordström pointed to his ear muffs.

"FORGET IT!"

"WHAT DID YOU SAY?"

"I SAID, 'FORGET IT!'"

Nordström cocked his neck, leaned his head toward Loring and pried up the near ear muff. "What did you say?"

"I said, 'Forget what I said.'"

"Well, what the hell did you say, man? If I didn't hear it, how can I frickin' forget it?"

Loring pried up his own ear muff. "It doesn't matter."

"What the hell doesn't matter?"

"What I said."

"Yes?" His chubby cheeks reddening in pulses, the burly Norsky pulled his ear muffs off completely and scowled.

Loring screamed, *"IT DOESN'T MATTER. I'M VERY SORRY!"*

"Well, why in hell did you think it would matter? Eh? Maybe you ought to just frickin' forget about what you're thinking and put your mind on shooting that goddamn rifle you got in your goddamn hands, eh? What did you come out here to do, anyway? Didn't your father teach you anything about guns?"

With the ear muffs off, Loring noted the bulges in Nordström's temple veins. Again, he pitied the Staff Captain's brain. If Loring hadn't already agreed to meet Stig and the Captain, he would have walked away. "Let's forget about it," he said.

"You already said that. Are you trying to bust my frickin' ass, eh Doctor? We're not throwing frickin' children's darts out here, you know."

Loring was about to ask the Staff Captain what he meant by that second statement. He paused, however, when he caught the glaring intensity in Nordström's eyes. Loring smiled.

Nordström shook his head. "No, we're sure not throwing frickin' darts out here, are we?" It seemed the Norsky felt as if the statement bore repeating to emphasize its profundity.

Despite himself, on the second mentioning of this absurd image – throwing darts at a clay pigeon off the *Atlantic Deck* stern – Loring succumbed to an overwhelming surge of hilarity. "Ha-*ha!*"

The Norwegian scowled. "Oh, now you really are bustin' my frickin'-a ass, aren't you?"

"I'm sorry."

"Sorry for what?"

"Ha-*ha*! *Ha!*"

"You sure don't look sorry!"

"No, I mean it, Staff. Wouldn't it seem funny what you said . . . to throw darts off the stern of the ship? Think about it. Just hurling dart after dart out over the ocean, one after the other . . . "

The rage in Nordstöm's eyes seemed to glaze over slightly, and Loring felt glad he was not actually on a long walk in the Norwegian woods with this humorless, low-threshold-for-violence creature. Better to have the Cablevista blimp gazing down at the potential crime scene.

Yo blimpmeisters! Over here! Yo international eye witnesses! Train that lens aft!

To his relief, Loring spotted little Stig Storjord and the Captain striding toward the stern with their shotguns over their arms.

"Captain!" Loring shouted.

Now those men look like they are out for a walk in the woods!

Stig Storjord approached with a smile. "I'm sorry we're late, Doctor. Good that you started without us."

The Captain, too, seemed amiably disposed. He offered Loring a cordial handshake. "I'm pleased to see you have some time now for some enjoyable activities. You deserve them."

Storjord gave Loring a reassuring wink. "Yes, you need to relax, Doctor."

"Oh, yes!" Nordström said. "The Doctor's having himself a good time out here. Problem is, he can't shoot for shit."

"Are you talking about your memorandum to me, Captain?"

"Yes. Mr. Storjord felt you were strung out. Maybe too many serious responsibilities."

Stig Storjord cleared his throat and nodded to Loring. "Hildegarde, too."

"Hildegarde?"

"Yes, Mrs. Snippet-White suggested the idea to me."

"Hildegarde told you to fire me? And is that why you invited me out here to shoot skeet with you?"

"Yes, Doctor," the Captain added, confirming the words with his sensational smile. "We thought you might not understand the reasons behind it, and perhaps you want to talk about it. Shoot a few pigeons, talk, shoot a few more pigeons. You see, that's the way we do these things in Norway."

Storjord searched Loring's eyes. "We're sort of kicking you upstairs. I think that's the way it's said. "

"Yes, I guess I understand now."

"Were you surprised?"

"I was worried I had done something unforgivable."

"Not at all." The Captain rubbed the faint bruise on his cheekbone. "Everything you've done has been more than correct."

"Kicked upstairs?"

"Call it that," Stig Storjord said. "Yes, enjoy the rest of the cruise."

"Do you have any questions?" the Captain asked.

"Well, yes. My ears are ringing like crazy right now. Besides, I have an appointment to meet some friends for lunch in a few minutes. Would you mind if I decline on the skeet stuff? We've had our talk, haven't we? And I guess I should say . . . "

"Oh, you've said enough, Doctor," Stig Storjord nodded. "Go have lunch. By the way, they're serving flying fish today in the *Officers' Mess*."

"Oh, I know. I love that flying fish dish! Every Thursday."

* * *

At noon Loring walked into the *Officers' Mess*, aft on *Riviera Deck*, with Tosco and Tulov. Partly in gratitude for the *Claridad* bouillabaisse, Loring had promised to treat his guests to the very excellent Thursday special on the Officers' lunch menu – *poisson volant à la Martiniquaise*.

Mr. Park, the elegant elderly Korean Head Waiter, poured them a nicely chilled Etruscan pinot grigio and sent his portly young Filipino trainee, Fernando "Guapo" Montoya, out to the *Galley* with their order.

"To the fish who tries to fly!" Loring urged, as the three friends clinked goblets.

Flying fish, no matter how predictably delicious as Thursday's *plat du jour* in the *Officers' Mess*, always sent Loring into an imaginative frenzy about the nutritive effects of a fish who couldn't claim rights to fly, yet didn't feel entirely comfortable in his own natural saline element.

Why uncomfortable? Why a fish? Ha-ha! Why not a bird?

The whole natural pretext seems ineffable!

One afternoon off the beach of the Private Island in the Bahamas, Loring had witnessed a split-second maritime wildlife tragedy: a *poisson volant's* graceful glide down toward the tip of the white caps that was suddenly

273

interrupted by a 4-foot long barracuda. The nimble-finned predator thrust right up out of the waves and ambushed the flying fish in his steely jaws then brought him back down into the choppy brine.

That'll teach a fish to fly!

N'est-ce-pas, Monsieur poisson?

Though the wings/fins were fibrous and almost tasteless, the delectable bulk of the animal was pure, white, and abundant – a nourishing protein served traditionally with a fond tip of the spatula to the Caribbean palate: cold snap beans, grated Jamaican goat cheese, crushed garlic, finely minced parsley, sliced onion, zested lemon rind, and oodles of Haitian red pepper.

They were early, the first ones to enter the *Officers' Mess*, Mr. Park pointed out and asked if they were comfortable at the round table near the starboard portholes. They were, Loring answered, although his ears continued to ring from his abortive skeet shooting expedition. Of course, there wasn't much Mr. Park could do for that, Loring commented after draining his glass and helping himself to a second glass of pinot grigio.

Most of the real (*i.e.* non-kicked upstairs) Norwegian Officers were about to engage in a safety exercise involving the lowering of several of the port side lifeboats, Park explained. The drill was being performed for the Cablevista cameras and was likely to last most of the afternoon.

It pleased Loring that his colleagues were out and about performing their duties for the cameras *and* that he had been "kicked upstairs" and, therefore, didn't have to participate in the important, albeit mindless, activities. (Trygve Storjord, no doubt, was now manning his post in the *Hospital*. Thanks for that, Doctor Trygve. Hope to meet you soon!)

This also meant Loring and his *Cirque Ineffable* friends could enjoy their repast in the *Officers' Mess* without the suspicious glances which might otherwise have greeted the tall, white bearded Russian with the Satanic eyebrows and his mustached, sway back dwarf accomplice with the messy network of scalp scars.

"This is not *Claridad*," Loring apologized, at which Tosco and Tulov nodded in understanding. "But may I also toast to *Claridad* and to Eden itself."

"And I toast to participation of Doctor in Eden Restoration Project," Tulov said with a fond twinkle in his eye as their three glasses clinked.

Loring was full of questions – things he hadn't had time to ask during the night. The wisdom and warmth in Tulov's smile suddenly overwhelmed him. As the soothing pinot grigio seeped into his blood, his chest quivered. He closed his eyes, heard himself sob in front of them. "I'm sorry. I'm . . . so . . . fatigued. I often cry when I'm tired."

"You're more than fatigued," he heard Tosco say softly.

"Yes, Doctor," Tulov added in his deep basso. "Anytime we receive new member, often find they pass through delicate time, when feelings raw and strong."

"But I'm not sure if I've actually joined you."

"We not give card membership!" Tulov chuckled, sympathetically. "We not keep list members. No initiation ceremony."

Tosco cleared his voice and smiled. "I think though, that volunteering to perform in one of our most important manifestation offerings tells us of your commitment."

"Thanks," Loring replied. "Well, at least to this flaming transcendental gyroscope, I'm committed."

Tulov chewed a morsel of fish with apparent delight and swallowed. "More I think, more good your . . . innovation."

"Do you?" Loring sniffed and gulped. Then he giggled with pride. "And do you like the flying fish?"

"Excellent," Tulov nodded.

"And so is your innovation, *Docteur*," Tosco added. He sipped his pinot grigio. "Let us explain."

Caught in the crossfire between Tosco's deep black, resonating latin eyes and Tulov's stern steel-greys, with the brows arching out in white filigree at the edges, Loring soon felt his own eyes blink open in dry, relieved concentration.

Both men had taken his display of emotional fragility – here, of all places, in the *Officers' Mess* – in stride. They seemed to accept his tearful outburst as proof that he was with them. Loring himself doubted, despite his recollection of the events of the past several days, that he could have allied with a radical fringe metaphysical group, which had planned a global demonstration. And he was the self-recruited key member. And yet, it all was true and was surely to happen. And now that Stig Storjord had relieved him of his official duties, Loring could concentrate on his non-medical duties.

"So, in a way, you fellows are taking your product to the market," Loring concluded. "By putting it out there on the whole Cablevista planet-wide panorama."

"Precisely," Tulov said. "Is shameful?"

"Shameful?"

Tosco shook his fork. "Failure is shameful. And honestly, *Docteur*, we are worried of failure."

"But is *not* having the tiger in it shameful to both of you? I need to know. Seriously."

"You've offered yourself as the alternative," Tosco said. "And the availability of Colonel Snippet-White seems almost providential."

Loring nodded. "Hildegarde has been on your side from the start."

"If it were *not* for Madame Hildegarde and her connections with the owner of the Nordic Star Line, our chances to present our cause to tens of millions around the world would have been impossible."

"Was it because she saw your show in Paris last year?"

"Yes. Ulla brought her, and she was amazed. In fact, it was her idea that we perform here on this cruise. She cleared the way for us."

"Through Stig Storjord?"

"*And* through Ulla."

"Then to Ulla!" Loring said.

Tosco and Tulov smiled and raised their glasses.

"To Ulla!" the three men echoed.

For several minutes, Loring silently savored the *Poisson Volant à la Martiniquaise*. And he appreciated the convivial peace in the *Officers' Mess*.

To Ulla, he repeated silently to himself.

Yes. To Ulla!

Loring smiled. He could feel the flying fish sliding around his gut, hitting his blood, mixing with the pinot grigio, and seeping into his nerves. He *always* felt lighter when he ate flying fish. He imagined himself shooting out the nearby porthole, spreading his wings, coursing merrily through the sea air above the fields of white caps all around. Toss in a dash of table top finger work with some recollected Scriabin – "*Ba-baaaam, ba-ba-ba-ba ba baaaaaah ba-bam!*" – and nothing at all seemed ineffable about *Le Cirque Ineffable,* so cozily disposed was Loring to his lunch partners.

Oh, to be in such harmony with one's metabolism and imagination. To say nothing of one's ship, sky and sea! *And* one's luncheon company. But that is *exactly* how Tosco and Tulov made him feel.

And their silence helped Loring digest other, now less ineffable, matters – even as his winged spirit juked and bobbed above the waves, wove and fluttered in the misty spray, out there over the tasseled blue Caribbean carpet. *So!* Using Cablevista's TV Valentine Cruise on the *S/S Nordic Blue* as a venue for the *Cirque Ineffable* was originally Ulla's idea!

Ulla! The woman for whom he had purchased the mystical necklace! She had heard about the cruise when Hildegarde invited her to join the Snippet-Whites for a cruise, thought it the ideal opportunity for Tosco to get his *"Cirque Ineffable"* out before the global public, and for her to bid her final goodbye to Jean-Luc.

According to Tosco, Hildegarde herself had called Stig Storjord, promoted the *Cirque* as a highly unusual television experience for viewers all around the world. Storjord had then intervened with Farrely Farrell, insisted that Cablevista sign up Tosco's troupe sight unseen or the Valentine TV Cruise would be canceled.

Farrell had agreed reluctantly, but on the condition that he would have full freedom on the cruise to choose his own "contestants" for "Love Luck" – hence no objections or veto power for Storjord when Farrely tapped Snø for the interview, despite whatever aspersions might be cast on the esteemed Captain of the *S/S Nordic Blue*.

The Caribbean geography had worked out perfectly – San Juan was ideal for Tosco to slip his tiger (and Tulov) onto the ship Wednesday morning, a day prior to the big show.

And Oliver Loring had entered the mix as an afterthought. Farrely Farrell had always enjoyed the old TV reruns of the sentimental sitcom "The Love Boat," one of whose stock characters was the geeky doctor. Farrell had simply brain stormed that an identifiable dancing doctor on the ship might perk up the luster and the spirit of the entire pageant. Little did Farrely realize that the geek would become a "blast image" who should acquire an agent as soon as possible. Before the geek did something stupid.

Loring watched his spirit frolic above the waves, imagined Ulla skimming along out there in the salt spray with him

Yo *Ulla! You're the one who instigated this entire comedy! The mind of an executive in a ballerina's body! Ballerina, meet Monsieur Poisson Volant!*

And her very suspicious "platonic" with Flip Spinelli now was understandable: keep the monomaniacal Cruise Director flattered, trusting, and preoccupied, enough, at least, not to intrude on Tosco's night work in the *Starlight Theatre*.

Yes, live in his cabin if he insists (gulp!), but keep Cruise Director Flip busy and at bay! Quite a woman you are, Ulla! Your grandfather Willibald, the heroic under cover anti-Naziman, would be proud. Whether or not you are searching to reclaim Eden, your instincts about creating a larger profile for the Cirque might be correct. Even at the risk of collaborating with transparent hucksters like Farrely Farrell, sharing a bed with Flip Spinelli (mega-gulp!), you have made it possible for individuals around the world to witness the event and be affected deeply, to the spiritual bone! Oh, how I hope you like the necklace, Darling!

* * *

After lunch, the three went to the *Nordic Notions* and the *Gift Nook* to pick up a pair of sunglasses and a wave-and-sunburst baseball cap for Loring. Tosco and Tulov agreed to join him for a post-prandial stroll up on *Vista Deck*.

"Cigar, *Docteur*?"

"Why not? Hey! When I look up at those giant twin smoke stacks, I guess I just want to . . . "

In and . . .

Under a marvelous Caribbean azure, speckled with marbly tufts of egg white wisps (the polarizing lenses of Loring's sun glasses deepened the blue of the sky to a rewarding new hue), the *S/S Nordic Blue* thrust gracefully north. A gentle westerly wind licked the tops of cresting whiffs of foam across the surrounding horizon. A thousand feet above, against the airy firmament, the silvery blimp floated in tandem. *"LOVE MAGIC AT MIDNIGHT!"* blazed in red letters across her long shiny hull to remind the sunning power cruisers all over the decks of what was to come tonight.

Loring and his companions hardly needed a blimp to remind them. And Loring himself, as the tiger man on the gyroscope platter, would be a crucial element in the planet-wide message.

Loring looked down at the green strands of the astroturf and chuckled silently. How well he recalled his hellish ordeal up here on *Vista* Saturday, the first night of this cruise! He remembered his violent reaction to the image of the serpent spinning on Ulla's legs in the theatre and his immediate retreat up here to the *Vista Deck* smoke stacks to get a bearing on his place in the universe. And now, just think! He would be performing an even grander stunt than Robespierre had done – a trick not for a serpent, but for an Amur tiger, or at least a stand-in for an Amur tiger. Could the stimulus of Loring's acute vertiginous spell that night have been a premonition of what he himself would experience tonight?

Once you start cavorting with these metaphysical types, who knows what insights might develop?

As they strolled, he was glad for the cap and the shades. None of the passing power cruisers seemed to recognize him, including several who had waited over an hour for his autograph at the morning clinic a few hours earlier and now passed by without a nod or a smile.

No pleading for a snapshot. A relief, indeed. And hadn't Stig Storjord been correct in relieving him of his duties! Not unlike the frisky *poisson volant,* digested elements of whom were blending into his protoplasm, Loring felt free to skim above the surface of such concerns. Of *course* the power cruisers should feel entitled. They had paid the ticket price on this high profile cruise. Any doctor who didn't understand that the happiness (and safety) of the power cruisers was the name of the game should never have signed on in the first place. But if all they wanted was an autograph or an e-mail address or an epaulet to show to their friends back in Duluth or Winnipeg or Spokane, then why should Loring be promiscuous with his eye contact up here on *Vista Deck*?

Maybe it was the cigar. Who would expect a doctor to be smoking a panatella? Maybe that threw them all off. They did not recognize him.

"You not feeling nervous?" Tulov asked.

"The physics of the gyroscope is all calculated, right?"

"Would like see figures?"

"No. But since I've never done anything like this before, I would like to have at least one rehearsal before . . ."

"Yes," Tulov smiled, puffing on his panatella, "I hoping you like a rehearse. How about five this evening? All adjustments be made by then, and the *Starlight Theatre* reserved for us. Not nobody else."

"Excellent, Vladimir Vladimirovich. But to answer your question, no. I don't feel nervous. Guilty, perhaps. I was rather abrupt with Daria last night. Is there any way I could see her and apologize?"

Tulov smiled over at Tosco. "Yes. Could be arranged."

"I mean, is she upset about not appearing in the show tonight? I didn't mean to preempt her."

Tosco smoked and thought. "I think she understands, but if you want to see her, we can arrange that. Certainly."

Tulov stopped and looked up at the sky. He leaned back and pointed his walking stick up at the Cablevista blimp. "Know what?" he said, drawing a series of rough circles around the blimp. Then he grinned at Loring, a wrinkled smile that contracted his bearded face into a glowing squint.

"What? What about the blimp?"

"I like blimp. Is beautiful, don't you think? And look there . . . it give our work some advertising. Yes, I like the blimp. But if I designed? Would have true fins on tail. No artist there. None. Do you agree, Oliver? But still, I like blimp!"

* * *

In the *Forward Cargo Elevator* they descended down below the water line to the starboard section of *Car Deck.* This was one of the areas on the ship Loring had always been curious to see. They passed through a darkened storage area smelling of diesel oil and old zinc batteries and filled mostly with warehoused cafeteria equipment and appliances – mounded metallic paraphernalia threaded by cargo dolly tracks and dimly lit by an occasional bare bulb. Most of it was dust-covered steel – ancient espresso machines, old Waring ice cream blenders, dish washers, half a dozen soda shop swivel stools, a cafeteria steam counter, even an old medical examining table with sturdy stirrups that still looked functional.

All now was ballast – cluttered objects nobody wanted or even remembered, abandoned here and accumulating dust for decades. Over the years, the material had been wedged into this forward and least accessible hold of the ship and was too bulky and voluminous to junk, except at a full-scale dry dock gut-out of all of the *Car Deck* compartments, perhaps not a cost-effective effort.

As Loring perused the forgotten relics and pressed his fingers to his ears (the high-pitched ringing now was countered by the deep, subtle rumble of the ocean passing on the other side of the hull), they came upon Tosco's storage area – a large, wire-cubicled space camouflaged by walls of discarded plumbing fixtures.

Behind a barricade of old porcelain bathtubs, urinals, and bidets, the *Claridad* panel truck workers had on-loaded and neatly arranged a vast cache of equipment in padded trunks and reinforced drums, all of it – in contradistinction to the dusty clutter stacked around it – organized in a double-locked functional order.

Most of the equipment for the performance tonight was already up in the *Starlight Theatre*, Tosco explained. But directly off the central *Claridad* section stood a long fiberglass panel clearly marked, *"Danger! Do not disturb. Dangerous animals."*

Loring watched Tosco insert a first, then a second, longer, key into the padlock. "All of my children are in here. We keep the air perfectly filtered and fresh."

"Even here on *Card Deck*? How? I don't see any ventilation ductwork."

"It's all self-recycled and convection-current purified, Doctor," Tosco said.

"System perfected in laboratory Paris," Tulov added.

Tosco opened the door. "We have to travel with our animals, and we like to keep them happy and healthy. Of course, they don't get much sun down here."

"*Bien sûr,*" Loring agreed.

"*Mes enfants!*" he called. "We have a visitor! Robespierre! Daria! Birds, all of you! Wake up, everyone!"

Loring's eyes blinked in surprise as he followed Tosco inside. The self-contained microclimated space, engineered and prefabricated by Tulov and then secreted aboard, was easily four times the size of Loring's *Viking Deck* cabin and as fresh and sparkling as though Mr. Kim himself had just been in to scrub, dust and spray. The small central chamber had a desk and a simple bed and was lit by a comforting, pink-hued light. Through round glass-panels off the central chamber, Loring saw the animals lounging in their separate compartments: python, doves, rabbits, three geese, a pair of . . .

"Pigs? Are there pigs in the act?"

"Actually, no," Tosco said. "But we brought them along in case we want to improvise. Pigs are good for humor, too. Sometimes you need them. Besides, if the ship were to sink, you could grab the back of the pig and he will swim you to shore."

"Really? Like a natural life boat?"

Tosco smiled and shrugged his shoulders. "Old fashioned? But you know what? The pigs make us all feel a bit more secure. True, Vladimir?"

Loring watched four small black and white, square-nosed porkers snoot around in a straw-filled, barnyard style pen of chicken wire. "Cute. But how did you get all this stuff aboard?"

"Magic," Tulov smiled proudly.

"And you stay down here on this little bed, don't you? Looks awfully comfortable."

"Yes," Tulov winked. "I like sleep with animals, you know."

"Have a seat, *Docteur*," Tosco offered. "We'll bring Daria in to see you."

"It's so cozy down here," Loring yawned. "Like a pink womb."

When Tosco and Tulov disappeared through the thick plexiglass door that led to Daria's chamber, Loring sat down on the bed and yawned again.

He pressed his fingers into the thick, form-fitting latex mattress that slid up around his thighs and all around his buttocks. He welcomed the stillness, solitude, the pleasant pink glow that comforted the eyes and the body.

Just like down on the farm, ha!

The ringing in his ears diminished. He took a deep breath in the purified air, squeezed his nostrils, and the ringing was gone. He giggled, amazed that Tulov's engineering skills and the *Claridad* workers could create a cozy menagerie of such commodious proportions and atmosphere.

His eyelids felt heavy. Suddenly, like lead plates, they slammed down. He felt his cheek hit the pillow, heard his lungs expand and contract in slow excursions, as if someone were sleeping beside him in another body, not his. No ringing at all now. The ringing was gone.

He wrestled himself up off the pillow, propped his eyes open with his thumbs. Perhaps that pinot grigio at lunch was taking its toll. Or was it the after-kick of the panatella? Or was it just the sudden, refreshing turn-off of that ringing sound?

Realizing that his senses were about to give out on him, that he probably should excuse himself, explain to Tosco and Tulov and Daria that he had not really slept in . . . now . . . how many nights?

Even flying fish need to take naps now and then, don't they?

He clutched the beeper on his belt, squinted to see the green bead light on it beaming.

Yes, the beeper's definitely on. If anybody needs me, I'll be available. Though I've been kicked upstairs, and I find myself down below the waterline, I should . . .

And when was the last time I slept? Not really, since . . .

* * *

Her whiskers prickled against his nose. The air issued from her nostrils in long heaves fragrant of sweetly marinated goat kid liver. From time to time Loring's eyelids batted up in disbelief, teared, tried to remain open.

She lay on the floor beside him. The pink light clearly defined her warm, mountainous form. He watched the blurred pyramids of her twin furry ears as they twitched above her jittery eyes in her big cat dream, whatever that fantasy might be. Who could imagine? Who could speculate, while there was a phantasm actively going on in the mind of a cold-nosed tiger, a whisker away from one's own dreaming organ?

Loring vaguely recalled Tosco and Tulov bringing her in. Her huge big-snouted face eclipsed the doorway like a giant orange and black and white mandala. In one glance those enormous agate eyes recognized, forgave Loring with one bobbing nod, and then – she saw his tears of fatigue – she moved forward to comfort him.

Then, sometime after Tosco and Tulov had excused themselves, she had rolled down onto the floor beside his bed, offered her abundant warm fur up to him as he lay beside her, flicked her tail up around his legs, tickled him behind his knees, enticed him down onto the floor beside her, and he rolled gently down over her shoulders and ribs and felt himself giving it up to an enormous and tender, responsive feminine feline who needed – yes *needed and appreciated* – his embraces.

And, oh, the grunting purr as he stroked her between the shoulder blades, under her belly, along the massive muscles of her thighs, even looped his forefinger and thumb up and down the length of her tail *(just as warm as the rest of her!)* And Loring could hear himself purring as his fingers intercepted the stripes, one by one, down her cervical, her thoracic, her lumbar – the magnificent curvatures of her body – all of it stair-stepped with scimitar stripes of luxuriant, warm fur.

After Daria had fallen into her own sleep, Loring continued to run his fingers along her, could not stop slipping them up and down her breathing thorax, all around her stripes in their paint drip pattern, down toward their white field of gentle disintegration across the belly. His fingertips touched, counted the fleshy dark nuggets of her eight breast nipples, played arpeggios upon them, wondered how soon Tosco would wish her to be bred by some magnificent Amur River valley sire.

Such a lucky sire!

Then he was in her dream, or was it his?

Fresh snow. Seven inches. Chill to the bone. Somewhere in frigid eastern Asia . . . in a faint pink . . . dawn light . . .

. . . I skirt over the moist whiteness at a pleasant loping pace . . . I feel the dampness on my paws, feel thirst, stop to push my chin . . . yes . . . down through the ice on the lake edge and lap up frigid water . . . I am very thirsty and I drink my fill, till the tip of my tongue numbs . . . and my throat hurts . . . I look up across the rolling white hills, the silhouettes of higher, mountainous . . . risings to the far horizon. I see a long white fish in the cold water . . . yes . . . under my nose . . . the fish swims fast . . . along the edge of the water . . . crystals . . . and then leaps . . . up and out of the ripples . . .

winks at me as he spreads his wings . . . I jump onto . . . the lake ice . . . and follow him as he soars along the surface . . . rising . . . falling . . . swerving away from my . . . snout . . . yes . . . as he turns and taunts me. "You look delicious!" I shout to him . . . "Wait! Wait, please! Poisson . . . volant!"

And he calls to me, "You can't eat me! You had my brother for lunch. But Tigers much prefer ungulates – deer and elk and things with horns, not fins or wings! Remember? Just fly! Yes, fly like me!"

"Tigre volant?"

"Mais oui! Push your paws off the ice and fly after me!"

And I lunge . . . up into the air and spread my forepaws . . . wide. At once I am far above the lake . . . up to the clouds and I look down to where . . . yes . . . some laughing fishermen with deep amber faces huddle . . . they huddle around a fire . . . yes . . . they wave to me, grinning, and . . . yes . . . I am suddenly falling . . . the flying . . . yes . . . fish is nowhere in sight . . . yes . . . I am falling and spinning and falling and . . . yes . . .spinning toward their fire . . .

* * *

"*Docteur! Reveillez-Vous!*" Loring heard Tosco's voice. "You were *so* tired, I thought it best to let you sleep."

Loring opened his eyes, peered around the pink-hued chamber, breathed deeply. His brain felt an extraordinary, post-purge clarity.

"Where's Daria? I was just getting to know her. *Really*! She had some questions she wanted to ask me. I was waiting to tell her till I knew more about myself. Something about her mother falling. Or was I dreaming?"

"Yes. I think you were dreaming. You were screaming in your sleep and I could see she was alarmed. I took her away."

"I scared her?"

"Could there be telepathy between you two? But you can confer with her later about your dreams. It's time to go up to the theatre and fit you and Colonel Snippet-White into the gyroscope. Then you have a rehearsal with Ulla in an hour, don't you?"

* * *

Positioned center stage in the *Starlight Theatre*, and bolted upright by an over-sized steel c-clamp, the huge transcendental gyroscope spun slowly on its vertical axis and gleamed in the single overhead spotlight. The bare central disk rotated lazily, glimmered an eerie metallic silver-blue. The spotlight reflected at tricky angles, undulated from the flat circular surface in pulses – vibrant, alluring, transcendental.

As Loring walked down the central aisle, Tulov crouched by his apparatus, squinted through a flickering red laser scope that strobe-timed the revolutions.

"Come closer," Tulov urged. "Now should fit. I want you know my creation well."

"It's exquisite, Vladimir Vladimirovich."

"First gyroscope, and then gyre. Finally attach you and Colonel onto disk. I want you be accustomed all."

Refreshed from his snooze, Loring mounted the stage and drew close to the gyroscope, imagined himself splayed out and spinning in his spandex tiger suit.

Tulov picked up his cane and moved slowly toward the stage door. "I will leave you alone with the gyroscope for a few minutes. Please, Oliver, get to know her well. I will try to answer any questions when I return."

When the door slammed shut behind Tulov, Loring stepped back from the gyroscope and circled the apparatus slowly. Just minutes ago, he had shared telepathic dreams with a tiger, and now Vladimir Vladimirovich wanted him to "get to know" an inanimate metallic sphere!

Sort of a critical "bonding period." Ha-ha!

And Tulov had called Loring by his first name. Very flattering. Even Tosco didn't do that! With each step he took on the darkened stage, Loring's affection and reverence grew.

Tulov and Tosco! Men of imagination and bravery!

Close to it, Loring noticed aspects of the transcendental gyroscope he had not considered before. There was no central spool, a fundamental Loring had failed to grasp when he witnessed the demonstration at *Claridad*.

No central spool! Does that defy physics?

Instead, the inner spinning of the fluted central disk was supported by a wire-thin structure not visible from more than five feet – two rigid domes of monofilaments (upper and lower hemispheres) attached to and supporting the rim of the disk (superiorly and inferiorly) and yet knuckled into the northern and southern poles of the gyroscope. As flimsy as it appeared, this filagree cage was able to support 900 pounds of moving tiger and tiger carcass (or 380-plus pounds of moving human and human dead body) along with the three-inch thick, slitted metal plate to which the transcendental travelers were fixed. What metallic/porcelain superfiber (Loring hoped the *Cirque Ineffable* had secured the patent on this substance) could possibly sustain such stress?

Also, the rotating central disk had unusual inscriptions laced into both its surfaces. The disk was, in concept, a huge spinning coin. But the splitting of the coin itself into fluted, chevron-shaped musical valve-like openings, was embellished also by decorative engravings on the surface of the metal – long unreadable passages in Sanskrit, several rolling scrolls of Russian/Cyrillic derivation, some Hebrew quotations, a smattering of Arabic, Greek, Latin. Mayan glyphs? There were images of animals, fish, birds, insects, humans involved in copulation in various and extraordinary positions (all species-specific).

And the greater aesthetic effect of the object at rest?

Stepping back from the rotating disk in its orb, attached as it was in its giant steel C-sclamp, Loring noticed an inspiring glint to the entire surface. Yes, it was egg-like, as he had perceived briefly at *Claridad.*

Like the Russian Czars used to commision!

Or was Loring reading too much into all of it? The imagery, the physics, the linguistics, the ethical conundrum of his own involvement, even the beauty of it all confused him. He was glad when the stage door opened and Tulov returned.

"Any questions, Oliver?"

"I wouldn't have any idea of where to begin."

"Is the Doctor ready for fitting?"

* * *

As his chin squeezed against the metal platter, Loring pointed his toes. He felt Tulov yank his ankles firmly into the velcro straps. The sturdy restraints stretched his shoulders and hips out to the painful limit.

"But my crotch is killing me!"

"I must make velcro band tight. So sorry."

"Ouch! You're sure these will release after three revolutions?"

"That's what try make sure about. Give leg. Give more leg."

"I don't have more leg!"

"You not quite size Daria. Last night said were same as Daria."

"Thought I was."

"Not."

"I'm sorry."

"But Colonel not quite the size Veda! Ha-ha! Colonel already fitted. Maybe all balance perfectly. Can spin now?"

Painful as the fitting was, Loring realized he was at the mercy of Tulov's calculations. For consolation, there were enough technological devices all around the gyroscope – strobe timers, video cameras, a large panel full of blipping controls – to launch a moderate sized sputnik.

"Okay, spin me."

"Just one quick. Full 360. Ready?"

Loring saw Tulov's forefinger stretch out and torque the gyroscope. In a silent whirling movement that lasted no longer than two seconds, the platter flicked gracefully through a full circle. The bones in Loring's spine tugged gently to a new and pleasant alignment. He felt and heard several soothing cracks.

"Would you do that again?"

"Like it?"

"God, that feels good. Did you ever do chiropraxis?"

"Surprise?"

"Keep doing it for a while, okay?"

"But need finish test."

"Just a couple times more? I'm not sure I'm fitted in just right. Could you tighten these wrist binders a bit? Yes, that one feels loose. You want a little more leg?"

* * *

Loring had just returned to his cabin when his phone rang. He felt slightly giddy from his twirls in the *Starlight Theatre*. He really loved that gyroscope! Ominous and foreboding appearance? Yes. Kinesthetic high? Also yes! He waited then picked up the receiver.

"Doctor? This is the *Radio Station*. We have a phone call from a woman in Vermont for you. I'll patch her through, Doc. She says she's your mother. Shall we proceed?"

"Ha-ha . . . ugh . . . hello?"

"Oliver, what's wrong? You don't sound right."

"Mom! Oh, Mom! Ha-*ha*! I'm just stretching."

"Yes, don't ha-*ha* me, please! Your mother. Remember me?"

"Olivia! Are you alright?"

"Well, yes, I'm alright. I was going to call and thank you so much for the box of chocolates. They came this morning. But then a little while ago I was watching the Cabelvista broadcast and they showed a picture of three men on the top deck near the smoke stacks walking along. They were smoking cigars. Was one of those men you?"

"So you liked the chocolates?"

"Was that you smoking, Oliver? You were wearing sunglasses and a very foolish-looking baseball cap."

"Yes, Mother! A cigar."

"Well, I'm not pleased at all. And don't say you're not inhaling! That's not even funny anymore!"

"Mother!"

"Smoking regularly, is that it? Besides, Son, don't you know you're on television? People recognize you. All my friends are glued to their sets, watching every day and night. What will I tell the neighbors? And what would your father say?"

"Mom! I'm almost 40 years old. Didn't Dad ever smoke a cigar?"

"Don't get smart on me and try to shift the blame, Oliver. And that baseball cap does not flatter. Your father would certainly never have worn something as hideous as that!"

"Mother, you're angry."

"Oh, I'm not angry. I'm just proud, I suppose. I've been watching round the clock, when you gave the tour of the medical department and how you saved that woman from Texas with the chip in her throat and now you'll be dancing tonight and then volunteering for the late night magic show. You seem to be getting along fabulously, Oliver. How should your mother feel?"

"Mom, I love you."

"And I love you. But really, Oliver! I don't want this sudden fame going to your head. I don't mind the sunglasses. I suppose they're necessary. But a cigar! I'm sorry to harp."

"Mother, I have to tell you something serious. I met a woman. A wonderful woman."

"Is my fool in therapy again? Is that what you're telling me?"

"No, Mom. The therapist thing is all over."

"And do you still bite your nails?"

"Mom, forget the therapist. And the nail problem. This woman is from Salzburg, Austria."

"An Austrian? Does she dance? You don't mean that beautiful Ulla woman!"

"If you watch the show this evening, you'll see us. Mambo. With knee slides at the end. At eight . . . we'll . . . Mother, are you crying?"

"All this week I've been so concerned about you. But tell me the truth for once. You really found a woman who can dance? Really dance? Because that woman Ulla can dance."

"We have a rehearsal in a few minutes up in *Club Atlantis*."

"Well then, run to her! Don't tell me anything about her. I'd rather get to know her by watching her . . ."

"But Mom, she's got a lot more than the mambo in her."

"Well, half the town of Coventry is coming over tonight to watch you. All the old Academy students will be here. The drink of the day on your ship, we're told, is the '*Cupid Cooler*.' I got the recipe, and I'm serving it! Have you had one yet?"

"I wish Dad could watch, too."

"Don't say that. Now run off! And . . ."

"Yes, Mother . . ."

". . . and make sure your mambo . . ."

" I know . . . that it tells a story."

"And please, son. Don't take up tobacco. Not at your age. And please don't bite your nails in front of the cameras."

"Mom, are you crying? Mom? Dad would love her. You will, too! Mom? Are you still there? Hello? Olivia?"

* * *

Loring arrived in *Atlantis* to find Ulla dancing by herself on the parquet. The band was gone, the club deserted. She mamboed slowly, tested each move. Low cut, sleeved black leotard. Fish net stockings. Stiletto heels. Such ideal rehearsal raiment for the mambo high priestess!

Manny Rodriguez, the Panamanian Bartender, straightened the long rows of liquor bottles, topped off his fleet of peanut dishes, lined up a row of specially-labeled "*Cupid Cooler*" tumblers, and evened the stacks of wave-and-sunburst napkins on the mahogany bar, all in final preparation for the V.I.P. Cocktail Party.

Loring stepped up to the dance floor, placed the *Flair* gift box containing Ulla's necklace on a table.

Ulla came over, smiled and put her hands in his. Her eyes were soft, welcoming. "I went over the music with Barry and the band. And then I sent

289

them off. I thought you and I should run through the routine silently. Okay?"

"No music?"

"No music," she echoed in his ear. "Just lead me through it once, very slowly, won't you?" She kissed his cheek and dipped her brow, put herself into mambo partner position. "We want to keep it fresh."

"Keep the story new."

"I like that."

"Slow motion at half tempo?"

"No, let's take it down to a quarter."

"Okay, let's mambo."

The *Atlantis* parquet was smaller than the floor-show dance area in the *Starlight Lounge*, where they would appear later. But they trimmed their steps, measured the turns and twirls to fit the space, all in slow, blissful solitude and silence.

Step, rock, double spin, rock twice . . .

Loring glanced up along the portico at the mute deity statues – Poseidon and Venus, Dionysus and Hermes – and hoped they didn't mind sharing the rarefied air of their pantheon in silent meditation with the mambo gods. This was, after all, the day to celebrate the joker cherub, the wily naked imp who tormented the gods themselves with his capricious pranks. Despite Cupid's celebrated mischief, Loring felt serene as he slid through their routine in slow motion, felt Ulla's poised muscles flex through dynamic postures and positions.

"Dip again, slide, thrust, and slide," she whispered, her eyes flashing.

Oh, how Loring adored this – weaving his body and spirit with her in slow, exaggerated movements, a pageant, a rite in their own silent temple, a hushed terpsichorean prayer. Later, when they danced up-tempo in the *Starlight Lounge*, with the crowd and the band and the cameras all around them, their vivid capers would burn with a pagan fire. But for now, in their lingering steps and mute tandem maneuvers – his hands on her waist, her elbows, crisscrossing above her breasts – the invisible flames licked deliciously slow, tantalizing, holy.

Double spin, double rock, step . . .

In climax, as Loring's final triumphant knee slides led him across the parquet with his right palm silhouetting the curvature of Ulla's advancing thighs and tightening buttocks, she strutted before him with slow pelvic thrusts in flagrant carnal pulses. He watched her muscular hips pump forward and her firm pubic mound jab beside him – at his nose level.

Oh, turn your eyes, gods! You mere statues! Here is beauty, flesh, dance, the source of all mortal rhapsody!

Here is slow mambo! Oh yessssss!

When they finished, Ulla stood panting, her cheeks flushed and moist. "You're lighter than yesterday, Oliver."

"I'm what?"

"Your step is lighter. You're less tense."

"But the routine is more familiar, and we were moving through it at quarter speed."

"Not only that. You do seem more agile. What happened?"

Loring stretched his arms up, arched his spine back, wiggled his ankles, one by one. "Tulov put me through some spins on the gyroscope. Do you think it pulled my spine out a bit? Maybe it was the flying fish at lunch."

"I knew there was something. It's clear to me. I mean, you were good before, but you're just," she wrinkled her lip, "much lighter now."

"For one thing, I'm getting exhausted. But I think the gyroscope has improved my . . ."

"Why should you be surprised?"

"Yes, why should I be surprised with the metaphysics of mambo. Ha!"

Ulla giggled, her eyes sparkling. "You know, I liked what we did last night. And I want to kiss you again. Come here."

Loring stepped back and took the *Flair* package from the table and offered it. "Do you mind if I surprise you first?"

She peeled off the golden bow and paper, opened the box. As she took the necklace in her hands, her eyes moistened. Tiny wet rivulets dripped down both her reddening cheeks. She held the necklace to her face, bathed the smooth pearls and blue lapis spheres in the teardrops. She shook her head slowly with a glistening grin. She held it out to him and said, "Could you?"

She turned away from him, and Loring fastened the tiny silver links at the moist nape of her neck. She turned back and put her arms around him. She pulled herself close, and as they kissed, he felt her tears seep onto his tongue.

So is this how happiness tastes?

"I love it, Oliver. And thank you for what you're doing tonight for Tosco. You are an unusual man."

"I hope I'm ready for it."

"Don't be silly. It's a magic trick. That's all."

"But there's so much physics and metaphysics. Daria really should be the one doing this, not me. She's so much better equipped."

"Daria will get her chance in Paris. Forget about that cat. Kiss me again. Oh, and do you mind if I give you my Valentine gift tomorrow?"

"Will I see you tomorrow?."

"Be sure of it. My gift takes some preparation. Oh, and Hildegarde has something for you, too. Now kiss me."

* * *

Fresh from a steaming hot shower and a meticulous shave, Loring stood before the full-length mirror in his cabin and carefully donned his uniform. Mr. Kim had returned a crisply starched tuxedo shirt and a shiny new pair of epaulets from the cleaners, had also buffed up Loring's pumps and polished the golden wave-and-sunburst jacket buttons.

Studs and suspenders plumb straight, Loring lightly gelled his thinning blonde hair and brushed as much as he could up into a partial pompadour. He spit pasted his sun-whitened eyebrows smoothly into place. He pulled up his socks, slid into his pumps, snapped the new epaulets onto his white gabardine jacket and fitted it over his shoulders. He fastened his Chief Medical Officer nameplate on his left lapel and clasped the waist button over his shining silk cummerbund. Then he picked up the frosted glass *vaporisateur* and shot a spritz on each cheek of Nino Cerutti 1881, rubbed the sweet fragrance around his cheeks and down onto his neck.

I do look a bit tired. But I'm tan. Say that for me, mambo gods!

Final step? He cleaned all ten fingernails with a stainless steel wave-and-sunburst letter opener (a gratifying milestone experience), rubbed each ungual surface with kleenex till it shone. Then he popped a scarab pill.

Loring stepped back, stood erect, inspected his tan again, smiled into the mirror. Now he was ready for tonight's three television broadcasts: the V.I.P. Cocktail Party, the dance show in the *Starlight Lounge*, and then the *pièce de résistance* and *grand finale* – the "Love Magic" Flaming Transcendental Gyroscope.

Oh, the responsibilities of a blast image! Who needs an agent, really! Ulla's smile and tears when she received that necklace are all I need. Let that necklace be my agent!

Yes, Ulla had received the necklace with obvious deep emotion, promised to give him something tomorrow as a Valentine gift, too.

Yo, Oliver Loring!

He glanced toward his porthole, watched the dimming pink shadows of the day fade as the spent sun sank below the watery western horizon. His eye caught the brooding mellowness of the reflected rosy light – darkening night itself seemed to creep, wave by fleeting wave, over the unsteady surface of the sea that moved past his porthole at a brisk 17 knots. "Time for all flying fish to be tucked into their nocturnal aquatic mode," he giggled to himself and faced the mirror, again liked what he saw.

Then he peered out the porthole again, sensed some odd shade of doubt creep in, as if some little cynical little *poisson volant* out there (perhaps a schoolmate of the fish he'd had for lunch?) was playing the vengeful skeptic.

"But I've already avoided the worst case scenario," Loring said to the mirror. "I stuck by my convictions and canceled the tiger trick. That act alone may well have prevented a horrible sequence of events. So please *shut up* about what happens if something goes wrong. I've already dealt with that. I don't wear these three stripes purely for show you know, even if I have been kicked upstairs."

As he stared back out the darkened porthole and waited for a reply, he heard a knock. Jarvis Lee was at the door with a another letter from *Viceroy Deck*.

Viceroy Deck #7
Thursday – 17.00 hours

Darling Oliver,

I hope you don't mind if I butted into your situation, but I suspect you received some good news from the Captain. I was talking with Stig, and I mentioned to him how actively you have involved yourself with the entertainment aspects of this cruise – the dancing tonight (I hear its a mambo, can't wait!) and also with the Colonel in Tosco's magic show. (By the way, I went down and checked him out in the tiger suit: he's divine! And loose as a goose, too, thanks to your wake-up Scriabin this a.m.)

I've glanced at some of the Farrely Farrell stuff coming over the Cablevista channel, and it seems to me you've become quite the adored swain. There was a clip of you signing autographs outside the Hospital, and there must have been two dozen women, several as ancient as me, panting for your attention. By the way, I understand you're called Dart Doc. Why is that?

I suggested to Stig that, if there were any way possible, you should get a break from your medical duties, so that you can concentrate on your dancing and your Tosco stuff. Stig said his nephew Trygve, who came along (and who has served before on this ship as the doctor) would be happy to fill in for you.

Thank goodness all this television stuff will be over by tomorrow at sunset when we bury the Colonel! I'm so glad about tonight, Oliver. Thanks to you, Rocky will be going out in a blaze of glory.

Love and many kisses,

Hildegarde

P.S. (Addendum): Oh, and if you'd like, Stiggy said you and Ulla could zip over tomorrow to his own private island (it's only a 30 minute launch ride from the ship's private island.) He'll call over and have the launch come pick you up. We'd go ourselves, but Stiggy is helping me with all the arrangements for Rocky tomorrow. So the place is all yours. Enjoy.

* * *

"Now tell us, Blanche Cruickshank, how does it feel to know that your name is a household word? They call it the chip flip seen round-the-world, and you're known as the Chip Chick."

"Farrely, I should say that instead of a brush with death, I would rather have won one of them beautiful roadsters up on the roof. But gosh darn, my husband Clyde already owns three and he's got two dozen more of those dynamite babies shined up and sittin' pretty in our lot out in Odessa, Texas. I can drive one of 'em 'round town whenever I please. Any color I choose."

"Fan-tas-tic, Blanche! I'm sure you do and you will."

During the V.I.P. Cocktail party in *Club Atlantis*, Loring stayed away from Farrely Farrell and his side-kick, Spinelli. Later he would have plenty of exposure as a dancer and as a metaphysical stunt participant. He preferred to sit back at the bar, munch on peanuts, listen to Barry Cox and the Atlantans, and sip his iced Perrier.

All the while, a very foxy Anita Rothberg stood by the cameras, never more than an arm's length from Farrely Farrell. Her blonde curls perfectly fashioned, her slender shoulders wriggling in a sheer black silk cocktail shift, she wrinkled and nodded her intelligent brow in wistful amusement at Farrely's slightest gesture or *bon mot.*

When he caught her eye, Loring raised his Perrier, winked, mouthed a friendly *"Skåll!"* to her across the room. But she ignored his salute, concentrated instead on her current paramour and professional consultee.

But why should Loring waste his time dwelling on Anita's cash-in on this cruise? All the better that she and Loring were finished and she on to someone else!

Skål anyway, Anita! Cupid, it's your night! Do your stuff!

And likewise, Loring should not jaw to the Cablevista audience. Though that might attract some late night viewers to tune in to the *Cirque Ineffable* display, he worried that any teasing blurb from him might jinx the act. Tosco wanted everything kept quiet.

"He who knows does not talk and he who talks . . ."

Loring pulled Hildegarde's note out of his tux pocket to read it again. He tingled with delight at the invitation to spend the afternoon with Ulla on Stig Storjord's private island. Legends about Stig's tropical retreat abounded. As far as Loring knew, nobody had ever been there to report what the island really was like.

Each Friday, when the *Nordic Blue* anchored off the lush, palm-fringed Grand Key island in the Bahamas, the ship's tenders ferried passengers and crew over to the island for a day of beach sports, snorkeling, barbecue sandwiches, and rum drinks. And at 10.00 hours, each Friday morning, a sleek, blue and white 120-foot power yacht named *"Sjøstjerne"* (Norwegian for *"Starfish"*) appeared from out of the northern horizon and pulled up alongside the cargo hatch to take on mail and supplies. *Sjøstjerne* never moored for longer then ten minutes, before her sullen Bahamian commander pulled her back from the ship and headed north again.

But one detail about the supplies for Stig's island was known: many of the crates and insulated barrels contained horticultural materials, fertilizers, gardening implements, refrigerated rose stalks and other sundry specimens. This led crew members to suspect that the fleet owner's island was a retreat where he tilled his rose fancier's dream garden. It tickled Loring to imagine that tomorrow he and Ulla would board *Sjøstjerne* and zoom up to the north to explore that mystery island.

Loring glanced fondly up over the bandstand at the oil portrait of the bearded fleet owner. He remembered his first evening of this cruise here in *Atlantis,* how that portrait's cheery smile had seemed alive. And there Stig was, in the full flesh, standing proudly on the parquet beside Hildegarde, his Imperial Fiat rose pinned to his white dinner jacket. Ever since he arrived on the ship, he had been a constant comfort and adoring presence with Hildegarde. And why not? Had not Stig Storjord once rescued and restored another rather celebrated and stranded *grande dame*, this very ship, in fact? The man who fancied roses clearly had an eye for enduring quality.

As Loring took a deep sip of his Perrier and considered the potential for a future shared by Hildegarde and Stig Storjord, he felt an elbow poke in the back.

"So Doctor," Nils Nordström leered over his Aquavit shot glass, "would you like to try some skeet shooting again tomorrow? Eh?"

The Staff Captain had sat down beside him at the bar. The gruff barb in his voice had not diminished since the unpleasant encounter earlier.

"Good evening, Staff."

"I said, would you like to shoot some skeet? Can't you hear me? I might be able to teach you something."

"I'm sorry, Nils. Thanks. I have plans for tomorrow."

"Suppose you'll be busy throwing darts or something, heh? Isn't that why they call you the Dart Doc?"

"Yes, something like that. Ha-*ha*!"

Loring sensed Nordström's contentious remarks were not likely to subside. Hearing a high-pitched ringing in his ears again, he quickly drained his Perrier and stepped away from the bar. "Excuse me, Staff, but I need to head down to my cabin. I have to perform soon. But thanks for the shooting lesson today."

"Dancing for the frickin' television, are you?"

"Yes. A mambo. And thanks for taking an interest."

"Yea, and I heard from the Captain that you're not the Doctor any more. Maybe you better just stick to darts. Or dancing, eh?"

"Yea, ha-*ha*!"

"Yea, I guess you're more of an entertainer than a real doctor."

"It's a cruise, Nils. Nothing more and nothing less."

On his way out of *Atlantis*, Loring did not look back at the bar. He had no reason to dislike Nordström, and he did not know why the Staff Captain resented him. Was Nils one of those surly Vikings who, loyal to his clan, simply resented an outsider? Did the Staff Captain somehow perceive Loring's therapeutic interventions with Trond Ramskog as a block to his own promotion? A career deprivation issue?

Hey, let the new Ship's Doctor worry about Nordström. I've got a mambo story to tell.

* * *

The *Starlight Lounge*. Darkened. Jam-packed. Silent.

Loring wiggles his toes in his dance pumps, leads Ulla – she's in a low-backed silver shift of silk with gleaming stiletto heels – to the center of the dance floor.

They take positions. She reaches her right arm above her head. He stretches his open palm to meet hers. They pose, frozen in silence as the spotlight starts to swirl over the ceiling and around at the hushed crowd and then shoots random glinting periphery glances at Barry and the Starlight Boys, then back into the audience.

Ulla's new necklace catches the spotlight flash, glows gently, silver-blue. He sees the shimmering gems rise and fall in time with her neck pulses. He can feel her breathing in voluptuous, fragrant heaves.

In . . . and . . .

Spinelli at the microphone: "Yes, ladies and gentlemen! Aren't our Starlegs Dancers fab? But we're gonna' give the girls and guys a break and bring on a very special couple. She's visiting from Austria, where she's principle ballerina for the world famous Salzburg Dance Circle. And he's the dancing doctor from Boston, the guy you've all come to know and love during the past few days of your cruise here on the *S/S Nordic Blue*. Ulla and Doctor Oliver have a little something special in the way of a mambo for you tonight, so let's all put our hands together and give it up for . . . ULLLLLLLLA . . . AAANNNNDUH . . . . DOCTORAH . . . OLLLLLLLIVERAAAAA!"

Full spotlight. Peppering conga drum crescendo as *Señor* Uribe heats up.

Loring's forefinger draws back along the full length of her arm, traces the curve of her shoulder, down the angled side of her shoulder blade and then up again. She spin reverses – still close but now in his left arm. She cocks her head, fixes it in haughty, glaring, puckered-lip insolence. His left hand clenches slowly to a fist in front of his heart, starts to pound with the conga and then her knee sticks out from the slit in her silver shift and begins to bounce up near his crotch. Her silver stiletto comes up around his calf, and they stare at each other.

Catcalls and whistles from the audience as Uribe's conga boils over.

She flings back her head, and he places his left hand in the small of her back. She arches back her spine till her head almost touches the floor. Still posing, she beams her icy blues up to him.

More high-pitched whistles.

Then she sneers up at him and her spine springs forward in a feathery Cuban float spin and then she locks into him in tight shadow position.

Her cheek is against his and he feels her face widen into a firm smile, as his hands descend to her waist. They both stare forward as they invoke the mambo gods to full power now, her hips writhing back and forth against him, rocking higher and higher with each beat. Her shoulders arch back against him, and he releases his hands. She glides around, struts in tandem with him toward the corner, swivels and, hands now flying in giddy circles, she elbows back from him and dares him to pursue.

Her feet flash and sparkle. Her hips are the conga as Uribe pops and undulates, lurks and levitates.

Under the silver liquid of the silk, her perfect buttocks – dazzlingly strong and defined – flow like hot mercury.

Yo! Mambo gods and goddesses! Carrrrrrrrrrrrrrumba! Your high priestess is up to her best tonight. Watch! The audience will be talking in tongues when they leave this lounge. Latin American tongues!

They finish the first and second sequences, enter the third. The audience is up on its feet.

And as for you, Tulov and Tosco, with your transcendent gyroscope. And all you other Eden Reclamation Project junkies, potential or otherwise out across the Cablevista planet! Check out this Fraülein with the transcendental figure and the eyes from Olympus. Would you care to try and abstract a realm of existence more pure and pulsatile than this glowing force of nature? And Fernando Uribe! Barry Cox! You guys! Just keep doing it! Yes . . . Mas . . . que . . . nada . . .

As the fourth sequence begins, the story is rippling and flowing before them all.

Behold, the gods are at work on this stage. Ulla and I are not performers. We are kinetic channelers in touch with the invisible ethers that lie within and without, above and below. And this is our story, that around the gloriously controlled turbulence and glitter, deep imperative rhythm, there is a search for the interior stillness which every god – mambo or otherwise – must share with all creatures, be they silver-dressed or silver-winged flying fish.

Oh, let this go on and on and . . .

And then, finally, Loring strikes off into his triumphant knee slide procession. His hand high on her moist shoulder blades, he trains back his jaw and angles his head at her pubis, looks up to meet her glorious glance. With each pace, her long legs striding beside him, the audience roars louder and louder, screams, explodes . . .

Oh, blessed sacrament! Yes, gods! Take us!

* * *

Loring dodged through the *Crew Bar* and out the rear hatch to the *Poop Deck*. After the miraculous mambo, he had wanted to share a moment with Ulla, but she had to suit up immediately for another production number with the Starlegs Dancers.

"We'll spend tomorrow together?" he had whispered, as she was about to run off to the dressing room.

She kissed him quickly. "Yes. Alone." She squeezed his hands and disappeared.

On the *Poop Deck* Loring stepped carefully around the anchor cables and leaned down over the stern rail. The mambo gods had infused him with a sustained adrenaline boost, and his heart hammered happily to those final imperative runs of Uribe's thundering conga. The thought of spending a day with Ulla tomorrow on Stig Storjord's mystery island sent surges of mambo megawatts throughout his body. He wanted to spread his arms and soar straight up over the spangled white wake, just as he and Ulla had soared over the *Starlight Lounge* dance floor.

He looked up at the stars in the black tropical sky and breathed the misted brine rising from the propellers. Indeed, they *had* been incredible. Never had this Dart Doc felt more securely ensconced in the bull's eye zone of kinesthesia than tonight with Ulla. It was a dance he would have been proud to have the entire world witness.

And guess what!

He sent a triple latin bump and grind out to the waves.

The entire world had, in fact, witnessed our story, surely must have felt our passionate circles with each erotic gyration of Ulla's silver-sheened hips.

He felt the cool salty mist against his face, breathed it in slowly, closed his eyes and cherished the vision of Ulla's muscular limbs turning and flashing before him.

He glanced up at the myriad eyes in the sky.

You out there! Was our mambo not incredible? Will tomorrow not also be incredible?

I am the tropical wind itself! I am that westerly, yes . . .

Stars! Let me climb up there amidst your mystical black firmament and connect all your dots, fly from glitter ball to glitter ball, soar in your surreal, billions-of-years-old radiances. I want to bathe my spirit in your infinities!

He recalled Tosco's description of the founding of *Cirque Ineffable* and how the new members of the circus cult realized higher levels of achievement and new clarity in their art with their first performances after joining, as if the commitment to the cult had ratcheted up their skills. Had that same upward bolt occurred tonight with Loring's rendering of a definitive mambo?

What do you think, stars? And you, glittering waves? Did I hit new peaks a while ago with the mambo gods shaking their moroccas and their high priestess knocking the audience silly in her shimmering silver raiments? Did that final knee slide sequence not rip apart the viscera of any skeptics?

He surveyed the constantly retreating horizon as it swept back and tucked in under the southern stars. But neither the firmament nor the moving ocean seemed willing to comment.

"Could I say something?"

"Who is it?"

"It's me."

"Who?"

"Your lunch. Le Poisson Volant. Remember me?"

"Speak up."

"If you don't mind me saying it, you sound blatantly schizophrenic to me."

"I do, don't I. Ha-ha!"

"To begin with, you're describing the layout of the universe in simplistic and narcissistic terms."

"So I'm narcissistic. I'll give you that. But schizophrenic? I'm not hearing voices or anything."

"Aren't you having a conversation with a flying fish?"

"That's just the way I think."

"So schizophrenics don't think? Maybe a little too much? Busy minds? Like you?"

"Shut up about the schizophrenia. I'm dealing with metaphysics."

"You asked for somebody to comment, so I did. This is the thanks I get. And are you absolutely sure you want to go ahead with this gyroscope stunt? Don't say I didn't warn you."

"But I trust Tosco and Tulov."

"Any questions you might want to ask them before you go out there? Remember? Tosco asked you if you had any questions. You said you didn't know where to begin."

"Well, as a matter of fact, yes. I do know where to begin."

"Question?"

"Once I'm strapped onto the platter, am I supposed to mentate in any special way to make the phenomenon even more transcendental in appearance? Will the image in the eyes of the audience and the tens of millions out there on the Cablevista planet be enhanced by any interior exercises on my part?"

"Hey, now you're thinking like a true metaphysician! You know, somebody slapped me on a platter earlier today. Want to hear about that?"

"No. This is different. I think. And once I slide down the invisible chute and the Colonel whirls around in my place and hits the flaming spike, should I cry out, shriek in agony, give the primordial scream that Daria did at Claridad?"

"These are fairly basic questions, Dart Doc."

"That's why I'm asking them."

"But why are you asking me? I'm the one who's trying to warn you not to do it! Life isn't all triumphant knee slides, you know. Take it from me, your lunch."

* * *

Loring tried to sneak back through the *Crew Bar* without being spotted. But as he passed by the starboard row of booths, a grinning Jacques Chemin popped up and intercepted him. The Haitian had on a stylish, high-cut French black tuxedo – thin lapels, elaborate pleat work on the sleeves, and a row of gold studs down the front of his shirt.

"Hey boys!" he shouted to Pearly Livingstone and Rupert and Robert Carrington, Jamaican Bellhop twin brothers. "Is it not the suave dude we just saw on television? The famous Fred Astaire himself? *Mais oui!*"

Loring slapped high fives. "Looking awfully natty yourself tonight, Jacques."

"But you are the star now, *Docteur*! As you can see, we're all celebrating down here."

"I'm due upstairs again for the magic show in ten minutes."

Pearly grinned and shook his head. "Always on the run, Dart Doc!"

"I'm sorry. Hey Pearly, I saw you on the tube today."

"Oh yes, Doc!" Pearly gave a huge smile. "I think all my children will be very proud. Their daddy is famous now, too. So maybe you would like to have just one thirst quencher with us? We Jamaicans are having our Red Stripes tonight. Would you like one?"

Chemin lifted his Aquavit glass. "You know, Pearly. We cannot detain *Docteur*. He has to go up to do some fine magic. But *Docteur*, Voodoo Jacques will tell you a bit about magic. Yes, you may reach into the top hat for a rabbit, and you pull out a tarantula." The Haitian's fingers fluttered in mock pain. His face twisted with his thin lips pursed around the glistening diamond in his front tooth.

"Ouch!" Loring grimaced, as the Carrington twins laughed.

Jacques shook his head emphatically. "You had best believe me, boys! There is danger if you don't believe old Jacques!"

"So, we'll be watching you, Doc!" Pearly said. "Good luck! But *mon*, maybe you can drop by later. Pearly is bringin' his girlfriend down here."

Loring frowned skeptically.

"Yes, *mon*. He's having a late date with Fatima."

"The woman is busy till after the magic show. But then she said she will meet me and we will come down for a sweet drink together. The *Crew Bar* is open late tonight."

"So she's finally giving in?"

"Yes. She will be my Valentine tonight. And I have a special Valentine in mind to give her. I am sure it will win her heart."

Pearly swigged from his Red Stripe bottle. "Will it make Jacques lucky in love?"

Loring gazed into Chemin's face. He seemed to have an agenda working somewhere inside him, but Loring couldn't see it in his eyes.

"You know, Fatima sold me a necklace yesterday."

"Oh yes, *Docteur*! She told me all about your necklace for the Ulla. And we all saw her wearing it tonight on television when she danced with you. Matches her sad eyes, doesn't it?"

"Why, thank you. I think it does."

"In fact, you gave me the idea for a Valentine necklace for Fatima."

"Something from *Flair*?"

"I cannot afford those fancy prices up in *Flair*, so maybe I do my shopping somewhere else. Maybe even on *Car Deck*? My necklace will be more exotic than yours. And I have a very special way to present it to her, immediately after the magic show. Would Jacques ever do anything that was not dramatic? Especially when he is trying to prove his love for a lady?"

"Interesting."

Chemin licked his tooth diamond and gave a teasing pout. "Oh, it will be more than that, *Docteur*."

"Feeling your caraway seeds tonight?"

"I am also feeling my love. Yes, it will be a very special necklace for my African beauty. *Trés magnifique*! I want the world to know I love her. I was out earlier on the *Poop Deck*."

"Blowing your conch to the waves?"

"Oh, yes. I told them everything."

"But no hints for us, eh? I guess we'll never know until we know?"

"Run off and do your magic, *Docteur*. You will see mine later."

"Promise you're not going to do anything silly, Jacques?"

"How about you, *Docteur*? You're not on your way to do anything silly yourself, are you?"

* * *

"Whiskers? Does the Colonel have whiskers?"

"Seven on each cheek. Like the dead tiger. God, you look just like that old stiff."

"That's what we're shooting for."

"Yea. I guess we are."

Loring stood in front of the full-length mirror in the *Starlight Theatre Dressing Room* and inspected his reflection. Ruby Decosta's final addition to his costume was a striped bathing cap with tiger ears. She painted in the details of his face.

"Perfect, Ruby."

"Now the whiskers. You realize, you're really goin' out on a limb with this one? Even for Halloween it's kind of a stretch. But for Valentine's Day? I still don't get it."

"This isn't trick or treat, Ruby. It's magic for a good cause. It's called the Eden Reclamation . . . "

"Shut up and hold still. Damn! I'm glad this show is only running one night."

* * *

Alone backstage, Loring squatted on a stool in his spandex tiger suit and listened as the steel doors of the *Starlight Theatre* opened. A noisy throng of power cruisers filed in. They tittered and cajoled far beyond the nervousness of the usual *Nordic Blue* audiences.

Or was Loring only projecting his own fear? Ha-*ha*! Or had they all had too many *Cupid Coolers*?

Kidding aside, and with due respect to Nadine Tulard and her fabulous scarab regimen, he would have loved to gnash into his nails, give them a good, bloody, tigerly mauling. But the painted mittens the perfectionist Ruby Decosta had stuck on his hands at the last minute (along with the painted socks) preempted even the thought of a late-in-the-cruise oral orgy.

What do tigers do when they are nervous? Loring wanted to know. He also wanted to find out a lot more about being a tiger – things not fully telepathized during dreams – but he reckoned he was as close to being a tiger as most human beings had ever been, and perhaps that permitted him to ad lib.

Nervous? Pace.

Who knows where the idea came from? Or was it actually an idea? He supposed it didn't matter, since his tiger-stockinged feet started moving on their own.

Step . . . slide . . .

Walking like an Egyptian didn't seem particularly original, but most of the rest of the act was highly novel, and it did serve to relax Loring, give him perspective. He realized, of course, that a tiger walking like an Egyptian clashed stereotypes. But why should any of that academic folderol apply currently? Most tigers did what they damn well pleased, Loring surmised. Just like the ancient Pharaohs.

Actors he had met on previous cruises had often discussed with him the various methods of "getting into character." Such meditative drills were not the type of mental exercise he was used to. But there were no spoken words to his role tonight. He was to be, if anything, a metaphysical effigy, partly of his own invention.

Nobody out there wants a fidgety effigy!

And his task, while he walked onto the stage and then ascended up to the Transcendental Gyroscope, was to represent a human *first* and a tiger *second*. (The Leonardo thing.) To step out onto the stage as a tiger walking this way would, of course, create a hybrid kinesthetic image and perhaps violate the tenuous performer-audience trust, the critical link which *Madame* Olivia Loring had long lectured her Academy classes to establish.

Better keep it simple. Feline.

He broke from his Egyptian gait and experimented with an up-on-the-toes cat prowl offering that seemed to blend a little of the bump and thrust characteristic of Daria with his own natural arm-swinging, quick-down-the-corridor stride.

"Surrender the ego!" Olivia had often preached, whether she taught the foxtrot, cha cha, or Lindy.

No problem here, Mom! But I didn't ask Daria how much of her ego she was willing to give up to me.

He was still nervous, and he felt he had a right to be that way. All this pacing had not quieted his fears in the least. What was a metaphysical effigy supposed to feel?

Yes, he realized many of these concepts should have been defined long before he had donned the costume and striped bathing cap. Why be daunted, though? It would all be just as new to the audience in the *Starlight Theatre* and around the Cablevista world as it would be to him and the Colonel. Of course, the Colonel had it easier – he was already strapped on the wheel. All Rocky had to do was . . .

Tosco walked in wearing his top hat, his performance wig and blue tuxedo. Tulov followed him, moving slowly on his cane, but clearly excited. He was dressed in white tie, striped trousers and mourning coat.

After eyeing Loring up, he grabbed his tail. "Must fasten this!" Tulov said. He pinned the tip of the tail between Loring's shoulder blades. "There. How feel?"

"It feels alright, but I think it might look stupid."

"Must live with!" Tulov smiled. "Aerodynamics problem. You have no any muscles in tail."

"But neither does the Colonel."

"Of course not."

"But isn't that good? Aren't we supposed to be symmetrical?"

"Yes, but you not symmetrical as Daria is Veda. And tails of you and Snippet-White not weigh heavy as tails of tiger."

"Isn't this a little late to be telling me this? Have you cleared this tail thing with Ruby?"

"We already pin Colonel's tail," Tulov explained, "and Colonel already..."

"Yes, I think I understand," Loring said. But the stern looks Tulov was giving Tosco disturbed him. "Or do I?"

"Not to ask questions at this point," Tulov insisted firmly, and he again shot an adamant stare at Tosco.

"Wait a minute," Loring said.

"No time wait."

"But you must answer something that I hadn't thought about till now."

"*Docteur*," Tosco interjected, "it is much better at this time to save the questions for later."

"Isn't this as late as it gets?"

"Farandouz start ask too many questions."

"But that's one of the questions. Farandouz. You guys never told me . . . "

"Not questions!" Tulov scolded. "Tail pinned. Stay pinned! Mouth, too!"

"But Jean-Luc! After he died, parts of his body were never found. His tissues vaporized or something. I want to know more about that."

"The show is going on, *Docteur*."

"Farandouz hot head," Tulov barked.

"And I want to know about that red smoke that broke out around his race car when he flew up into the air."

"No time talk smoke. Not sure where smoke came from."

"Did you see it?"

"Of course. Everyone at Spitzring sees it."

"Well, guys, is there anything I can do to avoid . . ."

"Is coming Ulla."

Each of them took one of Loring's paws in hand and, as if on cue, Ulla walked in wearing her snake dance costume. She joined them, completed the circle. "Oliver," she said, "you are with us."

Before Loring could confess his surprise, Tulov stared firmly into him. He felt his feet playing under him, as if the tiger paws were dancing to Tulov's power.

Tosco's bushy brows knitted together under his wig and top hat and his eyes closed. He began to murmur a hymn-like meditation in an idiosyncratic, faintly Caucasian tongue, and the four of them, their hands clasped and raised, began to turn in a circle.

Loring closed his eyes, too, and drifted with them. He realized that this was all the direction he would receive from Tosco or Tulov. Whatever sense he could make of it, as he felt their fingers clutching him while they danced around, he knew they trusted him.

And he trusted them, though he did open his eyes long enough to see Ulla staring constantly at him, her icy blues piercing into him above her lapis necklace.

He had to believe that she would not allow him to meet a fate similar to Farandouz. And this was not a race track in the German Alps. This was the *Starlight Theatre*, a performance stage. Only.

Suddenly Jacques Chemin's chant popped into Loring's head, and before he could think twice, he spouted it out at high volume, above Tosco's utterances.

"MY, MY, MY! LORDY, LORDY, LORDY! THE GOOD AND THE BAD! IT ISN'T OVER UNTIL IT BE OVER! YOU NEVER KNOW UNTIL YOU KNOW! OH YESSSSSSSSSSS! OH YESSSSSSSSSSSSSSSSS!"

Tosco and Tulov nodded in affirmation, continued their dance. They apparently considered Loring's outburst a sign of enthusiasm. How else would one prepare mentally for a caper intending to reclaim the Garden of Eden? And from the delight in Ulla's marvelous gaze, Loring sensed that she, too, enjoyed his blessing.

So he said it again, and he heard her echoing his words. *"MY, MY, MY! LORDY, LORDY, LORDY! THE GOOD AND THE BAD! IT ISN'T OVER UNTIL IT BE OVER! YOU NEVER KNOW UNTIL YOU KNOW! OH YESSSSSSSSSS! OH YESSSSSSSSSSSSSSSSSSSSSSSSSSSSSSSSSSS!"*

* * *

"Thank you Farrely Farrell! Ladies and Gentlemen! It's Flip Spinelli again, your *Nordic Blue* Cruise Director, welcoming all our millions of Cablevista friends all around the world to the last stop on our tour of the fabulous *Nordic Blue*. Here it is. It's the one and only *Starlight Theatre* – the largest, most glamorous stage on the high seas! We call it our Broadway on the Blue!"

(Kettle drums roll hard then hum again.)

Loring watched the beginning sequences of *"LLLOOOVE MMMAAAGIC!"* on the backstage TV monitor – Tosco's singing, the doves, then the Starlegs with *"Black Magic."* He averted his eyes from the screen during Ulla's cartwheel sequence with Robespierre. No need to be gripped by a fit of vertigo and stagger onstage in his tiger outfit and try to enter the gyroscope. Even though he loved her. And in a way, he loved Robespierre, too.

He wondered how much of Tosco's subliminal message would be lost by

307

transmission. Would it seem obtuse? Would millions of confused Cablevista viewers around the world suddenly snap off their sets, baffled by a bizarre assortment of abracadabras and animal tricks? But apparently Tosco did not care about the viewing masses around the planet. His target was the select few, the discriminating elect, who would sit back and marvel, feel their inner cores resonate with surprise, amazement, perhaps epiphany.

Tosco and Tulov were casting their nets far and wide for new adherents to the Eden Reclamation Movement, but would the message come across? Would curious individuals pick up their telephones and ring Cablevista in New York to find out more about the little Tosco and his *Cirque Ineffable*? Would they surf the web for Tosco's homepage?

None of these questions could be answered, of course, and Loring realized the futility of pondering them, as Tulov and Tosco had wisely warned. In any case, the flesh-and-blood audience of power cruisers seated out there seemed fully captivated. Loring heard gasps of astonishment, moans of disbelief, nervous snickers, powerful pulses of applause. As far as he could tell, nobody had stumbled out the door in the grips of an acute inner ear dysfunction. No vomiting. It seemed that they all were stunned, locked in their chairs while Tosco's emotional roller coaster carried them on.

And whatever worries Loring had harbored earlier about the starkly comic effect his tiger/human outfit might make on the audience quickly dissipated. As he watched Tosco's magic on the television screen and heard the warm responses from the audience, Loring realized how astutely the mesmerizing tapestry was woven. If somebody ran out into the audience and asked what they expected to come next, he was sure most of them would answer, "How about Dr. Oliver Loring dressed up in a tiger suit?"

It seemed that expected, that natural, that inevitable. And didn't he look magnificent? He stood before the mirror and turned slowly, took in every last detail of Ruby's striped masterpiece. Of course he looked *magnifique*! That's they way everyone looked in Eden, didn't they?

See! You're getting there, finally! The mere anticipation of this exercise puts you into the Eden frame of mind. Tosco and Tulov have paved the way. Step forward, you feline, you! Do you hear those kettle drums rolling for you? Your cue.

* * *

Loring still did not know whether or not he should scream when the Colonel hit the flaming spike, but when he walked onto the stage, there was no feasible method to communicate his question to Tosco. The Cuban dwarf pounded the kettle drums while he lifted his cleft chin and sang a story intelligible only to individuals with a sense of what a hundred generations past might have known as a testament to the human condition. Not the current *Starlight Theatre* audience, Loring assumed. Yet they all were mute. All of them gaped as he stepped before them, the spotlight hot on his whiskers.

He wanted to feel in his whiskers, but they were grease, mere elements of his make-up, and did cats actually feel in their whiskers? Tosco, beating the drums, wasn't revealing a smidgen of his knowledge of cats. Again, Loring would have to improvise.

Step . . . slide . . .

The Egyptian style hit him as appropriate, emphasizing the two-dimensionality of all realities. Nobody in the audience laughed, because it seemed natural, expected, inevitable. Even as he mounted the hydraulic platform and ascended, his mittened paws stiff, he was aware that the audience was fully with him. He could feel their thousands of eyeballs revolving slowly upward with the levitating vision in front of them.

Oh stop thinking, put your busy mind to work on the simple kinetic task at hand. Don't worry. Let the physics and the metaphysics work out for themselves.

* * *

And then *there* he was – splayed out in two dimensions on the mystical metal disk, his wrists and ankles locked in by the sturdy velcro bands. Through the thin slits of the disk, he saw the crusted eyeballs of the painted Colonel. If he raised his own brow muscles, he could barely make out the lights of the hushed theatre and the catwalk above them, but he refrained from doing that – the movement placed extra strain on his neck and also on his nose and forehead, pressed firmly against the cold metal. Abruptly a passivity fell upon him, and he looked deeper into the Colonel's eyes, glued open now, blank, turgid pupils, unblinking. He saw the glinting gold incisor between his pink-painted lips.

Nice whiskers, Rocky.

As Tosco's kettle drum rolled powerfully below, Loring eye's surveyed Ruby Decosta's detail work on the Colonel – the gorgeous filigree orange and white lines around the eye lashes, the individually textured black markings on the cheeks signaling the follicular origin of each whisker, and the cleverly fashioned *trompe l'œil* depth shadows of the tiger jowls – all of these embellishments completely lost *(quel dommage!)* on the audience.

Observed or no, did not all these details also belong here on this metaphysical vessel? The audience surely could not see all the symbolic engravings on the gyroscope itself – the bizarre copulating animals and endless scrolls of obscure scripture writings. But the fact that they all were there, willed into the vessel itself, was more important than the audience's seeing them. Loring had pondered them earlier, of course, and they had baffled him. But all the detail work added, ultimately, to the grand gesture itself.

As Loring considered the Colonel's face, he recalled the famous death masks he had seen in European museums of Beethoven, Chopin, Wagner, Napoleon Bonaparte. He wondered why he never had seen any of those grim death masks, so inexpressive and white, painted over with colorful artistic flourishes, such as Ruby's work on the Colonel.

Why not let death speak for itself? For example, allow the mask of the dead Ludwig von Beethoven look like a full-maned lion? Paint him up in royal leonine style. Everybody thinks of Beethoven as a lion, so why not make him look even more like one?

KING OF THE KEYBOARD JUNGLE!

Uninvited, the voice of the embittered *poisson volant* rang in Loring's brain: *"Well, chum, how do you want your own death mask painted?"*

"Who asked you?"

"Feeling slightly schizophrenic again?"

"I wish you would shut up."

"How about it? Which animal would you like painted on your death mask?"

"Not a flying fish. You barely have a face at all. And neither do all the members of your school!"

"Thanks. Guess who also got left without a face? Jean-Luc Farandouz."

"Ouch."

"My schizoid pal, let's talk about shattering of the personality!"

"Yes. I admit, even Ruby couldn't have put a face on that poor . . ."

The door on the gyroscope clamped closed, and the hand near Loring's stockinged ankle thrust the apparatus into motion. Loring felt the giddy, wafting exuberance he had experienced earlier when Tulov sent him through his practice spins. Then a marvelous centrifugal jerk on the bones in his back snapped his spine with several delightful pops.

The blood surged into Loring's swollen fingers and toes. His head flushed, bloated. His scrotum and penis felt numb, shrunken, but pleasurably so. Then pins and needles seemed to sprout from his crotch up each leg and arm.

The voice of the *poisson volant* piped up again, *"I'm glad you're enjoying yourself. But what happens if something goes wrong here?"*

Loring tried to ignore the snide, pesky fish.

"Yo, Oliver!" the fish insisted. *"Did you notice there aren't any brakes on this contraption?"*

Loring had not noticed that detail, but he felt confident that Tosco's magical visions and Tulov's engineering should not be called into question. It was too late for that, especially at the prompting of a fish he had eaten that day for lunch. Besides, a sense of raw ebullience seemed to be taking hold of him as the spinning wheel torqued him around. Apart from the stretching sensation up and down his limbs and the peculiar numbness in his crotch, was he also experiencing a physiological mood lift?

He waited for the flip and then the apertures in the thin spokes of the gyroscope to open, as they had in the practice sessions, but they did not. Instead, Loring found himself spinning ever faster and face to face, with a tiger-costumed corpse of his exact dimensions.

Through the fluted plate that separated him from the Colonel, Loring distinctly saw the Colonel's stiffened lips part for a brief instant. Then they split apart somewhat wider, as if the corpse wished to speak.

"Oh, right!" said the voice of the fish. *"Now you think the corpse is talking to you, don't you?"*

"Why are you so sarcastic? If I can talk to a fish, why can't I talk to him?"

"Did you ever think about the gases that have accumulated in his gastrointestinal tract over the past several days?"

"What about them?"

"Those gases in his gut are being forced out of the Colonel's mouth. He's not talking, he's only burping."

"I do smell a rather unpleasant odor. Slightly sweet, too. That's odd."

"It's called necrolysis, Dart Doc. Dead tissue eaten up by all the bacteria inside him. He's been out of the freezer for a day now."

"Pew. Smells like it has a touch of methane in it."

"Sure does."

Disconcerted despite his giddiness, and not a little annoyed at the snipes by the *poisson volant*, Loring trained his eyes on the Colonel's lips. He felt the centrifugal forces of the blood rushing to his head, the pulsing reports in his fingertips of each heartbeat. It was as if Rocky Boy Bebalzam wanted to tell him something, wanted to open Loring's mind. "Don't listen to that idiotic flying fish in your brain, Oliver," he seemed to say. "Be with me now, please."

"But you're dead. And you certainly smell dead. How can I be talking to you?"

"Weren't you just talking to a flying fish?"

"I pretended to talk to a flying fish."

"So pretend to talk to me. We never had that chat over tea, you know."

"I'm sorry. I went down to see you in the *Galley Freezer*, but I got mixed up and I never had a chance to tell you how much you resemble my late father."

"I do?"

"Yes. You don't smell like my father. He used Nino Cerutti."

"You mean the 1884? From the frosted glass *vaporisateur*? Great fragrance. But I'm afraid I smell more like methane gas tonight. Can't help it. But it's odd that you should confuse me with your father, because the very first moment I saw you, I thought, 'Well, now, there's the son I always wished I had.' Would you be my heir?"

"Pardon me?"

"I sense in you an unusual generosity of spirit, and I need someone to take over my philanthropic interests. We have quite a few clinics in the third world, and a person like you would be . . ."

"Shouldn't we clear this with Hildegarde?"

"Son, it was her idea in the first place. Ha! Oh, and I'm sorry for the odor. I can't help it, you know."

"Yes, I know."

The spinning force pushed Boy Bebalzam's lower lip up over his tooth, and his caked eyes drifted upward in a sinking desiccated sag.

Despite the egregious smell, Loring felt a strong urge to hug the Colonel. And while his arms strained against the metal disk that separated them, he looked through the slits and watched the Colonel's eyebrows rise with the increasing force of the spin. They peaked at a devilish angle – the very slope of Orson Loring's brows. And once again, the Colonel had called him son.

For a fact, Rocky's face fused into Orson's. Loring seized the moment – his dear father had spun down that cliff at Killington, and this moment in the Transcendental Gyroscope was a chance to reclaim some valedictory rights.

"So long, son. This is where we separate."

"I love you, Father!" Loring whispered.

The hatch in the gyroscope opened. Loring slid down the chute.

* * *

Loring landed gently and silently on his back. He was in a small padded compartment of black velvet invisible to the audience but behind the spike apparatus, in the exact middle of the stage. The hidden nook was covered completely with heavy black drapes, and a peep slit among the folds allowed him to witness the entire sweeping trajectory of the gyroscope. The orb's magnificent spiral course gleamed directly over him in all its fabulous chrome brilliance.

He had the best seat in the house, at the eye of the gyre. Relieved that he had touched down without injury or even discomfort (the sweetly rotten odor of the Colonel's unpleasant mouth discharges had faded quickly from his nostrils), he listened to the eerie drone of the machine and heard Tosco's exuberant baritone echo to the roof of the theatre.

As the whole audience gazed on in paralytic wonder, a strong shudder swept through Loring's tingling limbs. The fantastic image above him mesmerized and dominated his senses. Glowing, glorious, consuming, even humbling in its baffling drones, it was perhaps the most beautifully conceived *object d'art* he had ever laid eyes on. Its proportions and textures seemed of an otherworldly essence. It looked alive, as if it moved with its own rhythm, a giant, pregnant egg about to crack open with transcendent realities.

Oh, Tosco! Oh, Tulov! Let's make this moment last. Let's make this fabulous trajectory of the majestic sphere pass slowly.

And it was many things – both actual and abstract. There above him spun Leonardo's man in the circle, yet also a tiger, also a Hindu or Buddhist mandala. It was the astrolab, the alien space ship, the Colonel, his father, the planet earth, Oliver Loring. So many confluent identities bombarded Loring as he lay there in the center of the circles, his brain synapses discharged like tiny charges of gunpowder. His heart pounded hard, seemed to want to break right through his chest wall.

And it didn't seem fair that Tosco and the Colonel were doing all that work up there and out there, and here he was, the individual who would receive the accolades for having spun down right onto the flaming spike, now lying flat on his back enjoying it all from the choicest and most

313

comfortable of any positions. The only thing Loring had to do was make sure he found his way out of this little hiding place and onto the stage at the right moment.

This was heroic activity? *This* was a transcendental mission that led one back to Eden? Lying flat on one's back in a comfy nook after a quick spinning joy ride with a corpse?

The logic was elusive. But who ever said metaphysics was logical?

More tympany, Tosco! More enchanting strains from your lungs, please! Oh, how beautiful! I wish I could do more on my way to Eden!

As the gyroscope loomed ever larger over his head, Loring saw the spike rise ominously just above him. Then he felt a surge of dry heat, and serpent-like flames slithered in long, fiery tongues up along its stainless steel shaft. The audience instantly perceived the peril of the spinning globe, and a loud involuntary groan rose in the hall. Tosco sung above it, pounded the tympany with even greater authority. Loring now listened carefully to the mounting sighs and whimpers in the audience as the *Starlight Theatre* crowd, though still power cruisers on the the world's grandest and most legendary cruise ship, now became participants in a revelatory ritual that was reminiscent, perhaps, of ancient civilizations.

This was not magic. This was, rather, a visionary pageant.

Tosco himself, the charismatic channeler for the vast spectacle, surely now was accepted, even for this briefest of exquisite moments, as the priest.

As the glowing gyroscope proceeded above him, each time circling closer to the flaming spike near Loring's eyes, the globe enlarged, and Loring felt himself surrender to it, to the flaming spike itself. The message in Tosco's lamenting voice seemed also to submit, to allow this all to happen.

"You realize that everyone in this theatre thinks you're still up there in that spinning contraption? They really do."

"You again? You keep bothering me. Why? Especially now?"

"Remember? You had me for lunch. There is no such thing as . . ."

"Shut up."

"Oliver, they're all rooting for you out there. They think it's you up there. They think it's a human sacrifice they're about to witness. Their favorite cruise ship doctor is about to . . . "

"That flame is very hot."

"Yes. And even more the pity, since the Colonel just invited you to be his heir."

"He's dead."

"Who else has heirs but the dead? Are you missing the whole concept of this pageant? Oh yea! Maybe you're supposed to be the guy up there in the spinning silver sphere that everybody's rooting for, but you don't have the slightest clue about what this trick is supposed to reveal."

"It reveals wonderment, the excitement of life, the communality of all living things, stuff like that, doesn't it? Oh, it's so frustrating to put words into something of this magnitude."

"Might it reveal that you could have a new job, if you decide to make a move for it?"

"What, as a philanthropist?"

"Exactly."

"I'm beginning to think that conversation never happened."

"Why?"

"His lips were moving, maybe. But I probably put my own projections into them."

"But those words might *be his. Do you think this whole project is just a huge and magnificent artistic gesture? Remember, you are a fully responsible component of it."*

Down came the gyroscope, spinning lightly off the final tip of the last gyre and hovering for a long instant – balanced, buoyant, and sovereign. Directly under it, and above Loring's eyes, the giant spike stood straight in the flames, ready to receive and skewer the gleaming, gyrating sphere.

The Colonel's words were very kind. But maybe they were just so much imagining on my part and so much . . .

"Rotten gas on his part?"

"Well, yes. Rotten gas. Ha-ha!"

"What kind of rotten gas, Oliver?"

"Well, a broad mixture, I assume. Some of it smelled of methane."

"Combustible?"

"Of course, it's combustible. It's natural gas. It's one of the major products of necrolysis."

"And the Colonel's filled with it, isn't he?"

"Smelled it myself on his lips a minute ago."

"And isn't the Colonel about to touch down on a flaming spike?"

"Yes, any mini-second now."

"Did you think about that ahead of time?"

"Well, there had never been any problem with Veda. I saw the trick at Claridad. There was no . . ."

"Veda is a taxidermist's masterpiece. She has a hole drilled right through her spine, with a metal cylinder to protect her hide, and she's not filled with combustible gas. She can't explode."

"But you think the Colonel . . ."

"Another thing. Didn't you forget to ask Tosco about whether or not you should scream when the gyroscope hits the flaming spike?"

Before Loring's mind could respond, a bizarre sound came from somewhere far away, from sometime long ago, and from someone Loring had never known till now.

"YEEEEOOOOOOOOUUUUUUWWWWWW!"

The sound was his own voice groaning, shrieking, and bellowing with terror as he looked up at the silver orb, watched it slide down onto the flaming spike and then, as the hole in the central axis support filled with flame and rudely thrusting steel, a bright, glowing nimbus of brilliant explosive blue and yellow fire sprouted out around the sphere in a shower of awesome tentacles.

A concussive wallop shook the *Starlight Theatre* stage.

"YEEEEOOOOOOOOOOOOOOUUWWWWWWFFFFFFFFFFFF!"

* * *

"Pssssssssssssssst! Docteur! Allez!"

Slowly Loring realized he had the task now to slip out from behind the shroud and prance around in front of the audience as if absolutely nothing had happened.

As if nothing had happened?

"Pssssssssssssssssssssssssssssst! Allez, Docteur!"

Tosco sounded impatient. Loring heard the concerned murmurs from the audience rumble louder around the hall.

Hey, Houdini always prolonged the suspense, milked the moment as long as he could, before he appeared to his audiences. Of course, Harry Houdini could untie knots with his toes, whereas I'm having trouble just now trying to locate me feet, let alone find the slit that will let me loose from this darkened, black velvet hideaway spot.

Had he experienced a convulsion? A full-blown epileptic fit? Alien abduction?

He put his fingertips on his abdomen, felt for any telltale surgical staples or scars. No missing organs, anyway! Not funny.

Not a big convulsion. A little *absence*, as the neurologists called it. He did not have a post-ictal headache. He felt around his genitals. No, he hadn't soiled his underwear. He rolled his tongue around his mouth, did not sense any bite wounds.

For several seconds he lay dazed and pleasantly spent. But there did seem to be an odd odor wafting around in the air. Usually the smell and the aura precede the convulsion, rather than coming afterward.

What was that odor? Burnt human flesh? Of course! The methane gas built up inside the Colonel had caused a minor explosion and torched his venerable flesh. That's what all the noise and flash and lingering smell were from.

"Psssssssssssssssssssssssssssssssssssst! Docteur! Allez!"

And then Loring heard a unison chant rising slowly from the audience in a resonating and urgent voice. It was the voice of the power cruisers.

"OL-IV-ER! OL-IV-ER! OL-IV . . .

Everybody out there knew his name, had followed his course through the plummeting gyroscopic impalement and boom. And now they chanted to coax him back to life. Anybody for some Scriabin?

"OL-IV-ER! OL-IV-ER! . . ."

He wiggled his toes. It seemed that his feet were functioning. Slowly he stood up. He jiggled his legs and wrists. All twenty digits present and accounted for.

So there, silly poisson volant! Nothing went wrong, after all! Ha! So much for your pessimistic advice.

Had he made it to the Garden of Eden? But Loring had hardly expected for that to happen. He had to admit his hallucinatory experience up on the gyroscope, conferring one-on-one with a dead body who offered him a multi-billion dollar inheritance constituted an untoward psychiatric state of mind. And if a temporary dissociative psychic reaction was all part of Tosco's *hocus pocus*, then wasn't that a small price to pay? Or even some sort of out-of-brain ecstatic epileptic moment. Luckily, nobody out there had seen him have it.

"I saw it."

"Shut up, lunch."

"OL-IV-ER! OL-IV-ER! OL-IV-ER!"

"PSSSSSSSSSSSSSSSSSSSSSST! DOCTEUR! ALLEZ!"

Loring looked up at Rocky Boy Bebalzam – the Colonel smelled like the battlefield Scriabin might have intended in his *Etude.* But thank goodness,

317

there was only a moderate-sized crater in his abdomen all around the spike shaft and a blackened tangle of charred intestinal loops visible from under the wet black cloaks thrown upon him. Otherwise, Rocky Boy Bebalzam still looked every inch the model for Leonardo da Vinci's radially stretched out Renaissance tiger/man in the circle.

Ba-baaaam, ba-ba-ba-ba ba baaaaaah ba-baaaaaam!

Time to greet the audience.

"So long, Colonel. Sorry for the mess. You'll meet the sharks tomorrow. I'm sure you'll taste just fine to them."

* * *

Step . . . slide . . .

Loring approached the audience slowly, his favored two-dimensional Egyptian stride directed straight forward in the spotlight. With each gently slipping toe-heel-toe pace, the loud chants of his name gradually diminished until the entire sea of faces stared on in mute amazement.

Yes, he had survived.

They had witnessed the dizzying descent, the flaming impalement and the unexpected explosion. They had smelled burned flesh. Yet here he was. Not a stripe or whisker scorched.

Loring posed, inscrutable in his Pharaoh-like hieroglyphic fixity, and realized with an internal tremble that the entire audience had briefly fallen under a thick, trance-like reverie.

No applause. No cheers.

With the Starlight Orchestra dazed and silent, the entire hall seemed as hushed as a cathedral. The stunned faces stared on, transfixed in wide-eyed awe, as if they were watching Lazarus rise and walk in his bandages. The vibratory churning from the distant *Boiler Room* seemed the only movement anyone could sense.

They had all been startled to their very souls.

And now, unified in a communal daze, they stared on at Loring seeming like the waves of the ocean – each with a fleeting independence, but also a part of a much larger consciousness. That's what they were, both random individuals and the greater totality of humanity. But out there, as he stared forward in his frozen Egyptian pose, they looked like waves, their breathing rhythmic.

In . . . and . . . out . . .

318

They were breathing together. And they were breathing with him. What had captured them? Tosco's evocative conducting of the gyroscope stunt? Tulov's engineering and artistic expertise? Loring's own apparent defiance of peril?

And . . . in . . . and . . .

Or was it, rather, the faint tinge that hung in the commonly inhaled *Starlight Theatre* air of the Colonel's own burnt flesh – bitter, unmistakably human, and redolent of the precious protoplasm shared by all? They seemed unified in a trance even to the back corners of the upper galley levels, to pause for a shuddering moment and hearken inward to their own mortality?

At this still moment in the burning heat of the spotlight, Loring felt his own tissues wanting to melt off his poised skeleton. Scary. He hoped he was not having one of those *Cirque Ineffable* manifestation moments Tosco had talked about.

New visions of existence? Red smoke anywhere? No thank you. I don't mind if the grease paint drips a bit. After all, the stunt is over. But what do I do next? I'm afraid to break the spell. All these people out there are coming into touch with their own mortality. I can't drop my hands and collapse everything. Just like that. As if it hadn't happened. They are out there as the sea is, each a wave, each a part of me, I a part of each of them, all of us commanded, indeed the product of our own life-sustaining inhalations and exhalations. Actually, this is getting troublesome. My paw is outstretched, my neck is kinked forward, my eyes won't even blink. And the spotlight is beginning to scorch every muscle.

Loring realized he was completely paralyzed, locked in the frozen Egyptian hieroglyphic pose, imprisoned in his own tiger-suited body, exactly as the red bearded Harvard grad student he had once treated had presented years ago at the Boston Samaritan Emergency Room.

I'm stuck!

In . . and . . .

Really stuck. Can't those people out there do anything but breathe? Can't somebody come and get me to an emergency room or something?

Though Loring could not divert his gaze, he became acutely aware that some person had jumped onto the stage and was now holding a microphone and standing directly beside him.

Who is it? Help me, please! I know this seems like grandstanding, but I really cannot move a muscle.

"You were *fan-tas-tic*, mate!" Farrely Farrell shouted into his microphone.

319

"Simply *fan-tas-tic*! And you know what? I love that curious position. Let me see, the front hand goes up like this, then the head gets slanted forward, am I doing it right? You look a bit like one of those old Egyptian tomb pictures. Now let's take a step forward, what do you say? First, let's do a step, then a slide, then a . . ."

I can't believe it. Farrely Farrell is actually doing Mimic Empathy Therapy on me. And, thank goodness, it's working. Yes, and I am very glad to hear his voice and feel him standing beside me, urging me to walk, making me believe I can . . .

Step . . . slide . . .

"Mate," Farrely Farrell whispered, "for a minute there I thought we'd lost you. Let's take a few more steps together, eh?"

* * *

The tumult deafened.

Wobbly from his brief but frightening lapse, Loring gripped Farrely Farrell's hand and smiled out feebly at the ecstatic throng.

A dozen jowl-to-jowl Egyptian steps with Farrell had thawed him from his ancient hieroglyphic pose and brought him back to the here and now in the *Starlight Theatre*. The two of them stood center stage and bowed, while the audience, now on its feet, clamored and raved with relief and joy.

It was as if that tricky paralytic moment at the end of the gyroscope act – when Loring thought the muscles might melt off his skeleton and Farrell adroitly read the problem and jumped up on stage to rescue Loring with a bit of tango-like Empathy Mimic Therapy (EMT) – had been scripted.

Scripted? Right! All of it planned well in advance?

Question: how does one script a meditative paralysis? How does one plan ahead for a contemplative nose-dive into the realm of dissociative free-fall, while millions of people all over the world gazed on and wondered if the geeky doctor in the tiger suit was about to overdose on Egyptian and metaphysical symbolism and autocombust. Would the red smoke show up on their screens?

And another question: how does one script the instincts of a publicity-crazy Australian talk show host who jumps on stage and applies an obscure British psychodynamic to the flagging doctor and saves the event? Scripted or not, Loring felt indebted to Farrely Farrell for bringing him back. As the huge blue wave-and-sunburst patterned curtain came down behind him and

Farrell, Loring gazed out at the rampaging eruption before him with gratitude and a cathartic sigh.

As Barry Cox in the orchestra pit waved his arms and the Starlight Orchestra blared out a rousing refrain of *"That Old Black Magic,"* Ulla and all the Starlegs Dancers jumped in from the wings. Then Flip Spinelli stepped up in front of the cameras. (Ulla slipped over and kissed Spinelli on the cheek.)

Loring stepped forward, took off his tiger hat and mittens, bowed again. Once more, the audience raved hysterically, started to chant his name again. *"OL-IV-ER! OL-IV-ER! . . ."*

In the on-stage confusion, Loring saw Stig Storjord and Hildegarde step up and join the performers as they all waved to the cameras. Anita Rothberg came up, too, and put her arm around Farrely Farrell.

At last, Tosco stepped forward from the part in the curtains. Tulov, cane in hand, limped in from the wing. Loring waved them to the front spotlight. The *Starlight Theatre* audience, as if in a single thunderous motion, literally leaped and shouted. The booming applause resounded and the chanting began again. Now the cheers were for, *"TOS-CO! TOS-CO! TOS-CO! . . ."*

Loring clapped and chanted along with the audience. As Tosco received the adulation, Loring watched the dwarf nod, his teeth biting on his lower lip, his dark eyes set forward in a bright twinkle under his heavy black brows. Lightly his stubby fingers fluttered proudly as he bowed.

Beside him, Tulov gazed with a faint smile across his face. The Russian's head and his white beard trembled with delight, and his cane shook in front of him so hard, that he had to force its tip down onto the stage to stop it.

Proud they both could be. For the spectacle. For the success. For the incredible feat of leading this audience – and the Cablevista audiences the world over, one presumed – on the most dazzling and unconventional vision into new realms of the sub-psychological deep. The effect on the *Starlight Theatre* audience was more than tremendous, and they could, Loring reckoned, anticipate that the entire exercise – the powerful and astonishing demonstration for the world to see here on the *Nordic Blue* – had probably attracted enormous international interest for their *Cirque Ineffable*.

Who wouldn't want to travel to Paris in the spring and see the grand opening? Who wouldn't want to read all about the *Cirque* and the Eden Restoration Movement? Wild and radical it was! But look what wild and radical had done for this Cablevista Valentine TV Cruise! The whole audience was in a frenzy of amazement and unanimous approval. Even their chant was in perfect unison: *TOS-CO! TOS-CO! TOS . . .*

As Loring clapped beside Tulov, the Russian winked slyly and brought his lips close to Loring's ear."Explosion was incredible! *La pièce de résistance!* Exactly what we needed. How you figured out? Thank you!"

After minutes of exultation during which the crowds had started to chant in the aisles, Farrely Farrell, microphone in hand, tried to hail the audience above the din. "Ladies and gentlemen! And wasn't it a fabulous Cablevista Valentine TV Cruise, folks? Are we not all lucky in *luuuuuuuuv* and then some?"

In the midst of the hubbub, Loring felt overwhelmed with affection toward everyone, even Farrely Farrell. And he was not troubled in the slightest when Clyde and Blanche Cruickshank made their way up to wave at the cameras. Yes, in a way, they had all been lucky in love, Loring most of all.

Loring looked in Ulla's direction, had just caught her eye, when a loud and high-pitched whistling noise struck his ear. At once the shouts and clamoring began to subside, but then they gave way to an even louder, confused clamor. And above the howls and screeches, Loring heard a penetrating sound that filled the hall with an eerie, dominant trumpeting. Sweet as a French horn, piercing as an ambulance siren.

At first Loring thought it might be one of Tosco's high-pitched Siberian melodic riffs. But then he looked out at the crowd and noted that they all gazed high above the stage at a figure dangling from the ceiling catwalk of the *Starlight Theatre.*

Lowering himself slowly down onto the stage on a long rope, with swings from side to side, Jacques Chemin now descended with his royal conch shell to his lips and with Robespierre, the reticulated python, slung around his neck like a necklace.

The lower he came, the louder he blew the conch. With his legs curled around the rope and the snake writhing out in all directions, Chemin appeared Vishnu-like, a reptile god who had decided to crash the mortals' party.

The audience, confused but willing to believe anything now about the *Cirque Ineffable*, must have assumed the acrobat Chemin was an encore bit of the magic show – some off-beat athlete showman whose antics were not inconsistent with the earlier tricks. They'd already seen that long, thick python early in the show, hadn't they?

As the spotlights found him, Chemin spun round and round above the heads of the other performers. Just before he lit on the stage, light as a spider, he jumped off the rope beside a stunned Farrely Farrell, handed him the conch and took the microphone from his hand. Then Jacques shouted into the Cablevista cameras, *"FATIMA! FATIMA! FATIMA! I KNOW YOU ARE WATCHING IN THE CREW BAR! HOW DO YOU LIKE THIS BEAUTIFUL NECKLACE? I PICKED IT OUT FOR YOU SPECIALLY. I LOVE YOU! PLEASE SAY YOU WILL BE MY VERY OWN VALENTINE!"*

The charmed audience laughed and clapped.

A gigantic smile on his face, Jacques took advantage of his position in the spotlight to cavort around the stage, stretched Robespierre out over his head and pretended to limbo under him.

Farrely Farrell loved it. "Amazing, mate!" he shouted into the microphone. "Yes, I certainly hope you and your beautiful girlfriend Fatima are luuuucky tonight in *luuuuuuuuuuuuv*! And big time! I mean it, mate! And who is this fabulous *Fatima*? Will you tell us all about her? But first, I want to know, who the hell are you?"

"Oh, just a common Jacques, Mr. Farrell!"

* * *

In the dressing room with the other performers, Loring cold creamed the stripes and whiskers off his face, peeled out of his tiger outfit, and listened while Farrely Farrell stood together with Jacques Chemin on the *Starlight Theatre* stage for a spot interview. The herd mania out there after "Love Magic" lingered. Nobody in the crowd wanted to leave the party, even after Barry and the Starlight Orchestra played their final bars.

The power cruisers were hungry for more, and Farrely Farrell was more than willing to provide it. Obviously the Cablevista producers had given him *carte blanche* to extend the broadcast as long as he wanted into the night. And why not? Especially now that another last-minute "blast image" in the colorful persona of Jacques Chemin with his gorgeous python necklace had appeared out of nowhere to fascinate the Cablevista world audience.

"Welcome back, folks, from our commercial break. And I'm still here in the *Starlight Theatre* with the acrobatic intruder in this show, the man with the amazing conch shell and the python, Jacques Chemin. So, Jacques, are we all going to get a chance to meet this mysterious Fatima? Our viewers would love to get to know her."

"Oh, yes. I hope so, Farrely. She is waiting for me now, I believe."

"Fatima! We certainly hope you are watching!"

"Yes, Fatima! Je t'aime, beaucoup, beaucoup!"

"And how, may I ask, did you first encounter this ravishing creature? I'm not talking about the python!"

"Well, Farrely, when I first had the idea of starting a restaurant in Paris called Fatima's, I was waiting for the right woman to come into my life. And then, guess what happened? A woman by the name of Fatima came into my life!"

"It sounds almost impossible!"

"I feel the same way. But almost anything can happen on this great cruise ship. You see, Farrely, when I first . . ."

Back in the dressing room, Loring stood by the mirror and donned his tuxedo uniform. He marveled at Chemin's timing, artistry, balls. He must have planned the whole caper: commandeer Robespierre, climb up to the theatre cat walk, drop in at the last minute of the show for maximum effect.

Looking back, it could only have been expected that Jacques would eventually butt into the limelight, and how else, but trumpeted by his glorious conch shell and adorned in an exotic serpent. On the dressing room monitor screen, the grinning Haitian wiggled his shoulders and tossed his shiny round head, while Robespierre restlessly wound over his limbs. The scaly reticular diamonds writhed around the new blast image's handsome, mugging face in a gloriously ornate and living frame.

High impact television, Loring had to admit, right down to the tooth diamond.

Diamond man and diamond-patterned snake! Maybe even metaphysical! Next trip to Paris, who would not want to dine at Fatima's?

Loring expected that the coy Fatima, down in the *Crew Bar* watching this round-the-world demonstration by her Valentine wanna-be, might be more horrified than charmed.

Loring tightened his bow tie, brushed back his hair, and fastened his cufflinks. Then he checked his watch.

Almost one o'clock. Time to find Ulla. He wanted urgently to spend the rest of the night talking with her, till the sun came up. He had to go over everything that had happened and find out what her take on it all was – their mambo, his tiger costume, his weird spins with the Colonel on the gyroscope, his hallucinatory chat with the corpse, all of that part. The explosion, his daze, the chants of the audience, his terrifying Egyptian posture paralysis.

Could she make sense of any of it? Had Loring's journey for the sake of Tosco and Tulov and the Eden Restoration Movement proved anything at all? Had he, in fact, perhaps done it all for her – in the same way Chemin was out there right now in front of the Cablevista cameras hamming to win Fatima? (And possibly to find backers for a Paris restaurant venture?)

Had Loring lost his mind a little? If he had, was he back to normal now? What would Ulla say? Of course, they had tomorrow to talk. But Loring wanted to see her now.

He looked into the mirror and wiped a tissue over his face, pried out the traces of greasepaint that stuck in the deeper wrinkles of his forehead and under his eyes.

About that hieroglyphic paralysis? He wanted to talk to Ulla!

But more than anything, he wanted only to look into her eyes and hold her close to him, feel the air come in and out of her nostrils against his cheek. Was he really back to normal? She would tell him he was. She might suggest that he swear off metaphysics. She might insist, perhaps, that he never again try to walk like an Egyptian.

Ha-*ha*!

And if he were to embark on a passionate relationship with Ulla, shouldn't he tell her everything he could about himself? Would she mind, for example, that he sometimes spoke to imaginary creatures, like that ill-humored *poisson volant*? Should he run the risk of dragging old baggage from a previous rotten relationship into a fresh, pure and potentially lasting one? What good would that do?

First things first. Was he back to normal?

He had to do his own check. The dressing room was clearing out, so he stepped back from the mirror and watched his patent leather pumps run through Olivia's Loring's six-dance latin warm up – rumba, tango, cha-cha, samba, bosa-nova, lambada. Lower body fully intact! Then he stepped closer to the mirror, arched his back, grimaced in a silly, twisted frown, and wiggled his arms through the macarena. Upper body fully functional, too, actually felt exuberant.

While his elbows were raised and his hands flipped back and forth, Loring glanced over at Jacques Chemin on the television monitor – clowning in a similar macarena-like position with Robespierre draped over his shoulders. Such synchonicity! Jacques was right! Only on this amazing cruise ship did things like this – two people doing the macarena for totally different purposes – occur at the same time, if only to . . .

Abruptly it occurred to Loring: how had Jacques confiscated Robespierre? Where had he found him?

Jacques said in the *Crew Bar* that he was heading down to *Car Deck* to shop for a necklace for Fatima.

A nauseating ache hit Loring at cummerbund level. In the mirror his face blanched and then turned a faint shade of green.

Loring knew that Tosco had made careful plans to lower the snake onto the *Forward Cargo Elevator* down to *Car Deck* as soon as Robespierre's early appearance with Ulla was finished. They had rehearsed the transfer on the elevator and into the *Claridad* storage area repeatedly. It was to last no longer than six minutes, plenty of time for Tosco to return for his next act. Robespierre was supposed to be locked and tucked neatly into his *Car Deck* environment during the second half of the show.

Chemin, the Parisian pick lock, had pilfered his way into Tosco's secret *Car Deck* lair to filch Robespierre. But had he made certain to secure the place when he left? Was there any chance Jacques had left the door to Tosco's secret hideaway open? Most thieves never locked up again after they had made off with the goods. Perhaps Parisian cat burglars were more discrete and polite.

Loring looked around the dressing room. No Ulla. No Tulov. No Tosco. Perhaps the *Cirque Ineffable* team had shared Loring's fears and now were on their way down to *Car Deck* to check on things.

Let's hope so! And get down there fast, will you?

Loring watched in the mirror as the green-tinted skin of his forehead beaded up in glistening balls of sweat. His heart began to pound as the ache in his abdomen twisted and churned.

Get down there, folks, check on things on Car Deck, okay! We wouldn't want anyone with four legs to wander out of the door left open, just perhaps to snoop around the ship, would we?

Although everybody out front in the *Starlight Theatre* continued to watch Farrely interview Chemin, Loring heard a fishy voice give a private interview in his ear.

"You didn't think anything would go wrong. But now the big cat's out of the bag, isn't she?"

"We don't know that."

"You should have told the Captain as soon as you knew there was a tiger on the ship. Now look what's happening! Look who just walked into the Dressing Room!"

"What do you mean? Who's walking into . . ."

Loring's chat with the *poisson volant* came to a startled halt, as three large men in black mylar masks and flack jackets slipped into the dressing room. Their eyes were afire, and they spoke secretly in Norwegian through their hamburger caddie headgear. Each man carried an attack rifle. Loring had seen these outfits before during the surreal *Code Commando* exercises.

"*Code Commando*, Doctor," grunted the largest of the three. It was the Staff Captain. "Are you familiar with the protocol? The Captain wants you out of retirement and back to work. We may need you, Doctor. You are wanted at your station in the *Hospital* immediately."

"Something wrong?"

"Move it, Doctor. I will explain on the way to the *Hospital*. They need you down there. *Viking Deck*. You know where that is, don't you?"

"Nils, what the hell's going on?"

"We don't know for certain. We think there may be tigers running around on this ship, and I goddamn plan to shoot them before they start killing the passengers and crew."

"Tigers? You're not serious."

"Don't play stupid, Doctor. I said move it. Doctor Trygve is already down there. They need you in the *Hospital* now, too. Move it!"

"Has anyone been hurt?"

"We don't know. But we already marched that dwarf and his friend from Russia in irons up on the *Bridge*. Your Austrian dance partner, too."

"Ulla? In irons? Why?"

"You should tell us. Somebody said Dart Doc is in cahoots with these weirdoes. I feel like strapping you into frickin' irons, too, but we're probably going to need you to stitch up victims. I sure hope Nurse has got lots of thread down there. You're gonna' be sewing your frickin' ass off tonight!"

Nordström waved his weapon menacingly, and Loring jumped toward the *Dressing Room* door.

* * *

In *Code Commando* drills, Loring had watched the Norwegian Officers don their flack jackets and load their automatic assault rifles. When they fastened the headphones and jaw-level microphones over their black face masks, no question: they were fully committed to defend the ship's passengers and her sovereignty on the high seas, even if deadly force were required.

Loring had dreaded an actual *Code Commando* scenario might ever unfold on the ship. He had never dreamed that he might be blamed for one.

"Can you move faster?"

"My dance pumps. They won't let me run."

"Such a frickin' sissy!"

"I'll take them off."

"Now move it!"

The Chief Medical Officer's assigned station during a *Code Commando* was the *Hospital*. Any victims of on-board combat would be brought there for triage and life support, perhaps emergency surgery. In the case of a fire fight or a disaster with more than a few critical injuries, the *Hospital* staff would be quickly overwhelmed. That was assumed. But all efforts would be made to sustain the victims until med-evac vehicles and personnel arrived from the Navy or the Coast Guard.

Theoretical *Code Commando* scenarios involved assault and invasion of the ship by terrorists or pirates. Several cruises ago, Loring had skimmed the *Code Commando* Manual. He recalled that the two-pronged basic strategy of defending the ship used a pneumonic known as I.P. and I.D.:

(1) *Isolate* and *Pacify* the passengers and then

(2) *Isolate* and *Disarm* the terrorists.

Rigidity was required to coordinate the I.P. and I.D. through a common language. In the event of hostage taking and/or threatened detonation of explosives, the *Code Commando Manual* had special strategies, none of which Loring had ever read.

"I bet you didn't even review the 'Loose Tiger on the Ship' strategy. Did you?"

The fish was right. Now, because of Loring's preoccupations, a disaster was about to happen, perhaps was happening. And on world-wide television, so everyone could watch.

"You even fell in love. Isn't that precious!"

"Couldn't help it."

"Soon there soon may be many things you cannot help, Dart Doc!"

The Norskies rushed with Loring down the corridor and past the *Starlight Theatre* entrance, where two more mylar-clad guards stood at the door.

As he passed, Loring overheard Spinelli announce that, at the request of the Captain, the audience all should please return to their seats in the theatre. There was a "disturbance somewhere on board," and he had some "really special" new stand-up material to share with them for a few minutes, if they would only be patient. Actually no, they would not be allowed to leave the theatre until the Captain gave the command from the *Bridge*, and "Don't worry, the world's grandest cruise ship has not hit an ice berg!"

Meanwhile, as Loring hustled down the *Promenade Deck* corridor, Nordström at his bare heels, his mind raced feverishly. He peered down the long hallway, imagined Daria bounding fatefully toward them over the crazy-quilt pattern of the carpeting, only to be greeted by gunfire. He gasped loudly.

"What's wrong, Doctor?" barked Nordström.

"I have to ask. Has anyone been hurt?"

"Gonna' find out soon enough, won't you?"

The first prong of the *I.P.* and *I.D.* protocol said to isolate and pacify the passengers. Fortunately, almost all the power cruisers were already under Spinelli's spell of schtick in the *Starlight Theatre* and away from the sight of automatic assault rifles and black-masked commando troops.

The second prong of *I.P.* and *I.D.* required the isolation and disarming of the "terrorists," and soon the Captain issued the warning over the public address speakers that the huge, water-tight iron doors on the lower six deck bulkheads and cargo holds would be closed.

Wherever Daria was on the ship, Loring hoped she was not caught between a pair of those slamming iron doors – they rammed together with the strength of industrial pile drivers. Her powerful anatomy would be crushed instantly.

Then, as he heard Nordström puffing hard through flared nostrils behind him, Loring realized he also was part of the second prong of *I.P.* and *I.D.* Otherwise, why would they be running behind him and muttering into their microphones in Norwegian with rifles in their hands?

"There's only one tiger on board," Loring said.

"Why should we believe you?"

"I know."

"If you're so sure there's only one, you can be sure I'm gonna' get him."

"The tiger's a female and she's harmless."

"That's not gonna' keep me from shooting. Be sure of that, Dart Doc!"

"If you want to get that tiger under control, you'd better let out the dwarf."

"I know goddamn well how to bring a tiger under control. Shut up and get ready to do your sewing in the *Hospital*, Doctor."

They reached the *Central Stair Tower* and began their four-flight descent to *Viking Deck*. Loring hated to think what he might find waiting for him down there.

As his feet spun down the landings, step after step, the Norwegian Officers' boots clattering loudly behind him, he thought of Daria. He dreaded how she might respond to this cluttered maze of corridors and stairwells. The complexity was baffling. Surely Daria would not attack anyone. But what if she felt cornered or threatened in this puzzling jungle of naval architecture? What if she encountered a panicky power cruiser who reacted in a hostile way?

Loring wondered where, within the intricate labyrinth of the ship's passageways could Daria be? The fact that the Norwegians had clamped Tosco, Tulov and Ulla in irons, made no sense. Except according to protocol. The only individuals who might talk Daria down from any angry outburst and prevent a bloody confrontation and mauling had been locked up.

But why shove blame onto the *Code Commando* authors? Or onto the Norwegian Officers for following the dictated strategy? Why blame anybody else? Loring himself was responsible. And he, more than anyone else on the ship, was well aware that there were two functional operating rooms on board and only two doctors, neither of whom was a trauma surgeon.

Absolutely no blood bank!

Despite Tosco's earlier promise of some mystical, Eden-like state, achievable through heroic action in a fantastic circus act, this trick tonight had landed Loring as far away from paradise as anyone could get.

Nordström stopped to catch his breath on the *Viking Deck* landing.

"By the way, Dart Doc, if any of our passengers get hurt, I think you and your magician friends might be going off to prison in Norway. We got rules about manslaughter on this ship. And, you should know, we got some dark and cold prisons back in Norway."

"Thanks, Staff."

"Oh, yea. Our prisons, they're cold. Way up above the Arctic Circle. Sun she don't shine for six long, cold months. I hear they need doctors in those prisons. How's your Norwegian, Dart Doc? Guess you're gonna' learn some, hey? Those prisoners, they like sissies to warm them up. You gonna' be real popular there, man."

* * *

"When was the last time you cracked a chest, Oliver?"

"I did two at the Samaritan last year."

"You ready to fix up some tiger damage?"

"I better be."

Maggie McCarthy stood outside in the *Viking Deck* hallway in her blue scrub suit with her clip board and a dozen *Code Commando* disaster tags. Seeing Loring in his proper disaster post, Nils Nordström charged back down the corridor with his rifle-toting sidekicks.

"Trygve says he done a dozen before, so that's lucky. And if we have to intubate, I got the two code carts ready. What do you like for anesthesia? "

"Midazolam. How much do we have?"

"Ten vials, twenty milligrams a vial. I hope we don't frickin' need that much. Put on your shoes and sterile covers, please. This is a hospital."

"Where's the Midazolam?"

"I got it right here on the code cart. All ten vials."

"Keep it handy."

"I got Kevin and Guy in the operating rooms ready to assist, and I figure you and I can do the triage right here. That's what the frickin' *Code Commando* manual says. Trygve's already scrubbed up and ready for the first victim."

"I'm glad I got some relief."

"You better be. By the way, how the hell did that bunch of tigers get on board? They say you might know something. Hey, are you okay, Oliver? You look freakin' white as a sheet. You do know something, don't you?"

"I'll be alright. This all just seems . . ."

"But you've seen this heavy trauma stuff in Boston, haven't you?"

"But I never caused it."

"You *caused* it? Why do you say that?"

"I could have been more careful. I've been foolish. But have you heard about anybody getting hurt so . . ."

"So far not. One tiger was seen on *Car Deck*, another on *Dolphin* and then another on *Biscayne*. No victims. Captain's up on the *Bridge*. He'll let us know. And we got most of the power cruisers isolated in the *Starlight Theatre*. All the others have been ordered into their cabins. Four *Code Commando* units are out looking for the tigers."

"There's only one tiger. Her name is Daria."

"Oh, you know her name? Christ, Dart Doc! Did you really shit the bed on us big time?"

"I hope not."

"Well, what the hell were you doing up there in the *Starlight Theatre*? Captain went, but I had to stay down here. I watched it on the TV."

"Did you like it?"

"What the hell was all that stuff about?"

* * *

331

The two-pronged *Code Commando* strategy did not account for a third factor on board: Cablevista. And though most of the power cruisers were either sequestered in the *Starlight Theatre* with Flip Spinelli or locked in their cabins, Farrely Farrell had slipped out onto *Veranda Deck* to broadcast the moment-by-moment events.

As Loring put on his surgical gloves and trauma suit, he glimpsed the TV on Maggie's desk: a panoramic view from the blimp of the *S/S Nordic Blue* plowing through the Caribbean waves with her raked funnels and sloped hull basking in the blimps's floodlights. As the aerial cameras focused closer – the *Bridge*, the green astroturf of *Vista Deck*, the three silver Mercedes roadsters spinning on their carousel platform, the sweep of the decks, the pools on the rear decks, the individual portholes glowing with cheery light – all of it appeared fantastic and ideal, just as the Cablevista world would see it and imagine it.

Farrely Farrell's voice, however, reported as the story unfolded. "That's right, ladies and gentlemen around the world, you're watching a catastrophe in the making! You've all heard of the *Loooooove Boat*. Well, folks, this isn't it. Not tonight. We've heard that as many as five or six tigers – maybe a dozen – have been smuggled aboard the *Nordic Blue* and let loose by some fiendish terrorists. Very original, I would say, for a terrorist operation. And nobody's admitting to the deed so far.

"At this point, there is no word on any victims or injuries, but I just spoke with Captain Trond Ramskog on the *Bridge*, and he tells me they are preparing for the very worst. Three U.S. Coast Guard rescue helicopters are heading our way out of Miami at this time with qualified trauma surgeons on board. Let's just hope they can get here on time, mates. I'm advised that all passengers and crew members have been told to stay in seclusion until the Officers have isolated the terrorists and their tigers. And we have two of our courageous Cablevista camera crews out searching the decks for those tigers, so stand close by your sets, Cablevista viewers, it's all happening right here and right now!"

The screen switched to a jiggling view from one of the crews patrolling down *Dolphin Deck* corridor.

"Folks, we're waiting for one of our crews to spot one of the tigers, and we're not breaking for a commercial until this situation is under control. Stick with us. Believe me, nobody on board, not Captain Trond Ramskog, not anyone, has any idea how this happened or how it could turn out! So, as I said, stick right here. Things could get very interesting and very bloody and suddenly. None of us, of course, could have predicted that, after all the incredible things we've seen this week on the *Nordic Blue* that anything like this. . . "

Loring's stomach churned. He stared fearfully at the screen.

Any moment now, dear Daria was sure to prowl around a corner and run into one of the television cameras or, much worse, one of the attack squads. Once she was spotted, it would take very little time for Nordström or one of his commandos to destroy her.

What was she thinking? What was she feeling? Wasn't Tosco's metaphysical exercise supposed to develop some human/feline telepathic bond among the performers?

Welcome to this mess! My own original creation!

And hadn't Loring actually entered her mind earlier in that dream he shared with her down on *Car Deck*? Couldn't he enter her mind again? Loring closed his eyes for an instant, tried to communicate through some visceral connection with Daria.

Nothing. But what good would telepathic communion with Daria do now, anyway? Especially if Nordström was about to look through his sight and squeeze the trigger on his assault rifle and render all of Loring's meditations pointless!

"Whoooooooooaaaaaaaaahhhhh! Folks! Look at that!"

The *Hospital*'s TV screen screen showed Daria's muscular hind quarters and her curled tail leaping up a stairwell. It appeared to be the *Aft Stairwell*, not far from the *Thor Heyerdahl Pool* on *Sunset Deck*.

"It looks like one of the tigers is literally high-tailing it up the stairs. Does he have something in mind? And what a magnificent looking animal! Folks, that big cat is moving far too fast for our camera crew to catch up, but we're sending another crew up to the top deck, that's *Vista Deck*, I believe, to check that all out. And as I've just heard, one of the crews of Norwegian Officers, headed by Staff Captain Nils Nordström, is on their way to meet that tiger and bring . . ."

On the *Hospital* TV, the floodlit ship moved through the black sea, but now at a slower pace. The navigators on the *Bridge* always revved her down for helicopter evacuations – less risk of an accident when the chopper hovered over the rear decks near the tall wires on the ship's electrical rigging.

As he stood there gawking in his blood-proof gown and latex gloves, Loring felt helpless. Here he was, watching the same image on the screen that people on the other side of the world were staring at, and he might as well be in Tokyo or Sidney for all the good he was doing.

Protocol was protocol. He might as well be frozen in his Egyptian hieroglyphic posture, watching and waiting for Farrely Farrell to interpret the catastrophic events about to occur right here on his own ship. And why didn't Loring just allow his muscles to melt right off his bones, as he had sensed a few minutes before up the *Starlight Theatre*?

Of course, there was a significant difference between Loring and the millions of others around the world who were watching this televised catastrophe: he was responsible for it. His watching and waiting for the bloody fiasco to unfold was somehow more poignant and, arguably, less forgivable. No. Not forgivable in any way.

He glanced out the circular porthole for some type of inspiration. Nothing – looking anywhere except the TV – but blackness out there beyond. No visions. No stimulation. No infusion of cues to develop a creative therapeutic mode. (Not even a flying fish to advise him.)

All Loring could see was his own static reflection – masked and gloved in a yellow, blood-proof trauma suit with Maggie McCarthy standing behind him in her scrubs, drawing a vial of the injectable anesthetic Midazolam into a syringe.

"Dart Doc, I sure wish we had more of this stuff. There's no telling how much we might need. If we get more than six or seven victims, we're gonna run out. We got morphine. Gallons of that. And the Coast Guard helicopters will have anything we need. But by that time, it might be too late."

Loring watched Maggie's long, expert fingers top out the barrel of the plastic syringe as she squirted several drops of the clear liquid out the tip of the needle.

"Don't waste that stuff, Maggie!"

"Okay, okay! I know. But I still haven't heard from you how we got into this whole mess. Come on, Dart Doc, fess up. Last time I saw you, you were in some ridiculous tiger suit. Now we got frickin' tigers ready to kill people here on the . . ."

"Maggie, can you get me the Captain on the phone?"

"Why Captain?"

"Don't ask why."

"Here, don't use the phone. Use one of these head sets." Maggie pulled out of her desk a *Code Commando* radio headphone with microphone, like the ones the Nils Nordström was wearing. "They give us these for the drills. Just touch the button up here, and you'll be in touch with Captain."

"And Nurse, please fill a thirty cc syringe full of Midazolam."

"You just told me not to waste any of it. That's enough to put a six-hundred pound patient asleep."

"You heard me. And we're going to need the widest and longest endotracheal tube you've got."

"Are you sure you're okay, Dart Doc? Did something happen to you in that crazy gyroscope ride you took?"

* * *

Loring's patent leather dance pumps had never moved faster. He lunged up the *Central Stair Tower* four steps at a stride. He had on his hamburger caddie headphones and microphone and was in contact with the *Bridge*. Destination: *Vista Deck*. Contents of the syringe in his fist: thirty cubic centimeters of Midazolam, the potent benzodiazapine anesthetic, capped with a plastic needle guard.

Behind him ran Maggie McCarthy in her sneakers and with the full resuscitation code kit in the knapsack on her back. They both had removed their precautions gowns in the *Hospital*.

Loring knew his brief pitch to the Captain over the headphone set had been absurd. Most of the conversation had been implied.

Loring had banked on Trond Ramskog's gratitude for Loring's slap, the gesture that had straightened out the Captain's senses the day before. Leveraging his renown as as the "Dart Doc,"Loring had tried to convince the Captain he could hurl a syringe filled with Midazolam, the knock-out medicine, at the neck of a Siberian Amur tiger, hit the big cat's carotid artery, and "disarm" the beast, to borrow the *Code Commando* jargon. The Captain, after several silent moments of deliberation up on the *Bridge*, had reluctantly agreed to give Loring a chance.

If Trond had not put some stock in Loring's reputation, then Loring would have been ordered to stay right there in the *Hospital* and prepare himself to do surgery on the victims of the fray, according to Code Commando.

"But Captain, I swear on my honor as a physician, there is only one tiger. And if we disarm her, there won't be any human victims."

"You're sure, Doctor?"

"It's the best medicine – prevention. By the way, Captain, Daria is one of the most fabulous creatures you'll ever meet. If my plan doesn't work, then let the Staff Captain shoot her. But it would be a horrible and unnecessary loss."

"I've already given the order to shoot any tiger on sight."

"I'm on my way up there, Captain. Please. Don't let them shoot her. Not till I've had a chance."

"I'll give you one try."

* * *

Vista Deck, the top of the ship, had to be where Daria would go.

She'd been confined down on *Car Deck* for almost two days, and surely she desired to find space to stretch and romp, let loose and look up at the sky, inhale fresh air, especially if she'd been sampling some of Maurice's goat kid liver. *Vista Deck* offered the only spread-out space on the ship, and Daria's nature for wandering would lead her up and up, finally to *Vista*.

So Loring reckoned. He had slept beside her earlier that afternoon and shared her dream. In that dream, in her form, he was flying high and restless above the frigid Eastern Siberian landscape. Definitely, she would find her way to *Vista*. That's where Loring's instincts would say to go, if he were a tiger.

"Dart Doc! I don't mind tellin' you, I'm scared shitless!"

"I am, too, Maggie. But we have to do this."

"I suppose you're gonna' ask me to trust you."

"Look, we've got the Dart Doc and the Attack Nurse. What's the problem?"

"You really gonna' throw that thing? What if you miss?"

"I'm not going to miss. But we have to get to her fast."

"I'm right behind you. Remember, the oxygen tank in this knapsack is frickin' heavy. We are going after a tiger, right?"

"Do you believe what you saw on that TV screen?"

Neither Captain Ramskog nor Nurse McCarthy had questioned the physics of Loring's plan. Loring had fibbed and said he knew just the exact amount of torque to spiral the syringe through a direct trajectory from fifteen feet away. Otherwise, the barrel-heavy object was likely to topple end-over-end through the air with no hope of landing anywhere near the intended target. "We used to throw loaded syringes at targets all the time in medical school," he had said to the Captain. "I still practice it once in a while."

"Oh, so that's how you got your nick-name of Dart Doc?"

"Now you know."

There simply had not been time to convince the Captain to release Tosco and Tulov. A snap of the fingers from either of them, and Daria would have rolled over and allowed the Norwegian Commando Squads to restrain her with all the rope or chains they wanted to use.

But Loring knew Viking mentality. Logic often ran against the grain of their national character. The Code Commando protocols now in force required prompt action. That was what Loring had to do. Even if the physics or the wisdom of it did not make sense.

What if Daria suddenly snapped? The glare and confusion of the lights and cameras might torture her mind. After wandering through this indecipherable matrix of a giant cruise ship and then climbing to the upper decks for a view of the sky, she would look up and see a huge silver Cablevista blimp hovering over her. Her noble temperament mighty very well split, go berzerk. Daria had the grace of a metaphysical performance artist ready for her Paris debut. But she was also, by species, the most powerful predator on the planet. Eons of evolution had created her massive haunch muscles to spring when threatened. Her giant white teeth and long black claws were ready to rip, tear, kill, and devour.

Big cat evolution, one must assume, had proceeded with next to no metaphysical questions asked.

"But Oliver, what happens if you miss?"

"May I ask what you had for lunch?"

"Flyin' fish."

"Thought so."

"Why?"

"Maggie, I'm not going to miss. And please think positively now."

"Well, what happened to those other tigers? Did somebody . . ."

"I told you. There is only one tiger."

"But they said somebody saw five or six."

"Six people saw the same tiger. That's how panic works. Listen, we've got trouble enough with one real tiger. Don't worry about the imaginary ones."

"Don't get pissed. I'm behind you all the way. We got one more deck before *Vista*. I sure hope you know what you're doing."

"Of course I know what I'm doing."

Loring did not know what he was doing.

If Loring had known what he was doing, he would never have agreed to sign on for this Cabelvista Valentine TV Cruise in the first place. Nor would he have danced with Ulla. Nor listened to Tosco's story about childhood in

Cuba and the founding of the *Cirque Ineffable*. Nor would he have visited *Claridad*. Nor volunteered for the metaphysical gyroscope. In fact, he hadn't known about doing any of this. He just did it. And when he got to *Vista Deck* with the syringe full of Midazolam in his fist, he would proceed in the same manner.

Because Daria was his responsibility. He could not help but do this thing that he did not know how to do. Otherwise, Staff Captain Nordström would aim his rifle at Daria and do what Nils did know how to do. After which, Nordström would probably saw off her head and hang it over the fireplace, along with the Lion head from Africa, in his cozy trophy den back in Bergen.

"Captain speaking. Where are you, Doctor?"

"Doctor speaking. *Central Stair Tower*. Approaching *Vista Deck*."

"I've tried to get through on the remote to the Staff Captain, but he doesn't seem to be hearing me."

"He's planning to shoot the tiger?"

"Affirmative, Doctor."

"But Captain, there are only about five thousand Siberian tigers left in the whole world."

"We didn't invite this tiger on board, Doctor. Wait a minute . . ."

"We're up on *Vista Deck* now, Captain."

"Yes. On the TV I can see the tiger. Yes, I see the tiger. Running this direction, forward, toward the *Bridge*."

Loring shuddered when the Captain's voice blared out over the public address system. *"LADIES AND GENTLEMEN! THIS IS CAPTAIN RAMSKOG! AS YOU PROBABLY KNOW, WE ARE EXPERIENCING SOME TROUBLES ON THE SHIP! THE PROBLEM IS ALMOST SOLVED, BUT I ADVISE ALL OF YOU TO STAY OFF VISTA DECK UNTIL FURTHER NOTICE! I REPEAT! ALL PASSENGERS AND CREW, DO NOT GO OUT ON VISTA DECK! THANK YOU! AGAIN, THIS WAS YOUR CAPTAIN SPEAKING."*

* * *

Panting from the charge up five flights, Loring and Nurse Maggie emerged from the *Central Stair Tower* hatch and out onto *Vista Deck*.

Blinding floodlights flashed in their faces. A Cablevista camera crew stood directly in front of him, and Farrely Farrell's voice boomed down from giant speakers from somewhere immediately above: *"THERE HE IS, LADIES AND*

GENTLEMEN! WE'VE SPOTTED THE DOCTOR RIGHT IN FRONT OF OUR CAMERAS UP ON VISTA DECK!"

Loring's eyes blinked with pain and bewilderment. His glance jerked upward.

As if a giant silver lid had been placed over the sky, the massive silhouette of the Cablevista blimp loomed over the entire length of the ship and hovered dangerously above the funnels. Three giant spotlights whirled around from the blimp's belly, and powerful loudspeakers from the cabin bay blared down with Farrely Farrell's voice.

"WE'RE WATCHING EVERY MOVE, FOLKS! IN ALL MY YEARS IN TELEVISION, I DON'T THINK I'VE EVER SEEN ANYTHING QUITE LIKE THIS! STICK WITH US, WON'T YOU, MATES? THE DOCTOR SEEMS TO BE CARRYING SOMETHING IN HIS FIST. WHAT IS IT? IT'S NOT A GUN, IS IT? IS IT A GUN HE'S CARRYING?"

A high-pitched ring stung Loring's ears from the deafening blare. A fierce spinning sensation shook through his bones briefly, as if he were back in the gyroscope with the Colonel. His heart pounding, he looked down at a plastic object in his right hand. Yes, what did he have in his hand?

Midazolam, 30 milligrams, he remembered.

"Make way!" he shouted to the cameramen in his way. He and Maggie began to sprint forward.

For an instant, Loring wished he could stop and slip two or three innocent little milligrams of Midazolam up into one of his own forearm veins, slump down on the astroturf, and snooze deeply through whatever was to come about.

Not an option. No more letting the muscles melt off your bones, Doc! The hieroglyphic posture is extinct. You did this to Daria. Now get her out of it.

"AND ISN'T THAT TIGER MAGNIFICENT, LADIES AND GENTLEMEN? A REAL BEAUTY! WHO KNOWS WHAT AN ENRAGED ANIMAL LIKE THAT CAN DO? GOSH! LOOK AT THAT! HE'S UP ON HIS HIND LEGS, GNASHING OUT AT THE AIR! FOLKS, STICK WITH CABLEVISTA! WE NOW HAVE TO TAKE A QUICK COMMERIAL BREAK."

Farrely Farrell's thunderous commentary did not help. And imagine what the blimp and the noise and the lights were doing to Daria? She probably ascended up to the top of the ship, hoping to take a grip on her bearings by looking at the stars. And once up here, all she can see is more shining metal above her with blinding floodlights, while a deafening voice blares out of the blimp.

No wonder she's gnashing out at the sky! There is no sky! And where is Nordström and his hit squad?

"I SAID MAKE WAY!"

As he ran along the astroturf, he knew he could not allow any distractions to divert his intention to find the tiger. He must proceed carefully and with an intractable will. How many invasive procedures had he performed during his career in the emergency room? How many times had he steeled his nerves like this and narrowed his vision? In his job, conviction and well-honed clinical habits had always substituted nicely for courage.

Admittedly, this situation and species was unique to him, but he had never shied away from innovation before. Especially under adversity and, of course, when he wasn't sure what he was doing.

Remember Mozart: INNOVATION!

"YES, FOLKS! WE'RE BACK. AND LOOK! HE'S ACTUALLY STALKING RIGHT AFTER THAT TIGER. THE GOOD DOCTOR MUST BE OUT OF HIS MIND! AND WE CAN SEE THE HUGE ANIMAL NOW UP ON THE FORWARD RAILING. RIGHT OVER THE BRIDGE, FOLKS. LOOKS VERY JUMPY! AND MAYBE A TAD HUNGRY! DOES THIS MAN KNOW WHAT HE IS DOING? LOOK AT THE WAY THAT BIG HEAD JERKS BACK AND FORTH!

"BUT WAIT A MINUTE! YES, FOLKS! I THINK YOU CAN MAKE OUT AT THE BOTTOM OF YOUR SCREEN THAT GROUP OF MEN WITH RIFLES CHARGING UP THE LADDER THERE ON THE SIDE OF THE SHIP! THREE, FOUR, FIVE OF THEM HEADING FORWARD NOW. YES, LET'S HOPE THIS MAY BE THE SOLUTION TO THIS VERY DANGEROUS SITUATION, AFTER ALL. AS FAR AS WE KNOW, NO INJURIES HAVE OCCURRED TO ANY OF THE PASSENGERS UP UNTIL THIS POINT. SO FAR, WE'VE BEEN LUCKY. AND IF THOSE HEROIC NORWEGIAN OFFICERS CAN GET TO THE TIGER QUICKLY, I THINK THE WHOLE SHIP WILL BE SAFE. BUT STICK WITH US! IT'S NOT OVER YET, NOT BY A LONG SHOT!"

Loring's eyes leaped over to the starboard rail. Twenty yards ahead of him, immediately forward of the aft funnel, Nordström's chunky black silhouette mounted the stairs. He shook his burly shoulders and yelled behind him, waved his rifle barrel forward. Four officers followed closely. The five men jogged forward along the stacks of deck chairs.

Loring shouted, but they seemed not to hear him. As he ran to catch up with them, he passed the Cablevista computer consoles immediately forward of the smokestacks. He sprinted past the Mercedes roadsters, where another camera crew had clustered. They ran with him, pointed their camera lenses forward as they tried to keep up.

"THE TIGER LOOKS LIKE HE'S GETTING CROSS! HE'S PACING BACK AND FORTH, STILL JERKING HIS HEAD UP AND DOWN, FOLKS. CAN YOU SEE THOSE TEETH, MATES? HE'S GOT HIS MOUTH WIDE OPEN NOW. NO, I DON'T THINK THAT TIGER HAS LONG TO ROAR, NOT IF THOSE NORWEGIAN OFFICERS HAVE ANYTHING TO DO ABOUT IT!"

Loring saw Daria. She had come as far forward as possible on *Vista Deck*. She stood directly over the *Bridge*, paced furiously, her fur a spectacular, spiraling orange and black as she twisted against the green of the *Vista Deck* astroturf.

"Jesus Christ!" shouted Maggie. "How the hell are you gonna' get close enough to throw that syringe, Oliver?"

"Now we have to slow up a bit. Don't rush at at her, Maggie."

Loring was about to approach Nordström to try and make eye contact, but the Staff Captain unaccountably pointed his rifle out over the starboard rail. His gun barrel blazed as he squeezed off seven or eight fast blasts.

The tiger leaped into the air, shocked and terrified by the flashing explosions.

"WHAT THE HELL ARE YOU DOING?" Loring screamed.

Nordstrom laughed, amused at the tiger's response. *"JUST A FEW WARNING SHOTS, DOC!"*

"YOU'LL SCARE THE LIFE OUT OF HER!"

"BEAUTIFUL HEAD. NICE HIDE, TOO! HOW ABOUT I GET THE HEAD AND YOU GET THE RUG?"

"I PLAN TO PUT THE TIGER TO SLEEP."

"SURE, DART DOC! YOU GO AHEAD AND THROW YOUR SYRINGE. WHEN IT MISSES, WE'LL GIVE HER SOMETHING TO MAKE HER SLEEP GOOD!"

"AND IN CASE YOU JUST TUNED IN, CABLEVISTA VIEWERS FROM AROUND THE WORLD, WE'RE – YES, WE'RE HERE – ON VISTA DECK, THE TOP DECK OF THE LEGENDARY S/S NORDIC BLUE. I UNDERSTAND OUR VIEWERS IN GREAT BRITAIN ARE JUST TUNING IN NOW. WELL! WHAT A SIGHT TO WAKE UP TO, MATES! NOW WATCH WITH ME CLOSELY FROM OUR CABLEVISTA BLIMP. PROBABLY THE MOST UNUSUAL SITUATION YOU'VE SEEN LATELY IS UNFOLDING

RIGHT IN FRONT OF YOUR EYES AS SEEN DIRECTLY OVERHEAD FROM OUR CAMERAS. WE UNDERSTAND THAT, CONTRARY TO PREVIOUS REPORTS, THIS TIGER'S NAME IS DARIA AND SHE IS ACTUALLY A PART OF THE CIRQUE INEFFABLE OF PARIS, AN AMAZING PORTION OF WHICH WE WERE ALL LUCKY ENOUGH TO WATCH DOWN IN THE STARLIGHT THEATRE WHEN . . .

With a two-inch, large bore,14-gauge needle on the business end of the syringe, Loring would have to infuse the entire contents – all 30 cc's – into Daria's carotid artery as fast as he could push the plunger. That would send the Midazolam up into her brain in less than a second. There was a danger, of course, of an overdose and respiratory depression. Daria could stop breathing. But Maggie McCarthy was right behind him with a size #9 endotracheal tube on hand to put into Daria's wind pipe.

Should Daria fall and stop breathing, Loring would have to open her mouth and slide the tube (about the caliber of a garden hose) down into her lungs. Then they would resuscitate her with the rubber bellows in Maggie's knapsack to keep her alive till Daria started breathing on her own. All of that depended on whether Loring could get close enough.

"Doctor speaking. Captain, I request permission to approach the tiger."

"You're sure you know what you're doing?"

"Certain, Captain."

"Permission granted to Doctor. Staff Captain, please hold your fire until the Doctor has made an attempt to anesthetize."

"Doctor speaking. Request permission for the Nurse to follow behind me at five paces."

"Granted."

"Ready, Maggie? This may not be easy."

"I knew that already."

"Just think of it as a regular old cardiac code. Same rules as in an emergency room."

"You think it's going to be that routine?"

"Otherwise, they'll kill her."

"Maybe they should."

"Think positive."

"How close do you have to get?"

"Very close."

Loring looked over and saw the five Norwegian Officers, rifles aimed at Daria, a firing squad primed to execute.

Daria backed up against the forward rail – immediately over the huge *Bridge* windscreen. Nordström's "warning shots" had spooked her horribly. Her agate eyes peered crazily around, and her neck twitched desperately in every direction. Her giant white fangs snapped at the air and for a moment she crouched in terror and fury, ready to spring and attack.

Eye contact with her was impossible, and Loring felt a grim hollowness creep into him.

And to think that Tosco and Tulov – the only individuals in the world who could possibly pacify her – stood in irons with Ulla, immediately below them on the *Bridge*, while the Captain and Nordström conferred over their microphones in Norwegian. No doubt, Tosco was standing with the Captain and watching every move on the *Bridge*'s Cablevista monitors.

As the brilliant floodlights from the blimp fired down from above, Loring paused. He was a dozen yards in front of Daria. This time the Dart Doc had to be nothing less than *magnifique*.

He had to take all of Daria into his consciousness, zone into her as he did with the striped target in the *Crew Bar*, and then go for the quick, direct puncture. To concentrate better, he went up on his toes and breathed slowly, sniffed the Caribbean wind for all the rich, Amur River-scented tiger dander he could possibly absorb. He raised the syringe over his right shoulder, as if he stood at the *Crew Bar* dart firing line.

Slide . . . step . . .

The moment required meditative concentration, and his favorite kinetic posture felt natural, seemed to engage Daria's attention long enough for Loring to fix his eyes deeply into her. Also, with his pointed weapon raised, he was in the classic posture of the old Viking spear bearer – probably an effective image to convince the Norsky hit squad that, in a way, he was speaking their language. Surely they would hold their fire while this spear bearer took his crack at the animal, he hoped.

Slide . . .

Daria's furry ears twitched. Her huge head turned with curiosity. The syringe was poised behind Loring's neck, out of her sight, and he saw her eyes blink for recollection. Her lips slipped up over her fangs as he neared to within five yards of her.

Step . . .

She panted fitfully, her breath redolent of goat kid liver. As he stared closer and closer into her huge eyes, he could feel her body beginning to tighten up briefly, and then she retreated toward the port side, putting Loring directly between the Norwegian officers and her.

"ARE YOU GONNA' THROW THAT DAMN THING, DOC, OR ARE YOU GONNA'. . . "

Daria's ears pricked up and her eyes darted around, confused. Loring listened closely and heard a familiar voice over the loudspeaker.

"Eeeeeeeeeeeeeeoowhafrhatravereeeeee!" It was the dulcet baritone of Tosco – transmitted over the public address system from the *Bridge.*

"Eeeeeeeeeeeeoowhafatfratraverrrrrrrrrrrrreeeeeeeeeeeeeeeee!"

The tiger's eyes scanned port to starboard. She crouched on the astroturf and gazed up at the blimp. She stared at Loring, her eyes blinked with befuddlement, as if to say, "Where is he?"

And then the sweet, enchanting strains of Tosco's voice slowly drifted into a familiar melody. Three-quarter time. "LA- la - LA la - la LA - la La..."

It was the haunting, impassioned tune to Tchaikovsky's *Vagabonde* in *A minor*. Before three bars had passed, Loring could hear a deep feminine contralto join him, and then Tulov's basso. They were a trio, after all!

"LA- la - la, La - la - la . . ."

Step . . .

Right on cue, Daria rose on her massive haunches, assumed dance position.

"LA - la la - La - la - la . . ."

Slide . . . step . . .

Slowly and intently, in time with the waltz tempo, Loring closed the space between him and Daria. As the floodlights from the Cablevista blimp burned on the two of them, he embraced the tiger. She placed her forepaw in the palm of Loring's left hand, her head cocked back at a regal angle, exposing the neck. Loring's right hand, clutching the syringe, settled into the fur along her muscular back.

Just think of our waltz at Claridad, girl!

"LA- la -la . . . LA- la - la . . ."

The trio on the *Bridge* sang in unison. Daria seemed soothed with the familiar melody. Loring could feel the tension in her back melt away. No question about it – Daria was a performer. *And* a natural dancer. Loring watched her eyes close as they started to spin slowly on the astroturf.

A huge blimp hovered above. Spotlights glared down. Men pointed loaded attack rifles at them. And half a dozen yards away stood a nurse whose mouth hung open in disbelief. Yet Loring felt that he and Daria were back at *Claridad,* Tchaikovsky's beguiling *Vagabonde* waltz their channel to sanctuary and to peace.

As they turned on the astroturf, Loring lost himself for several heartbeats in the waltz. His eyes, too, closed in the waltz trance of *Claridad*. But then he felt strange pressure on the back of his wrist – Daria's tail rubbed up and down on the hand that held that midazolam syringe, as though she had to remind him that their waltz could not last forever.

And neither would Nordström and his *Code Commando* troops be satisfied with an alert tiger, whose mood could quickly change from a ballerina in a celestial spiritual state to big cat ferocious.

Loring had to put Daria to sleep.

"LA- la -la . . ."

Loring grasped the syringe tightly, and then he realized he had a problem. His left hand contained Daria's paw, and in order to remove the plastic cap from the syringe needle in his right hand, he required another set of fingers to tug off the cap and expose the needle.

"LA - la - la . . ."

In the Samaritan emergency room there was always a nurse to perform this simplest of functions for him, or sometimes he would stick the plastic cap between his teeth and tug it off. Neither of these options was available to him. He had four hundred and sixty pounds of peacefully enchanted tiger in his arms and a knock-out dose of Midazolam in the syringe, but how could he pry that cap off, make the needle naked and effective?

He did not want to risk Maggie coming any closer to the tiger.

He felt Daria's heart beating strongly on his chest, and he watched her eyes open with contentment. He glanced into the deep phosphorescent agates and hoped that she would not sense his tactical confusion.

"LA - la - la - LA - la - la . . ."

His right palm sweated. The syringe had become slippery.

As he twisted it moistly in his fist for a better grip, it almost slipped out of his hand. As he tightened his grasp, he suddenly felt something odd and new on the end of his thumb. He touched it with the tip of his index finger. It was his new, fully-grown thumb nail – firm-edged, scarab-enforced, and a full quarter of an inch of leverage.

In a twinkle, Loring's new thumb nail pried the cap off the syringe, and his fist had moved away from the back of Daria's chest. She didn't notice. Slowly he brought the syringe low under her foreleg. He began to sing with Tosco and Tulov and Ulla. "LA - la - la . . ."

The syringe barrel tight between his thumb and index finger, and his pinky finger resting on the base of the plunger, he slowly inched the needle up

345

toward Daria's neck. She seemed entranced by the music and by Loring's movements. While her eyes were closed, Loring's middle and ring fingers stroked the fur on her neck, while the syringe needle gleamed directly under her chin. He could feel her purr – a huge, vibratory mountain of a purr. This was gratifying, but it also made it difficult to trace the pulsations of her neck artery.

Slowly they turned as a couple with the music, and Loring felt her white and amber neck fur, palpated further up toward her ear. He tickled her whiskers slightly, and her eyes opened as if pleased by the tease. Then they closed again, and she danced.

Mom, if you're watching, this dance is telling a story!

When he found the pulsing bulge at the angle of her huge jaw, Loring turned the syringe and readied it for the stab.

"*Thooooooooooooooooooooommmmmnng!*" he whispered and then jabbed the needle firmly through her fur and into the artery. In the same motion, his little finger pressed the plunger fluid up through the syringe barrel and out the 14-gauge needle orifice.

Straight to the brain, great god Midazolam! Please, straight to the brain! Dazzle her, man, with Midazolam! Please.

Daria's neck muscles convulsed with pain against his cheek. She grunted. Her jaw jerked away from the stimulus. As the strength in her haunches gave out, she slumped abruptly to Loring's left. Her forepaw went limp in his left palm. He watched her eyes blink up at him three times before her tongue, a wet quivering rag, protruded from her mouth and instantly became a purplish blue against the astroturf.

As he withdrew the syringe from her fur (only ten cc's had done the job!), Loring dropped the syringe, took off his earphones and microphone, and piled on top of her.

"I'm with you, Daria," he whispered, as he felt her muscular body turn to warm, fur-covered dough. He cuddled her closely on the astroturf, heard her slow breaths become deeper as she prowled the Amur river basin, through the reeds, through the wind, through the brightening Siberian dawn.

"You've got to stay with us, girl!" Loring whispered in her ear. "Help me get her jaws open, Maggie! Remember, it's just like a human code. Hand me a flashlight."

Maggie squatted by Daria's head. Her hands reached out with the resuscitation code kit flashlight. The portable oxygen tank was out and ready.

Feeling Daria's muscles relax, Loring pried down on her jaw and beamed the flashlight down her throat. Far down he saw the anterior orifice of her trachea.

"Grab her tongue, Maggie. Damn! She stopped breathing."

"What?"

"I said grab her tongue and pull for all you're worth."

"Hell, I forgot to put my rubber gloves on."

"Forget the gloves. She's clean, Maggie. Do you have the breathing bag ready?"

"Ready, Dart Doc."

To pass the tube into her trachea, Loring had to peer deeply into Daria's throat. This meant he had to stick his head in her mouth and, with the flashlight in his left hand and Maggie yanking on Daria's tongue, his right hand carefully passed the tube down along the hollow cave of her throat and into the trachea.

I started this day with one resurrection, now I'm doing another.

Come on Scriabin. Ba-baaaam, ba-ba-ba-ba ba baaaaaah ba-bam!

Damn is this as oral as I ever want to get!

"Let's bag her now, Maggs!" Loring shouted. "Hook up the oxygen. Do you have a stethoscope?"

Maggie attached the bellows to the free end of the tube and began squeezing the inflated bladder of the bellows, then letting it release, then squeezing it again.

Loring lay beside Daria and listened through the stethoscope to hear the flow of oxygen to her lungs.

"Come on Daria, we'll keep you oxygenated till you can breath on your own."

With the first three puffs of oxygen, Daria's tongue pinked up. He watched her amber and black chest fur heave lightly up and down with the force of Maggie's thrusts. He listened with the stethoscope to her heart – thundering thumps under her ribs.

"Come now, Daria," he whispered. "Come on girl, be good. Start breathing on your own. Come on Daria. *In and out . . . and . . . in . . . and . . .*"

FRI/FEB 15
Ersatz Eden Earned

"Open your mouth. Now close your eyes."

As if a delicate fairy princess had flown down to pirouette on his tongue, the flaky, light-crusted dough in Ulla's fresh-baked *Äpfelküchen* settled onto his taste buds, began to massage and arouse them. She dropped sweet, sticky nectar that drifted and flowed and trickled in a flavorful melody that blended with the fluffy rich cream and the glazed golden delicious apples and swirled rapturously all through his mouth.

Cinnamon. Clove. Nutmeg. Was there also some tincture of almond/ praline nougat in the strudel glaze? And all of it nestled deliciously into a tender, crumbly crust with a dainty whisper of shortening, light on the palate as honeyed gossamer.

"Mmmmmmmmmmmmmmnnnnnhhhh."

From cheek to cheek, his salivary glands spurted with pleasure. The tip of his tongue slid eagerly along his jubilant palate and teeth, searched every crevice for tidbits of the enchanting confection. He sniffed and puckered, licked his delighted lips. Never had golden delicious apples, picked from an earthly orchard, known an apotheosis so resonant and definitive. Loring had not yet swallowed, but it seemed the bewitching *Äpfelküchen* was finding an alternate route into his senses.

"I've never tasted anything like this. Please, may I have some more?"

"As much as you want. Happy Valentine's Day, my love. I'm sorry this is a day late. I didn't have time to bake till this morning."

"No apology! It's fresh. It's perfect. In fact, everything here is fresh and perfect."

God, are you fresh and perfect!

From his boyhood Sunday school readings in *Genesis*, Loring recalled the original Garden of Eden had four rivers. Here on Stig Storjord's private island in the Bahamas there was only one water source – not actually a river, but a potent natural outspilling of an icy cold Bahamian aquifer. The unique spring gushed up nearly a thousand feet from below the ocean bed to feed the lush palms and blossoming tropical flora on the verdant, private, 400-

acre compound.

The manor house was early French provincial, crafted of shipped-in granite and slate shingles. There were three attendant guest bungalows. There was a huge formal garden with several hundred varieties of exotic roses.

Smell those roses!

Other appointments: a pair of grass tennis courts, a botany laboratory and abundant green houses, servant and groundskeeper quarters, a boat house, an oval-shaped marble swimming pool, and, at the end of a mile-long, flowery path through a palm forest, the fern-circled, shady glade where Loring and Ulla now picnicked on a wave-and-sunburst beach blanket spread out on the downy green grass.

The cool water bubbled in the spring-fed natural pool at their feet. The soothing ripples floated melodic and cheery in the afternoon's gentle westerly breezes. The hushed bower felt sacrosanct, disturbed only by the occasional rustlings of the sleepy python, Robespierre, who basked in the therapeutic sunshine high among the fronds of a poolside coconut palm.

Tosco had begged Loring to take the python along for the afternoon. The confusion and trauma of the kidnapping the night before had emotionally shaken the temperamental snake. Emotionally fragile even on his very best days, Robespierre desperately needed some high-dosage natural healing rays from the sun, or else he might fall into a deep reactive depression and start to molt or tie himself into knots. Or worse. So said Tosco.

Loring opened his eyes.

The pool in the green bower. The snake up in the tree. The gorgeous, pouting-lipped woman offering him her own preparation of essence of apple with tender, crystal blue glances.

Biblical substitute or not, this was Eden enough.

And thank you. I would not want to change anything. You never know until . . .

Their picnic of raw tuna *salade Niçoise* with fresh-baked garlic bread and a lusty white Bordeaux *(Château Mirabeile)* had been a nourishing prelude to Ulla's promised *chef d'oeuvre*. Now she leaned over the picnic basket in her white string bikini and sliced up more squares of her succulent *Äpfelküchen*. She had baked it early that morning in Jacques Chemin's pastry oven – secretly and especially for Loring.

Eden! Love the menu.

He lay silently beside her and blinked back more tears of pleasure.

Nothing makeshift about this place! Okay, the snake's a bit fake. But it

*wasn't easy hauling Robespierre over here on Stig Storjord's power yacht
and then lugging him down through the garden. So what! If reclamation
needs to be done around here, let's begin!*

Ulla's tresses wafted gently across her shoulders. Her eyes were a dazzling
blue tease beneath her raven locks. Her smooth, muscular arms glowed with
supple strength, and with each downward slice of the knife, her tight waist
undulated above her enticing hips and thighs and knees. He watched her
tongue lick a white wisp of cream from her forefinger.

*Bring on the forbidden fruit! Especially the full curve of your buttocks –
just as it breaks into two muscular hemispheres of palm-shaded melody. And
that smooth tanned valley that narrows and steepens so succulently between
them. More! More! More!*

There was little use in disputing the academics of whether he had *earned*
his way into this ersatz paradise. Foolishly or not, he had done Tosco's
transcendental gyroscope trick, saved the tiger's life – through decisive
(Farrely Farrell called it "heroic" on the air) action – and now he found
himself landed smack dab with the woman he loved in a nutritious and
sensuous epiphanyland. Exactly as Tosco and Tulov and the other *Cirque
Ineffable* theorists had postulated!

It would be folly on a par with the original Adam's to debate his own
credentials (or impending nudist activities) here, no matter how jury-rigged
or trumped up the circumstances on the evolutionary continuum. What's more,
this Eden possessed another improvement over the original: a very special
and tantalizing ladybug who bounced inches away from his nose.

Ulla stretched her hands behind her back to release the snap of her bikini
top. "Do you mind?" she asked. "I feel so comfortable with you."

"Oh do! Yes, so do I. With you, I mean."

OH YESSSSSSSSSSSSSSS! DOOOOOOO!

Ulla's dove white breasts with their erect amber tips now played before
him in all their smooth, orbicular majesty.

*Talk about fresh and perfect! Talk about ineffable! Or oral impulses! Who
needs fingernails?*

She slipped another cream-topped square of *Äpfelküchen* between his
lips. "So you really like it, don't you? I made plenty. My grandmother's
recipe calls for a half a kilo."

*See! Another improvement: the original Eve didn't have a grandmother
to bequeath her fabulous recipes.*

She dabbed on more *Schlagsahne* and set the delectable morsels on a plate beside their wine goblets. "For later. How about if we swim first? Doesn't the water look wonderful?"

She peeled the bottom portion of her bikini down her legs, kicked it onto the grass, and stepped into the sand-bottomed pool. As she stood knee deep in the cool water, the sun gilded the lines of her smooth silhouette in a shimmering glow against the deep blue of the sky and the lush green of the glade. He watched the sun and the ripple reflections play on the gently trembling raven hairs of her pubis. She looked back over her shoulders toward him. "You won't be shy today, will you? This is our afternoon together, darling. Our first afternoon. I want you to forget all about last night."

She jumped further into the pool, dipped her head into the water.

Loring pulled off his polo shirt and his swim suit. He stood up and glanced around sheepishly at the lush grass at the sides of the pool: no, there were no steamer trunks full of electronic sex paraphernalia anywhere to be seen. Not a single vibrator or mechanical dildo in sight. Yes, for the moment, he would forget about what happened on the ship last night. But eliminating the traumatic memories of the past six months of Anita Rothberg's elaborate machine-enhanced sexual pageants was more difficult just now.

Particularly for the last two months of their relationship, on a nightly basis, Anita Rothberg had orchestrated their intimate encounters with her rococo scriptings: of when and where Loring should apply certain aphrodisiac ointments or orifice-stimulating devices, of when and how long his erection should be maintained or diminished ("You tell Mr. Buck-Buck to behave himself till Missy is ready!") and of how often repeated orgasms could be achieved. Sex *per se* had taken on for Loring (and for the confused participant known as "Mr. Buck-Buck") multiple-prong strategic trappings not totally unlike last night's *Code Commando* scenario.

How grateful he was for this return to an Eden-like simplicity! Simplicity had always seemed to Loring a sign of health.

Fresh. Perfect. Ineffable.

And under the category of personal health, more good news in this Eden: earlier that morning during the ride over on Stig Storjord's power yacht, *Fraülein* von Straf had charmingly confided to him – she said she knew he might be curious "as a doctor" (innocent wink) – that she took birth control pills and had always tested negative for all possible infectious diseases.

Loring said that as a doctor ("but not *your* doctor, ha-*ha!*") he was pleased to hear of her hygienic purity. What's more, he was happy to confess that he, too, had recently been tested for every possible communicable disease and, in fact, enjoyed the same fortunate state.

Yo hygiene! And venereal housekeeping matters! You can never have enough of either. In Eden or anywhere else! (Meanwhile, we can leave that pack of condoms in the rolled-up napkin in the picnic basket.)

"Oliver! Are you coming in? It's wonderful! Look! The little fish are biting my toes."

"What kind of fish?"

"Please! Don't be shy! I want to be with you. Forget about last night! Things worked out fine!"

Loring stretched his arms up and arched his spine in the sun. He rolled his head and smiled. A pleasant wave of goose bumps showered over his back and thighs, as if his very skin sensed the relief of being *au naturelle* with the *natural* elements: only a gladed bower and the woman he so desperately loved.

No extras. No machines. No pre-written script. And, up in the barren blue Caribbean sky, no snooping Cablevista blimp to spoil it all!

As for forgetting about last night, as Ulla wished? He wanted to forget sticking his head into the tiger's mouth. But he had two reminders that probably would never leave him: a pair of puncture wounds that would surely turn to small scars just above the temples – Daria's fang marks. (He could throw away the rest of his scarab pills, for he realized now how horrible his finger nails had felt all these years. *Wow!* Talk about Mimic Empathy Therapy! How could he ever have done that to them?)

But as for the rest of last night, yes, he would be able to forget that.

Once Loring and Maggie McCarthy had anesthetized and bag-breathed Daria back to respiratory stability, Captain Ramskog had taken over and the situation had resolved rather efficiently.

Deftly appraising a situation that baffled almost everyone else on board, the Captain ordered Pearly Livingstone up to *Vista Deck* on his fork lift. As Loring pumped oxygen into her lungs and Staff Captain Nordström rode shotgun on Pearly's rig, Daria's sleeping form was conveyed slowly and carefully down the *Forward Freight Elevator* then along the *Car Deck* passageways to Tosco's hidden hideaway compound. Tosco, also at gunpoint and in handcuffs, was allowed to attend the transfer.

After Daria had recovered her full tigerly consciousness and was breathing on her own, the tube extracted from her lungs, the Captain ordered all the principle parties involved to an impromptu dawn debriefing on the *Bridge*. Cablevista personnel strictly prohibited.

The rising sun's rays beamed bright on his brow, as Trond Ramskog sat mute in his high Captain's chair, twirled his golden mustache, and listened to each of the participants describe the extraordinary actions over the past days and hours. Occasionally he winced, at times a mute smile rose and fell around his mouth. But for the most part his fjord-blue eyes were implacably stern as everyone spoke – Tosco, Ulla, Tulov, Jacques Chemin, Loring, Maggie McCarthy, Flip Spinelli, finally Nordström.

When everyone had finished, the Captain stood down from his chair. For several moments he looked out at the sea, his hands folded behind him, and paced along the length of the *Bridge* windscreen. His eyes gazed then at each of the individuals, as if he were searching their souls to be sure each was telling the truth.

"First off," he said, "none of our passengers or crew was hurt. That's the most important thing. I suppose we have God alone to thank for that."

As the group stood and watched, Ramskog's lips pursed and his voice grew tender. "Secondly, the show I saw at midnight last night in the *Starlight Theatre* was the most magnificent spectacle I have ever seen in my life. I was sitting in the front row with Mr. Storjord and Mrs. Snippet-White, and I would like to thank all of you people who were involved in it, especially you, *Monsieur* Tosco.

"I have never been moved so deeply and shocked by the beauty of the dance and the demonstrations. Doctor, your appearance as a human tiger and then your apparent death on that gyroscope and your reappearance fully alive affected me to my very inner feelings. I *mean* that. Along with many of the people sitting near me, I wept in my chair. I must admit, I was quite skeptical about this show when I heard about it. But, *Monsieur* Tosco, I do hope you will invite me to the grand opening of your circus in Paris this spring.

"Believe me, I am very proud to have had you here on the *Nordic Blue* on this cruise, and I look forward to following the progress of your circus. There is no question in my mind, that you have touched millions of people around the world with your visions. Your circus is, frankly, what this world needs more of. Thank you."

The Captain then fixed his glance at Staff Captain Nils Nordström.

"Finally," Ramskog said, with a quick tightening of his jaw muscles and a deepening of his voice, "apart from the fact that nobody was injured during this past night, there was quite clearly an inexcusable breach of security on this ship. Although the intentions of these performers were obviously of a spiritual nature, those intentions could easily *not* have been. I am shocked

353

that such a violation of our security protocols could have occurred right under the Staff Captain's nose without his knowledge of any of this, until a potentially catastrophic situation was at hand.

"Staff Captain Nordström, these people are obviously not terrorists, but they *could* have been. Now, I'd like to dismiss all of you, except for Staff Captain Nordström. Everyone else is forgiven. No more questions asked. Now everyone, run off and get some sleep or enjoy the rest of this beautiful day however you like."

Didn't the Captain say you're all forgiven? Yo forgiveness! Isn't that a new item in Eden!

"*Oliver! Darling!* Please stop thinking about it! It's over. Come in and get wet!"

"It's all forgotten! Ha-*ha!* All of it."

"Why don't I believe you?"

Loring stepped into the water, lingered with each step at the enlarging view of Ulla's head turning, laughing, turning again. She cupped her hands on either side and splashed him, giggled as he blinked the water out of his eyes. The silky coolness rose above his thighs as he came closer to her. He felt his scrotum clench with the chill.

"Hold me, Oliver. I want to kiss you everywhere!"

He looked down and watched the pale white reflection of her breasts in the pool. Bobbing in the sun, the lady bug's twin twittered before Loring's eyes.

He felt her hand on him, cupping his scrotum. Was it the chill of the icy aquifer water? Was it the fatigue of an exhausting, nearly sleepless week? Or was it the power of his passion for her?

For whatever reason, though he was in the arms of the most voluptuous creature he had ever known, and though he had danced with Ulla in a series of precise and demanding choreographies for the whole world to see, here in the nourishing intimate setting of the Garden of Eden, his member was embarrassingly limp. The artist formerly known as "Mr. Buck-Buck" seemed to suffer from stage fright and did not want to come out of the dressing room.

"Let's just swim," she said.

"You know, I love you very much."

"I know that. You're still a little shy, that's all." She ducked her head under the water, and her marvelous mouth was all over him, her tongue up and down him in quick, teasing licks. Her head came up and she smiled as she held him gently, warmly, brushed her thighs up against him. "I want this afternoon to last forever, darling."

"It will."

He leaned toward her, put the tip of his tongue onto her ladybug. He kissed her there, then began to lick lower and lower, down across her tight nipple and lower.

She pulled his chin up with her hand. "But how do you know?"

"Because we can always find our way back here. But next time I'm not sure we need to lug the snake along."

Ulla laughed a foggy, musical laugh and glanced up in the palm tree. "*Shhhhhhhhhhhh.* He might here you. He's very sensitive."

"May I kiss you again?"

Ulla's pale eyes glistened under her dark lashes. "Isn't that why we're here? But first let's swim. Let's get really wet."

He watched her glide along the surface, her legs kicking frog-style. The perfect pale mounds of her buttocks clenched and released in the sun. He watched the rippling water trail in her wake. Yes, he worshipped everything about her, her wake included. He dived forward and followed her, closed his eyes in the wet bliss of pursuing her.

When they had swum for several tantalizing minutes, cutting a circular path in the pool, they both emerged from the chilly water and toweled each other as they stood in the sun. He tenderly drew the white terry cloth over her muscular back and across her shoulders. He touched it to her breasts, felt the nipples pucker tighter with each stroke. He went to his knees and drew the towel down across her smooth, dripping belly, caressed each of her thighs. Gently he touched his lips to her.

"I feel wonderful with you, Oliver. So clean."

He looked up. Her eyes were closed. Her head swayed against the sky, and her nostrils flared with pleasure to his touch.

He pulled her down to her knees. "Do you think Eden ever really happened?"

"Of course I do." She opened her eyes, looked down and smiled. "And I see you are getting less shy."

"Do you think it's happening now?"

"Eden happens all the time, Oliver." She put her arms around his shoulders and brought him down onto the towel.

He loved her smiling eyes, strangely dark against the sky as she leaned over him. "I'm pretty strong, aren't I," she said. "May I kiss you?"

"You don't think it was only a one-time shot?"

"Not at all. *Oooooooooh!* You are definitely less shy."

"But what do you mean it happens all the time?"

He closed his eyes and felt her lips around him, felt his artist grow strong. She looked at his eyes. "I'm sorry. What did you say?"

"I asked what you mean about Eden happening all the time?"

She leaned away from him and reached over to the plate of *Äpfelküchen.* He watched her bite off half of a cream-covered square, chew and swallow it. Then she leaned back down and put the rest of it into Loring's mouth.

"It's simple." As her magical *Äpfelküchen* fairy danced in his mouth, she watched his lips. "Time. Just eliminate it. As long as you look past the concept of time, we are all simply part of the same biology. We are all part of the same fabric – you and me and everyone else. Oliver, someday I think I would like to add to that fabric with you."

Loring breathed in and out with pleasure. He looked up at the sky, heard Robespierre slithering in the palm fronds. "I'm very not shy right now."

"See, it's all simple, Oliver. Not like baking *Äpfelküchen.*"

"Or riding a flaming . . ."

"Forget about doing that ever again. Let Daria do that. I'll be your gyroscope. I'll keep you spinning. But right now, I want you to hold still."

"I can't hold still. Not right now."

"Let me teach you a trick, Oliver. Just close your eyes and take some deep breaths."

"Like this? In . . . and . . . out . . . "

"Yes, just like that. Now close your eyes and let me take you somewhere you have never been before."

"If I like it, can I come back."

"Oh, I know you will like it. Now let me hear you breathe."

In . . . and . . . out . . . and . . .

* * *

At sunset, the *S/S Nordic Blue* slipped north and west through a vast pink field of smoothly shimmering waves.

The broadcasts of the *Valentine TV Cruise* were officially done, and the Cablevista blimp had flown away north and west to Florida – to cover the annual car race up in Daytona. Now the Caribbean sky, rim to rim, was blessedly empty. As celestial company to the sinking red sun, a single star glowed low in the west – proud Venus, whose untwinkling white presence ruled an otherwise endless, gradually darkening firmament.

Far aft on *Promenade Deck*, a black-veiled Hildegarde Snippet-White sat with Stig Storjord in the front row of the funeral party. She and each of the guests held a single Imperial Fiat rose bud in hand. Tremulous and tearful, but resolved, Hildegarde prepared to bid a final, elegant farewell to her husband.

The Colonel's huge death bust rested on a high, rose-bedecked platform between the coffin and Barry Cox's band. The slanting rays of the sun in the west penetrated the giant ice head, imbued it with a glowing scarlet, as if the genteel and self-effacing Rocky Boy Bebalzam might be blushing from the attention.

Mahmoud had meticulously arranged the particulars to the widow's preferences: a small parquet dance floor by the band, a large sterling silver tub filled with bottles of Dom Perignon, a rose for each guest to toss, and two sliding board ramps to convey both the Colonel and his death bust over the edge of the *Promenade Deck* rails at the ceremony's climax.

Mahmoud's skills at restoring the corpse to a life-like semblance (no burnt flesh odor, whatsoever) were impressive, especially after all Rocky had been through since his death – including the scorching and skewering of the previous night. Hildegarde had stipulated no artificial chemicals or embalming preservatives, in deference to the Caribbean's tenuous ecology, so Ruby Decosta had finalized the presentation with biodegradable make-up ingredients – the Colonel's pink cheek flush came from a special carnation petal oil derivative, and the plum extract on his lips gave Rocky's persistent grin, with the glint of his gold tooth, a confident and reassuring final luster. Trond Ramskog, Maggie McCarthy, Tosco and Tulov sat with the widow in the front row, several Norwegian Deck Officers right behind them. (Nils Nordström was absent).

Hildegarde had insisted that Jacques Chemin attend, and Jacques had brought Fatima along. Farrely Farrell with Anita Rothberg in the back row rounded out the small, but elite, group of mourners.

Loring had offered to play some elegiac Elgar or perhaps a fond and deep-reaching Brahms *Intermezzo* for the ceremony, but Hildegarde had preferred that he and Ulla pay tribute instead with Strauss – by waltzing one last time for the Colonel to the *"Blue Danube."* Now as Venus herself glowed in the pink western sky and Barry and the band tenderly reprised the Colonel's favorite Viennese, Loring twirled slowly on the parquet with his Eden picnic partner in his arms.

"Ich liebe Dich," he whispered.

"You learn German quickly. This afternoon was so beautiful, darling," she whispered back and closed her eyes.

"Ich liebe dein Äpfelküchen," he whispered.

She shook her head with a soft wink.

"I told you I was oral," he said.

He recalled, of course, his first dizzying waltz with Ulla for the Colonel. And to think, earlier this sacred and delicious afternoon, they had shared for the first time the full pleasure of each other's feelings, had poured turbulent and insatiable passion out of their mouths and hearts and glands, again and again.

At Ulla's insistence, he had said nothing about last night. But now that the Colonel was about to be whisked away from them and sent off to meet the sharks, Loring wanted to speak to her about what might happen tomorrow. And shouldn't he at least mention to her some of the conversation he had shared with the Colonel in a hallucination when they were pinioned together on the gyroscope platter? Like when the Colonel suggested that Loring become his heir?

Loring glanced over Ulla's shoulder at the giant red ice image of the dignified Colonel. Rocky Boy Bebalzam looked full of confidence and wisdom, as though he were as good as his word, even if last night it had been uttered under extremely extenuating, perhaps perverse, circumstances.

As he held Ulla in position and slowly circled in front of the coffin for their final twirl and bow, he felt Ulla's hand reach behind his neck and push his ear forward to her lips. "Whatever you are thinking, Oliver, the answer is yes."

"You're sure?"

"I know we have the Colonel's blessing," she whispered as they bowed.

"I hope you're right."

As the band completed their final phrase, no applause was offered. The waltz had not been, after all, a performance. And Hildegarde seemed pleased with the silence as she stood up and approached the Colonel. She leaned over the coffin, lifted her veil, and kissed Rocky on the lips, turned back to the funeral party and said, "Well, Captain? Will you do the honors?" Her face was calm. Her mascara was intact.

Trond Ramskog stood and nodded to Mahmoud, who wheeled out a tray bearing two dozen champagne flutes. Adroitly, the Egyptian clasped a large magnum of Dom Perignon under the stump of his left arm and, with uncanny ease, popped the cork with a polite, froth-free bang. He filled several glasses and passed the tray for the guests to help themselves. As the party rose from their seats, the Captain held his flute to the sky. Mahmoud stood near the coffin, as the Captain shouted, *"Skål!"*

The mourners echoed his word all around, *"Skål! Skål! Skål!"*

With a flick of his wrist, Mahmoud tugged a gold tassel at the bottom of the coffin, and at once both the boxed Colonel and his death bust tilted slightly and then began their descent down their respective waxed wooden ramps.

The resourceful Mahmoud had seemed to borrow a chapter from Tulov's notebooks on this one – so precisely, gracefully did the two large objects move in tandem. And the mourners, as if in awe of the sight, stepped along toward the port rails, flutes still raised, to watch the trajectories.

The movement was slow at first, but gradually the coffin and the ice bust both picked up speed. They glided silently beside each other, and at a small barrier just over the edge of the rail, the coffin stopped with a thud. The hinged lid on the head end flipped open, and the uniformed Colonel, whose lower spine had been transected the night before by Tosco's flaming spike, emerged in flight. He plummeted down a dozen decks in a triple back flip, maintaining perfect pike position as he slipped smoothly, almost without a splash, into the smooth pink brine.

It was an instance that verified Galileo's famous Leaning Tower of Pisa physics experiment, for the huge ice head flew off the *Promenade Deck* rail smoothly at the same time as the body. It then lofted in glistening flight a dozen feet behind – but at exactly the same diminishing vertical altitude – as the stiffened corpse.

Rich with sunset radiance in its descent, the brilliant red head spun upright on its vertical axis in a slow, falling pirouette, as if Rocky Boy Bebalzam were taking several 360-degree valedictory surveys of the ship and the tranquil pink sea.

Exactly when the corpse pierced the water, the bust hit the surface with a loud, popping splash. The head submerged below the waves with the adjacent body for several seconds and then bobbed up alone, a big glowing buoy. The head bobbed back and forth in the waves, nodded up to the funeral party as if Rockwell Snippet-White hoped his final flourishing antic had come off to their satisfaction.

Her glass raised to the sunset, Hildegarde shouted for everyone to hear, "Oh, thank you, Rocky! It was all such fun!"

The witnesses on *Promenade Deck* could not hold back their admiration.

They put down their champagne flutes, tossed their Imperial Fiat rose buds after the corpse, and applauded. Mahmoud was probably not the only individual who might have enjoyed – for once on this cruise – a television camera to capture the event. After all the televised detailing of the week's events, this was clearly the most deserving of preservation.

Alas, the *Valentine TV Cruise* was all over.

The Colonel had gone to meet the sharks, and his rocking red head with the harpoon-shaped nose trembled in the *Nordic Blue's* expanding wake. Rocky's ice effigy gazed after them as their ship honed north and east toward Miami. He remained, still bobbing in approval, to begin his own molecule-by-molecule, melting reunion with the warm mother sea.

SAT/FEB 16
Troll on a Roll

"Wedding March of the Trolls" by Edvard Grieg was not part of Loring's memorized repertory. But lack of familiarity with the odd syncopations of the little A minor pianistic jewel did not prevent him from developing it as robustly as he could for the wedding reception guests.

He had purchased the sheet music for *"The Collected Folk Dances by Grieg"* a few hours before at a music store in downtown Miami – two doors up from the Flagler Street formal wear shop where he rented a white dinner jacket. Now his fingers pranced and jiggled through the oblique, Nordic-flavored chords and tricky trills as fluidly as his sight reading skills and one hour of practice allowed.

"Ya-ta-ta-ta. Dah-dee-dee-boom. Ya-ta-ta-ta. Dah-dee-boom-boom!"

The grinning groom was delighted that his request for some native Norwegian folk airs was being honored. At 87, Stig Storjord looked tanned, fit and trim, every inch the proud, white-bearded nubial hero, as he strolled among the guests with his new bride on his arm.

The private ceremony had occurred that morning in Miami at the office of a Justice of the Peace, but there was nothing private about this reception – all the passengers on the ship were invited to dance and enjoy the champagne, all as the generous Fleet Founder's treat.

And Hildegarde could not have seemed more radiant – purple veil, rich satin gown, blinding boulder of a diamond on her ring finger, and an engaging smile to everyone she beamed it upon.

Oh, how she beamed!

"Ya-ta-ta-ta. Dah-dee-dee . . ."

The *Sky Club* on the *M/S Nordic Pearl* could not compete with the elegance of *Club Atlantis,* divine statuary and all. Here on the *Pearl*, however, simplicity and plate glass created a stunning celestial effect. Port to starboard, the *Sky Club* offered unlimited water views. On *Sky Deck*, the highest of the ship, stationed atop his commanding position at the Steinway concert grand's concert platform, Loring played as if perched in the clouds. He glanced out at the fading gold lights of Miami that dipped gradually under the misted western horizon and at the brilliant string of white dots across the water that winked a mile off to starboard.

He sighed to see the glowing silhouette of the *S/S Nordic Blue*, speeding eastward on her weekly Saturday night course down toward the lesser Antilles.

"Dah-dee-boom-boom . . ."

The *Nordic Pearl* and her happy passengers, of course, cruised toward their own appointed Sunday morning destination, the Bahamas, where Loring planned to enjoy yet another intimate picnic with Ulla – again deliciously alone – tomorrow afternoon in Stig Storjord's gladed Bahamian bower. This time raspberry tort. And no snake.

A tingle of delight shot up his spine when his eyes spotted her near the buffet table. She was offering Stig a second sliver of wedding cake, and those icy blues gleamed on the groom. She tweaked his cheek affectionately, and the giddy Stig obviously enjoyed the tease by his newly adopted goddaughter. Apparently sensing Loring's attention, Ulla then glanced up toward him, turned her head and winked.

Loring felt his cheeks blaze hot at her gaze, and he power chorded the next three measures that led into a dizzying arpeggio interlude and then let the ten bold and nimble digits dance under his hands fly round in an ecstatic dervish crescendo up the keyboard.

"Ya-ta-ta-ta. Ya-tee-tee-tah. Rakaraka ffffffeeeeeeeeeeh!"

Ulla laughed and shook her head at his pianistic clowning, while Stig and Hildegarde glanced at each other, delighted to be the new conjugal couple. (Wasn't it nice that Hildegarde had finally married somebody her own size!)

Yes, all the trolls were on a roll – had been on a celebratory rampage all day. Loring felt lucky to channel into their mysterious musical and spiritual dynamics. Not a single mischievous poltergeist lurked among them, it seemed, thank you very much Edvard Grieg and all your inspired peasant composer predecessors!

Thank you, also, Troll of Trolls! Stig Storjord!

"Ya-ta-ta-ta. Ya-tee-tee-tah!"

For the past 24 hours, Stig Storjord had proceeded with trollish singleness of purpose. As soon as the Colonel's corpse had plummeted stylishly to briny eternity and the bobbing ice bust had faded miles behind the long wake of the *Nordic Blue*, wily Stig took Hildegarde aside and pulled the boulder out of his pocket. Talk about sculpted ice!

"Well, what could I say but, 'No time like the present!'" Hildegarde chuckled later in her suite up on *Viceroy Deck* while still sipping on Rocky's funeral bubbly. "At our ages, we certainly cannot afford to waste time on a prolonged engagement, don't you know!"

Quickly she contacted friends in Miami, and Stig phoned the *Pearl* to prepare for a week-long wedding celebration cruise. Loring and Ulla were invited to occupy the *Penthouse Suite* on the *Pearl's* exclusive *Olympic Deck*, two doors up from the *Owner's Suite*, where the joyful bride and groom would preside for the week.

Loring had immediately phoned the Boston Samaritan to see if there was any chance that he could tack on an additional week's vacation here in the Caribbean. The administrators at the Samaritan said, as a matter of fact, they hoped he would. Their public relations department had been bombarded with hundreds of calls from Boston and national newspaper and television reporters who wanted to interview Loring as soon as he returned to work. Apparently Loring's appearances on Cablevista had made him so popular to the media, the administrators complained, that the Samaritan staff was frankly not looking forward to handling all the attention.

An extra week off in the Caribbean would be absolutely no problem for them, and if he could add on a third week, that would be fine, too! They would fill out the emergency room schedule. They also suggested that Loring consider retaining his own publicity agent.

Ya-ta-ta-ta. Dah-dee-dee . . .

When Loring called Novak, Bart did not seem surprised. "Not getting married yourself, are you, Oliver? The nurses want to know."

"Not quite. Ulla and I are getting to know each other."

"The Austrian doll I saw you dancing with on Cablevista? No wonder you want to spend another week in the Caribbean. We may never see you again."

Rakaraka ffffffffffffeeeeeeeeeeeh!

Bart Novak might not have been far off the mark. Once Ulla and Loring had moved their luggage from the *Nordic Blue* to the *Nordic Pearl,* a package arrived at the *Penthouse Suite* – a thick perspectus of the Snippet-White Foundation's world-wide operations, along with another handwritten note from Hildegarde:

Viceroy Deck #7
Saturday morning, February 16

Dearest Oliver -

Have you ever considered a career in international philanthropy? Look this over and let me know if you would consider taking the dear Colonel's place as Chairman of the Board. We desperately need someone as generous as you to give away our money wisely. Think about it this week on the Pearl, won't you? I know you have a busy practice up in Boston and all, and you probably think you don't know anything about philanthropy. Guess what! Rocky didn't know peanuts either when he started, but he learned fast. You will, too. (We don't deal with peanuts, you know!)

Love and smooches,

Hildegarde

P.S. I also want to talk to you about Rocky's will.
P.P.S. By the way, of course I should have told you this earlier, but Rocky and I always had a solemn agreement that, should something terrible happen to him, Stig was to step in immediately in Rocky's stead. Remember how Rocky's ice bust nodded to us approvingly in the water yesterday? I took that as a sign of his blessing. I hope you will, too.
P.P.P.S. This other package is a belated Valentine's gift to you. Obviously the Colonel won't need it any more.

The package was wrapped in white tissue paper and golden ribbon. Inside was Colonel Rockwell Snippet-White's deluxe, alligator skin encased traveling manicure kit – a dozen beautifully crafted silver instruments with ornate tortoise shell handles.

Daa-dee . . . Boom-Boom . . .

So many changes to think about! But Loring reckoned, when benevolent trolls came into your life, offering dozens of Imperial Fiat roses and deluxe suites on ocean liners, you really didn't have a choice but to change, especially if you entertained at their wedding receptions.

So many changes! Did he really want to spend the rest of his life in the Emergency Room putting up with arrogant and confused medical students and concocting multiple-lettered theoretical psychiatric intervention techniques to propel his career?

Daa-dee . . . Boom . . .

Also, so many farewells that morning!

Fortunately, the Miami police and the Immigration and Naturalization Service had barricaded a large section of the dock in the Port of Miami to keep the media at bay, enough to allow the tremendous off-loading process of all the Cablevista equipment, the satellite dishes, and the Mercedes roadsters. This also gave the crew and passengers some much needed dockside breathing space to sort out their papers and belongings.

Tosco's disembarkation went surprisingly smoothly. The *Claridad* staff had arranged the specifics far in advance – all the documents were in place, stamped by customs, and the officer from the Department of Agriculture quickly cleared Daria and Robespierre and the other animals straight through to the huge moving van that would take them and all of Tosco's equipment to the Miami airport for their charter jet back to San Juan.

By the *Crew Gangway*, Tosco and Tulov embraced Loring and thanked him. Loring said he was certain he would attend the grand opening of the *Cirque Ineffable* in Paris in April, when Daria would be allowed, finally, to show her true stuff without the annoying influence of any meddlers. Tosco said he would convey those sentiments to Daria, and Tulov said he was sure Daria would be grateful. Would Loring and Ulla be able to fly down and visit Claridad any time soon?

Ya-ta-ta-ta. Ya-tee-tee . . .

Jacques Chemin and Fatima had waved at Loring as they headed off to an off-ship day in Miami. Shopping? Lunch? The horse races?

YOU NEVER KNOW UNTIL YOU KNOW! OH YESSSSSSSSSSSS!

And Pearly Livingstone had stepped off his forklift to give Loring a huge, sweaty hug. "Next time you come back, Dart Doc, I expect you down in the *Crew Bar* every single night! And Pearly will be buying all the Ringnes."

"Is that a promise?"

"You know you can rely on old Pearly, Oliver."

"My best to your family."

"Oh yes, I called them already. They are very proud, Doc! Very proud indeed! Their daddy is a star. Hey! Now don't go freezin' yourself up Boston!"

"I'm not going back to Boston for at least another week. I'm spending a week on the *Pearl*. And I still have the fever, Pearly, so I won't get cold."

"Good for you, Dart Doc. But that little dinky ship? Hell! Their *Crew Bar* is barely big enough for Pearly to turn around in. No space for snake dances."

"I probably won't be spending much time there. I'll only be a passenger."

"A power cruiser? Don't believe it!"

"Hey, Pearly. Worse things could have happened."

"*Mon*, you got that one right! By the way, did you know they named that ship after me? Just kidding. So long! Have a great time with the ballerina!"

Loring had left a very generous tip to Mr. Kim, but as usual on Saturday morning in port, the busy valet was nowhere to be found.

Anita Rothberg and Farrely Farrell had phoned Loring's cabin and said they were flying together back to New York. "If you need an agent, mate, I can make the connections. You're a blast image now, mate, remember. Like big time cash in the bank! I've already set Flip Spinelli up with a fabulous firm. Give me a jingle. Whenever, mate."

"You will call him, won't you," Anita added.

"Yes, whenever," Loring replied.

Ya-ta-ta . . .

The happiest goodbye that morning was to Trond and Maggie. Loring had stopped by the *Hospital*, where Maggie was finishing up her cruise reports and restocking the pharmacy. ("We need a whole frickin' shit load of Midazolam, thanks to you, Dart Doc!")

The grinning Captain had just come by, and he announced that Snø had phoned her lawyer in Oslo to start divorce proceedings. Snø's appearance on *Love Luck* had so convinced her that releasing the Captain from their marriage was the right thing and that her boyfriend in Oslo had flown over to meet her. Snø and he would be taking the new Mercedes on a trip across America, wherever their hearts might lead them.

"Ain't that special?" Maggie winked. "But I sure don't begrudge her the car or the man. I got the guy I've been waitin' for. And as long as I can keep him from catchin' the hiccups, I think we might have a future together."

Loring congratulated Maggie with a kiss on the cheek and the Captain with a respectful salute. "Thanks for being my Captain, Captain."

Daa-dee . . .

Loring watched Ulla approach the stage. She was dressed in her silver lamè, as requested, and her crystal blue gaze fixed steadfastly on him. Her shoulders glowed and her smile sparkled. So did her necklace.

In Miami she had happily agreed to join him for the week on the *Pearl* and said she could rearrange her schedule to fly with him back up to Boston after the cruise. She had also consented to take a quick trip up to Coventry,

Vermont, to meet his mother, that is, if Loring agreed to fly with her soon to Salzburg and meet her parents.

"The little things," Ulla had said with a smile, "will take care of themselves." At 32, she felt more inclined to devote her artistic skills to choreography than to the athletic rigors of dance. She might want to use her body for other creative purposes, she had said. Her philosophy of the great fabric of humanity – and adding to it – had struck him as awfully true, and not unduly metaphysical.

"Why not a Paris wedding in April?" Hildegarde had suggested that morning. "Tosco and Tulov can attend. First we'll do the *Cirque Ineffable*, then we'll do you two. And don't worry about making a career decision. You probably think you don't know anything about giving away money, but neither did Rocky and I when we got started. Or did I already say that in my letter? Well, you certainly can't be a cruise ship doctor for the rest of your life, can you?"

Daa-dee . . . Boom!

Ulla stepped up onto the stage behind him, put her hands on his shoulders as his twenty rollicking trolls danced into the final quirky sections of their march. He loved the knowing touch of her fingers down along his collarbones. He felt her chuckling softly against him. Her belly bumped onto his spine and worked a swinging thrust against him with each of Grieg's final triumphant measures.

If this is how trolls marched, Loring was delighted to move in their ranks. *"DAH-DEE-BOOM-BOOM-BOOM!"*

When the final echoes of the Grieg chords faded and the brief applause had faded, the bridegroom rose and offered a cordial *"Skål!"* toward the pianist and Ulla.

Then Ulla took Loring's hand, and together they walked out the starboard exit and onto *Sky Deck*.

"Will you dance with me now, Oliver?"

"And for our music?"

"For music we'll listen to the stars."

"Please, darling. No metaphysics on this cruise."

"Don't worry, my love," she said. Her warm cheek nestled close, as she melted into him. With the lady bug above her heart tight on his chest, Loring looked out at the waves, at the distant glow of the ship – the tiny *Nordic Blue* – now cruising many miles off to the south.

The sultry wind rushed against them, and he listened to the stars. He thought about the week, then the life, they would share. Tomorrow, for starters, they were returning to the Garden of Eden. Eden was certainly wonderful. He and Ulla had been there yesterday. But they had many other beautiful places to go together, as well.

"Oh, Oliver," she said as they strolled. "This feels like a night for a tango."

"Yes, a tango."

"Sing to me, Oliver. Sing to me, please."

"What shall I sing for you?"

"I don't care. Just sing."

"Well, I once wrote a song called, *"Shuffleboard Tango."* Would you like to hear it? It goes with a silly dance. Sort of like this . . . "

Acknowledgements:

The author would like to thank Jib Ellis, Brett Coty, Christopher Keane, Theresa Hummer, Jennifer Kish, Stan Hart and Charlotte Horovitz for help and inspiration.

Vineyard Haven, April 1, 2003

Printed in the United States
1365800004B/55-57